James Wade Harrah
MEET THE AUTOR

Maria Mueller

James Wade Harrah was born in northern Idaho and spent the majority of his youth in the Great Northwest, including a long stint in Eastern Washington. He then spent a couple high school years in the Tampa area and headed back to the northwest for his college education. After meandering through college in Southern Or-egon, he graduated with a journalism degree and headed out to the big bad world to make a living, which he barely did at first. The first years in the real world were spent snapping photos at professional and not so professional sporting events as well as everything else associated with surviving as a starving artist. He then went on to an illustrious career as a salesman, which shot him around the United States in hyper speed. Throughout it all, he maintained a deep desire to travel adventure style and he always consumed people and places in large quantities, hopefully writing down contact information like recipes to his favorite flavors. He is now a proud father of two and a citizen of the world, residing wherever the world justifies that he be, as of this book it happens to be Athens, Georgia.

Visit the official James Wade Harrah website at www.jameswadeharrah.com.

Too Much Is Never Enough

JAMES WADE HARRAH

 Published by SO&SO Co LLC

Too Much Is Never Enough
by
James Wade Harrah

Copyright © 2012 by James Wade Harrah

Cover art by Aspen Kuhlman

Author photograph by Maria Mueller

Published by: SO&SO Co LLC

59 Damonte Ranch Pkwy., Ste. B163
Reno, NV 89521

www.soandsoco.com

For permission requests, write to the publisher, addressed "Attention: Permissions Coordinator," at the address above.

This is a work of fiction. Names, characters, businesses, places, events and incidents are either the products of the author's imagination or used in a fictitious manner. Any resemblance to actual persons, living or dead, or actual events is purely coincidental.

The author wishes to acknowledge his family, especially Maria, for their support during the writing of this book.

Publisher's Cataloging-in-Publication Data

Harrah, James Wade; 1975-.

Too Much Is Never Enough / James Wade Harrah

p. cm.

Summary: A young man with two important overriding principles, lust and intoxication, sets off for Europe in the late 1990's.

ISBN 978-1-938332-94-4 (1st Edition—English)

[1. Erotic—Fiction. 2. Travel—Fiction. 3. Europe—Fiction.]
I. Harrah, James Wade. II. Too Much Is Never Enough.

*This is dedicated to Maria Anne Mueller and Kristina Keogh,
the two women who stood by me as I wrote this book.*

Chapter 1
ACROSS THE POND

This trip was meant to be an enlightening experience for the young man boarding his first flight overseas. Enlightenment — who the fuck knows what that is, right? Just a group of events that add up to an experience that turns into a memory that may or may not have been learned from. Anyway, this kid is getting on a plane. Twenty-one and full of an adventurous attitude and completely devoid of fear, yet in reality slopping around in a mass of ignorance. A fearless man must be ignorant of danger at least. And this particular young man understood nothing but pure exhilarating enjoyment — physical, psychological and out-of-body. Jimmy, the young man in question, was headed off to Europe for a summer jaunt with nothing more than a couple of backpacks and some Birkenstocks.

Of course, there were another one hundred thousand spoiled American brats setting off to do the same, but for some reason, Jim's trip didn't have quite the same flavor as his counterparts'. He wasn't planning a sightseeing expedition; he was setting out to experience the world in his head, but with different ports of call. He planned on travelling through much of the continent alone, but would be making an exception for part of the journey; his classmate from high school, Elizabeth, was planning to join him for a little stint. This young lady, who was now a woman in every sense of the word, would be waiting at Heathrow. Liz was studying at Oxford on an exchange program and Jim was planning to spend his first couple of days visiting her there.

There had been a minimum of planning done for the trip. Jim had a train pass and a guidebook — what else do you need to maneuver your way through twenty foreign countries? He felt that he would let the wind blow him wherever he needed to be. He surely didn't intend on spending a lot of time in museums or churches, but wanted to enjoy the people of each new destination. He converted all the cash he had in savings into traveler's checks and hoped for the best. Actually he expected the best — it was like his God-given right to experience the best of all things and if they weren't really the best, well he would deem them as so and that was that.

Jim was an independent young man with a vicious hunger to live and he devoured every opportunity to gorge himself in all the pleasures he could endure. Jim was a drunk, a drug addict — well, maybe not an addict, but an abuser of anything that could be smoked, snorted or eaten to cause an alternate state of reality. An intellectual teetering on the verge of insane, he carried himself in such a way that he came off as "the good ole all-American boy." He wasn't trying to fool anybody; he really was the all-American boy, especially if perception is reality. Jim thought of himself as a rock star without the band or the massive, cheering crowds. He could imagine that he was living in such a way that deserved a raucous audience. He had let his hair grown long and had a full-fledged goatee leaving him with the grunge look that marked the time. Over six feet tall with piercing orange eyes and olive skin, he could pass for southern European without a problem as long as he didn't open his strictly American mouth.

Jim boarded the plane in Seattle on a trip that would take him to D.C. and then on to London. Once the plane was in the air and the seatbelt sign dinged off, Jim undertook his first mission, which was to win the confidence, and hopefully admiration, of one of the flight attendants. He knew that drinks would be free on the international part of the trip, but he sure didn't feel like paying four bucks a pop on this leg. He sauntered back to the galley and picked out the most receptive, smiling young lady, and addressed her with his usual charm. "Miss, I was hoping I might be able to cajole a light beer from you and that you might be kind enough to think of me whenever you're headed my direction." He handed her a twenty hoping that that would be enough for the entire flight even though he was planning on drinking double what that would pay for.

She smiled and said, "I'll take care of you, sir, as long as you promise not to get out of control."

"Ah, but I am much more civilized than I appear."

This brought a polite chuckle from the crew of female flight attendants and by the end of the flight young Jim was helping himself to beers in the galley. He had the girls turning their heads the other way as he supplied several of the patrons near the back of the plane with free brew compliments of the airline. Jim had flown enough to understand the protocol of the flight attendants. They didn't fancy being waitresses and were not held accountable for stocks of alcohol. He had been intimate with a flight attendant from Denver the year before and she paid for their whole night out with cash she had stashed from alcohol and headset sales. She turned in a paltry sum and kept the rest to make each new destination interesting. Good thing they didn't give her a breathalyzer before she got on the plane the next day because she and Jim had also had their share of minis the night before. Sometimes that's how important information is acquired — an intimate exchange while passing through a busy city in a busy world. Jim charmed the flight attendant into a couple free drinks on the plane while she charmed him into her room at the airport Marriott. He was supposed to be catching a connecting flight to be with his family for Thanksgiving, but his priorities changed for an instant; he still made it in time for the turkey. Knowledge is power, or is it just useless information on how to get drunk. Jim wasn't about short cuts; he was about realistic ways to avoid reality.

Jim's understanding of the situation and ability to win over the staff made him many friends on this particular flight. The rear of the plane became a social, lighthearted event that encouraged many to chatter about their destinations and their reasons for going. This was the spice of life that Jim took credit for creating and he loved to take part in, the human interaction and the quick friendships that could be limitless or dead on landing. Jim adored people and for the most part they adored him back.

The plane touched down in D.C. and Jim was off and on to a big DC-10 that would whisk him across the Atlantic to the next stop in his one-man show. The flight was an all-night affair, designed for people to sleep for the eight hours before touching down on the outskirts of London. Jim really wanted to take advantage of the free liquor and he probably would have got the whole fare's worth of Jack Daniel's down him if his eyelids had not faltered. He awoke with the sun smashing into his face at an ungodly time in the morning and was quick to get a screwdriver in front of him. The pounding in his head would subside with an alcohol injection.

"I could have guessed that you would be the first to order a drink." The flight attendant gently stated as she handed him his early morning wake-up call.

"I'm on vacation. I don't have time for hangovers. You must take these things head on, if you know what I mean."

"Do you think that's healthy?"

"No, but I do appreciate your genuine concern and would be very flattered if the next round could please be a double." Jim said with a glimmer in his eye that showed little concern for health and an absurd amount of mischievous intent. Jim was carefree with an alcoholic buzz and he had an amazing aptitude for maintaining such a state of mind: a soft haze that made the edges of the world softer, less abrasive. By the time the plane touched down at eight A.M. London time, Jim was good and soused. He was excited to see his old friend at the airport and knew that she would be amazed, but not surprised, at his ability show up at any waking hour fucked-up.

Liz, or as she now preferred being called, Elizabeth, waited patiently outside of customs for a man who caused a lot of emotions to rise up within her. She was not going to let him charm the pants off of her. Jim had every intention on getting in her pants so there was a slight conflict there. Elizabeth was in love for the first time in her life, with an Oxford man, and even though she welcomed the arrival of her long-time friend, she was concerned that his visit would test the relationship that she was deeply committed to. She had not told Jim about her romantic involvement, and she was sure that even if she did he would dismiss it and regard it as unimportant. Jim and Liz had feelings for each other, but Liz was scared to death of the antics that followed Jim wherever he went. Neither of them knew the true feelings of the other, so they just danced around it and guarded themselves from ever divulging too many emotional secrets.

She caught sight of him first walking out of customs. As he walked towards her, all the magical memories of adolescence came rushing through and a smile rose from within and sparkled on the outside. Jim noticed her as she began to wave frantically and he pushed the sunglasses down his nose so that he could get a clear look at the now full-figured woman. Jim locked this image in, replacing the skinny young girl he kept stored in his memories.

The long walk through the airport had sobered him up a bit, but he was still rip-roaring happy to be alive. He strutted up to his friend with the best James Dean impression that he could muster and dropped his bags at her feet. She could smell the vodka as he embraced her and planted a big kiss smack on her lips, which she certainly was not prepared for.

"You look fantastic. You're not still a virgin are you? Because it would be a shame if you weren't putting that sensational body to use."

"None of your business. Are you drunk?"

"Yes. You want to join me or what?"

"I can't play too hard today. I have a ball to attend this evening so we have to head to Oxford pretty soon. We can probably catch some breakfast here in London. Are you hungry? But then we have to catch a bus."

"A ball? But I didn't bring my tux."

"You're not going. I'm going with my boyfriend and it is very important that you are nice to him."

"Boyfriends, fuck boyfriends. I came half way around the world to see you and I certainly should be the guest of honor at the ball. What? We're taking a bus; I thought you would have a car for me to drive on the wrong side of the road." Elizabeth laughed and locked arms with Jim as they began to stroll towards the exit signs.

"Take a left. We have to catch the tube into the city first, then we'll catch a bus. Don't worry about tonight, though, I've got some very fun people lined up to take care of you. You wouldn't have any fun at a formal anyway."

"Fuck the formal. Let's shack up in London for a couple nights and start this trip off right. I can make you forget that there are any other men in England."

"God, what an ego, you haven't changed. Love the hair." Liz said with a spry smile and the interlocked couple giggled and hopped on the train to downtown London.

Elizabeth and Jim had spent a lot of time together the previous summer, but then they had gone their separate ways and their thoughts about each other had strayed to more immediate things. The previous summer was full of flirting, but it had been kept platonic even though they constantly groped each other with physical touching and signs of mutual attraction. The truth was Jim needed sex and Elizabeth was very clear that she wasn't going to provide such a thing until she heard wedding bells in the background. She was an idealist and he was a perversionist. Jim did not know about the boyfriend before arriving and he wasn't really fond of the idea. He should have expected it, even though he truly hadn't even considered it. Elizabeth had had boyfriends in the past, but Jim avoided her when she was with her men and therefore he always had the feeling that she was available. When he was around her, she allowed him full access to her most intimate feelings and thoughts, so he always felt that if he put enough pressure on her, and respected her stance on abstinence, that he could win her over.

Elizabeth had an unbelievably perky personality with a voluptuous body topped off with strawberry-blond hair. When she walked, it seemed like she might walk straight up off the sidewalk into the sky. Her body was built like a sprinter with a high butt, wonderfully long legs, and perfectly proportioned breasts. Her facial features were very petite and were a unique part of her enduring beauty. Jim had been very attracted to her the summer before, as she had grown to be a young woman, but he could not quite understand the concept of her wanting to remain pure, whatever that was. He liked challenges, but when it came to sex, he would much rather have an enthusiastic participant than have to struggle to get to that point. Jim went through sexual partners while Elizabeth stayed committed to one man at a time, but their relationship grew as others came and went. They had never expected anything from one another except friendship, so the complexity of most male to female relationships didn't exist between the two, but that was before this summer in Europe.

"I just realized I'm pretty hungry," Jim stated as they walked off the train into the pleasant summer air of London. "I also need to get some pounds with one of these travelers' checks."

"You can get the money at the station, but don't worry about it right now. We'll find a little café and I'll buy us some breakfast."

Jim was served a thick, hearty piece of ham with two eggs over easy even though he could have sworn he ordered bacon. Liz explained that the ham was the bacon. "Fuck if it is. Bacon is bacon. Ham is big hunk of pork like I have on my plate now, not that it is a nightmare or anything, I love ham —I just was expecting bacon. There's a slight oddity here, but I'm sure I'll get over it."

"I'm not so sure you'll like the food here. It's quite bland. Really standard meat and patatoish, if you know what I mean. Not a lot of flare or spice. Enough about the food, though. What do you think of London so far?"

"I think it should give my girl back and serve bacon when the damn menu says bacon. There's not supposed to be anything lost in translation between English and English. How do you like it over here?"

"I love it here. All the people are stuck up snobs just like me and I have fallen quite in love with the man I'm seeing. I think I might marry him."

"You've finally let someone have a piece of that fine ass. What a letdown, I'm just a nanosecond too late. You're not so innocent anymore, are you?"

Elizabeth blushed. She turned the most intense shade of crimson as she slowly shook her head up and down with a childish grin.

"You know I really did want to be first. I wasn't just coming over here to see Big Ben. How did it go? Are you a sex freak now?"

"The first time wasn't really that pleasant, it was more painful than anything, but I'm starting to get the hang of it now. I'm not a freak as you suggest, but I think I'm beginning to understand why people like it so much."

"Does he go down on you? Does he get the job done or what?"

"He does quite well, I believe."

"You don't have any idea what well is, you have nothing to measure it against. You've gotta give me a chance to show you how it's supposed to be now that you're broken in. Just one night with me and you'll forget about all this marriage shit," Jim exclaimed with a playful, mischief twinkling in his eyes.

"You'll never marry anyone and you're a full-blown male slut. I'm not giving you anything. Anyway, I love my little Danny and I'm not going to cheat on him."

"We'll see about that. You're not taking him to Italy with us, are you?"

"No, it's just going to be you and me, but I promised him that nothing would happen, so don't even try anything."

"I have no respect for the wishes of British boyfriends who steal our girls without the common courtesy of providing us American blokes with a reach-around or at least some snappy little English vixens."

"What? You think you deserve a fair trade for me? You can't trade me I never belonged to you, you just have this semi-grip on certain parts of me, but I think they're the morbid parts anyway. I want you to give this guy a chance. I think you'll really love him once you get to know him and once you like him, you will respect our relationship, right?" And with that Liz was convinced that her fidelity was secure and that her friend would make an effort to like her first true love. The sexual tension was a little deep though, so the couple made an effort to steer to more mundane topics. They went through the highlights of their last year in school and sat around chatting in the café as if they were comfortable old friends.

After breakfast and a little walking tour around downtown London, the couple boarded a bus headed for Oxford. The bus marched out of the city and began to weave through the green English countryside. The cool colors and the gentle swaying of the bus put Jim to sleep quite quickly, his head resting on the shoulder of his old classmate.

"You were snoring like a chainsaw on that bus and you dropped a couple of ounces of slobber on my shirt."

"So are you upset or does the combination turn you on?"

"I'm ignoring that. Do you want to get some sleep at my flat? I need to go pick up my dress."

"Do you live with some other chicks or what?"

"No, I live with a guy. His name is Nathan. He's just like you except with an accent."

"What's your little Danny think about you living with a dude? This just keeps getting worse. You're shacking me up with a dude, going to some ball without me, and you don't even have some English slut lined up for me to shag."

"Nathan is a lot of fun. You'll like his company. His girlfriend is always at the pad; maybe she can hook you up. I didn't know I was signed up to be your pimp."

Jim shut up and started to pay attention to his surroundings. The streets of Oxford were lined with stone buildings that looked like medieval fortresses. The ancient walls of the university spread a scholarly quietude during the days and added and elegance to education that Jim had not witnessed before. Jim was exited to be in a new land and figured when he sobered up and caught some shut-eye, he might have a little time to absorb some of the culture and take some pictures before he began to tie another one on or he could tie one on and still make pictures and they just might have some interesting creative properties. He was really not as discouraged by the situation as he let on to Liz. He was quite comfortable with her company and was also sure that whatever friends she introduced him to, he would blend with well. His sarcasm was his defense to everything.

Elizabeth put Jim to sleep with a powerful back massage, which Jim had been whining to receive since he hit the ground in London. She felt completely at ease with her old friend and was glad that they had had such a playful, easy venture so far. She left Jim snoring in her single bed and left a note for her roommate that there was a large American man in her bed and not to be startled if he should stir.

Nathan didn't show up until much later in the afternoon. He knew Jim was coming and that he was in charge of keeping him entertained for his first night in England. He spent the first part of the day picking up his lovely, fire-topped seventeen-year-old girlfriend from the fine city of London. Katrina, was a shy beauty, but she could rise to any occasion and Nathan knew that she would be of great assistance in pulling off a fine night for the American stranger. He liked Elizabeth and when asked to perform the duty, took charge of the situation and made it his own. He would treat Jim like an old school chum, no doubt.

Jim awoke in an empty, very modern and stylish little apartment, which really wasn't so little. It consisted of two stories with two bedrooms and a bathroom upstairs and an office, kitchen, and living area downstairs. "Not bad for two college students," Jim thought. He cleaned himself up and decided to take his first clear-eyed steps around England. He grabbed his camera and a handful of British currency, shoved the money in bright plaid shorts, slid on his wise sandals and headed out into the world as if he had just been born to it.

Oxford was a medieval fair in the park and Jim's camera shutter clicked at every turn. He walked through the grounds of the university in absolute awe of the perfectly manicured gardens and the dark, prestigious buildings. It was as if the buildings and the grounds were well educated, just like the inhabitants of the university. The lore of Oxford swirled around him as he lackadaisically followed students through security gates and found himself wandering through dorms and the college of this and the college of that. "So many colleges, why not the college of everything and be done with it," He thought. "I wonder if I can get smarter through osmosis. If I just open myself up, maybe I can absorb the intellectual greatness." Everybody looked at him quite strangely as he meandered through female living quarters and medical libraries, none of which he should have been freely allowed to wander around, but Jim portrayed a smooth sense of belonging that allowed him to boldly press forward to the places that interested him most.

"What are you doing wandering about here?" A female student asked him in a curious but not necessarily accusatory tone as Jim walked into a laboratory and grabbed a white coat from a hook on the wall.

"Oh I'm just a mate of Professor Twilley's. You know, from the College of Indifference or something like that. Anyway, he told me to wander about, you know, make myself at home and whatnot. What are ya all doing in here?" The young lady looked at Jim in disbelief. What on God's earth was he talking about and who the hell was Professor Twilley, come on? She began to giggle, which turned into a full laugh and ended with a light snort.

"You're bloody loony tunes, mate, but it takes all kinds I reckon." She completely let down her guard and spent a half-hour explaining to him her intricate biological experiment.

Jim excused himself after the girl got too seriously back into her work and he was back into the labyrinth of the interconnected Oxford buildings. After a couple hours of sightseeing Jim came across a small, dungeon-like pub that bordered the campus and decided he might pop in and see if he could strike up an intelligent conversation and swig down a couple pints. He wanted to make sure to absorb the environment in which he was present, to a certain degree, so he ordered a fine English ale and pulled up a stool to the dark mahogany bar. For the entire trip through Europe this would be a common scene for the young, drunken intellect, or so he thought of himself. He was quite keen at finding a local watering hole, befriending the barmaid and extracting the best sort of local knowledge from his new companion. As Jim's eyes searched the dim light of the pub, he realized that he didn't really fit in with the Oxford natives when it came to dress and his personal grooming. The men were dressed in button-up shirts and slacks and the women weren't too far off from their counterparts. This was no Southern Oregon campus where the only standard for style was to look as if you were completely disinterested in the subject all together. Oxford had clothing named after it and it wasn't flannels or t-shirts, it was something with clean lines, something Jim had no knowledge of.

After sitting at his barstool for a short period, Jim realized that the clothing was just a façade, not an actual manner by which to judge these natives. The vulgar obscenities flowing out of these young peoples' mouths were much like the rhetoric that he would hear at his favorite hole-in-the-wall bar in Oregon. The book's cover was shiny and pristine, but its interior was full of the same smut that his pages breathed.

"Lovely bar mistress, might I get another pint of this fine English ale?"

"Don't ever call me a bloody bar mistress again and I'll serve you all you want."

"Just having a little fun. No need for violence."

"You Yanks think you're so charming, don't ya?"

"I'm Canadian, eh. Why do you take me for a Yank?"

"Oh you're a Yank all right. You couldn't keep a straight face with that Canadian shit."

"Mighty observant, my sassy lady. I need someone to show me around. I came to visit a friend, but she's ditching me to go to some formal tonight and it's my first day in a foreign land. What do you say? I need a guide to show me how to act right around here. I'm not very refined, as you can see, but I can be pretty entertaining and I always treat women with the very highest level of respect, no shit. So you think you might be interested in showing an ole Yank around? I'm not nearly as arrogant as the masses, I assure you."

"I get off at eight. Swing by here at ten and I'll be cleaned up and ready to get a bit pissed. Please wear some decent clothes. There are dress codes at a lot of spots. You definitely can't accompany me in that attire."

"I will not let you down, my lady. I clean up quite well actually." With this short, direct conversation Jim had secured some female companionship for the evening. He felt pretty good about himself considering that he thought his chances were very slim with the ice-cold temperament of the barmaid. He thought asking her out might warm her up a bit, but it was actually a successful way forward. Never straight, just forward, you've always got to press forward. Her quick submission was a good sign for the young man with a thriving libido and signified the prosperity of quality friendships that would flourish on his walk-about. She told him her name was Linda and that she usually didn't go out with any of her patrons but because Jim was so pathetic she thought she better help him get acclimated to his new surroundings. She warned him the English had a much drier sense of humor and that his boldness might land him at the butt of certain groups' jokes. The problem, or maybe the solution, was that Jim didn't give a damn if he was the butt of anything as long as the pint was full and the violence limited. "I'll tone myself down a bit." Jim thought. "I don't always need to be so fucking beautiful. Maybe a little under-statement will be good for me."

Jim had a couple more pints watching his female companion work the bar. He watched her fluid movements and easy gestures and let himself fall in love with her. He always liked to let his emotions go to extremes. There was no need for any emotions other than lust, love, passion and disgrace. After he had drunken off his sobriety he bid Linda farewell and headed back to the flat to try to put himself to-gether in Linda's image of a decent date. She hadn't really made clear what that was, but Jim thought himself a good judge of such things, so he would give it his best. He was also hoping to run into Elizabeth in her formal gown or, better yet, maybe get there right in time to help her get into it.

When Jim returned to the apartment there was no sign of the young Elizabeth, but there was a very interesting redheaded creature sipping red wine on the couch. She blushed and spoke with a soft voice and viscous British accent, "Elizabeth already dashed. She left us to keep charge of you for the night. You're Jimmy, right? I'm Katrina."

"Did Liz leave you as a gift?"

"Not quite. I'm Nathan's girlfriend."

"Nathan the roommate?"

"Yeah, he lives here with Elizabeth. He's off in the toilette; he'll return momentarily."

"Is there any beer in this place, Katrina? I'm quite parched." Jim slung open the fridge before the girl could answer and was happy to find a large supply of chilled beer bottles, "Is it all right to drink these?"

"For sure; I think they're for you. We were told that you had a large appetite for alcohol. Nathan does too. You'll get on well, I'm sure." Jim popped off the top of his beer bottle on the edge of the counter instead of looking for a bottle opener. The beautiful Katrina giggled as she brought her wineglass to her sensuous freckled lips. Jim was overwhelmingly attracted to her, as he was to most attractive red heads, brunettes, blondes and even those girls that dye their hair green, but he had just enough class to not blazingly show it. She warranted a quickening of the heart rate that almost gave Jim the goose bumps, but he managed to stop staring and direct his eyes to the television.

Katrina, on the other hand, was so shy that she was inwardly screaming for her Nathan to make his appearance and as if her wishes could be made true, he appeared.

"Hey mate, Nathan." He stuck his hand out for Jim to shake as if he were long lost friend. "You go by Jim or Jimmy? Elizabeth calls you Jimmy." Nathan had listened to many a tale about Jimmy from his loving roommate and he was intrigued by the lore of the fellow. He knew that he would like him before meeting him and felt like he already knew him once he saw his first smile.

"Call me whatever you like my friend, I'm not picky. Stick with Jimmy. It doesn't sound as serious and I'm certainly in no mood to be taken seriously."

"Sounds good, Jimmy. See you found the beer. What do you think of it?"

"It's fantastic and quite cold. I was under the impression that the English preferred their beer warm. At least that is what the only English person I know back in the states told me."

"Some of the pubs serve their beer a bit warm, but for the most part, we keep beer chilled."

"You guys won't believe this, but I scored me a date for the evening. I was wandering around the campus snapping photos and bullshitting people when I stumbled into this dark bar in a basement. It was like a dungeon. It was cool. All the academics were kind of scared of me or something. I guess cause I look like a fucking head banger or something, I'm not really sure, but the bartender was exceptionally cordial. I mean, it didn't start out that way. She kind of got mouthy with me, but then I put her in her place and she melted like butter in my fingers. Or maybe I just threw a dart and got lucky, cause it stuck in the bull's-eye and now she is going out with me tonight. Show me the town, you know. What do you say? You guys up for a double date? I work fast and furious."

"Fucking hell, mate, you're out there. Got to love it. Katrina is only seventeen, though. She can't go out to the pubs and clubs and whatnot. We pretty much just hang out here and get pissed."

"She's only seventeen. My God isn't that illegal?" With this Katrina's cheeks blushed a deep shade of violet and Nathan let out a hearty laugh.

"I get on great with her family and they don't seem to mind. I even sleep at her parent's house from time to time. Seventeen is legal anyhow, but we were getting it on when she was sixteen too, no worries." Nathan was proud of Katrina even at his twenty-four years of age. Smooth elegance flowed from her and put her far beyond her years. Her modest shyness let her beauty take center stage.

"Fantastic, what a country. Do you have any friends that might make their way to the party later this evening? I wouldn't mind a little forbidden fruit myself, if you know what I mean."

"You're awful." Katrina spouted, "Elizabeth didn't tell us you were a perv." Katrina's youthful eyes portrayed an endless playful spirit that was just right for the mischievous Nathan. She didn't really think Jim was awful, she thought he was like an extra piece of color, a new color, thrown into her life to make the dreary day come alive.

"Like I said earlier, you call me what you like just as long as you don't mean it. Under these circumstances, I guess we are going to have to have a little pre-party here. This woman I met said that I had to dress nice in order to get in some of the joints around here. I was hoping that you guys might be able to find me something appropriate for a night out in Oxford without completely ditching my non-style style. I don't have much to choose from in my pack and I'm certainly going to have to score some shoes because all I have is these sandals and a pair of sneakers."

"Yeah, you got to show a bit of style around here. People are very fashion conscious and they are even a bit snobby about it. I got plenty of stuff you can borrow for the night, but you are going to have to get some shoes because those feet aren't going to fit in anything I've got. And don't worry, I kind of stay on the "don't give a shit" side of the fashion spectrum so it shouldn't deviate too much from your fuck-all attire." Nathan began to joke with his new friend. He knew that he could handle even the bluntest of English discourse. Jim did not have any of the emotional tenderness that his friend Elizabeth was so famous for.

"Which direction should I go for a little shopping?"

"It would be best to go by car. I'll take you to a shop where we can get a good deal on the proper styles for an Oxford evening."

"I'm all for some shopping," Katrina exclaimed as she was the first to rise off the couch, slug down her entire glass of wine and grab her purse.

"You two are too kind. If I get lucky enough to bring Linda home tonight I'll be sure to share her with you guys."

"Don't say that too loud, Katrina loves to go both ways." Nathan stated and Katrina sported a huge grin in agreement.

The crew returned to the flat in less than an hour. Effective shopping landed Jim a pair of slick, black Italian shoes and a pair of forest green dress trousers that were an odd mix of rayon, cotton and polyester. Jim liked them because they felt good on his balls. He didn't much like wearing underwear in the summer, so it was important that his pants were of comfortable material. The dressy attire would be needed on his European jaunt, yet he had not calculated having to dress nice while living out of a backpack and it was never an easy feat. He readied himself for the evening to come by putting on his new acquisitions and adding a black silk shirt that Nathan suggested he wear. He had also clipped his goatee to tame the wild beast and had put on some of Nathan's cologne. He was as refined as the world could make him at that particular moment. He left the shirt unbuttoned as he sat back down on the couch to attack a cold beer. He was ready to put on a buzz and converse with the interesting couple of Nathan and Katrina, but didn't want to slobber any beer on his borrowed shirt. The couple had quite a hunger for each other. They sat on the couch intertwined as if a luscious pretzel. They enlightened Jim on many of the attitudes of the English people and kept him well amused with their slanted accents. Jim and Nathan polished off twenty beers between the two of them while Katrina gently devoured an entire bottle of wine. All three found themselves in an easy loving state of mind, completely accepting of one another and happy that their paths had crossed. Nathan thought Jim fit the description that his roommate had drawn — that he was similar to himself. They both had an easy sense of humor that was always turned on. Katrina thought Jim was a bit sexy and she had the slightest urge of lust for him, but it was just healthy attraction, not something she had to act on. She thought of him a little brasher than her smooth English lover, but he had a thicker physique, which she liked. Jim was enjoying his company tremendously, but it was time for him to track down Linda for a little Oxford nightlife.

Linda had two men sitting at the table with her as Jim took his seat in-between them and interrupted the conversation. "You look ravishing my dear. I hope I'm on time." Jim made sure that the two men knew that she was expecting him.

"We were just leaving. Enjoy the little slut. Don't let her fool you into thinking she's a lady." One of the men stated.

"Oh, fuck off Ronnie, you wanker, let us be." Linda shot back with a viscous eloquence.

Linda was dressed in a pair of tight black polyester pants and a beautifully snug, red silk sleeveless top that was cut extremely low to allow the maximum amount of cleavage to be on display. She might have been a dirty slut, but Jim believed he was just a pure charmer who had lured a beautiful English woman to his side for the night. Her brown hair fell to her shoulders and her lightly freckled face was splashed with just a touch of make-up. She was simply stunning in Jim's eyes and he really wanted to taste her so that he could have his senses filled with her. But he thought he better get to know her before he jumped in her lap.

Linda was impressed with how the rowdy American had cleaned up. He had shaved his face, trimmed his goatee, slicked back his hair into a ponytail and had definitely improved his wardrobe. She would have taken him in his plaid shorts, but at least this way he could be presented in public. Linda was quick to escort Jim out of the pub and to a more engaging, nightclub-like atmosphere, which was one of the few such places in the quaint Oxford area. Linda explained that London was an unbelievable city for nightlife, but that Oxford's high-brow socialites kept the town somewhat muted from its full potential as a raging college town. Jim was just glad to be going out; as for the venue, he wasn't really concerned because it would have little to do with the true feeling of the evening. He and Linda were the only two people on earth as far as he was concerned. If all the silly college students wanted to study for their finals instead of partying with him, it was their loss. Maybe he would catch them on his next trip through Oxford. The two flowed through an evening together, dancing, drinking, discussing their different worlds and when it was all done they had developed a chemistry that could have set a laboratory on fire.

They wandered the streets of Oxford drunk and entwined in each other. Their first stop was a kebab stand where they were served a mound of steaming animal flesh mixed with onions and slathered with sour crème. This was the English version of the hot dog stand and Jim was happy that drunks everywhere could count on the late night entrepreneur to feed them something guaranteeing a future heart attack. The couple attacked the kebabs while Jim directed their stroll to Elizabeth's flat where he knew he had his own room for the night. After their hunger had been put at bay, there was definitely another desire that was burning within them both and they barely made it back to the flat without molesting each other. Every so often, they threw themselves onto the grounds of the university, wrapped up in an embrace and explored each other with curious hands. Eventually they made it to the flat without being arrested and with their clothes still, for the most part, covering their bodies.

Jim ripped open the door to Liz's place a little after one in the morning. He expected that his two flat-mates would be in bed, but to his pleasant surprise, they were sprawled across the couch smoking a funny-smelling cigarette. "Ooh, I love to smoke, that will make the sex even better." Linda said as she invited herself into the smoking circle. Jim was also ecstatic about the new mind altering substance that had suddenly been incorporated into the night. Marijuana was a drug that Jim preferred to use daily if it was accessible, but he was concerned that he might not be able to obtain it in some areas.

Just happens that there is almost always an underlying dope culture — a kind group of herbal enthusiasts that don't hide too far beneath the surface of society. Jim had run across a little luck and had stumbled head-on into one of his favorite pastimes within twenty-four hours of hitting the ground in Europe.

"These two are wonderful friends," Jim thought of his two roommates.

"Elizabeth told us that you probably smoke pot every day so I had a friend drop some off after you headed to the pub. I thought I would surprise you. Cheers, eh mate. Have a toke." Nathan stated as he exhaled a large cloud of billowing smoke.

"I love you two more every minute. I bet Elizabeth would be furious if she knew we were smoking in her flat." Jim said, exhaling his own cloud through his nostrils.

Nathan and Jim were now in the chairs as the girls commandeered the couch. Each couple had their own joint, the boys passing one between the two padded chairs that sat on the sun porch with the couch and the television and the girls snuggled extremely close to each other on the couch. Nathan and Jim noticed that the girls were getting on much better than strangers normally did and they encouraged the friskiness of the girls. "You girls are welcome to put on a show if you like," Jim stated with great anticipation that the event would turn into a full-blown sinful affair. "Nate, what do you think about these girls exploring each other in a creative way? I don't have a problem with sharing, you?"

"Fucking hell right. I ain't greedy. This is going to be a fucking miraculous night, mate. You wait and see," Nathan excitedly spilled out. He was sitting on the edge of his chair watching the girls like they were an intense movie.

The girls were in their own world driven by an instant animal attraction. Linda slid her hand up Katrina's sweater while Katrina began to unbutton Linda's blouse. The twenty-five-year-old Linda was being controlled by the seventeen-year-old hands of Katrina and the erotic nature of the interaction was a utopian bliss for the two male observers. Katrina was sucking, licking and biting the breasts of Linda as her hands were covertly sliding Linda's pants to the floor. As the pants hit the floor, Katrina began to make her way down the lightly freckled body of her new, instant lover until she was orally pleasing her.

Nathan yanked his shirt off and began turning out lights and lighting candles. He turned the shades down, turned off the television and turned on the stereo. The ambiance was set and he didn't even think twice about jumping into the action. Neither did he have any concern that his American counterpart wasn't as completely intrigued as he was. Once Nathan had set the stage to his liking, he winked at Jim and slowly slid down and began to finish the disrobing of Katrina, who had already lost the sweater. Her clothes thrown to the side, he began to rub her clitoris as she licked Linda's in vicious circles that had Linda crawling out of her skin. Jim followed Nathan's lead and lay down next to Linda, passionately kissing her. She pulled Jim's shirt over his head and then went for his belt while Katrina continued to make her body shiver. Linda wanted him in her mouth and he quickly obliged. Nathan was lying on his back with Katrina's thighs wrapped around his face. The moans of ecstasy began to escalate as the foursome began to pulse as one. Eventually, the group slithered its way up the stairs to the bedroom where there was a king-sized palette to continue their exquisite masterpiece of flesh exploring flesh. At this point the men had access to condoms and used them to sheathe their swords and penetrate their fair ladies as well as their new friend's fair lady. It was a complete orgy of the senses. When it was finished, which wasn't until light began to slice through the shades, the four lay abreast in the bed, each shaking from their core to their toes with pure exhilaration. They smoked a joint and fell into a deep slumber.

The four naked, tangled bodies were awoken by the loud shriek of Elizabeth as she cracked the door to ask where her friend Jimmy had run off to. There he was in all his glory. She had to look no further. "Oh my God, Daniel, come look at this." Jim opened one eye to see his friend, but didn't have the energy to cover his bare ass. His leg was draped over Linda's naked body whom had one arm draped over Katrina's bare chest, who was wrapped up with Nathan. Quite a pornographic sight for Elizabeth to digest, but she took it in stride and was rather amused at the mass of flesh. "Put on some clothes people. We've got some major work to do to get you guys through the pearly gates; there are some major sins that occurred here," Elizabeth said, trying to get a rise out of the lethargic group.

"Fucking Christ, what a motley bunch," laughed Daniel as he got his first view of Elizabeth's American friend. Daniel and Elizabeth had just returned from a quaint inn that they had stayed at after their long evening at the stately ball. The couple was in a jolly mood and had just enjoyed quite an exhilarating sexual experience themselves, so they understood how needy the human body was. They understood the body's desires, but neither of them would ever experience anything like what went on in that room just a few hours before they arrived. There was evidence of the mayhem, condom wrappers littered the floor, but there was no video, nothing but the hazy memories of the four participants to be kept locked away for rainy days when the world seemed doomed. That night could always give them hope, in the darkest shadows of monotony.

"Who's your friend, Jimmy? The brunette?" Liz asked.

"That's Linda." Jim lightly shook Linda. "Linda, Elizabeth. Elizabeth, Linda."

Linda wiggled her body under Jim's in order to show a little modesty, which really wasn't an honest emotion with anyone in that bed, but the clothed intruders broke the comfort zone established the night before. "Hello, my dear, I would introduce myself more cordially, but the circumstances are a wee bit awkward. If you would have showed up a couple of hours ago, I'm sure I would have hugged you rather erotically and tried to pull your clothes off and make you join the rest of us."

"No worries. I'm not really sure that I could handle whatever went on here."

"Bloody hell, we could give it a try, my love." Daniel chimed in.

Nathan came to life just a bit, "Oh, fucking hell Danny boy you two squares couldn't handle what happened here last night." Nathan's comment had a sarcastic bite to it as he had done some wild stuff with Daniel before hooking up with his American flat mate. They had been friends for years. "Now run off so we can get in a little morning stir."

As Liz and Daniel walked out the door, Jim got in one last request, "Wait. Can you grab our clothes from the sun porch? Please, princess." The question sprang off Jim's lips as they formed a crazy, gleaming grin. Liz's eyes opened to their widest point and she finished closing the door with an acknowledging nod.

After the door was closed, Jim fumbled for some sheets and wrapped Linda up, giving her a hard kiss on the lips as he did so. She kissed him back and giggled at their predicament. Nathan and Katrina had seized the comforter at the first sign of Elizabeth and were hiding out in the darkness of its cover. Katrina popped her head out of the hideout, "I bet she's never seen anything like this, Jimmy. She's such a proper girl, we may have shocked the holy shit out of her."

"You think I oughtta walk out there in the buff? Help her gather up the clothes like nothing is going on. She'll freak out, eh."

"Daniel's a good chap, he'll get a kick out of it, but you're likely to run Elizabeth completely mad," exclaimed Nathan in a muffled voice from beneath the comforter. "I can't face her, that's for bloody sure."

Elizabeth dropped the clothes inside the door. "Jimmy, will you please get dressed and come meet Daniel. I didn't expect you guys to be in bed at noon, much less together. You've already turned my quiet house into one of your chaotic portraits. Do you have any idea how traumatic this is for me? There are at least thirty beer bottles down there and it smells like someone has been smoking and I don't think it was cigarettes."

"Oh, lighten up. Why don't you strip down real quick, jump in bed with us and we'll show you how we had this thing working last night? I'm sure we can incorporate another body. There's plenty of lovin' to go around here." Jim tried to wind up his friend to the best of his ability.

"Nathan, are you under there? Are you in support of this maniac? Did he force you into this or slip something into your drink, or, or, how could you possibly go along with this? Katrina?"

Katrina answered in her quiet, but confident young voice; "It was fantastic. I think it was my fault."

"Bloody hell right. It was all the teenager's fault. She started eating pussy and the whole world collapsed from there." Nathan blurted out, but he still couldn't face Liz so he stayed in his blanket fortress. Linda, Jim and Katrina thought the comment extremely hilarious as they all began to giggle uncontrollably, but Liz was lost in haze of bewilderment. She couldn't quite picture what had happened; she could not even imagine it. She slowly walked from the room surrounded by playful giggles. Nathan popped his head out from under the blanket and offered one last comment, "We all love you, dear. Don't be concerned or angry. It's just youthful exuberance mixed with drugs, alcohol and some perfectly safe sex." Elizabeth ignored this and continued on her way.

Jim and Linda got up, leaving Katrina and Nathan rustling under the covers. They tried to conserve water and take a shower together, but the together thing resulted in an extremely extended shower. Linda left Jim with ten, three-inch scratches on his ass for his intense effort to please her before they began their day.

By the time they made it downstairs to visit with the sophisticated couple of Daniel and Elizabeth, it was time for Linda to be getting back home so that she could go to work later that afternoon.

"Sorry to be rude, Liz, but I've got to get her home. She's got to work later. I'm going to walk her home. I won't be too long. I'll clean up this place when I get back and properly introduce myself,

I promise." Jim and Linda headed out the door. Daniel and Liz were still basking in the perfect evening they had had the night before so they were able to absorb all the shock of the chaotic household. Daniel was especially happy and thought the whole situation quite amusing.

Linda and Jim shared a lot of awkward silences on their walk, knowing that they had definitely crossed certain borders for a first date, feeling the slightest amount of guilt and remorse, as well as the mounting lust and attraction. There was so much to digest in less than twenty-four hours of knowing each other. Jumping into a drunken pot-clouded orgy was not what either had intended at the beginning of the previous evening: it might have been what Jim was intensely dreaming about, but he never imagined it would come to fruition. That being the actual outcome the sensory overload was hard to put into words, hard to communicate. The two trudged all the way to Linda's without discussing the actions of the night before. It wasn't like either of them owed the other an apology, it was a fantastic event, it was just so far beyond what near strangers do that it gave them goose bumps to think about it. They would get over it. They were happy looking at each other in the sunlight, so they would surely find a beauty in their unconventional exasperation. "Sunshine," Jim said referring to Linda, "it certainly can't continue at such a torrid pace. We'll find something wonderfully mellow on the other end of this." He kissed her a long, gentle kiss. "I'll stop by and see you at the pub."

"That would be great," she said as he turned and sauntered back in the direction that they had come.

Jim made his way back to the apartment with a sense of confused joy, which was a common emotion in his life. But he didn't overanalyze it and was more worried about the vicious hangover that rattled his skull. When he arrived back at the apartment he shook Daniel's hand, apologizing for running out in such a hurry. After the shake, he headed directly for the fridge to indulge in a cold hangover cure.

"What do you think about the royal family, Daniel? I heard a lot of English think it's a God awful waste of tax money. Actually, I think I read it somewhere yesterday, like a tabloid or something. I didn't have any idea that that would be a problem. You know, looking in from the outside, I always thought that English people loved the royal family. I know Americans even get a kick out of 'em," Jim said, sitting in front of the tube which, displayed the Queen making some sort of public appearance.

"Fucking hell right. Get rid of the whole lot of them and build some golf courses on their bloody palace grounds. Their argument is that there are millions of quid in tourist revenue produced by the royal family, which justifies their continued existence. I think that golf courses would be just as productive and not make England such a bloody laughing stock. These people are just people like us. They are fallible and they make asses of themselves in front of the world's cameras. I think it's a fucking circus. It literally costs hundreds of millions of quid to keep up the façade of the royal family. I believe there are better uses for this cash: ways to make it work for the people in a much more productive manner. Not to bore the pants off you, mate, but that's what I think."

"Strong opinions are the spice of life my friend. Cheers, eh mate." Jim raised his beer bottle and knocked back his first one of the day. "Have a drink with me. We're on vacation. Well, I'm on vacation and you're with me so let's pretend we're all on vacation. I kind of like the attitude of vacation. It's a valuable resource to me, this attitude of freedom from making important decisions or acting in any way rational. I'm always on vacation, but don't tell anybody." Jim wanted to impress Daniel with his free spirit.

Elizabeth, Daniel and Jim spent the rest of the day together. Jim tried to be friendly to Elizabeth's new love and Liz tried to constantly highlight the finest qualities of her man. She wanted Jim and Daniel to get along so that they would respect each other and not feel threatened by one another. Neither man was jealous, so the interaction was smooth and natural. Elizabeth had the idea that if they became friends that Jim would not pressure her when they were travelling together later in the summer. He would respect her relationship and be a gentleman about it. Deep down Liz knew that there would be some sexual tension between her and Jim as they traveled through one on the most romantic countries on earth. How could there not be? What the fuck was she doing putting herself in this situation? Daniel didn't worry, though. He wanted to show his trusting nature and he truly believed in it. He was sure that he had won her over completely and that this hippie from America was no threat at all. She was too secure for his antics or at least that is where he stood on the matter, completely at ease.

Jim couldn't bring himself to truly like Daniel because he didn't want Daniel to exist. He didn't want to have to wade through the emotional baggage that Liz would display for her first lover. He was hoping for the same Liz he had experienced the summer before: the pure, amazing, beautiful young creature that was always in awe of his life. She had grown up, though, and he had to make the best of the reality. He wasn't rude in any way, he just didn't make the same effort to befriend Daniel that he did with Nathan, or for that matter anyone that he encountered on the streets. He preferred to keep a distance, to keep the relationship shallow, so that he didn't develop that respect that Elizabeth so desired. Daniel was aloof because the American had been described as a friend with no romantic ties to his beloved; a friend who lived on the same block and was never a boyfriend or even considered in that regard. What Liz left out in her description of the relationship between her and Jim was the extreme intimacy that they shared without actually indulging in anything sexual. Jim and Elizabeth shared a relationship full of physical contact, whether it be long massages in scant to no clothing or hours of laying cuddled together as if they were exactly what they never admitted being, a couple. They always spent time together sharing what was going on in their lives, but rarely did they intermingle those lives in a public manner, so their relationship was this secret kinship developed in the shadows of their neighborhood.

Jim was getting sick of being the third wheel early on in the afternoon and began to design an exit strategy. He had walked behind the handholding couple long enough. He lured the sickening couple to the dungeon pub where his sexy English barmaid was slinging pints. He knew it wasn't too long until Linda got off, so he figured he could duck out with her when the time was right and leave the love birds to enjoy their evening. What he didn't figure on was that they would stay the entire time and drink quite heavily. "Fuck all, I'm going to like this guy if I get drunk with him. I almost always fall in love with everyone I get drunk with," Jim thought as the night slid by and Elizabeth and Daniel became his drinking buddies.

"We never used to do this when we were kids, you know." Jim directed his comment to Daniel. "Liz was a straight-laced girl who used to like to live vicariously through me. I would go get out-of-control drunk and then on my way home I would stealthily park my car near Liz's house and climb up the back balcony where she and a friend would be sleeping on the back patio. Then I would educate them on the life of a bad boy and they would tell me about their recent exploits with good boys. We would be amazed that the other could live like that. Now we meet in the middle and my little Elizabeth is drinking like a fish."

"I haven't seen a pint she's afraid of yet," Daniel added.

Liz was a little tipsy and her lips were loose so she thought she would speak what was on her mind. "You know, Jimmy, I'm quite in love with Daniel and he completely trusts me when it comes to our trip, but I'm a little concerned with what we saw this morning. I mean, I can't figure out for the life of me how you could possibly end up naked with three other people, my roommate included, within twenty-four hours of arriving here. What's going to happen in Venice or Rome? Do you always act in such ways or can you be just a tad bit civilized for me?"

"Oh, stop whining. What am I going to do, get us involved with an orgy every night? We can't possibly have that much luck. Linda and Katrina had the perfect chemistry that started with a spark and turned into a raging fire. You're not willing to go down on another chick anyway, so don't get your panties in a wad about my behavior. I'll be your goddamn knight in shining armor if that is what you want. I'm not interested in making you uncomfortable. We've known each other too long for me not to respect who you are and not know where the boundaries of my actions can be placed when

I'm around you. Last night was a once in lifetime, well hopefully not, but maybe, occurrence."

"I'm not too worried. She's too much of a prude to get involved with anything too raunchy anyway," Daniel added as the alcohol made him speak before he thought about it.

"A prude, so that is what you call last night. You surely don't appreciate what I've given up for you. Maybe I'll just take it away, then you'll see prude," Liz retorted.

The three of them got pissed and developed a playful, drunken respect that made the evening enjoyable. The underlying tension about the future was washed away in English ale and even Liz showed a little of her wild side. Once Linda was relieved, she joined the group who were already well on their way to being fully greased. She couldn't possibly catch up in a safe manner, but she enjoyed the outlandish company as it was. Eventually, Liz and Daniel excused themselves heading back to his flat and leaving Jim with Liz's room once again. Jim tended to get quite lovey when he was drunk, so he was fully intoxicated by Linda. He was fascinated that she had kicked off the fireworks the previous evening and was fiercely attracted to her energy. Linda looked at Jim with piercing, wondering eyes that were taking in his every action and gesture. She did not want to grow too close to a man from so far away who planned to leave so soon. Neither of the couple expected the evening to finish like the one before and they both welcomed something a bit more civilized.

The tube in the pub kept showing highlights of the world famous grass-court tennis championships in London and Jim had a notion to see it in person, but figured it inaccessible due to ticket price and availability. "Hey Linda, what does it cost to go to Wimbledon?"

"Why, you really want to go?"

"It's gotta be too expensive and hard to get a ticket, eh?"

"Not at all. I have off tomorrow, we can go in the morning, queue up, and pay fifteen quid and we're in."

"What does queue up mean?"

"The queue is the group of people waiting to get in. There's a long-ass queue at Wimbledon, but once they open the gates it goes really fast and the grounds are so huge that it absorbs the people quite well."

"Ah, you've got to wait in line. That is what you mean by queue, right?"

"Sure, a line, whatever. Let's do it. I love to go. I haven't been since I was a girl and no one will take me."

"Cheerio, beautiful Wimbledon it is." With that Jim had designed a perfect exit strategy for moving his trip forward. He would take his favorite English mate to Wimbledon, which would end their love affair on high note, then stay in London and catch the best mode of transport to Paris. The overcast skies of England put Jim in a mood that made him want to run to the mainland and get off the dark, gloomy island, not that he wasn't having a fantastic time, just that his spirit yearned for sunshine.

Jim and Linda spent the evening back at the flat with Katrina and Nathan. The chemistry between the four people had been established the night before and it was as if they all had been friends for eternity. They cooked frozen pizzas and giggled about their exploits from the night before while they drank and smoked just a touch of doobage. The sexual energy from the night before had

been zapped out of them and they oozed into a mellow consciousness that brought them all to the conclusion that they needed some
sleep. The escapades from the previous night could not possibly
be duplicated so the couples remained couples and retired to their
perspective rooms.

The next morning Linda and Jim made love in the single bed that
they had so completely crashed in the night before. It was a slow,
deliberate kind of sex with each absorbing the feel and look of the
other in the morning light that streamed through the window. It was
like eating a piece of delicious candy; both of them wanted to savor
the taste and make it last as long as possible. Orgasms were achieved
in simultaneous fashion just as Elizabeth and Daniel made their way
into the flat. They didn't dare come upstairs to determine the sleeping arrangements, though.

Jim had called Elizabeth the night before to make her aware of
his plans to head into the city and continue on to Paris from there.
She and Daniel came to see him off, but were not interested in making their way to the tennis championships. "You certainly did light
up the neighborhood for a couple of days," Liz said giving Jimmy a
hug goodbye. He and Linda were in a rush to get to London so they
could get a decent spot in line. "I guess I'll see you in a couple weeks
as long as you can stay out of jail and make the rendezvous in Zurich.
This is real life stuff, don't leave me halfway across Europe without
my protector."

"Don't fret, Sunshine. I am dependable as a Swiss clock and shall
have Zurich scouted out for us before you even arrive unless I meet
some Spanish goddess who wants to make me her prince in which
case I'll give you a call. Just a joke, you know I'll be there."

"Hey mate. It was great meeting you. Take care of my girl when she gets out there with you. No orgies. I plan on marrying her some day, so don't let her stray too far from the path," Daniel added as Jim and Linda prepared to make their way to Linda's car. Nathan and Katrina had said their good-byes the night before, but they came tumbling down the stairs at the last minute anyway to give Jim and Linda a hug. They were still muddled in sleep and didn't say much, but the looks on their faces and kindness in their embraces almost brought Jim to tears. Leaving places was always a matter of leaving the relationships that were nurtured there and for Jim each relationship had a pureness to it: its own personality that would live forever within him.

"Cheers, eh mate," Nathan added as Jim was about to close the door of the car. This simple term of endearment said it all. Jim had picked up the term during his stay and had used it frequently after he had had a couple beers, everyone was his mate and they all deserved good cheer.

Oxford was in the rear-view-mirror and Linda drove the car as if they had robbed a bank in the university town. Jim had to whip out a joint about halfway there because the ride was making him very anxious. Linda toked and drove which made the situation even more hazardous, but at that point the harshness turned soft and Linda slowed down just enough to make the situation bearable. The gray clouds of England tried to spit just a touch of rain, but it wasn't enough to dampen the spirits of the couple who were determined that the tennis would go on.

The vast grounds of the tennis tournament swarmed with tribes of tennis fans as well as good ole English and Aussie hecklers of which Jim was proud to become the American representative. Jim felt in awe of where he was and was absolutely gleaming with excitement as he came up on the famous grunts of Monica Seles. "Do you believe this, we could reach out and touch her. This is jolly good fun, I do say. What do you think, princess?" Jim stated in his best English accent.

"I'm no princess, sweet, but I do believe you would make a fine Englishman." Linda was truly enjoying the day as well as her company and somewhere inside her she was wishing that she could just keep him on her home island for just a little longer. Two days wasn't enough to develop an overwhelming emotional tie and Jim wanted to keep it that way because he was as apt as a female to get tied up in his emotions. The journey could not be compromised. This was a search for his soul through the bloodline of his ancestors and it was no time to be getting sentimental. Jim was on an adventure and Linda was one of the many relationships that would occur and he cherished each and every person that flashed in and out of his life, but he made it a point to always be honest with each person he came in contact with. If he were to head on the next day, he would not lead anyone to think any different. He devoured people by the minute and lived for that minute only.

With Linda by his side they were royalty among the peasants, at least the fantasy was such in the young man's mind as he watched the tennis pros of the world exchange ground strokes. Jim cheered for the Americans while Linda supported the English, which were fewer and harder to find, so eventually she just took up opposition to Jim's picks in order to keep the day a bit feisty.

When the day of tennis action concluded Jim escorted Linda back to her Peugeot where he bid her a quick and delicate farewell.

"You're much more than an American man can handle, my dear. I'm honored to have met you and will make sure our paths will cross again."

"Don't bullshit me, just kiss me."

Chapter 2
FANNY IN PARIS

Jim was able to catch a bus out of London soon after he left the sacred grounds of the grass tennis courts. He entered the bus with his two backpacks and his newly acquired souvenir tennis shirt, his trusty Birkenstocks and two tightly rolled marijuana cigarettes stowed in the belt line of his trusty, plaid leisure shorts. "What a way to start off my adventure. Somehow I lure a bartender out on a date, that feat alone is nearly impossible, then I take her home and she is unconventionally attracted to a seventeen-year-old firecracker that has an insatiable hunger for every piece of human flesh. Now I have this fucking movie in my head that won't stop playing and I don't know that I'll ever create any other experience that will be able to replace it. I can't possibly trudge around Europe expecting to outdo such an experience. I must let it settle in a happy place and move on without lofty expectations. As for Big Ben and Buckingham Palace, fucking tourist haunts, I believe I saw the finer side of England," Jim thought to himself as he settled into his seat.

The bus would head to Dover where it would board a ferry that would cross the English Channel. Jim was seated next to the window and it was only a matter of time before someone plopped down next to him. He was interested in what fate would bring him. He believed in such things, that destiny fell in your lap and that you could choose to embrace it or reject it. There were skeptics and there were optimists; Jim was a super-optimist. Her name was Fanny. She had just come from working a cruise liner in the Atlantic where her shift was three months long. She was heading back to her flat in Paris for a little rest and to get reacquainted with the world. Fanny was a tall, jet black, Parisian woman with strong, beautifully chiseled features. When she smiled, her sharp features melted into one distinct emotion, pure kindness. She was poured into a tight pair of black jeans and wore a tattered winter coat in preparation for the nightlong journey to Paris. She spoke very broken and accented English, but she was so interested in her American seatmate that she constantly brutalized the language in an effort to communicate. Jim smiled and shook his head a lot at his mysterious French friend, but could pull little from what she was saying. By the time they reached Dover, the seatmates were playing a kind of charades mixed with single English words in hopes of understanding each other to some degree. Language wasn't too important; they both said everything in their smiles.

Fanny and Jim became friends and were watchful of each other as they made their way off the bus and onto the ferry for the short journey across the channel. Jim was quickly lured to the duty-free shopping and bought himself a bottle of Jack Daniels and a carton of smokes. He bought French cigarettes in the spirit of going to France and planted himself in a quiet corner with his new friend, Fanny, and his old friend, Jack. The massive late-night ferry pushed across the channel with a silent motionless strength that put the couple in a bizarre void of sound and motion. Most of the other passengers stayed on lower levels and there was no music blaring into the public spaces, just the cabin light surrounded by big black windows staring into the pitch black of an ocean night. Jim and Fanny drank shots of whiskey chased with Coke and smoked cigarettes in rapid succession. There was an announcement to return to the vehicles. The two seatmates stumbled down the stairs to the craft, boarded the bus and crashed into a medicated slumber. Fanny rested her head on Jim's shoulder; she was comfortable with her American friend who always smiled back at her.

Jim woke up to the bright sunshine coming through the windows and was amazed at the wide-open plains around him. The expansive, busy freeway and the rolling wheat fields could have been in Iowa if it wasn't for the French signage. Fanny remained deeply asleep and Jim lowered her head down to his lap, providing her with his fleece as a pillow. She was a kind-hearted youthful soul and Jim was glad to have a real life Parisian by his side as the bus began to hit the outer edges of the city with so much culture. "Hemingway found his muse somewhere in this mystic city — if I could just find a little piece of my own magic somewhere in these streets. Maybe I ought to get drunk on absinthe, point my camera to the heavens and follow the sounds in my head. Maybe I'll just stick with this Fanny girl; she could be the source of my enlightenment," Jim thought to himself.

Fanny woke up with the comfortable feeling of being embraced, her head resting on the fleece and Jim's arm resting on her side as if she was a dear loved one. She embraced the kindness of her travelling mate and at once invited the stranger to stay with her. "You stay with me, Jim. Yes, in Paris you stay with Fanny, oui. I show you the city, I show you all."

"You don't even know me. You can't just take me in. You should be more cautious."

"No, no, you are good. You stay with me American boy, I show you Pari'. You no spend money to sleep. I show you the real city," she tapped her hand on her chest, "the real heart of the city. You come with me, oui?"

"Merci' boucoup, Fanny. I shall surely stay with you my dear."
Jim now had accommodations and the most genuine tour guide one
could find. He was ecstatic about the situation and was sure to be
very thoughtful and generous to his host.

Fanny was also excited to have some company after working for
such a long time without any true time to develop friendships or to
enjoy others. She described the work on the cruise ship as very vigorous, where she only had time to work and sleep. She was engaged to
a man from South Africa, but he would not be in Paris for another
couple of weeks. Jim would be the perfect antidote to keep her from
getting lonely. She had no reservations about the American man even
though his appearance was quite shaggy and he liked to drink whiskey early in the morning.

The very different duo hit the streets of Paris with Fanny in the
lead. She had lived in Paris most of her life after being born on an
island off the southern French coast. She knew the city and she felt at
home in its streets.

"Man everyone has got a dog around here." Jim's first statement
in France referred to his first observation. "Don't they pick up their
shit? Fanny, watch out for the shit, my dear, it is everywhere."

"Come on Jim. No worry. We must get a train ticket. One week,
one hundred francs."

"Do you think I'm made of francs? One hundred, my God, are there
bullet trains around here or what? How much is a hundred francs? I
hope it's not like pounds 'cuz they kicked my ass."

"Not so much. No worry. You get francs at station. No worry,
Jim, come."

Jim got some money exchanged at the train station and realized that the subway pass was about twenty bucks, no big deal. Fanny was an expert at manipulating the subway and Jim just kept up, barely able to distinguish one tunnel from another. He very much enjoyed the ease of the travel, though. The crowds weren't too bad and the trains moved quickly to anywhere in the city. He liked Paris and as they came out from the underground, the sun was finally shining.

Jim came to France with preconceived ideas of what his reception would be. He imagined the French people would be cold towards Americans, or any outsiders for that matter, but the stereotypes came tumbling down once the ignorance was lifted. Fanny liked Jim's idea of saying he was Canadian, but didn't Canadians know how to speak French? Not the ones from British Colombia. "You no worry about French people, they will be nice because you with Fanny, the French girl, oui."

Fanny had already destroyed all of Jim preconceptions about the French, so he let his guard down and remained his easygoing self with a predisposition to love everyone and ask questions later. Jim was on a journey to learn about the people of the world and for him to be so absorbed with an actual Parisian was exactly the kind of experience he was striving to attain. Jim was going to see the Eiffel Tower, stroll along the Seine, walk among the artists and create his own art with his camera, but those were just the actions of his body; the people would give him the actual feeling for the place. Years after the adventure he would remember the people that walked by his side much more than the places he was walking. That was the way in which Jim understood the world, through the people. The Mona Lisa was simply a mysterious-looking picture unless you were able to have a conversation with Da Vinci about its creation, about the humanity that was breathed into it. Surely there were visions along the way that would remain awe inspiring and therefore remain anchored in the sensual memory bank forever, but Jim's memory was more likely to recall the common silences between him and Fanny, the comfortable silence that rested between the two because they didn't speak the same language. The hours on the patios of quaint cafes with the couple smiling broadly at each other as the world struggled by, a large draft beer and a French cigarette burning the day away.

Fanny guided him through the subway system to a Paris neighborhood that housed the busy bodies of the French working class. They entered a building that was older than most buildings, if not all buildings in America and there was no elevator in the ancient structure. Jim felt like he was getting to go home even though he was several thousand miles from his doorstep. Fanny opened the mailbox only to have it flood out on her and spray all over the floor. Jim picked up the mail, as any gentleman would, and followed the blushing black girl up three flights of stairs to Fanny's humble Paris home. The room they entered was just that, a room with two small appendages that formed a kitchen and bathroom, each not much larger than an average coat closet. The kitchen was comprised of a small white porcelain stove with a tiny oven and only two burners on top, a half-sized refrigerator that fit under the cupboard and a very small pantry that consisted of two shelves in a four-foot high cabinet. The space had about six square feet of linoleum, which gave just enough room to make a pirouette in the kitchen. The bathroom was similar in size except incorporating a stand-up shower and the flats only sink in its space. There was one bare light bulb hanging over the small mirror over the sink. The main living quarters consisted of five pieces of furniture: a foam couch that also folded out to make a bed, two chairs, a table and a stand-up bureau that was used as Fanny's closet. There was one window in the flat, which the gargoyles in the courtyard stared at the occupants through. There was a little fountain in the courtyard where Jim and Fanny had entered the building and when Jim opened the window he could hear the peaceful splashing of the water in the fountain. The courtyard reminded Jim of an inner sanctuary, a peaceful, quiet place just out of the reach of the busy streets of Paris.

"It is not much. Just for sleep and wash. I live in City, no need to stay locked here. You will like, Jim. We will see all of Pari."

"Merci, Fanny. It is perfect. You are a wonderful Parisian woman. We must track down some food and get a couple more hours of rest before we take on the mighty city," Jim said with a genuine hunger and wary eye.

"We go to the market in a minute. Sit down, sit down, get comfort," Fanny said pointing to the couch and demanding Jim follow her orders. Jim threw his bag on the floor and melted into the upholstered foam couch. He looked on in awe as Fanny stripped out of her tight fitting jeans, threw her top in the corner and stood in front of her burrow with nothing on but a g-string and a lace bra.

"I guess you're not modest?"

"Modest, what is modest?"

"You're not shy to show your body. You know, shy, timid," Jim said and then he covered his face with his hands and tuned his head away from Fanny trying to show a shy or embarrassed look.

"My body is good, yes? Not shy, but you no hanky panky, Jim," Fanny said with a wide grin extending on her lips. She retrieved a

picture of her fiancé and handed it to Jim. "I marry this man, so
not hanky panky, Jim." Fanny did not see Jim as a threat and she
even felt a certain secure comfort when he was around. She felt
at ease in his presence and he in hers. They didn't have to work
at being friends, they just had to be themselves. Jim thought of
Fanny as being completely innocent, playful and loving. The two
danced in each other's company as if they had been ballroom partners for a decade. Fanny did not make it habit to invite strangers
into her home for an indefinite amount of time, but with Jim, it
seemed like the right thing to do. Jim also felt the effortlessness
of the relationship and reveled in the convenience and the selfless
motive that allowed it to develop.

Fanny and Jim put on some comfortable clothes and headed back
down the stairs. Fanny escorted Jim to the local market, which was
about one quarter the size of the massive American grocery stores that
Jim was used to, but had a collection of cheese that was at least double
that of any American store. The cheese aisle was the backbone of the
French market. Jim was amazed at the emphasis on cheese, bread and
wine. Fanny glided through the aisles in a light, airy summer dress,
which she had changed into after peeling off her jeans. She picked up
fresh fruit, granola, yogurt and two kinds of cheese. She told Jim to
pick a bottle of wine and she grabbed a baguette near the checkout.
Jim looked at the vast selection of wine without a clue what to get.
He shrugged both of his shoulders up in the air to the woman next to
him as if he was completely lost and couldn't deal with this decision.
She took the hint and gently handed him her choice. "Merci, Madame.
Merci boucoup," Jim thanked the woman ecstatically for choosing for
him as well as making it something he could afford.

Back at the flat, Jim was treated to a very healthy breakfast of granola in yogurt with fresh fruit pieces. The bread was cut into slices and smeared with a stinky cheese that Jim thought unfit to eat, but he gagged it down as Fanny adored it and he didn't want to offend her. The bottle of wine also made it onto the breakfast menu and was the savior to Jim in washing down the flavor of the cheese and taking over the palate with a very smooth flavor. This would become a favorite tradition for Jim along his European travels, to uncork a bottle of wine for breakfast. He loved places that didn't frown upon drinking with all three meals. In France he would do as the French did as long as it wasn't too hard and conformed with his mantra, which was to have fun at all costs or if it was free, even better.

After their first authentic French meal, at least that is how Jim saw it, the foam couch was folded out into a foam bed about the size of a double and the roommates from different sides of the world were going to share it. "No hanky panky with Fanny, Jim," she reminded him. Jim thought that kind of a difficult request considering she had crawled into bed with nothing but a thong and a tee shirt on. Jim dropped his plaid shorts to the ground and took his shirt off flexing his muscles for Fanny to try to persuade her to break her own rules. He picked up his shorts from the ground and extracted his marijuana cigarettes holding one in front of Fanny like it was the finest piece of candy in the candy store. She took a look at the joint, smiled and produced a lighter to make it burn. Anyone who drinks for breakfast surely smokes a little pot.

The joint crackled to life and Jim had found yet another pot-head, or at least a casual smoker. Jim truly thought of marijuana as a peaceful substance that did the more world more good than bad.

The mellowing agent helped wash away his anxiety, which would creep into his thoughts and dominate them if allowed. The couple puffed and passed for half of the joint, then snuffed it out and kicked back on their separate sides of the bed for some restful sleep.

He slid his hand down her leg just to test the waters. "Maybe she's just saying that," Jim thought, but he found out the truth really quickly as he felt a sharp sting on his hand from a quick, hard slap from Fanny. She turned around in the bed so she was facing Jim. She was going to keep an eye on him. "I guess she meant the no hanky panky thing. Oh well, I'll be good," Jim thought as he rolled over and put his hands up in the air as if he surrendered. Fanny giggled and pinched his butt.

Jim woke to the sound of water running in the bathroom and figured his host was showering to prepare for a night in the Paris lights. He rolled over, did a couple push-ups to get his blood flowing, pulled out the cork from the bottle of wine, and lit the grass. Fanny came out from the shower to find Jim swigging wine from the bottle, smoking some pot and scratching himself with only his drawers on. Jim wasn't too modest either. Fanny was fairly amused by her new roommate's nonchalance and was not offended by his brusqueness. She took the joint out of Jim's hand, pointed to the shower and took a swig out of the wine bottle herself. "If you weren't already engaged, I swear I'd get down on my knee right now. You are a woman to love," Jim said with admiration in his voice.

Jim and Fanny hit the streets of Paris that night stoned and enthused about their cordial relationship and of their summertime excursion into the city. They jumped on the subway and popped out on a street alive with cafes that were splashed out into the sidewalks — the tables and the patrons becoming part of the streets, a very fashionable and trendy accessory, but never the less, part of the streets. The sidewalks were wide expanses, almost as wide as the streets. The buildings were designed to have this added expanse of space to allow its inhabitants to spill out into the streets and become part of the social environment. It was one of the finer characteristics of Paris, that when the weather was nice everyone partook without the least bit of guilt. The Parisians also took fashion to a higher level than their counterparts on the island next door, or at least Jim felt underdressed among the Parisian youth. Of course, he was wearing some pretty shabby clothing even for the states. His jeans had holes in them, a fashion accessory as far as he was concerned, and his tee shirt was ten years old and he finished the outfit with his sandals, which had some serious miles on them. The cafes would let him in for a drink, but as he had been told before leaving, the clubs would certainly not let him in. Neither Jim or Fanny really needed a nightclub, though, they were too fashion conscious and too expensive for either of them to get excited about.

The couple found some premium seats outside one of the cafes and ordered the largest beers the place had to offer. The air was smooth and the sky still clean blue, with a tint of orange as the sun was beginning to set. There wasn't a lot of conversation, they just watched the world slide by and it was a beautiful piece of urban art — the quintessential Paris with the cafes brimming with a world of people and the clear sky breathing life into the vibrant crowds of smiling faces — the wide stone sidewalks with tables, umbrellas, twinkling light posts and dancing candles.

The night wore on and different people kept surrounding them, people from all over the world as well as Paris. Jim struck up a conversation with some German men who were in town for a soccer match while Fanny had a conversation with some locals. She was explaining how she picked up a foreign roommate while Jim was trying to learn the intricacies of European football. Jim learned of the vicious rivalries of the football companies throughout Europe and of the extreme pride and respect that the Europeans carried for their regional teams. He saw the similarities of how devoted the fans were to those of American football teams as one of the Germans went on and on about his pure dedication to the sport in his sparkling clear English. "Football is literally my life at this point. I received a legal settlement a couple years ago, quit my job, and took to the rode following my squad about Europe. Sometimes my friends are along and sometimes they have to go back to their regular lives, but I continue on. This week Paris, next week Milano, Italia and then back to the beautiful green hills of the homeland for a match against the Scots, should be a bloody one."

"What do you do when football season is over?" Jim asked in hopes of getting the conversation to steer in a different direction, but the man was getting rather drunk and simply ignored Jim's question. He just continued on about his favorite players and their achievements as if he could bring Jim up to date on the entire European soccer league.

Jim excused himself from the soccer junkies and corralled Fanny. He hoped they could move on to another café to find a new set of world citizens that weren't so fanatical. At the next café, the couple requested outdoor seating and ordered large frosty beers again. Jim loved the fact that Fanny slugged down beer with the best of them. She had sort of a masculine, tomboy sense about her — the way she carried

herself upright and strong and the way she drank her beer in big swal-
lows, but when she opened her mouth and began to speak the most petite voice emerged. Jim and Fanny sat on the sidewalks of Paris letting
their imaginations whisk them away into the lives of the passers by.
Paris had a unique magnetism that filled up its streets most any time
of year, but in the summer especially. The couple let the evening fade
away into a drunken euphoria that carried them back to the flat while
the nightclubs were still pounding with rhythm.

The next day Jim woke up to the sun blistering across his face
from the courtyard window and soon realized that his bedmate was
not snuggled up with him nor was she anywhere else in the vast
expanse of her Paris flat. "She left me for another man," he thought.
Jim lay in his foam paradise and thought about how they would
spend the day in front of them. They had discussed some options
the night before, but had not made any concrete plans. Jim just
wanted to be out on the streets of Paris. He didn't care where they
went as long as it didn't involve standing in line with a bunch of
tourists waiting to see what he had seen a thousand times repro-
duced in literature and media.

Fanny came floating into the flat with a tray of hot coffees and
croissants. She had gone to the bakery across the street and retrieved
the perfect hangover cure when mixed with just a touch of marijuana, of course. "Breakfast in bed, merci, Fanny," Jim said in appreciation of such hospitality.

"You like chocolate, yes?"

"Very much, my love, it is one of my favorite things." But Jim was
confused because he did not see any chocolate and he had already
tasted his coffee, which had none. Things were made clear when he

bit into the croissant, which was filled with rich, wonderful chocolate. Jim loved Fanny even more for the splendid effort. How he had
stumbled across such dumb luck was beyond him.

The couple headed into the heart of Paris filled with goodies,
coffee and just a touch of cannabis, which clouded their minds just
enough to make the subway seem like a video game. With squinted
eyes and an open heart, Jim grabbed the hand of his tour guide
as they emerged from the subway somewhere in the Montmartre
district of Paris. Jim had explained to Fanny that he was willing to
let her be the guide with no limitations except for the line and tourist thing. Jim had his trusty Pentax 35-mm camera, some money
and a pack of French cigarettes to experience the city with. The day
was perfectly blue and hot with Paris blooming in full color and life.
Fanny pulled Jim up the largest hill in Paris, or at least it seemed
such since you could see the entire city from its crest, to the beautiful Basilique du Sacre' Coeur — a picturesque, domed church that
guarded the skyline of Paris. There was a long set of stairs leading
up to the majestic structure with fountains springing out of the
walls along the way. Jim made Fanny pose for pictures, with the
strong structure and the strong woman creating a unique composi-
tion that exuded confidence and beauty. The couple had certainly
not avoided tourists by coming to this location as the broad steps
leading to the Basilica were littered with picture-crazy tourists
snapping their own elegant compositions. It was hard to make a
bad picture with the Basilica framed against the blue sky, shooting
up the great staircase. There was no noise in the frame, no clutter
around the church, just the white, stone structure with immaculate
detail work in every nook and cranny.

Fanny had picked the perfect starting point to their day on the town with an awesome panoramic view of the city they were beginning to explore. From the apron of the church, she could point out all the famous sites in Paris and their relationships to one another. The streets near the church were cluttered with artists making their renditions of the Paris skyline and displaying all their work for sale. The artists had little canopies set up to protect their work, which lined the streets wherever there was a view. Jim made pictures of the artists making pictures and then turned his camera to the local people that he could pull out of the mass of tourism. There was a small child with deeply tanned skin sitting on a curb playing the accordion, his sister nearby collecting offerings for the show. The young boy wore a sad face as he played the music and both he and his sister were smeared with dirt. Jim dropped a coin in the offering can and noticed that the children would eat well that day as they had collected a good sum.

The next stop was the Louvre, but it was too fine a day to be herded through a museum, so the beautiful exterior became the touring ground. Fanny and Jim strolled through the Tulleries Gardens, which extended out in front of the Louvre like a huge, natural red carpet made of opaque pebbles and stretching out before them all the way to the Arc De Triophe. There were a lot of Parisians in the park enjoying the beautiful weather during their lunch hours while still dressed in their office attire. Jim made pictures of the scenery as well as its inhabitants. He made pictures of French children sailing their model sailboats in one of the garden's ponds and then he turned his camera on the fantastic architecture of the Louvre. He enjoyed the creative freedom of the glass pyramid entrance that stood as an incredibly modern structure surrounded on three sides by majestic castle-like structures. It looked like a playful child dancing in front of his smiling grandparent.

The couple was beginning to get hungry, so they looked to the near edges of the park for a quick bite, nothing fancy, just sustenance. They found a small sandwich shop and bounced out carrying large baguettes with salami, pepperoni, melted cheese and slices of tomato. Back in the park, they found a quiet bench along the Seine where they ate their sandwiches and drank a bottle of water apiece. The garden became everything that Paris was and the couple lounged around most of the afternoon watching and talking to strangers. They ended up walking up and down the Sienne a bit to catch some photos of Paris icons such as the Eiffel Tower and Notre Dame. There was no need to climb them or take tours within them; just seeing them from the outside was magic enough. Jim enjoyed capturing the famous French church in the same picture frame as a McDonalds, which was across the street. The irony of the French allowing the most American of things to intermingle with their most sacred structures was pure fascination to Jim.

"We go to Chinatown for dinner, yes Jim?"

"Chinatown in Paris?"

"Oui, it is very good."

"I thought I was supposed to have some fancy French cuisine while in Paris."

"Too expensive. Chinatown more food, less money. We go Jim. We not too far; I think you like."

"Lead the way, my dear." Jim responded. He was up for anything. Jim thought it very interesting to go to the Chinatown of Paris. It wasn't something that he thought about in association with Paris, but most large cities in the states had Asian areas called Chinatown, so why wouldn't European cities? Jim's mission while travelling in Europe was just to experience it as it came and not to force anything. There was no schedule — no limits or obligations for at least a couple more weeks when he was supposed to meet Elizabeth in Zurich.

The meal at the Chinese restaurant was very authentic and for Jim, much of it was repulsive and slimy. It wasn't the fried and sauce-drenched stuff that he was used to, but then he didn't get to order. The menu was in French, so he let Fanny order which turned out to be a mistake that he would suffer through one slow, aggravating bite at a time. Jim gagged down the food, but this time he made no comments to his kind and gracious Parisian tour guide. He didn't want to sour the day, so he ate a little of the food and supplemented the rest of his diet with bottled Chinese beer that was dirt cheap and washed away the dishwater aftertaste of the squirming animals that he was chewing to their deaths. The couple still had a lot of trouble communicating. Jim would tell stories of America that Fanny would want to hear, but her face would quickly look puzzled and lost as Jim expounded. This frustrated Jim to the point where he gave up on communicating freely and left all verbal communication to be instigated by Fanny. If she asked a question he would answer in as simple English as possible and leave it at that.

Jim could only handle one more day of the situation at hand. His gracious tour guide was a wonderful person and the free place to stay combined with a lifetime of experience in the city would have persuaded most travelers to stay at least a couple more days. Jim, on the other hand, had no patience for the struggle to communicate and the "no hanky panky." If he was going to beat his head against a wall trying to communicate, he at least wanted to be getting laid. Not only was she not fucking him, she wasn't introducing him to anyone that would fuck him.

"I like girls, Fanny. Can you find me a girl for tonight, maybe one of your friends who can meet us out or something? I need you to set me up."

"Fanny no have too many girlfriends. I know mostly men, not too many girls."

"I'm being kind of selfish, I know, but I have to leave tomorrow night I think. I need to head south, find a beach and some companionship. Not that you're not the finest host a man could have in Paris, 'cause you are. You're a sweet, wonderful woman and I still need another perfect day in Paris with you, but I think later on tomorrow I need to find myself a train. You understand?"

"Tomorrow you go?" Fanny asked with a somewhat hurt expression. Most of the time she smiled, but she left the smile out of this reply.

"Yes, after we see some more of the city. What do you think? Are there some more places you would like to show me?"

"Yes we will go. Fanny will show you more. You come back to Paris you call Fanny always, yes?"

"I'll never forget you, my dear. My Parisian angel," Jim concluded on their journey back to the flat.

Fanny didn't understand why Jim wanted to leave so soon and did not feel the same frustration when it came to the language barrier because she was actually trying to become better at speaking English while Jim had little interest in learning French for his short visit. Fanny was kind and simple and truly enjoyed nourishing a platonic relationship with what she considered her sweet American friend.

Jim wasn't blind to the purity of Fanny's gestures, he was just ambivalent, because his loins were a stronger driving force than his brain — this would be his weakness for many years to come. There was one truth that Jim knew to be self evident and that was the fact that he could not bear to sleep with a woman in her panties, especially a woman with the fine figure of Fanny, without trying to remove said garment. Two nights was all he could stand of such torture.

The next day the couple woke up and went through the same routine of breakfast and coffee, but on the way out Jim carried his packs. They would drop them off a locker at the train station before beginning their day of sightseeing.

Their first destination was a maze of cobblestone streets used only by foot traffic that made up the wonderfully free-spirited Latin Quarter. The vendors were crammed into tight retail spots pitching everything and anything one could imagine with the smells of world cuisine wafting through the market-like atmosphere. The Latin Quarter was alive with guests from around the world selecting souvenirs as well as Parisians buying rare spices and incense as well as hard to find fruits and vegetables. Jim loved the lively, tight spaces full of arts and crafts. There were also a lot of purely French items such as wine shops displaying all the best of French wines, berets and designer clothing boutiques. The food ranged from American style pizzerias to Thai to rich, strong Indian curry that all mixed with the smell of bakeries making fresh bread and pastries. Jim and Fanny snacked on numerous dishes as they wandered through the market haggling with the street vendors for a couple of Parisian keepsakes. Jim would haggle with the vendors just to get them frustrated and then walk away with the item at an extreme discount because the vendor would just want to get rid of him. Fanny even employed him with items that she wanted to purchase even though she was embarrassed by his brashness. She would walk across the street with her back to him as he did his dirty work so she wouldn't have to be a part of the pushy American's antics.

By the time lunch officially came around, which became a time to rest instead of eat since they had been nibbling all day, the two had met their spending limits as well as their belly's limits. They headed to the nearby Luxembourg Gardens to rest and digest. Jim and Fanny rested in the Paris sun knowing that their time together was limited. Jim was headed to the train station soon and Fanny would be catching the subway back to her part of town, but there was a satisfaction within them both — a feeling that they had a little piece of each other slivered away in their memories forever. Jim felt good that he had acted as a gentleman and that he would leave his new friend with the perception that he had some self-control. Fanny saw Jim as a kind, fun-loving man who came along just when she needed some company. She was amazed how two people from such different worlds could come together and become a functional unit of pure, enjoyable friendship. It truly was as simple as that — an instant of friendship that brought two different souls together to share the warmth of being human.

When Jim kissed Fanny on both cheeks as they said their goodbyes in the lush landscape of the gardens, Jim felt a sad nostalgia that glistened his eyes just a touch and Fanny let one tear slide down her cheek before wiping her eyes and putting on a smile. Jim turned and walked away from the shadows of Luxembourg Palace into the bright Paris day planning to catch the TRV heading south.

Fanny watched her unique friend walk away wondering if they would ever cross paths again.

Later that afternoon Jim caught a train to Bordeaux. "I wonder if I'll ever see her again. I should have stayed another day. I think she liked my company and I could have tried harder to communicate. Sometimes I wonder what kind of person I am — how completely self-indulgent I can be? Is there more kindness somewhere deep down inside me or am I just along for the ride? Do I like me? Sure. Chill out, Jimmy. Have a beer and relax."

Chapter 3
JOEY

Jim got on a train headed to Bordeaux, but he was planning on continuing through Spain and into Portugal. He had some Portuguese blood and wanted to see how well he fit in. Portugal also had some mystery to it and you didn't hear of a lot of the other backpacking travelers heading that way, so Jim chose Portugal to try to blaze his own path. He wanted to extend his dominion on unique destinations. Sure it was "the running of the bulls" in Pamplona and surely every other drunken college student would be risking their life to soak up the culture, but Jim would be in Portugal being careless with his life within the culture.

The French train glided along on its rails at a miraculous speed and in a very smooth, soothing manner. The interior of the train was very neat and for the most part was filled with French businesspeople with the occasional backpacker mixed in. The seats were in groups of four with two facing two others, so that half of the seats were zooming along going backwards. Jim put his bags at the storage area in the front of one of the cars and made his way to a lightly populated part of the car. He made himself comfortable and took a nap to recover from the two long days of tromping around Paris with Fanny. She kept him moving the entire time he was in Paris, so the train ride was a welcomed time for relaxation, which was made easy on the French luxury train. There was no sound of rails screeching or thumping through transitions, just a quiet floating like a phantom railway car. The train would race though the countryside unbridled and then as it began to bear down on a populated area, it would slowly decelerate until it stopped at the town station. Then, it would sprint out of the station without jerking or swaying—one fluid movement that the passengers hardly even noticed.

About halfway through France, Jim awoke and found himself parched and in need of alcohol and nicotine. He got up and made his way to a car selling refreshments. His journey took him through four cars before he hit the payload. He noticed one of the cars was a smoking car and as he was walking back towards his car he plopped down and lit a cigarette while swigging his first Amstel Light of the day. He enjoyed the utility of the smoking car, but he didn't want to sit there throughout the journey. It was hazy and depressing, while his assigned seat was located in a lively car that seemed to be more bustling with life. After an infusion of nicotine, Jim made his way back to his original seat. Now this is a very important moment in his summer journey. He could have interacted with anyone, and almost anyone would have been a healthier acquaintance than the blond-haired man across the aisle, but it was this exact man that Jim decided to strike up a conversation with. It was the beginning of a long journey that would tunnel through darkness and come spitting and coughing back out into the light only after the devil himself had been at the table.

The man's name was Joey. He was English and lived in a German castle with his American wife. Jim had observed Joey for a while before engaging him and noticed that he was quite opinionated and outspoken. He was just waiting for someone to jump in with both feet—someone with a craving for alcohol and drugs who wanted to make this trip much more than just a train ride. Joey offered Jim a Valium and a beer within the first couple minutes of their conversation.

This catered to two things Jim enjoyed the use of, drugs and alcohol. Someone offering him both in the first five minutes of knowing them was sure to be a lifelong chum.

"Where ya headed?" Joey asked.

"Lisboa. Lisbon, Portugal. What about you?"

"Ah, Portugal myself, but not the boring capitol city. I'm headed to the south, the Algarve. You don't have any business in Lisbon, do yuh? You should come to the south with me. It's a constant party, my friend, you can't beat it. By the time we get to Lisbon, I'll have you convinced. We'll be all night on the train. Switching trains once in Spain and then again in Portugal. Stick with me and the journey will be a breeze. I make this trip several times a year. I prefer the train to the plane, it is always so much more interesting."

"Appreciate the hospitality. It's good to know someone with your resources and I'm sure your dashing good looks will come in handy if we come across some Bettys."

"Bettys? For Christ sake, lad, where in bloody hell did you get that? I guess you're talking about females and I can't do yuh any good there, I'm married. Got to be good to the wife, she puts up with a lot of shit. But let me tell you what, if they come begging for my services, which is known to happen, I'll send 'em your way, lad."

"You're not shy, right?

"Correct," Joey replied in a sarcastic tone that matched Jim's.

Joey was built similar to Jim, about six feet tall, slim with well-defined muscle structure, but overall he was much prettier and much better groomed than the youthful deviant was. Joey had golden bangs, a sweater vest with a white tee shirt on underneath and

some khaki Dockers with deck shoes and no socks. He was traveling lightly, carrying a couple CD cases, along with one small, black,
leather duffel. His personality had an attraction to others that drew
many in nearby seats into conversations with them. Joey had made
room for Jim in his section of seating and it seemed as if they were
on the journey as a unit, combined to make the train ride as purely
enjoyable as possible. Jim was ten years younger than Joey, but their
spirits were identical, carefree and ready to enjoy every second. The
two began to slide into a medicated comfort that was such a large
part of both of their lives that they began to play off each other in
order to entertain the surrounding passengers. For four hours they
drank heavily, with Joey passing Jim different pills every so often to
encourage further intoxicating results. He just wanted someone to be
as fucked up as he was.

"What's your story? I mean, really, what gives you the right to just
wander about aimlessly? Are you just fucking off or is there something more that I'm missing?" Joey asked Jim as they torpedoed to
the southern border of France.

"Yeah, fucking off maybe, but it's more than that—more like an
in-depth experiment in life. I wanted to come to Europe to test my
hypothesis that people are the same everywhere. I care most about
the people, the human interaction. I don't want to be seen as just
another American tourist, even though it is hard to escape that with
all the bumbling college students tromping through Europe with
their backpacks during the summer. It's hard to escape the stereotype, and maybe I'm being a little self-important by even thinking I
can, but I damn sure want to avoid the stereotypical experiences. I
don't want to live in the pages of this guidebook I'm carrying around.

I mean it's a great resource, but I don't want to live the same journey that its pages entail, I want to add my own volumes. I've always loved to travel and this kind of freedom may not be available after I finish school and I have to make it in the real world. I want to see the entire globe in my lifetime, all of it, and all the people that come with it. I want to know them so that I might understand myself a little more. Supposedly I have some Portuguese blood, so I thought that I would come check out Portugal. I have no real agenda. I just came from Oxford and Paris. I've definitely had some interesting experiences so far. Had an orgy in Oxford. Ended up with a prude in Paris, but she was a great girl, don't get me wrong, I just couldn't handle sleeping in the same bed with a female with a nice ass and not be able to fully take advantage of said ass. Am I talking too much or would you like me to elaborate?" Jim babbled in a self-important haze. He loved to talk about himself and would ramble on for extended periods of time if anyone showed the least bit of interest. He went on to tell Joey the details of his adventure so far, including a complete, boastful depiction of Linda going down on young Katrina. Joey sensed a little immaturity in his traveling mate, but he also was taken in by a keen wisdom, a confidence and self-acceptance that Jim exuded. "This kid is a blast. Just what I need to jump start this trip and he'll be good cover if he sticks with me," Joey thought as Jim continued to make him laugh. From this point forward, Joey was sure to keep Jim by his side. He was confident that Jim would travel all the way to the Algarve with him and the young man was a good source of preservation as well as amusement. Jim would never truly know the reason for Joey taking him under his wing and treating him with so much interest, but he liked the attention and what seemed like genuine friendship. He also liked that Joey was packing a pocket full of goodies and that being around him was like being part of a rolling party. Whether Jim was gullible or just not concerned with the underlying intentions of his shady English traveling partner was not important because they were both committed to party and they befriended everyone around them to join in on the joyous occasion.

"Jimmy boy, we're headed to the Algarve. You're the first mate, you can't jump ship now," Joey said as he and Jim were switching trains in Spain. They had turned the French train upside down, drinking one of the concessions completely out of beer and making a complete ruckus out of their entire cabin. Most anyone who had an inclination to drink and get loud joined them, and that turned out to be a good portion of the travelers.

"I'm just going to let the wind blow me where I need to go, mate. If momentum carries me onward with you then so be it. If there is a beautiful Portuguese woman that wants to bathe me in her Lisbon apartment, then you're going to have to make the trip solo to the Algarve. As it stands now, though, it seems that we are a pretty good team and you paint a pretty picture of the southern beaches. I never thought to go there. It sounds exotic to me."

"That's the spirit. By the way, the rolling party is just getting started. This train will be much more casual." The Spanish train that they were entering was not as luxurious as its French counterpart, but it had private cabins that were cozy and casual, as Joey had described them. Jim enjoyed the new surroundings because it brought a whole new set of characters to the stage. Joey enjoyed the new environment because the more intimate setting allowed for more mischievous behavior. The two men went to the bar car first where they met up with a crowd almost as jovial as them. After a beer or two Joey proposed,

"Why don't we all go get stoned?" The proposal was a great success with the three new friends that Jim and Joey had acquired, so the group headed through the cars looking for an open cabin to spark one up in.

Once in their very own sanctuary, Joey pulled out a wad of what looked like black tar. "It's Nepalese hash. It will take you to another dimension, no doubt." He asked Jim for a couple cigarettes and pulled out a large rolling paper. He then took the hash and rolled it into a long snake and laid it the whole length of the paper, broke up both cigarettes' worth of tobacco and rolled it all together in one big, long spiff. The finished product was an enormous joint that looked dangerous before it was even lit up.

"So, we're smoking the tar shit, huh? That's got to rough on the old lungs. It kinda looks like a big ball of opium, but it's got that pot smell," Jim said after Joey had passed him the remaining chunk of Nepalese hash to examine for himself. Jim had never seen anything like it before and was excited to experience its effects. Sometimes Jim was a little too eager to experiment with new drugs, but the fearlessness was part of his persona and it was actually ingrained and rarely thought about. He had started with cocaine at sixteen and if he was able to overcome the extremely negative stigma that accompanied that drug, then a little hash just seemed like a soft drug to him. He was young and invincible and if someone with ten years on him, like Joey, could enjoy the buzz, then Jim was pretty sure that it would work for him as well.

When the smoke began to thicken there were four men and one woman in the train cabin with the window cracked and the Spanish night forced to take each exhale. The woman was in a light summer dress that reached just below her knees. She had mid-length brown hair with no bangs that split down the middle and was tucked behind her ears. Her eyes were hazel and her face open and expressive. She was not shy, but bold, unique and kind. Her other half was much the same with a kind face that always had a smile on it. He was blond-headed with hair as long as his girlfriend's and bright blue eyes that sparkled with delight. He was shorter than Jim and Joey, but wider than both of them with a thick, muscular stature that he pulled off with fluidity. The third man was very small and his black eyes were very beady. All his expressions were so intense that he would make everyone nervous if he weren't traveling with two such kind spirits. His hair was clipped military style and he wore jeans with a tight black tee shirt that showed off a well-defined yet wiry physique.

The two men were Belgian and claimed to be in the French Foreign Legion, which is an elite military force that is actually made up men from outside France, but is an institution of the French military. Many of these men, it is sometimes said, are escaping persecution in their own countries and have joined the Legion as a form of shelter. It is not a free pass by any means, as the Legion has extremely strict physical and mental standards and many drop by the wayside trying to join its ranks. With all the lore surrounding the Legion, its members are somewhat glamorized as extremely tough mercenaries or so it was said by Joey as he explained what his idea of the French Foreign Legion was. Joey laid out an extraordinary tale that left Jim with the feeling that they were on some super-secret spy mission working their way to right some world injustice or maybe even create one. Joey whispered to Jim as he passed him the joint, "These are some seriously bad-ass motherfuckers. We don't have to worry about getting in any trouble if we stay close to these guys, they're fucking fearless." This was stated after Joey had a long conversation with the two men in German, which they spoke better than English.

Jim thought, "These Europeans are amazing with all the languages they can speak. I took Spanish for two years and I can't speak a lick of it. I surely didn't apply myself, what a fucking surprise. I guess these people start younger and it is much more important to their educations. It is more necessary here with so many languages packed into such a small area. I could probably understand tongues right now. I'm out of my fucking mind." And so the productive thoughts kept racing through the young man's head. He spoke to the group in English, his mind coming back to the people surrounding him, "Can we get involved in some cloak and dagger shit or what? I'm in, whatever it is. My code name is Jackass and I do my best work completely intoxicated," Jim spoke with an enthusiasm that brought the whole group in on his mysterious thoughts.

Joey began to feed the dragon. "These guys are involved in some serious shit, no joke. They just told me that they're going down to Portugal for some kind of state-sponsored dope deal, then they're headed to Morocco for some shady weapons deal. Drugs and guns, man. This is how governments do their dirty work with guys like this, man." Joey told Jim while the Legionnaires sat and grinned, exhaling the toxic hash smoke and nodding their heads as if to agree with every word that Joey was spewing.

"No way, dude. I knew governments were all wrapped up in the drug shit. They're feeding it to the public to keep the power structure intact. Don't yuh think, Joey? I mean if we keep smoking this shit, we sure as hell aren't going to do anything about it. And these bad-asses here are the instruments of the chaos," Jim said still going along with the very interesting conspiracy theory. The Belgian Legionnaires and their female companion were quite amused by Jim's gullible nature. The whole group was getting far too obliterated to keep up the charade much longer and eventually the cabin turned into a sanctuary for the slant-eyed giggles. The composure was out the window and the child within each individual was let out to roam free.

Jim declared after a long fit of laughter, "So you guys aren't really secret agents or what? I need to know what the fuck is going on here. Are you going to shove a bag of heroin down my pants and tell me to make a run for it or what?" There was sarcasm in his voice to let them know that he had caught on to their buffoonery. Jim allowed himself to be the gullible idiot as long as the deceiving was good-hearted. He always went into a situation trusting fully and learning who was prone to joking as relationships progressed and those few who had mean spirits were left to their own evil ways.

By this time the group was in complete submission, like a weight had been lowered onto all their bodies creating total lethargy. They grinned at one another and began discussing topics other than those deceiving one within their ranks. The Belgians began to speak in English so as to not leave Jim out and the topic of pompous Americans came up as it did many times along Jim's travels.

The young Belgian woman spoke to Jim as if he was someone who could rectify the problem by carrying the message back to his fellow countrymen. "Most Americans come to Europa and think that everyone here is to serve them on their holiday. You can always spot the loud American shouting orders, not to say you are like this, Jim. You are very nice man, I see. Very funny, very, how you say, relaxed, or maybe it's just this, huh?" She held the joint in the air as an example of the mellowing agent. Jim didn't answer. He was glued to his seat wishing that the young girl would just come sit on his lap.

Eventually the group worked itself to a complete fervor with energy spilling out the cabin door. The conversations became light hearted and meaningless with lots of laughter to distinguish that things had completely gotten away from them. Everyone became great friends and hugged and drank and smoked more dope together. It was an instant in time where the whole world was inside one train cabin and it didn't matter if that was the only place on earth because it was a perfect, floating bliss. As the party wound down, Jim and Joey finally had to give into weariness and search for another cabin to get some shuteye in. The Belgians had no intentions of sleeping and were still popping open fresh beers when Jim and Joey retired. Joey handed Jim a little blue pill as they lay down on their own bench seats in an empty cabin. They slept soundly as the train glided through northern Spain headed on a southwest course for Lisbon.

In the morning, the loudspeaker squawking at yet another train station rousted Joey and Jim. This time they had to jump on a Portu-guese train to carry them the rest of the way. On the platform outside the train they were reunited with their Belgian Legionnaire friends who still had beers in their hands and were smoking madly, looking like a misplaced rock band. So the group of five from the night before was once again united for another raucous train ride. The train was another step below what they had ridden in Spain in terms of shine and speed, but the cabins were very similar, just a little more worn. For Joey and Jim it was the infamous "wake and bake," which they did gladly with their friends from the night before. The hash smoke rolled out of the train window as they churned through the Portu-guese countryside cracking an early morning cerveza and rehashing the revelry of the night past. By this time the Belgians were get-ting quite boisterous; considering they were completely out of their minds and hadn't slept a wink that was not a surprise, but Jim and Joey had had some sleep, so were not in the same stumbling man-ner. They were not all on the same page anymore and Jim and Joey became less and less comfortable with the group that they had been hugging and cheering with the night before, so they gently distanced themselves from the group once they landed in Lisboa.

Joey didn't have much trouble convincing Jim that it was in his best interests to head to the southern tip of Portugal with him. He painted the southern region, called the Algarve, as better and just as much fun as the French Riviera. The resort town that was their destination was called Albufeira and Jim was excited because of the word "resort," which just made the place sound like a paradise. He was also very encouraged by the hospitality of Joey who had shared absolutely all his drugs with Jim and was on the up side of the beer buying as well.

Joey moved swiftly from the train station in Lisbon to a ferry that would carry them across a bay that split Lisbon in two. This was Jim's only opportunity to see the capital city, and the panoramic view from the ferry was a good spot to take it all in. Lisbon was a large sprawling city that was mostly flat, but had a few rolling hills that carried the mass of humanity slightly up above the sea. There were large white beaches wrapping around the bay and drawing a white line at the edge of the city, which softened it and made it seem more inviting. Jim had been planning to explore this city and to enjoy the beaches, but the allure of an unknown utopia pulled him southward.

The ferry port was within blocks of the train station serving the southern routes and Jim and Joey were on another train within an hour of leaving the last one. The train zipped directly south from Lisbon and when it hit the southern coast, they were in Albufeira. Jim and Joey were finally done with a train journey that had lasted over twenty-four hours. The small town, everything reachable by foot, was bustling with beach-goers, mostly people from the northern reaches of Europe on holiday. The architecture of the town was Latin and white with everything finished in white stucco. It was clean and quaint, but it had a real vibrant energy, like everyone was ready to dance. The flat-roofed buildings climbed a steep hill that shot up from the beach. The vast beaches extended to each horizon with at least a hundred yards of deep white sand reaching from the edge of town to the water. In every direction there were large sandstone structures that had turned into natural arches or large boulder-like structures that jutted out of the beach. They were perfect perches to climb up and watch the sunset, which was happening as Jim and Joey pressed up the hill to find lodging. The village seemed to be serene, but as the night moved in the nightclubs began to turn up their music and it was more noticeable that the streets were lined with clubs and the town sprinkled with bars. It was designed for sun filled days and intoxicated nights and that is what Joey and Jim were looking for. Joey had a good idea what was in store since he made this journey quite often and even owned some part of one of the pumping nightclubs. Jim planned to get to know the little spot very well over the next couple days and build memories that would resonate for a lifetime.

"We've got to stop just up the hill. I go way back with the owners of this place and I've got to conduct a little business with the boys, so stay parked at the bar until I come back down. I've got a great place for us to stay, we'll get to it right after this," Joey explained to Jim as they were walking into a nice open-air bar called The Twisted Turtle, which would be their base of operation for the next week. "Hey boys, good to see yuh. This is Jimmy, a straggler I picked up from America. He's not as bad as he looks. We've had quite an eventful ride from Paris. We were across the aisle from each other on the TRV and I haven't been able to shake the little fucker ever since, especially after I got him polluted on some of the world's finest hash. Jimmy, meet Jimmy as well, and this is my long lost buddy Charlie. Jimmy here is always in a shit-ass mood, so don't mind him, but Charlie here, he should take care of you. Over there, that's Salvador. Make sure you get to know him really well. He's the local that can keep your ass from getting into any trouble in you happen to stumble into the wrong situation." Jim smiled at the owners of the bar and extended his hand. Jimmy, who was closest, ignored the gesture while Charlie jumped over the bar, gave Joey a rough hug and then grabbed Jim and pulled his handshake into a hug.

"I've got to make up for this cocksucker here, huh Jimmy boy? We're going to have to tag you with Jimmy boy so we don't get you mixed up with the old grouch back there. Don't mind him, though, he don't like anyone but Joey and myself and that's even marginal at times."

"You're right, I don't, especially little American pricks," the older Jimmy stated in his crisp English accent and without any hint of sarcasm.

"Lighten up there, old-timer. I come to spend money in your bar.

You don't bite my head off and I sure as hell won't bother you." Jim figured if he spoke straight to this guy that he might get him to treat him with some civility. Even though Jim felt a little uncomfortable and a little pissed, he wasn't going to let this old grump ruin his time in this little Portuguese paradise. When Joey told Jim that Salvador was an important man to know, Jim took heed and befriended him as soon as the other men had left the room. They discussed Jim's trip so far and his reasons for ending up in Albufiera. Salvador instantly joined Jim's forces and offered some him some pertinent advice in his smooth, Latin-accented English. "Don't you worry, my friend, you can have much fun in Albufeira and don't worry about too many rules. My uncle, he is head of police. You get crazy all you want and if you get thrown in the tank, I get you out."

"I don't think that I need to get that out of control, but it is good to know," Jim replied.

"My friend, you'll be surprised what can happen in this town," Salvador added. He was quite the presence behind the bar as Jim spoke to him. He stood six feet five inches and weighed nearly three hundred pounds with very little fat. His full Portuguese blood gave him the dark tan skin of a sailor and he had let his black, curly hair grow down below his shoulders and wore it pulled tightly back into a ponytail. Salvador liked to wear tropical button-up shirts with only half the buttons buttoned, leaving his massive chest exposed for female wonderment. He finished off the outfit with deck shorts and flip-flops, super-casual. He reminded Jim of some of his big Samoan friends, but with much more chiseled features and none of the body fat. His personality was like a bright light that refused to ever be extinguished.

Jimmy and Charlie were one and the same as far as their physical makeup and choice of clothing was concerned. They both had middle-aged smoker-creased faces with sandy brown mops on the verge of thinning as hair. They had medium builds of a little less than six feet and around one hundred and fifty pounds. Jimmy wore a straight-faced frowning expression while Charlie always sported a smile and some dark shades no matter what time of day or night. The men were exiles from England who had settled down to live the latter part of their lives in a tropical, inexpensive environment where they could support their drinking and drug habits without being hit in the head with too much persecution. Joey was their younger partner who owned part of the bar as well as his own nightclub down the street and who kept the flow of drugs constant. At the Twisted Turtle if you asked for a coke they might think twice before serving you a liquid beverage. Cocaine flowed like whiskey, which kept the nightclubs full of lively patrons until the sun came up.

Joey disappeared with Charlie and Jimmy to their apartment, which sat on top of the Twisted Turtle. Joey set a large sack of narcotics on the kitchen table, which lead to a frenzy of drug abuse, or simply use, whatever you want to call it. Once the dope was secure in Albufeira, most of the selling chores went to the trusty, and conveniently above the law, Salvador. While Joey was upstairs completing his transaction and testing the goods with his buddies, Salvador was downstairs tending the bar and asking its solo patron, Jim, if he ever partook of any cocaine. Salvador figured since he arrived with Joey that the odds were pretty good. When Salvador saw Jim's response, which was a slight, knowing grin, he quickly pulled out a small baggy and waved it in front of Jim.

"If you like, I can provide," Salvador assured Jim and then, to Jim's amazement, he poured a good amount of the powdery drug onto the shellacked surface of the bar and expertly arranged two gigantic lines. Jim pulled out an American fifty-dollar bill, rolled it up into a straw and snorted one of the lines in a swift, obviously practiced move. He then handed the fifty to Salvador with a nod for him to keep the snorting device once it had served its purpose.

"Hook me up, amigo. Drugs are my specialty," Jim said, followed by a gagging gesture caused by a large amount of cocaine streaming down his throat. "Hooah, you got to love cocaine to get a night started off right. I've been here all of one hour and I'm already snorting coke with the police chief's nephew. What a bizarro world, but I won't complain. It's like some fucking Al Pacino movie or something, snorting coke right off the bar. I'm very happy with the way things are developing."

"Here you go, Jimmy boy. This'll get you started. Come back whenever you run dry." Salvador handed Jim a good size bag of the powder they had just ingested and Jim immediately returned the favor by laying out two more mouth-watering lines. Jim and Salvador sucked down their second lines, choked, gagged and slapped high fives while laughing at the insanity of it all. For the next hour, Jim talked Salvador's face off telling him a quick summary of his life story and going into great detail about his friend Elizabeth, who had been on his mind.

"She's sexy as hell and was a virgin until just recently. I was hoping to be the first on this trip. I'm meeting her in Switzerland and then we're traveling through Italy and Greece together. That's perfect, right? I mean, that's when you're supposed to lose your virginity, while traveling through Venice and Florence with a man you've known most of your life who really cherishes your vigilance in remaining pure until your twenty-first birthday. This English wanker that she gave it up to doesn't know what he's got and now I've got to wrestle her away from him, cause she thinks she's in love or something."

"It sounds like you really have feelings for this girl, am I right?"

"Man, I don't know what I feel. I wander around this world in a haze and I'm never really sure what I want. I party so fucking hard that it's always like I'm teetering on the edge, just one slip and I'll fall to some awful demise, but if I can keep my balance, then I'm on top of the world. Not too many people can live like that and I surely can't expect her to walk that line with me. I feel like I'm too young to settle down with one girl, yet that is what she would want, a commitment to sanity, a commitment to her— both of which I would have a tough time making. I have some deep feelings for her, don't get me wrong, but there's a long ways to go before we can bridge the gap between our lifestyles. I'm going to leave my mind open, though, man, and let her dictate the rules. She's the one who has to have them and I'm the one who was born to break them, so you tell me if there is any hope for us. What do you think? Do you have a woman?"

"Many women my friend, many women. It's the only way to go. Maybe some day I'll slow down, but for now, I'm looking over the edge like you." As Salvador commented the three older Englishmen came down from their version of a cocaine binge. Jimmy and Joey's eyes were glued wide open while Charlie still hid behind his shades. They all had a little case of the sniffles.

"Let's go Jimmy boy, we're off to our lodging. We'll be back in a flash, boys," Joey stated as he lead Jim out the door and up the hill directly behind the bar. They passed a restaurant, which Joey pointed out as the best place in town to eat, and then came to a two-story, white stucco hacienda. An older woman came out to meet the two men as they approached. She obviously knew Joey and carried a key in her hand. She asked only one question and Joey relayed it to Jim, "You okay with a whole week or what?"

"Works for me," Jim replied. Once inside the house Joey led the way up the stairs. The top floor had three guest bedrooms and a family-size bathroom, which the guest rooms would share. Jim and Joey were assigned to the bedroom directly across from the bathroom, which had a small veranda overhanging the street and an unimpeded view to the sea. The room was tiled in white Spanish tile and had two double beds, a bed stand between them and a small table with two chairs. There were no luxuries, but it was very clean, comfortable and affordable. Jim was reminded of bed-and-breakfasts back in Oregon, but without the breakfast. Jim had noticed a lot of poorer communities from the train window on the journey from Lisbon and was surprised that Albufeira was so modern and seemed devoid of such areas.

Jim and Joey showered and put on some fresh clothes. They still had a couple of cold beers that they had carried from the bar and they made their preparations while downing the cold suds. Joey rolled another hash-laced joint and had it smoldering on the veranda when Jim came back from the shower. The pollution continued after the joint was burnt to their fingertips with Jim dumping a pile of cocaine on the bed stand and offering his buddy a sniff.

"Where the fuck did you get that?" Joey asked in amazement.

"I've got connections in this town, man." Joey soon realized that Jim must have scored from Salvador and that it was probably his dope to start with. It wasn't until later that night that Jim found out who the source of the drugs really was. The two men were now slicked up in their nightlife duds and were also fired up on a plethora of substances washed down with their favorite frothy beverage. The ticking time bomb had been wound and was bound to go off at some time, but for the time being, the two men were functioning pretty well. They looked like the bad guys from an episode of Miami Vice; kind of seedy, but definitely cool. They skipped the restaurant for the evening and headed right back to the Twisted Turtle, which was beginning to show some life.

The Twisted Turtle consisted of two large bars at either end of a big room with one whole wall of windows that were left wide open and a set of stairs that bisected the whole space. The darkest back corner opened up to a cozy patio, which was enclosed by two-story stone wall. The bar was designed for heavy drinking and little else. It had no food, no dance floor, no pool tables or any other distraction that would slow down the main task of putting back beverages.

Jim started a tab with Salvador at the bar nearest the back door to the patio. Jim and Joey set up camp on the back patio where the tables were made of polished. The police would leave the Twisted Turtle off their patrol loop anyway, so the area was pretty safe for illegal activity. The shiny, hardtop tables made it awfully tempting to do lines of cocaine in-between drinks. "Break out some shit and line it up, Jimmy boy," Joey requested after they had both knocked down at least five whiskey and cokes.

"Right here, don't you think Jimmy will have a shit fit?" Jim asked as Salvador came around the corner with another round of drinks and joined the couple for his break.

"Don't worry, I'm going to do one too and I'm their fucking insurance policy so they won't get mad," Salvador exclaimed, eyes bright and smile ripping from ear to ear. "Nothing to worry about senor, no worries, bro." With the reassurances Jim dumped out a pile and lined it up. Salvador went first, and then Joey took his time slowing sniffing half up one nostril then switching nostrils so that each inhaled exactly the same amount of cocaine granules. He showed no worries of sucking down the white powder in a public place. At the very moment that Jim bent down to inhale the final line, Jimmy came out on the patio.

"What the fuck are you thinking, you little prick," Jimmy grunted with a pure look of furry and disgust consuming his face. Salvador jumped up from his seat and put his arm around Jimmy, dragging him back through the door from which he had come.

"It's my fault, you can fire me if you want." Salvador tried to settle his boss down, but the older Jimmy had it in for the young American and this incident gave him perfect ammunition to blow the kid to shreds.

"I want that little shit out of my bar, now!" Jimmy hollered as he was dragged off the patio.

At that, Joey got up and went to cool his friend down. "Hey, loosen up. We've been doing shit out there for years and all the sudden you want to throw a fit. Leave the kid alone. I don't give a shit if you don't like him, he's with me and I'll be responsible for him. You're not kicking him out, he's fucking harmless and a lot of fun if you'd give him a fucking chance, but I can see you're not going to do that so just stay the fuck away from him." Jimmy walked off in a fervor and left the group alone on the patio. Jimmy didn't like the way the young man carried himself. He was too carefree and his confidence level seemed to teeter on the verge of cocky, so the old bar owner instilled a grudge that for the life of him young Jim could not dislodge. Jim didn't understand how someone could dislike him so much without even taking the chance to have a conversation with him. It was disturbing and unsettling to him, but he carried on with his friends who had fervently stood up for him. The fact was that the older Jimmy didn't care that they were doing cocaine on the back patio, he knew that it was the safest place in town to get high, with the fortress walls and the only one entrance, it was simply the fact that the Yankee was having his way with his friends and employees in his bar with an ease and enjoyment that should only be available for those he had directed it towards.

Jimmy left them alone on the patio and as time passed, the patio became more and more crowded. There were Germans, English and even some locals that gave the patio an international ambiance. The night was beginning to have an electric feeling as the crowd built stronger and stronger buzzes. Whiskey was drunk by the shot with beer and cocaine chasers. There was no need to experiment with traditional Portuguese drinks like port; the American whiskey, Dutch beer and Colombian cocaine seemed to be the perfect mix. Jim and Joey's table was large and after a while either Jim or Joey had asked a group of strangers to join them. This is when Joey broke out a large bag of cocaine, poured a good-size pile on the table and offered it to all comers. Surprisingly, the narcotics did not scare anyone off and were ingested by almost everyone at the table except for a few who politely denied as if it was simply a strong beverage that they were not interested in choking down. Jim thought to himself, "Why shouldn't it be like this, cocaine flowing freely at the bar, a little pick-me-up to keep the mind a little sharper, probably even a little safer than blithering idiots polluted on alcohol alone. The world is crazy how it regulates what you can and can't put in your body. This is my temple; I should be able to burn it down if I please. I know that this shit is extremely addictive and can tear you down and leave you with nothing, but it's there anyway, it's easier to get than a drink in some cases, just let it go. Let it be—let the world be what it will, cause it will anyway. I've got to get out of my head. I'm starting to think in circles and I think I'm talking out loud to myself." Jim wasn't talking out loud to himself, he was mumbling, but nobody noticed. Jim looked around the table and wondered how he ended up with a crowd just like the one he used to end up with in the Oregon hills. The kind of people he gravitated towards were always in the back room or on the back patio up to no good without any fear of repercussions—the invincible youth.

The night wore on and Jim and Joey made their exit from the Twisted Turtle accompanied by a very vibrant Scottish drug dealer who worked directly for Joey. His job was to supply everyone outside the Twisted Turtle, especially in the nightclub that Joey owned, the ecstasy and cocaine that Joey kept the town supplied with. The Twisted Turtle acted as its own drug depot of which Neil, the Scot, was not allowed to sell in, nor was he truly under the protection of Salvador. Neil was loud, fearless and funny, as long as you stayed on his good side. Joey described him as the toughest man he had ever known even though that was hard to believe since he was only

about 150 pounds and no greater than five-feet-nine-inches tall. The
three men became the best of comrades that evening and all spoke
nonstop, interrupting each other frequently to profess bigger and
better stories of masculine superiority. "Did you know, Jimmy boy,
that the men from Glasgow, Scotland are considered the toughest in
all the world, huh did you know, Jimmy boy?" Neil exclaimed with
a matter-of-fact air and a goofy-looking seriousness that put Jim on
the floor of the nightclub laughing.

Joey backed his friend up, "He's right mate, they say the Glasgowe-
gian man is the toughest on earth. It has been proven time and time
again when you put a Scot up against anybody, he'll walk away without a scratch with a poor, bloody bastard lying on the floor. I've seen
it with me own eyes, my boy." Both men kept unbelievably straight
faces while attesting to their sworn truth and it sent Jim into an
uncontrollable fit of laughter that got the cocaine and alcohol pumping ever more efficiently into his brain, which was amazingly lucid
considering the amount substances he had dumped into his body.

After he got control of himself Jim had top comment, "I would
wipe the floor with your skinny little Scottish ass. It would take a
whole herd of you little Scottish turds to take down this finely-bred
American machine." Jim was two hundred pounds and had spent
his life wrestling and playing football, and he could see no way that
this little sawed-off man could be a threat to him without carrying a
large weapon.

"I'll allow you some youthful ignorance, my boy, but you'll learn
some day. You're lucky I like you or I might give you a little testament
to the true furry of a Scottish blow. It goes back to before your time.
You get a little more worldly and you'll come back to me some day and

admit that I was right. Everywhere you find a bloody Scotsman, you'll find that he's the toughest cocksucker in the place, no doubt."

Jim left the boasting alone and took it as pure comedy. The three men were playing pool on the upper floor of a lively nightclub that Joey happened to own. This allowed the group to enter the owner's office, which had two-way mirrors running all along one of the walls peering onto the dance floor. In the office, long lines of cocaine were chased with shots of fine whiskey, and all exaggerated upon the constant talk of male conquests, mostly about women and extraordinary partying experiences. With a perfect polluted state of being, drinking enough to make the constant nag of the cocaine subside, the three men exited the office and made their way down the half-circle carpeted stairway to the flashing lights of the thriving dance floor. The three crusaders melted into the gyrating space, dispersed from each other and found women to move their bodies against, increasing their momentum towards complete sensory overload. Hearts beat a million miles an hour as the coke mixed with the whiskey and marijuana. Moving to the rhythm brought beads of sweat to the brows of the men, which ran down the sides of their faces, skirting their cheeks and soaking into their already drenched shirts. They stayed on the dance floor though multiple dancing partners. Sometimes they watched each other, laughing and pointing at the unique gyrations that each was not shy to display and sometimes they were completely focused on the perfect women who were sharing their space. The men danced for over an hour, pushing their bodies beyond what would be possible without the chemical enhancement, but even the chemicals wore down after a while and the men found themselves recuperating at the bar. It was already broad daylight outside, a beginning of a new day, while the men were still lost in the previous one, as the club was enveloped in darkness that was specifically designed to elude the sun's rays. Jim was staring off into space when Joey patted him on the shoulder and said, "Step back a bit, I think Neil has found himself a friend."

Jim snapped to reality, took a step back, and looked toward Neil who was standing next to Joey, leaning up against the bar with his back to Joey. He was exchanging words with a blond headed, blue-eyed Dutchman who was Neil's size, but a little broader and friendlier looking. The conversation looked sensible with both men's faces not showing any sign of distress, but Joey had asked Jim to step back for some reason, so something must have been going on that Jim could not perceive. Then, wham, Neil took one hard step towards the man and sent him flying across the dance floor with a genuinely viscous head-butt. The man skidded across the hardwood surface, blood spewing from his forehead and nose, and collided with two large speakers that were stacked on top of one another. The speaker on top crashed to the floor and everyone nearby jumped back from the scene in horror. Two giant bouncers grabbed Neil, lifting him up in the air and depositing him on the street outside the club. Neil did not fight with the giant men. Jim and Joey followed behind the buzzing crowd that was migrating to the street.

"We've got to help him," Jim said, thinking that Neil was sure to pick a fight with a whole group of Dutch men.

"Yeah, we've got to help him get the fuck out of here." Joey replied with a whole different state of mind and sense of clarity. Joey had a cool head and was not one for street fights, even though he claimed to be very efficient in certain martial arts.

Jim and Joey came walking out of the club into the blinding light of the early morning sunrise without expecting any light at all and were nearly dropped to their knees by the unexpected shock to their eyes. Once adjusted, they each grabbed one of Neil's arms and escorted him away from the scene while he screamed obscenities over his shoulder to the man he had just bloodied in the club, who had also been dragged to the street by bouncers. The Dutchman was putting on a little show for the crowd, screaming for a good old-fashioned fist fight to restore his honor, but he wasn't motivated enough to chase Neil down and tear him from his two larger escorts. Neil, on the other hand, was itching to get free and cause some more damage. He was constantly squirming and jerking in an effort to race back and partake in the brawl. Joey laid out firm instructions to Jim, "Don't let go of the sorry little bastard. I can't have the club liable for his ridiculous fucking actions. Calm down you fucking deviant." Neil started to chill a little bit once Joey stated his concerns, but he continued to throw obscenities over his shoulder to the Dutchman who was still standing in the middle of the narrow cobblestone street with his arms bowed out and blood dripping off his upper lip. The macho show continued until the threesome was out of earshot, but the Dutchman never advanced on the group and surely didn't want any more of the psycho Scotsman. Neil had cleaned his clock in one quick, swift move. It was all over a woman on the dance floor, but it didn't matter, it had become legend.

"Did ya see that, Jimmy boy? That there was the Glasgow Kiss. Works every time no matter what the size of the motherfucker you need to take down and the beauty is, usually you break the fucker's nose as well," Neil exclaimed as they got a couple blocks away from the commotion.

"I don't think it is good to feed an angry man cocaine. I mean, you spoke about the furry in the blow of a Scotsman, well that has to come from somewhere and I'm pretty sure the stimulant increased the viciousness ten fold, or maybe you're just bloody insane. I don't really get it." Jim shoved Neil to see if he could get a little of the crazy stirred up, but Neil just shook his head and continued on.

The three men found a table to plop themselves down at a small bakery that had just opened its doors to the fresh new morning. The night had come and gone and there were no beautiful women by their sides, but they had acquired a life-long memory of Neil delicately applying the Glasgow Kiss on an unsuspecting Dutchman. They had also inhaled about a quarter-ounce of terrifically strong cocaine and were not about to go to bed. The men knew that the next major venue would be the beach, but they still had three to four hours before the sandy shores began to come alive. The café provided the entertainment needed by making ready an entire bottle of vodka for their early morning patrons to mix with their orange juice. Somehow Joey knew this would be possible when he took the lead at sitting down at this particular café. Jim got the feeling that he and Neil had shared an early morning cocktail at this establishment in the past; they were just too familiar with how to acquire liquor at sunrise.

Alcohol mixed with the drug and the clarity began to dissipate with a sunshine haze taking over that left the men floating around searching for just the right situation to make the day glide into bliss. There was no more violence on their minds and the topic of their increasingly deep conversations began to gravitate towards women. What made the perfect woman in each man's terms? They were fairly youthful perspectives, but Joey was the eldest and the only one married. Joey thought highly of his wife, or at least he spoke of her beauty and finer qualities, but his excitement on the subject of women was not directed at his bride. Joey allowed women other than the one to whom he had pronounced his faithful obligation to flow in and out of his life. He cheated, and he wasn't the least bit shy in describing some of these encounters. Joey had no scruples with morality. His description of a perfect woman was a lesson on this bent morality. "A perfect woman, lads, is completely independent, sure of herself, and able to use you just as you would her. She's got to be able to distance herself from her emotions, if just for an instant, to see the situation clearly. Most women can't do that, they're driven by their emotions and that makes them dangerous to us because we blokes just don't understand their basis for decisions, we don't understand their emotions. How can we? We're cold as ice, just want to get our dick wet and fuck all the sentimental bullshit. I like women who are driven and greedy just like me, that way I don't have to wade through any crap. You bleed each other for what you can get and move on," Joey stated with a nonchalant air.

Neil quickly replied with a vexed look squishing his eyebrows together, "You fuckin' wanker. How do you get a hard-on with ice running through your veins? That's the true definition of blue balls, aye mate."

"I'm not sure you have any respect for yourself or the women you're sticking it to. That's a fucking heartless ideal, bleeding each other. We're not vampires. You drain a woman and then go to the next, is that all I have to look forward to, faceless relationships serving my loins? I mean I love a one night stand as much as the next conceited prick, but I value the tenderness of a sweet woman who can break me away from logic for a while and take me for a swim in her emotional world," Jim announced with his youthful utopian perspective.

"What the fuck did he just say? Did you hear that babble, Neil? I'm not sure you've got a fucking clue, young Jim. This could go real bad for you one day, these pansy-ass feelings you've got. That is what a wife is for, once you get ready for such a thing. All these feelings and whatnot you're talking about, you can explore such ridiculous notions with a wife. That's why I've got one, so when I'm around her I can be a civilized human that looks like he has a place in society, but the reality is that it is just window dressing on the savage that I truly am. When I'm on my own, I revert back to my animal instinct. You're a naïve young man when it comes to women, my boy. They'll suck you dry if you let them get their talons too deep into your skin. Just like you said, a woman can make you lose your basis for logic and that's not a safe place to be no matter how good it feels. I've had a lot of experience in this game and I've come to find that it is a power struggle and the winner is the only one that is truly satisfied. Don't feed me any idealistic bullshit young Jimmy boy, I've already done it all; you'll learn."

But Jim's idealism could not allow such defacement. "I'm not getting married so that I can have a civilized side. Look at us, there is no civility here and if your wife strolled up to the table, that surely wouldn't bring the civility out of you. There is no way to wash away eight hours of coke and alcohol abuse or for that matter the forty-eight hours of complete debauchery that I've experienced since I've met you. We are the spirits of the ever-shifting winds, the kamikazes of the free world, there is no civility among us and I believe that the perfect woman is one that can fly the mission with you, not one that you have to put on a different pair of pants for. You live in your diluted nostalgia and I'll continue to live in the moment."

Neil put in his two cents, "I'll take 'em any way I can get 'em as long as they're still warm. Drink up fellas, pretty soon we'll be able to scan the beach for our own version of a perfect senorita and I believe my warm and willing version will win out even for you two freaks."

"Good luck finding the perfect little sweetheart, kid. I'm looking for a nasty little slut that'll take it in the ass," Joey stated, with drunkenness starting to slur his statements.

The three men stayed at the café until the entire bottle of vodka had been polished off. Then they stumbled down the street towards the beach, stopping at a small market to purchase giant cans of Fosters beer. The cocaine was put away for the time being and each man slowly began to sway downward to a drunken indecency that was amusing to some while completely obnoxious to others.

By noon the men had managed to change into beach attire and were standing by the steps that led down to the beach packing fresh cans of Fosters, shirtless with sunglasses and swimming trunks. Neil was a white, skinny scarecrow while Jim and Joey sported impressive physiques with muscular statures and tan skin. The three stooges of Albufeira attracted many women with their looks, but could only hold together for a very short time without saying something lewd. And so many women were waved down by the men and contracted for a minute of their time only to walk away speedily, hoping to put some distance between themselves and the three dysfunctional jackasses that could barely be understood.

At some point, completely defeated but quite amused, the men dragged each other up the hill to their rooms. Their dry throats and scorched skin hit the mattresses with three distinct thuds. Lights out for the toxic trio who had used every minute of the last twenty-four hours in order to deliberately pound themselves into submission. It was the natural mentality of each of these men to live life in an altered reality that was dependent upon extremes. Youth was perfect health and invincible chaos that was rarely met with any resistance.

Jim and Joey settled in their shared room while Neil made his way to a flat nearby. All three slept soundly through the night and into the next day when the hot sun began pouring into their rooms. Jim and Joey arose feeling quite queasy, but undeniably hungry—they had not eaten a meal since arriving in Albufeira. They popped a couple Valium to help the pain and shakes subside, took showers and headed to the café just next to their lodging.

It was a quaint little place with a sit down, diner-style bar and a couple mismatched tables, which were all full. The two men took seats at the bar on some bolted-down stools with round swivel-top seats and ordered a couple beers which they choked down; knowing that if they could get the first one down it would assist greatly in beating back the hangover with its own poison. Joey ordered the food and Jim was happy with the choice once it arrived in front of them. It was fried chicken that had been cooked in a pan with just the right amount of spices in the thin batter. The two men huffed down the food and worked their way into a second beer, which went down a little smoother, but still stung a little bit. With their bellies full, they hit their room for an adrenaline boost, choking down huge lines of cocaine so as not to bring any with them, what restraint. They both concluded that they could not continue on like the previous night; their bodies would not stand for it. Even though there was over ten years between them, they both had similar resistance levels as far as pushing their body's through excessive bouts of partying.

Jim and Joey made the walk one more door over after dinner and found themselves tying on a professional drunk at the Twisted Turtle. This continued for several days—drinking, doing drugs and chasing women who were generally turned off by the belligerence. The week was a haze—a flash of strobe lights from dance clubs, a pile of cocaine sucked down during most waking hours, a search for some marijuana that ended up with Jim getting ripped off and beach days with half naked women fading off in the sunset to a much firmer reality. Jim and Joey were always scavenging the town looking for some female companionship, but each time they would get close it would slip away like fog lifting from its morning cover. They would be on different schedules, wandering about the town on their own accord, but it seemed that each evening they would find themselves planted next to each other on barstools at the Twisted Turtle. Joey thought highly of the drifter he had picked up and defended him vigorously against the attacks of the elder Jimmy. They had long conversations while lying in their double beds at the conclusions of their drunken nights and if they ran into each other in town they would always track down a Fosters and chum around for a bit.

One evening, near the end of Jim's week in Albufeira, Jim got to the room exhausted from being in the sun all day and spied half a Valium in the side pocket of Joey's bag. "Perfect little come down for a long-ass week," Jim thought. He grabbed the pill and slid it down his throat with some help from a bottle of water nearby. The pill seemed to cool the steaming blood that was pumping through him and he was so thankful for the little shred of relaxation that it brought him.

Several hours later Jim woke to a frantic Joey, "Jim, did you take my last fucking Valium?"

"Yeah man, I'm really fucking sorry. I had no idea it was your last one."

"You fucking idiot, that's my medicine. I won't get a bit of fucking sleep and my wife is coming tomorrow. I'll be a fucking zombie and she'll have me pegged. You can't just take other people's shit, you little prick."

"Hey, wait a minute, man. I made a fucking mistake. You don't have to be a jerk about it. You've been handing those things out like candy all week and I figured that was just extra that you left lying around. I'm really sorry, maybe I can find you some in town. I saw a pharmacy down the way, maybe they'll sell some to me." Jim got himself dressed with serious intentions of finding some Valium. How hard could it be; the little blue pills were universal. Joey was steaming mad because he had been sucking down coke with Jimmy and Charlie, counting on that last half Valium to carry him until his wife arrived with a new supply.

Jim headed to the pharmacy that he had noticed several times during his visit—it was hard to miss with its bright neon first aid cross lighting up the night. He had no idea if he could just go up to the window and purchase the drug, "I'll just tell them that I've run out and that I have a prescription back in the states, but I don't have the bottle for proof. I think I need more of an urgent situation like my wife having a severe anxiety attack and she left her pills in Paris, there we go, that's it," Jim thought standing across the street, afraid to actually address the pharmacist. As he contemplated, Jim watched two young men go to the pharmacy window and walk away with a couple packages of pills. Jim thought it better to test his theories with the two young men than to go directly to the window. He was uncomfortable in his current predicament, but shyly approached the young men because he was desperate to make up for his bullocks with the Valium. "Hey guys, do you speak English at all?"

"Yeah, yeah, yeah, no problem. What's up?"

"Do you know if it would be possible for me to walk up there and buy some Valium, will they sell it to me?"

"No, they will not sell it to you, not without doctor's note."

"There is no way for me to get some? I have money. Is there any way one of you guys could buy some?"

"We can not get them, but we have these, which are just like Valium. They're German Valium, twice as strong, you want?"

"Alright, can I buy some of those from you?" Jim asked somewhat defeated. He felt like these guys were being honest with him and he hoped that Joey would be happy that he found something, but deep down he felt like he had failed and there was no way to overcome it. The pills being just like Valium, but twice as strong made sense to Jim.

"We give you some, no problem. Do you stay nearby? We want to smash some up—they work faster that way. Can we go by your room to do that? We'll give you a couple and you can try it our way, we snort them. Goes to your head real fast, you'll like it."

"Yeah, then you guys can explain to Joey what the fuck you got here. I ate his last Valium and he's pissed at me. I'm hoping one of these will calm him down." Jim and the two Portuguese men headed to the room. As they passed the Twisted Turtle, Neil came bouncing out and approached Jim.

"Hey, Jimmy boy, have you ever had any ecstasy?" Neil asked in a hushed voice so the other men couldn't hear.

"No. Why, you got some?"

"Yeah. Here are a couple of them; I think you'll like them. Get with me later to pay me for them. They're kind of expensive, twenty quid apiece, but they're worth every penny, I assure you."

"I'm only paying fifty American bucks. That's one of my travelers checks and it's way out of my budget, actually I fucked up and forgot to budget money specifically for drugs, so I really can't afford such luxuries, but for a new euphoric experience, what the hell. What is it like? Do I need two?"

"Two is better than one, mate and the fifty bucks is fine. These things will take you to the moon—I guarantee it. You'll fucking love it. It's kind of like an acid trip except it doesn't wind you up like a top and leave you twisted, but it makes your body feel great and you definitely go through a mental trip that's a fun ride," Neil stated with a salesmanship that put Jim beyond his angst of spending more money, which he was doing rapidly in the beach community.

"Alright, I'll get with you tomorrow if I'm not locked up for going crazy on this shit ," Jim said with a grin on his face, anticipating that he was in for a fun night. He had heard a lot about ecstasy and would have jumped at any opportunity to take it, which is exactly what he did. He slid the two pills in his pocket and marched up the hill with his two new Portuguese buddies in tow. He really didn't know them well enough to introduce them to Neil and Neil showed no interest in being introduced, so Jim just left it alone.

When the three men reached the room, Jim tried to explain him-self, "Hey Joey. I met these guys at the pharmacy and they said that they could spare a couple of these Domikan. They say they're just like Valium, except a bit stronger. Do you want one?"

"Give me a fucking break, Jim. I'm not taking some shit I've never heard of. Go out on the fucking balcony and let me try to get some fucking sleep."

"I'm sorry, Joey. I tried, man."

"You're alright, just let me sleep. I'll live," Joey responded in an ir-ritated, yet wiped out fashion.

The three men went to the veranda where one of the men began smashing the pills he had into a powder form, "We like to snort them. It hits you quicker that way. I'm Paunch, by the way and this here is Thomas, but I call him Tommy, he likes it better."

"I'm Jim, Jimmy, whatever you want to call me." Jim was looking at the line they had prepared for him— they had both already snorted theirs. "I've got some ecstasy that I'm going to eat, do you think I should mix this shit with it?"

"Go for it, man, no problem. We take you with us. We'll keep an eye on you. You'll like it very much."

"I appreciate the hospitality. It'll be cool to go out with some locals. I came from the states on a little summer jaunt. It's been a blast so far, and I keep running into cool people wherever I go. Sorry about my buddy, he's usually really cool, but he's just pissed about the Valium. I took his last one," Jim stated before leaning down to top of the banister wall to snort the white powder that had been made by pulverizing the pills. Jim had conveniently mixed cocaine, Valium, two hits of ecstasy, some German pharmaceutical that he had never heard of and the alcohol from the beer that he washed it all down with.

The cocktail of drugs and alcohol that Jim had ingested was enough to send him into a delirium of intoxication that was nearly impenetrable. Paunch and Tommy, in their downer and alcohol state, had to keep their American friend on a short leash and it was similar to watching a puppy that got into everything which created laugh after laugh. Jim slipped into a black hole of outrageousness that not even he could control, but his Portuguese brothers, as he referred to them throughout the night, stood by his side from club to club. They held him up when his equilibrium seemed to check out and they begged and pleaded with bartenders and bouncers to let him stay at each establishment. Tommy and Paunch dragged Jim along the corridor of clubs, quite amused at their new-found friend who danced in the streets and molested women on the dance floor, when his Portuguese brothers allowed him to venture there. Jim was bouncing off the walls enveloped in his own complete chemical meltdown that left him animated but completely incoherent at times. His mind was pure adrenaline where the thump of the music mixed with the flashing of the strobe lights into an energy that was bursting out his fingertips and constantly tapping both his feet. The true miracle of the evening was not Jim's ability to function through complete poisoning, but that all the people who journeyed through the chemical abyss with him did not try to take advantage of him. Jim's Portuguese brothers kept a cold beer and some ice water in front of him all night, and when he was unable to function at all and was propped up in a corner, they would send females over to comfort their sideways brother.

At seven A.M., Jim found himself in the backseat of a Toyota Corolla blasting through the countryside. He had gone on a journey of grabbing asses, getting slapped and kissing large women which, was just as well that he could not picture. His Portuguese brothers would grin whenever they thought about it for a long time to come, though.

"Donde esta mi hermanos?" Jim spoke what little Spanish he could recollect asking his brothers where they were. "Is it wise to be driving this fast, I feel like I'm on a space ship and we're fixing to take off. Are we traveling at excessive speeds or am I out of my fucking mind?"

"Paunch is top notch driver. He likes to hug the curves. You don't worry, we're going to the only bar open within a hundred miles, so you should be proud that you are with such tour guides," Tommy said from the passenger seat with a shit-faced grin beaming on his face.

"Obrigado, amigos. I don't know what I'd do without you guys, shit, I don't even know what I did with you guys. Why don't you fill me in, I haven't a clue where the night went. Should I be worried that my impeccable reputation has been blemished?"

"What? This is too much English, I like your Portuguese better." The top-notch driver answered while gripping the wheel like a mad man with just the slightest recollection for where they were headed. Tommy understood the question for the most part. "You make many girls in Albufeira very happy with your many kisses, but a couple not so happy. Many of the girls, they like you though, so you so well mostly."

When they arrived at the bar, Jim was having trouble with his newfound sanity in that it didn't connect with his physical functionality. He didn't feel like he had any control over his extremities, or at least not much. Tommy and Paunch pulled him out of the car, stood him up against the vehicle, and gave him a pep talk. "Come on, amigo. All you have to do is make it to the barstool ten meters from here and then we are home free. We can't carry you in like at the clubs. Can you do it? We've come a long way, we must try."

"Oh yeah, I feel better. I'm with it, no problem. One foot in front of the other, man," Jim exclaimed with the true will to get it done, but with severely drug-tinged coordination. He immediately pushed himself from the support of the car and began moving his body confidently towards the door of the cantina, which looked more like a diner with the early morning sunlight streaming in through the clear windows. The entrance and the walk across the smoke-filled room went well. Jim kept his pace going strong, just striving for the nearest barstool, but at the last second, with the stool in reach, there was a step down from the main floor to the bar level and Jim did not maneuver it well. He went flailing down, taking three patrons comfortably minding their own business at the bar, with him. Tommy and Paunch quickly grabbed Jim from the drink-soaked floor and headed for the door as the bartender threw several stern Portuguese phrases into the air.

That was it for the night. There was no need to belly up to another bar and to continue the deluge of sloppiness on more innocent people. The world was a bar and the Portuguese brothers could shape it as they pleased. Jim was begging forgiveness as Tommy and Paunch dragged him to the car and threw him in back. They were not upset, but amused—laughing uncontrollably at their friend's finale of many absurd incidents throughout the evening. Jim was coming back to reality from a place that he had not visited before—a place of chemical induced mayhem where lucidity was lost and replaced with a black hole. Jim didn't like where he had been inside his head, but he was extremely gracious for who had watched over him while he was there. Sure, they were part of the reason he had visited la la land with their huffing of pharmaceuticals, but Jim had walked into that with the same wide open arms that he walked into any mind-altering experience. Jim enjoyed alternate realities, but he was teetering on the edge of self-destruction from the chemical dump he had turned his temple into. It was time for some peace.

"Hey guys, thanks so much for taking care of me. I don't deserve it. I fucked up the whole drive, I'm sorry. Can you forgive me, my Portuguese brothers? I repent for my sins and won't ever mix so many drugs together. What do ya think fellas, do I deserve your friendship? Am I worthy of being chauffeured through the most wonderful countryside of the Algarve by my long lost Portuguese brothers? Huh, fellas, am I?" Jim rambled on seeking confirmation.

"Portuguese brothers for sure, my friend. Let's head to the beach for a soak, a beer and some tits. What do you think, brother, can you make it?" Paunch asked not concerned with the reply because he had already made up his mind that that would be the next course of action and if Jim couldn't make it, Paunch would simply drag him to the water's edge.

The three men had no swimming trunks on hand so they all stripped down to three different shades of boxer shorts and stumbled out into the deep Algarve sand. They laid down at the edge of the surf letting the water lap up onto them as they relaxed, sinking into the moist sand. Paunch had stopped at a fish market on the way there and somehow came walking out with a styrofoam cooler packed full of iced-down beer. Jim didn't ask any questions, he didn't even think it was odd, it was just part of an endless night that was winding down, sipping suds in the early morning surf with the sun streaming up over the horizon. The men had been drinking steadily for nearly twelve hours and were getting their second winds somehow, energized by the cool seawater. Laughter pervaded their every move as they recollected Jim's lunatic binge. The Portuguese brothers lived in the instant that a breath could be taken, that was as far as they wanted to go and as beautiful as they could realize it.

The sun rose to the middle of the endlessly blue sky and Jim finally got himself together enough to make it to the beachside market for more beverages and ice. He was still in his underwear when he did so. As he walked out of a store with a cigarette dangling from his lips and a cooler loaded with beer and ice he ran into his formerly grumpy roommate, Joey. "Hey there you big prick, give me one of those?" He grabbed the cigarette out of Jim's mouth, "How bout one a them, too." He reached into the cooler and extracted a cold one.

"Good, you've gotten over the plunder. Good old Joey, back in the action," Jim said with a beguiling grin and was thoroughly excited that his buddy had gotten over his bad behavior.

"You're in your bloody drawers, mate. You've completely lost it, eh? The Portuguese Riviera can do that to a man, send you to a strange land that you're not even sure how you go to."

"Oh yeah, an insane land with no sleep and no pants."

Joey joined the Portuguese brotherhood as they continued to sit in the surf watching the different shapes of female bodies and building a tin can castle of empty beer cans. Joey, of course, didn't really match the motley crew with his perfectly placed hair and bright blue knee-length swim trunks, but he had not been down the same road as the wacky trio and found it perfectly acceptable that he didn't quite fit in. He actually sat a little distance away so as to not be associated with their crazy antics, which included the mooning of women who refused to sit down for some slobbering conversation.

Once the cooler was at its second emptying, Paunch and Tommy had finally had enough. They stumbled to their car, dropping their drawers completely off for the last hundred yards to receive a colorful reaction from the passing beach goers and to give Jim and Joey one last vision to remember them by. "Those two blokes have a bit of your ancestry, I'm sure," Joey added as Tommy and Paunch turned around and waved goodbye with their peckers blowing in the wind.

Jim and Joey sat staring into the surf wondering what the rest of their holidays might be like—there was no way that the furious pace could be maintained for either of them. Joey would make the trek across town to the luxury hotel that he and his wife would be staying at while Jim would jump on the train and head east, escaping the fury to a relaxed fishing village. They eventually got up and sauntered back to the room together, passing the Twisted Turtle but not stopping for the first time. Joey watched Jim pack his backpack as his stuff was already neatly laid out on the bed. Jim was on the verge of exhaustion, but he had just enough steam to heave his bags and stumble back down to the city square. From the fountain that marked the center of Albufeira, the train station lie one direction while the hotel the other.

"You take care of yourself, mate, and get yourself some rest. Don't forget to call when you get to Germany, you're welcome at the castle."

"You don't want me around your wife, I don't have any table manners. I'll see yuh on the flip side, huh? It's been real," Jim said giving

Joey a firm handshake with half a hug. "I'm going to find the oppo-site of what just happened here. I need to put myself back together. I need some peace."

"You're a legend in my book. I won't forget the last week—I know that. It will never be repeated."

"Not if we want to live." Jim winked and headed towards the train. Joey jumped up on the side of the fountain to sit and watch his friend try to balance himself with a week's worth of heavy pounding trying to knock him down. Jim staggered a couple steps and then miracu-lously remembered that he hadn't taken one photo of Albufeira, so he took out his camera and snapped one of Joey looking at some wom-an's well-crafted behind in a swimsuit. "Perfect," Jim thought, "One photo to sum up a week." He snapped the case back over his camera and continued to the train.

Chapter 4
THE FISHING VILLAGE

J im's next destination was chosen because it was said to be a peaceful place and Jim was in desperate need of a smooth quiet place that could calm his soul. Tavira was another small town on the southern Portuguese coast, further east towards Spain, but it was nothing like Albufeira. The sleepy little town was a fishing village that revolved around its seafood market with the locals working hard until siesta time. The town was not lined with pristine beaches, but a short ferry ride brought you to an island that was an endless beach oasis.

When Jim got off the train his only concern was to find a bed and make use of it. A small Portuguese woman, much like the one who had rented Jim and Joey the room in Albufeira was waiting at the train station looking for a customer for her pension. Jim quickly accepted the offer of a room and was led to the front of the station where the woman's husband sat in an idling car. They zigzagged over the cobblestone streets and ended up in a back alley that didn't seem too promising, but when the woman opened the door and took Jim to the second floor where he would be staying, his mind was immediately satisfied. The veranda doors were open to a view of the river that split the town in two and further on was the Mediterranean that brought its salty, relaxed smell into the room with a peaceful essence. This was the exact spot that Jim was supposed to be. "I'll take it. How much for a whole week, siete days?" The price was much less than Jim expected, so he handed it all over and was given a key to a small room that adjoined the dining room where two matching verandas opened up to a beautiful view of the river and the sea. He never saw the old lady or her husband again.

The room was very small with a single bed, a nightstand and a lamp, but the overall second story pension was good size. A hallway that went back towards the alley had a kitchen through the first open doorway to the left, next came the bathroom and one more bedroom on the left while on the right side of the hallway there were two more bedroom doors. The kitchen had a small stairway leading to the roof where you could see for miles in every direction. The rooftop patio had a table, chairs and a laundry line that gave it a function as well as an aesthetic feeling. Jim walked around for a short time after the couple left getting acquainted with his new home. He was the only one there at the time and the town was resting during siesta, so the quiet sunk into his bones like the warm chicken soup that his mother used to feed him when he was sick. His body was worn down and abused, so when he hit the bed that late afternoon, he was planning on staying there until the next day.

Jim woke up the next day to the sound of a busy market that was just down the street and could be heard through the open veranda doors. The sound was not harsh, but like the constant moan that a seashell makes when put to the ear. Jim made his way to one of the balconies and stepped out to see what all the activity was about. The sun was somewhat blinding and Jim had to shade his eyes with his hand in order to see down the street. He saw an amazing scene as the town had come alive and was bustling with rows of tables stacked with fish, vegetables and fruit. The town's market was large and nestled up along the river where the fishermen could bring their fresh catches directly from the sea to the tables as if they could still be squirming around, struggling for their last breath. It gave Jim a better sense of what a true day was like for the people of Portugal and he felt welcome without having to speak to anyone. This was a kind, thriving place that politely woke him up and introduced itself.

Jim grabbed his sunglasses and a bag of weed that he had finally procured after being jerked around in Albufeira and headed to the rooftop patio. The smoke sunk into his barely awake mind and made the busy streets, the blue sky, and neon green seaweed that grew in the river melt into a soft velvet that would be his day. The river whispered his name and the locals invited him to roam their streets as he waited above for just the right moment to become part of the fluid world.

His stomach eventually moved him to action as it growled for sustenance and he made his way from his perch to the alley he had originally been dropped off in. From there he sauntered around the block to join the flow of people near the market, but he was too wore down to buy fresh items and take them back to the pension for preparations even though that flashed through his mind as the economical and healthy thing to do. Once his ravaged system was allowed to breathe, he might be able to function in a more sensible manner, but he was still reeling from the excesses of the last week. Jim took his foot off the gas and let his system idle into tranquility. He had taken himself to the brink of darkness and was allowing the fishing village to fill him full of a soft light that seemed to exude from its very existence.

He wandered the streets in search of a simple café that would serve some of the local seafood in a laid-back atmosphere. He was in no mood for complexity. His stroll brought him to a small, open-air bar that had a pretty extensive menu written in different colors of chalk on black boards behind the bar. The proprietors were Caucasian and looked as if they might speak English, which Jim preferred because he was limited to "thank you" in Portuguese.

"Cheers mate, you look like you need a refreshment?" The bartender inquired in a distinctively English accent.

"I can always use that, but what I really need is some nourishment. I've been lacking such a thing for the last week or ignoring it. I need to supplement the liquor diet with some actual food. I'll also have a cold beer, though, whatever's ice cold and light on the wallet. What's good to eat? I need something hardy, what do you suggest?" Jim asked as the gentleman snapped the lid off a cold Amstel and slid it in front of Jim who was now firmly planted on a stool at the cozy little joint. The bar's open doors faced the river, which flowed only a short distance further before dumping into the sea. The scenery was perfect for lunch and a drink.

"How bout fresh catch of the day. Some fresh fish from the market with a spicy sauce loaded with shrimp and some buttered potatoes for a little heartiness. Won't leave you hungry." The bartender shot back.

"That'll do senor, fire it up." Jim directed as he slurped down his first alcoholic beverage of a new day. The bartender went to the back to get the order started while Jim looked out into the fishing marinas that bordered the market and nestled up under the window of his quaint pension.

"What brings you to Tavira, eh mate? Not usually a destination of people from the States, you are from the States, right?"

"Yep, but I was told to tell everyone I'm from Canada and they would treat me nicer. I just can't betray myself like that though. The first impression that everyone would get of me is that I was lying—it would be written on my face, no question. I figure people will give me a chance before shooting me down. Maybe I'm lucky enough to be the exception to the rule or maybe the perception of Americans as precocious assholes is simply a perception and nothing more. What do you think? Do you have a preconceived idea of Americans or was it just my lush northwest accent that gave me away."

"I don't really judge anyone, especially if they're sittin' at my bar."

"So you do incorporate a general stereotype of Americans being assholes—you just don't want to say because I'm a patron. What about the English and the French? You're English, right? The English have stereotypes of the French and vice versa and they both think each other are stuck up know-it-alls and the rest of the world seems to agree with both of them. Don't you think there is a certain wrap for brashness and superiority there?" Jim asked the bartender feeling that he was easygoing and would certainly engage in the conversation.

"These are so-called successful countries, including the States by the way, that are extremely developed and seem to wield a lot of influence on the rest of the world. I think with success comes scrutiny as well especially from each other because there is such a fierce competition among us. This brashness you speak of may be an attitude achieved by a good amount of ambition that seems to drive people past good manners, oblivious, sort of. It's a shame, but capitalism brings it on and some values suffer in a free market, not that they have to, they just do because it takes all kinds and no one is locked out. Many times the most ambitious, sometimes equating with the most materially successful, are the basest of human beings and they seem to be on the front lines making asses of their countrymen. We came down here to get out of the whole rate race and now things are a lot simpler and I can see the world a little clearer being back a step or two from it."

"I'm flowing right through the heart of it, but I'm not taking anything seriously, so brash people don't bother me—I just discard them and search for the genuine folks, the kind of people that don't build barriers. By the way, my name is Jim—some people call me Jimmy. Use whichever you like. Nice place yuh got here, didn't mean to start things off so philosophical, but good conversation is crucial to my existence. I love to talk, don't be afraid to stop me if I need to put a cork in it."

"I enjoy a good conversation as well, mate. Name's also Jim, but my wife and mum call me James, so I guess you can as well so we don't get things mixed up. My wife, Betty, is fixing up your food in back. We came down here a couple years ago for an early retirement, but neither of us likes to sit around so we made sure to have a small business lined up. It's no Shangri-La, but it has been a wonderful couple of years. What about you, what brings you to this corner of the earth?" asked the bartender as he popped open his own Amstel.

"I'm on a self-guided tour of Europe and I have some Portuguese blood, so I thought I would come down here and see if I felt the ancestral aura. I'm just bumming around being free, meeting new people and experiencing whatever I can get myself into. I'm trying to make some pictures along the way to see if I've got the eye of a true artist—if not, I'll have a real nice journal of images. I'm also meeting a woman for part of my journey through Italy and Greece and I'm interested to see how things go with her. I can't figure out if we're made for each other or if that's just some childhood fantasy that I have to shatter in order to know that it's just that, a fantasy. The close proximity should start the fire of lust or loathe and we've been friends long enough to survive either one."

"Ah, you're too young to get bogged down with love issues; you still have a lot of time before you need to make any life long decisions. Let this thing play itself out, but don't put too much weight on it. Hey, it looks like your meal is ready, let's get you fed." The bartender bounced to the back and quickly returned with Jim's meal. His wife followed him back to the bar and the three conversed throughout the afternoon. Jim had definitely found his watering hole for the week and his hosts were glad to have him. Beers and meals were cheap and the conversation was fruitful and free. Jim was glad to have Joey and the crew behind him, so he could slow down enough to absorb the environment around him a little more. Jim wanted to be a little more connected with the environments he was travelling through, but he had to maintain his standard amount of intoxication in order to do so. A little pot and alcohol were standard operating substances within Jim's life, so he didn't believe them to hamper his ability to absorb the culture and remember it later. Jim was part of a massive culture of summertime travelers in Europe, but he was truly looking for and experience that was unique; he wanted to step outside the guidebook and create a new chapter for it. For this reason, Jim was very inquisitive with his new friends about what he could get himself into around Tavira.

"Well, this is the Algarve and our most redeeming feature is probably the beach. You have to take a short little ferry ride to get to it, but it is completely sublime once you arrive. It's not commercialized or mucked up at all—it's just miles and miles of pristine, deep sandy beaches. It really can't be beat for relaxation and long swims. If you walk to the side of the island facing the shore, the sea is ultra calm and you can take quite a swim out there. The other side of the island absorbs the surf if you're in need of a little ruckus in the waves, maybe a little body surf or boogey board, not enough for a surfboard though I don't think – pretty mellow seas around here. The other natural beauty we have around here is a good hike outside of town, but I highly suggest it. You just follow the river up into the farm country and you'll come to a natural oasis about five to seven kilometers in. There's a beautiful little waterfall and swimming hole that is pretty much reserved for the locals, but they're willing to share if you can track it down. That's about it for local treasures except for the daily sunsets and the excellent selection of port, which go great together." Betty explained.

James added, "The pace of life doesn't shift gears too often, we like it that way—might not be enough excitement for a young man like you."

"Nah, this is perfect. I need a refuge from shifting gears, I've had my foot on the gas for the last week and I desperately need to idle for a little while. I've got a great little spot across the river, there." Jim pointed out the open sliding doors of the bar across the river to the open doors of the second floor verandas. "It's only about fifty bucks a week, what's that thirty quid or so. Anyway, it's dirt cheap and comfortable and it has a kitchen and large patio on the roof. I could kick back all summer over there and drink over here and be perfectly happy. I don't need much; a little beauty and tranquility go a long way. I love the way the town wakes up with the fishermen bringing in their catch to the market. There's a peaceful bustle below my window that makes me feel like enjoying a coffee and a new day. I think that I'm going to have a really good week here. I don't have to follow any schedule or be in a rush to do anything and I'm sure I will come across some interesting people, I mean I already have."

Jim puffed on his French cigarettes and drank Amstels all afternoon. When dinnertime came, he simply ordered another meal from the bartender and kept on drinking and smoking. He was served his meal among a crowd of locals and tourists that had filtered in throughout the afternoon. The eclectic feeling of the place was soothing compared to the hard driving nights he had pounded through at the village down the tracks. After his meal, he was introduced to his first glass of port wine, a beautifully rich wine that is native to Portugal. Jim was surprised at the hearty and extremely sweet flavor and he instantly took a liking to the beverage. It was like drinking a candy elixir with a smooth alcohol burn chasing it down. He liked it so much that he bought a bottle at the small wine shop below his pension as he returned home. The warm feeling it created in his stomach was what he desired as he planned to watch the sunset from the rooftop patio.

"Oh what a life, a bottle of pure Portugal to get me acquainted, a river to wash away my sins and a sunset to drag up the moon. All I need is a Portuguese princess to share my bed." Jim sighed to himself as he climbed the stairs to his abode. When he reached the top of the stairs there was a couple walking down the hall towards him with two beautiful smiles that invited him to speak. "Hello, I'm Jim, I stay around the corner there off of the dining room. How are you this fine evening?" He extended his hand to the young gentleman with a similar complexion to his own and whom he figured could understand his English.

His assumptions were correct as the young man showed no signs of confusion and began to speak, "I'm Charles and this is Anna. We're right here, just got in today." He pointed to the room that they were all standing in front of.

Jim held up his bottle and asked, "Would you like to join me for a glass on the roof, beautiful view of the sunset. It's high quality port wine, lovely stuff. I've just had my first glass after dinner and I liked it so much that I thought I would indulge myself.

Charles then began to speak to Anna in a smooth, fluent Spanish that helped explain her olive skin and questioning eyes. Charles was a tall and slender man with relaxed brown curls covering his head. He was clean-shaven with a long narrow jaw, impeccably clear skin, and dark brown eyes that always told the truth. Anna was a lovely Spanish woman who lit up the pension with her smile and graceful movement. She was quite small with an exquisitely fit, petite structure. Her hair was a sandy brown while her eyebrows were a little darker and her eyes were a honey brown that fluttered in a way that could melt any man's heart. The couple looked a little odd together with Charles being over six-feet and Anna being under five. Anna was exotic looking and Charles upright, but the chemistry was definitely there, they were infatuated with each other. They clung to each other and constantly stared at one another with a longing that could be felt across the room. They were travelling around Europe in much the same manner as Jim was and they were the same age, so there was an immediate connection that was born out of the adventurous spirits that were within them all.

Jim made his way down the hall and into the kitchen where he began to grab glasses out of the cupboards. Charles and Anna finished their Spanish discussion, their only concern was that Jim was a little loaded, but he seemed civil enough so they were obliged to give him a chance. The three travelers climbed out of the kitchen to the rooftop patio where they took seats around an old table with mismatched chairs. Jim opened the wine with a simple corkscrew he had bought in the shop and splashed it into Charles and Anna's glasses first waiting for them to take a taste before serving himself.

"Ooh, I like it, smooth and sweet." Charles stated then asking Anna what she thought in Spanish. "She likes it very much as well." He conferred to Jim after speaking to her.

Jim took a drink of his own—it was as good if not better than the one he had been served at the restaurant. The wine shop attendant had been very helpful in picking out an affordable and exquisite port wine. Jim had simply shown how much money he was willing to spend and asked for a port and the attendant did the rest coming back to the counter with a big smile on his face, satisfied that he had done the traveler a great service, which he had.

"So where are you both from?" Jim asked with genuine interest knowing that he was going to get and interesting answer from the unique couple.

"Anna is from Spain, the Basque region in northern Spain and I am from Montreal."

"Wow, what a couple. How did you meet from such distant places?"

"School. I've been studying in Spain for the past year and Anna is hard to miss. She may be small, but her smile is gigantic and her body is delectable."

"So you speak fluent Spanish? I took two years of it in high school but I don't think any of it sunk in. I feel bad leaving Anna out of the conversation. Does she understand English at all?" Whenever Anna wanted to know what was going on she would give Charles an inquisitive look with her head tilted to the side as if ready for his explanation, he would respond immediately.

"Don't worry, I'll translate. She hasn't learned much English yet, but we're going to work on that soon." The three communicated in a slow, easy manner so that Charles could be the bridge.

Jim was in love with the couple, in love with their love. He devoured their story and felt at ease with their flowing compassion for one another. It felt good to be in their presence. Anna and Charles enjoyed their new friend as well—his free spirit, big laugh and free flowing generosity were attributes that were hard to deny and comfortable to absorb. They drank the entire bottle of port as the sun dropped down and floated on the water until it dove beneath the surface. As the night wore on they burned tobacco and shared stories of the rails. It was a simple evening in a serene location that suited them all as if they were staying in the finest accommodations in all the Algarve. Eventually, Charles and Anna's bodies got to the point where they could no longer resist becoming one and they made their way back to their room leaving Jim staring into the starry sky.

Jim knew what they were about to do to each other, or at least he could envision some possible erotic scenarios, and he was envious of their passionate existence. He envisioned Elizabeth and he becoming like the exotic couple, leaving a wake of longing wherever they roamed. "What the fuck is going to happen to us?"

His drunken mind spouted out. "I wonder if she'll let go and just let us be whatever we're going to be or if I'm going to have to fight to shape it into what I want most. Am I that manipulative? Can I actually shape another person into acting the way I want? I always have so much faith in myself, but that's kinda fucking ridiculous. I'm going to charm and romance her with genuine intentions and if she resists, then I'll have to slap her around a little. Hah, just kidding, Jimmy. I sure do want to have what they have, but I can't force it to happen. I'm not going to worry about it. Somewhere out there destiny is being formed and I'm not the artist of unique outcomes, so I'll let them sculpt the perfect tomorrow while I spark up a joint and go play with myself." Jim struggled with the idea of building a romantic relationship with Elizabeth. He had always wanted to have a physical relationship with her, but in the past she had guarded her chastity with great strength. He was a physical creature that fed his animal instinct and looked for females with the same hunger for sex. He didn't really prefer the long, hard struggle to get into a woman's pants, but enjoyed the mutual consent that devoured each other hours after meeting. He was willing to be more savvy and patient with Elizabeth. He dreamed of the perfect evening with the woman that he was sure he could love. He was drunk and a little sappy, but the beauty of the Portuguese night had carried him off the rooftop and into a raging love story that was very possibly out of reach. Elizabeth was in love with someone else at the moment and it wasn't going to be a cinch to undo that emotion.

The next day started with the same buzz of the fish market and a slight inner thumping noise created by what was left of the Port. Jim stumbled to the veranda in search of some fresh air, but what he really longed for was some caffeine and grease. To his surprise, there was already a scent of coffee in the air. Charles was brewing some in the kitchen and Jim was grateful to be quickly offered some. Anna was cooking breakfast on the stove and she had already figured Jim into the equation, as there was a place set for him at the table.

"Would you like to join us at the beach today?" Charles asked Jim as he settled in at the table. Both men were shirtless with only a pair of swimming trunks and no shoes. Anna was cooking in her bikini with a beach shawl tied around her waist like a dress.

"That would be perfect. I think we have to take a boat out there, right?" Jim asked.

"Check this out." Charles led Jim to the veranda and pointed just below the window. "The ferry stop is right there. We walk out the door and we're on the boat. I've been watching this morning and it seems as if there is a boat every fifteen minutes, so we have the perfect location for beach access. The boat ride is only fifteen or twenty minutes."

An hour later the three were in the little ferry with ten other beach goers cruising out the mouth of the river. The boat would drop them off at the barrier island that provided the fishing town with an immaculate beach that kept the tourist population fairly heavy. There were three languages being spoken on the boat and if Jim piped up he could make it four, but he just sat back and tried to decipher the German, French and Charles and Anna's Spanish. It was like an opera of sound—smooth and abrasive all at once. The people of Europe were much more learned when it came to language as the German, French and Spanish could probably communicate with one another in their own tongues as well as in English. Jim felt a little inferior at times and wished he had the intellectual fortitude to master another language. He had had the opportunity in school, but preferred to keep his mind focused on being unfocused. He reasoned with himself that his brainpower not be wasted when the world was learning English anyway. He really didn't understand until he arrived in Europe how learning another country's language was a sign of respect for that culture and could provide a lot of open doors that were otherwise closed to tourists.

The day went by lazily with the newfound friends soaking in the sun without too many worries in their heads. Anna mesmerized both the men in her miniscule bikini. Her olive skin glowed with the application of suntan oil making her radiant as she lay on the beach. The threesome had traversed across the long, narrow island and then made their way a good distance down the beach that stretched as far as the eye could see. They distanced themselves from others and were in their own little piece of paradise. The water was a deep shade of blue that was as inviting as a gigantic swimming pool, and for much of the day the group swam in the warm sea. Anna and Charles would end up entangled in each other pushing their way far out into the sea. Charles was holding Anna in his arms making his way far out into the horizon in the shallow water. Jim would lie back towards the shore with his shades on watching the couple gaze at each other like they were hungry for one another. He sat back on his elbows with the water lapping at his chest and daydreamed about finding the same kind of intense passion and lust. Jim dreamed about lust instead of love because he found it intoxicating and extreme. The newness of a relationship usually brought with it a fierce lust that rivaled any drug. Jim was great at feeding on this part of the relationship and then when it died down moving on to another. He wanted to be able to sustain it and turn the corner, but it never worked out that way.

At the end of the day they motored back on the people ferry and exited on the docks below their domicile. The only entrance was from the back alley so they had to cut through a slit between buildings to get to the pension door. As they climbed the stairs Jim commented, "I'll leave you guys alone. I'm sure you've had enough of me. Thank you so much for letting me tag along, and I really enjoyed the day."

"You haven't worn out your welcome at all. It was a great day and great to have you along. I think we're going to take a siesta, what about you?" Charles replied.

"That sounds perfect. Maybe I'll see you later tonight." Jim said as he passed the couple on the way to his room.

The pension was not air conditioned, but each room had a fan and the veranda doors were always wide open to let in a breeze. It was hot outside, and taking a nap was the best option during the hottest part of the day making the traditional siesta a wonderfully sensible option. Jim left the door to his room open so that the fresh air from the veranda could pour in. Charles and Anna were the only people he had seen in the pension even though he knew there were locals who stayed in the other two rooms, but who would be offended at seeing a large American snoring in his underwear. Jim slept for a couple of hours letting his sun drenched skin cool down.

When he woke, he headed to the house's only bathroom in hopes of getting a shower. He was not impeded, as he was the only one in the house. Charles and Anna had gone out to eat already and the other residents, a single man and woman, were working evening jobs. The bathroom was spacious and comfortable except for the slight smell emitting from the trash bin next to the toilet where toilet paper was disposed because the plumbing was not designed to handle paper. The shower was in a full size tub, and there was a window that brought in a nice light.

Once fresh and clean, Jim headed out the door to his favorite watering hole for a bite to eat and a few cold beers. His energy level was drained, but a little marijuana put him in a floating mood that used very little energy as a matter of practice. He ate another superb meal and enjoyed the company as much as ever. Sharing the bar with him was an older Portuguese gentleman who was drinking at a steady pace and kept a smile on his face throughout. James, the bartender, was talking to both Jim and the older gentleman and ended up brokering a conversation between them. Jim asked the old man through the mediator what his line of work was, did he have a large family, and where he made his home? The old man asked what had brought him to the sleepy town of Tavira, and was there enough excitement for him? The old man was a fisherman who had lived and worked in Tavira his whole life. He made his living by selling fresh fish at the very market below Jim's window at the pension. Jim explained that he was a college student who was travelling through Europe and that he had some Portuguese ancestry and wanted to see if he saw any of himself in the people. He was also drawn to Portugal because he loved the sea and knew that it was an integral part of the Portuguese way of life. Beers were consumed and bought for one another in a mutual admiration that spawned a genuine friendship between Esmiraldo, the fisherman, and Jim. Esmiraldo wanted Jim to get an authentic feel for the sea that he was drawn to and invited him to be his first mate the next morning when he set out to get his catch. Jim quickly agreed before he was made abreast of the four-thirty A.M. departure time.

"Well, I guess I better get back to the hacienda and sleep fast if I've got to be out to sea in the middle of the night." Jim and Esmiraldo both made their way out of the bar. Esmiraldo pointed his boat and his home out to Jim. The home was a block away from the bar with only a street between it and the river where his boat was gently bobbing in the moonlight. What a simple existence to be able to walk across the street to work in a boat that sells its catch at a market across the river and makes enough for beer money at the bar a block away. "I doubt old Essy even has a car. What would he need one for?" Jim thought to himself as he watched the man meander back to his world.

As Jim walked home, he realized that he had actually acquired a slight responsibility while vacationing, but was ecstatic about the opportunity to experience some authentic Portuguese life. Who knew there was more to travel than finding the best bars and nightclubs? Fanny had shown Jim some authentic Paris as well as the quintessential Paris, but Joey had pulled him off the path – how easy he was led astray. He felt that he was back on the path that would lead him somewhere special – to some life experiences that would resonate within him for a long time to come. Jim had an overwhelming urge to become one with others, especially kind peaceful people. He didn't put up any barriers and he crashed through other people as if they didn't even exist. He found that his partying lifestyle gave him the opportunity to come across a lot of laid-back people, who easily let others in. But Jim was confined to the raging alcoholics of the world, he consumed and entered all kinds of people's lives and that was the essence of his existence – a profound interaction with others.

The next morning Jim rose to the annoying electronic screeches of the alarm clock that James had lent him for the night. He had only been asleep for four hours and the grogginess weighed on him like a mudslide, but he quickly shook it off and replaced it with excitement and anticipation. He looked at the outing like a personalized charter-fishing trip without the exorbitant fee.

Esmiraldo was already scurrying around his modest fishing empire when Jim jumped down on the bow to greet him. They shook hands and Esmiraldo immediately pointed to the ropes holding the boat loosely against the dock. Jim recognized his orders, untied the ropes and gently pushed the bow out towards the center of the river as he jumped back into the boat. The engine had been idling and the muffled groans were turned into a drowning roar as Esmiraldo kicked the engine into gear and provided the hungry combustion with the fuel needed to lift the wooden bow out of the water. They headed out the mouth of the river in the pitch black of night with a lantern burning on each side of the center console. With the language barrier, there were few words spoken, but the human interaction was rich and the two men were comfortable with one another.

Esmiraldo hit the hammer down once they got out the mouth of the river and the wooden fishing vessel roared wide open to a maximum speed of around twenty miles-per-hour. The bay was fairly smooth and the boat slapped each wave softly as it split it in half. The night sky wobbled in the shifting water but stood firm to every horizon and was filled with a mass of stars that made it seem like the boat could keep going right into space. The boat clamored along leaving a gurgled stream of white like a florescent tail wagging in the night. The boat was directed southeast, and they could see the outline of the deserted beach island as they made their way to the prime fishing about five to eight miles beyond that.

When they reached the designated fishing grounds, Esmiraldo waved for Jim to take the helm and he began to feed large nets into the water. The nets glided into the water and were yanked out of the boat by the tugging in the water. Once the nets were completely out of the boat, they were allowed to silently fall over their prey with the line that ran around the entire exterior of the net falling freewheeling with them. There were two nets connected to electric wenches that sat on the back deck of the boat with the line running up poles that had arms attached to the top of them extending out over the water. When it was time to bring in the nets, the wenches would be engaged and the line around the outer edge of the net would be cinched tightly together trapping everything swimming within the perimeter of the net. The nets would be pulled up to the end of the arms that hung out over the water and then the arms would be swung in over the deck and the line released letting the fish flop onto the deck.

As the nets were descending upon their prey, Esmiraldo killed the engine and retrieved his thermos from the console. He pulled out two cups and poured them about half full of steaming hot espresso. Jim was not used to the thick, black espresso as he usually drank watered down American coffee, but it definitely gave him a jolt. The men sat in a beautiful silence sipping the steaming beverage watching the sun creep up over the horizon and illuminate the water from black to a golden orange. The depth of the silence and the vastness of nature with little influence from man made Jim think how peaceful it must be for Esmiraldo to come to work each day. He could get lost in his own thoughts out here. You would have to prefer solitude, which

I like myself, but maybe not to this degree. I think I would talk out loud to myself all day when I wasn't pondering on the inexplicable characteristics of human nature.

Esmiraldo thought Jim was the one lost in solitude – travelling around the globe like a lost puppy flailing in uncertainty. He perceived that the young man had little direction and needed an anchor to keep him from floating aimlessly in the seas of human desire. Esmiraldo had had an anchor and he reached for a picture to show Jim. It was of him and his wife some years before standing on a brand new fishing boat that was the very craft they were on. Esmiraldo pointed to his wife and put his hands together behind his ear and tilted his head as if to show someone sleeping, then he pointed to the sky. After that he made the sign of the cross and bowed his head for a little prayer. Jim gathered that Esmiraldo had lost his wife and indeed he had. She was usually his first mate and had manned the small fishing vessel with Esmiraldo for twenty-five years before passing away just a year before Jim arrived in Tavira. They had decided to work together because they had not been able to have any children. The traditional role of parents was something they were able to put behind them and dedicate their lives to each other and to the sea. Because of this, they had a larger boat than most of the modest fishermen of Tavira who stayed closer to the mouth of the river in their small skiffs.

With the sun almost fully exposed on the eastern horizon, Esmiraldo started the engine and slowly circled around the netted area, drawing the nets tight on the winch lines and then engaging the winches to bring in the catch. It took the nets five minutes to slowly be tugged out of the sea with Jim and Esmiraldo standing on opposite sides of the boat waiting for the net on their side to bust through the surface. They both burst through the water at the same time and were pulled up to the top of the arms that extended out over the water from masts on either side of the boat. Esmiraldo turned a handle on the mast and the arm moved its way over the back deck of the boat as he continued to wind the handle. Jim took that as a queue and began to crank the handle on his mast that slowly brought his arm over the rear deck of the boat. The nets met over the back deck and Esmiraldo pulled a release line on the bottom of his net that let the squirming bounty crash down to the deck. Esmiraldo's rubber boots were more suited for the job than Jim's flip flops, which he had bought the day before to go to the beach. Jim was instantly inundated with slimy fish and sharp scales cutting into his feet and shins, which made him jump in the air and high step it to the outer edge of the flopping pile.

"Shit Esmiraldo, this is quite a load. Mucho pescados, eh." Jim exclaimed with a look of disbelief as Esmiraldo laughed a deep belly laugh after watching Jim high step out of the fish pile. Esmiraldo had offered his wife's rubber boots at the beginning of the trip, but there was no way that they would fit Jim's extra large feet. "Now I know why you need the sapatos." Jim said to a nodding and still laughing, Esmiraldo.

The old fisherman had begun weeding though the fish and discarding the undesirable species that he would hold up in the air for Jim to see before throwing them overboard. Jim began to mimic him, tossing away the fish that were undesirable at the market. The fishing then became vigorous with the nets being lowered for only a short time before they were jerked back into the boat. The fisherman pulled in five more loads before the hull was loaded down with the catch of the day. Blocks of ice had been added before Jim's arrival in preparation of the flopping passengers and it quickly shocked them and made them more docile.

It was still early when they headed back towards the mouth of the river, but both men felt a little drained after humping it for two straight hours, wrestling the larger fish, and trying to keep their balance on the slippery scales that were left on the boat deck. They were both drenched with the slime of their catch mixed with sweat and sea water and felt worthy of taking a seat for the relaxing boat ride back to the docks.

The work was only halfway complete when they hit the shore, the fish still had to be wheeled to the market tables and sold—all of which the boat owner did himself. The boat came into the market docks where there were large carts available to haul fish from the boat to the market tables. Esmiraldo threw Jim a large shovel that Jim used to capture as many slimy creatures as possible and transport them to the cart. The first load was a little shaky with two prime fish getting dropped into the river between the dock ant the boat, but after that Jim took his time and delivered full shovel load after full shovel load to the cart on the dock. As soon as the cart was full, Esmiraldo took the fish to the market table he had used for the last gazillion years and shoveled the fish onto the table. He then went and loaded the cart with ice and covered the fish with it before returning to the boat to get another cart full. Three-and-a-half carts later the long table was brimming with the day's catch and the fish business was ready for the customers who were already digging into the ice and plunging deep in the pile to find the perfect fish. Jim even spied

Betty from the Parrot Eyes bar that he loved so much. She was purchasing the fresh fish that she would later serve.

The two men stood behind their catch proudly with shimmering fish scales covering most of their bodies and the free market began to churn. Jim mostly watched as Esmiraldo haggled with the locals and schmoozed the foreign restaurant and bar owners with his careful, direct Portuguese. He sold fish faster than the other fishermen, being that he was the senior fisherman with the best table location and the largest mound of fish for a one-man show. The pile dwindled down with little old ladies making off with one single fish and restaurants filling a whole five-gallon pale with iced down fish. When the pile had dwindled down to only a few sickly looking fish, Esmiraldo called the show and headed back to the boat. The Portuguese sun was glaring at mid-day and the old man's slumped shoulders were damp with sweat, his waves of black and gray hair soaking wet, and his thick eyebrows had beads of sweat dripping down from them. Esmiraldo eyed his young companion as they got back on the boat and before he shoved his wad of pesos in his pocket he peeled off some for Jim. The young man accepted the money as he was taught to accept generosity as a way of respecting the generous.

The boat still needed to be guided across the river to its home-port and Jim, being an expert first mate already, untied the ropes and shoved the nose of the boat towards the middle of the river as Esmiraldo fired up the engine. Once the boat was secured at its home dock, the men sat down for a little rest and Esmiraldo produced some cold beer from one of the ice chests. They drank the cold suds in silence and Jim began to feel the hot sun drying the fish scales to his skin, so, to the surprise of Esmiraldo, he gently rolled over the side of the boat and plunged into the river water. Jim wasn't fond of laundry mats and he hadn't seen one in Tavira anyway, so his best coarse of action was to clean himself and his clothes as thoroughly as possible before the scales dried and made an armor on his clothing. He swam vigorously out into the river and back to the boat gyrating himself like a human washing machine. Esmiraldo had a good chuckle and was happy that he had brought the energetic youth along. He reached down to give Jim a hand from the river with a wide grin on his face that showed appreciation of the action. It was a beautiful day for a swim in the river. Esmiraldo admired the young American for jumping into a Portuguese day with a truthful spirit and a hard working mentality. He also admired the adventure that each day was for Jim, but it wasn't something in him, just something he could appreciate. His adventures all took place within one hundred kilometers from his home where the sea could make any regular day into a full-fledged adventure.

As soon as Jim was loaded back in the boat, another beer was passed to the first mate. The work for the day was done and Jim's pay would come in liquid and a stringer of a couple of the finest fish. Of coarse he needed no pay for being able to experience a true Portuguese day, but the company was fantastic and the suds tingled the hard worked bones. There were plenty of beers to last until siesta and then there was a short cleaning exercise that included washing down the boat with hose and gathering the beer cans into a bag. Esmiraldo then shook the hand of his one-day first mate and patted his shoulder with the other hand. He then turned and began home, but only made it a couple steps before turning back towards

Jim. He took off his weathered fishing cap and threw it to the young man as a gift of remembrance. Jim didn't have anything to give in return, but he was truly moved by the gesture and made his way back to the old man and gave him a hug as if it was his own grandfather. Jim felt as if a piece of him was somewhere in Esmiraldo, somewhere in Portugal, and he was glad to have come halfway around the world to see it shine.

Jim felt like a true citizen of Tavira marching through the streets with his pristine fish flopping by his side and his weathered skin tanning to a dark brown as if he was a native. He was in great spirits as he walked up to the house and saw Charles and Anna waving at him from one of the verandas. He held up his fish and yelled out, "There's definitely enough for us all. Spark up the stove and we'll have a fish feast." Anna grinned and Charles went inside to meet Jim at the door.

"I'll go pick up some stuff to go with it." Charles said as Jim came in the door. "Some wine, some vegetables, maybe some rice, how's that."

"A fresh lemon and some garlic would also do me well if you don't mind." Jim added. Charles nodded and was off to the corner market. Jim brought the fish into the kitchen and searched for a filet knife. He left Anna alone on the veranda, as she was probably not excited to watch the decapitation and skinning of the fish. Jim proceeded with the preparations and ended up with four fillets longer than the cutting board and well over an inch thick most of the way through. Charles returned quickly and the two men worked together to create a home cooked meal a thousand miles from their homes. It was the traveler's delight to be able to feel so comfortable and at ease in the depths of their journeys.

They ate a beautiful meal on the rooftop patio, fish in a wine, lemon, and garlic sauce lay over a bed of rice and served with a fresh salad that Charles had whipped up. There were two bottles of cheap white wine chilled just right and consumed with each bite of food and for dessert there was conversation and trails of smoke into the evening sky. For Jim the day had been long, but each moment had a sense of community that he always longed for when he was travelling and that he had been successful in letting happen in Tavira.

The next day Charles and Anna were continuing on their journey and Jim was to be left in the pension by his lonesome. They were packed and ready first thing and had to wake Jim in order to say goodbye. Jim got up and grabbed his camera so that he could make some pictures of the couple before they were whisked out of his life by the eight A.M. train. They were receptive to his lens and he could tell that their photograph would do them justice as the beautiful couple that they were. The light was good as they stood with their backpacks consuming them, especially Anna who was carrying close to her weight in the bag. Jim made a couple pictures as they walked down the lonesome ally behind the house and then when they hit the more crowded street that lead to the station, Anna and Charles turned back to wave at Jim and were caught in one last image with a Tavira flare.

When Jim got back to his room, the stench of his clothing made him realize that a splash in the river wasn't quite enough to remove a million fish scales. There was a distinct odor of fish guts and traveling sweat that had to be dealt with. There probably was a laundry mat somewhere in Tavira, but Jim hadn't seen one and he knew that there was soap and water in the house, so he figured he could be creative and come up wit h a third world solution. He filled up the tub, threw in a bar of soap and then added his whole bag of stinky clothes. He stomped around in the tub for a while trying to simulate the washing cycle of a machine, then let the clothes soak a little while he fixed a couple eggs that were still in the fridge. Then back to the bathroom for the rinse cycle that consisted of letting the soapy water out of the tub and filling it with some fresh water and repeating the violent action of stomping the clothes. No one garment was given any more consideration than the other and nothing was scrubbed too diligently, just stomped. The water was then let out of the tub and each item was rinsed a little before it was rung out and thrown in a garbage bag for transport to the clothesline on the roof. The clothes still looked a little dingy when done, but they were on the line and presumed complete. Jim sat on the roof and watched the clothes cook as he cooked himself with some burning weed.

He spent the day wandering around Tavira tracking down some personal items and getting a flavor for the rest of the town besides his favorite bar and his comfortable little house. When siesta came around Jim was obliged to join the locals. "The siesta is a beautiful thing." He thought to himself. "It should be observed around the world, heat or no heat. Afternoon naps would make the world a more peaceful place." Jim was pretty sure the Portuguese, especially the Tavirians, had it all figured out and were able to extract a lot of the complexities out of life to allow a sort of stripped down simplicity to reign in a world that in most other places had no time for a nap. Jim stripped down and let the fan blow over his naked body for a completely relaxing siesta with no expectations before or after the nap, so there was nothing to keep him from floating far away into a deep sleep.

He awoke when he awoke and meandered over to Parrot Eyes for a drink and some conversation. "Hey James, I am the great white fisherman. Did Betty tell you about my catch yesterday? Betty was loading up the good stuff from me and Esmiraldo." Jim exclaimed as he entered his favorite Portuguese watering hole.

James slid a beer across the bar before Jim even sat down. "Yeah, Betty said the market was fully stocked and that there was a white boy flopping around like a fish out of water. You must have had a prosperous fishing day as you picked a good one to go. It looks like you enjoyed yourself there, mate."

"It was fucking brilliant, smashing I say, quite a blast. That might have been a little much, but it was very peaceful and I definitely enjoyed the experience. It's a good honest way to make a living and I'm sure some days are a lot more treacherous than yesterday. We pretty much went to one spot about twenty or thirty miles, caught all the fish we needed, and shot right back in. The weather was perfect and the sea was barely choppy. It doesn't get much easier than that. I've been on charter fishing trip where we had to scratch and claw just to come back with two fish. By the way, I wouldn't mind having some of Esmiraldo's fresh catch from today, I'm getting used to the fresh seafood diet."

"No problem, we'll get you fed." With that James went back to place an order for his wife to cook, which she did with a tenderness that came across in the food. The couple had found a way to exist in harmony in a foreign land and Jim made mental notes for later in his life.

After Jim finished eating he told James that he was considering going on a hike the next day and trying to find the waterfall that James had described to him a couple of days before. James made it seem like an easy jaunt just a couple of miles on the only ride heading north out of town. Jim figured that something as grand and beautiful could probably be seen from the road, so he didn't ask for too many specifics, which he would regret later.

The next morning after a relaxing bath and a morning bake, Jim slung his camera over his shoulder, threw on his authentic fishing cap and headed north on the only dirt road heading that direction. As soon as he hit the edge of town, things began to get interesting for his camera. He ran into an old deserted church that was beautiful in its old forgotten way with vines taking over the exterior façade, the old colorful tile patterns only halfway adhered, and ancient bird baths still standing strong in the courtyard. Jim shot pictures of the lonely scene and imagined the grounds hustling and bustling with the scurrying of the Portuguese faithful in the past—the faithful that had moved to a new shinier church in the town.

The countryside beyond the church was a rugged landscape dotted with farms, orchards and exotic looking trees. The river valley was a lush green agricultural area, but as the hills rose on either side of the valley the landscape became more barren and was patched with green bushes and brown grass. The eastern hillside, across the valley from Jim, was guarded by majestic looking stucco mansions that seemed to be keeping an eye on their land below. The road ran along the bottom of the valley, but not along the river as Jim had expected, so he was always peering through the orchards in hopes of recognizing the path of the river. From time to time the stream would show itself and then dash back behind a rocky crag or get lost in an orchard, but Jim continued top hike without a concern in the world while the sun beat down and his camera shutter kept blinking.

After the sun had shifted substantially in the sky, Jim began to get
a little concerned that he may have missed the oasis and he began to
look for any sign of life that may help direct him. At about the same
time a van came racing by on the dirt road, which had acted as Jim's
hiking path. He didn't pay much attention to it the first time it went
by, as it went too fast to extract any information from those inside,
but after about the third time, the van's occupants were obviously
as frustrated as he was. Jim began to think that these people were
looking for the same thing he was as they came hurling back for their
fourth trip past him. This time the van rolled to a stop next to him
and Jim looked into a face as befuddled as his, but obviously kind
and interesting. The man had hair down to his shoulders with short
bangs, a wide mouth and a long narrow nose. He was a father of four
and they were all in the Toyota van with him and his wife, the Swiss
Family Robinson.

"Do you speak English?" He asked in a very thick German-like accent.

"Yeah, that's all I speak. I'm kinda useless around these parts."
Jim said.

"We are looking for swimming hole, we were told it was this
direction."

"Yeah, I'm looking for the same thing. It must be some kind of joke
to send all the foreigners out here in the boonies and get them lost.
I've been looking for a local to ask where to go—I was going to try
a little Spanish. I think I will be able to give them the idea of what
we're looking for at least." Jim explained to the traveling family. The
children in the back, three young boys and a baby girl, stared at Jim
with open faces and welcoming smiles. The man's wife was a beautiful Bohemian looking woman with a much darker complexion than

him or the children and black hair that reached her waste. The family was from Switzerland and they were on a classic family vacation. The youngest boy and the baby girl were strapped into child safety seats while the two older boys ruled the back seat of the van. The kids thought Jim quite the site with his fishing hat, which looked like a New York cabbies hat, no shirt, dark shades and a camera strapped over his shoulder. But the Swiss family had no apprehensions about the longhaired, broad-shouldered young American hiker.

"Jump in, we'll find it together." The Swiss man said with an inviting smile. Jim jumped in after the woman reached back and swung open the side door. Jim sat down right inside the door next to the two young ones and politely waved to the boys in the back seat and smiled at the little ones.

"My name is Jim." He said as he extended his hand to the driver.

"I am Thomas and my wife, Monica. These are Domian, Keya, Vaughna and sweat little Vivian."

"You have a beautiful family. You're a savior as well. I was beginning to get a little concerned and I sure didn't want to turn back after hiking this far." The Swiss family began to crawl down the road again keeping their eyes peeled for the oasis. When Jim spied a man working in his field he asked Thomas to pull over and let him have a crack at trying to communicate what they were looking for. Jim jumped out of the sliding door and hustled to catch up with the man who was tilling the soil the old fashioned way, behind a mule. Jim ran up beside the grunting mule and politely waved his arm at the older Portuguese gentleman, who looked like a piece of the sun scorched earth himself. The old man pulled his concentration from the ground where he was intently staring as the plow dug in. The man pulled the reigns on the mule as soon as he caught sight of the misplaced American and shot Jim a look of bewildered confusion that got Jim wondering what he could possibly extract from this lonely farmer. "He doesn't swim." Jim thought. "He doesn't even like people who swim, especially trespassing foreigners." But Jim gave it his best anyway and started making swimming motions and waving his hands in the air like water flowing over a ledge and he used the Spanish word for water a lot. It was a simple and desperate attempt to communicate and the Swiss family got a good chuckle from the roadside charades. At the conclusion of the flailing, the old man raised his ancient arm and uncurled his cramped fingers to extend his index finger in a slightly crooked pointing gesture that unlocked the key to the forbidden city. He knew of the place and it was tucked in the center of his very property just a quarter mile away. There was a dirt road behind the farmer that led to a thicket of trees in the center of his property and he was just fine with the foreigners using it as the locals always did. The old man started tilling again and Thomas pulled onto the smaller dirt road at Jim's direction and Jim jumped back in the van. He wanted to wave a thank you to the farmer, but he was back to his duty and would not see Jim again. No one would have ever figured on driving down this road because it was on private property, but they had been lucky enough to be directed upon it by what seemed to be the proprietor so the license had been issued.

Jim hadn't expected to be on a daylong venture and did not have supplies to sustain him for a whole day. He had planned on taking an exhilarating hike, topping it off with a refreshing swim and then heading back to the town, but once he saw the oasis and after all the work it had taken to get there, he wanted to stay. Jim had fell into the perfect situation to solve all his problems – he was now in the fold of the Swiss family, and he had been successful in helping them find the oasis so he was easily accepted as part of the family. The Swiss family broke out a large picnic once the clan was set up at the small sliver of sandy beach that guarded one edge of the fresh water basin.

The spot was worth the entire struggle to find it and a lot more. The oasis was a little paradise surrounded by dense greenery with a luscious waterfall pouring into a basin that was deep and clean and cold. Jim followed a little trail to the top of the fall and, with his new family admiring his bravery, jumped the forty feet in a perfect symmetrical swan dive. He swam to the side of the lagoon where Monica was cutting up some fresh melons and laid in the sun with the happy parents eating melon and watching the three boys splash around at the water's edge. Little Vivian sat in the sand on the bank trying her best to gum a piece of melon with most of it spreading across her face.

The day was already perfect, but when two college-aged women came strolling up to the oasis in bikinis with big smiles, Jim was sure that heaven was near, if not right there on that morsel of Portuguese soil. A short haired blonde and a long haired brunette, both with voluptuous chests and shapely hips, spread their towels out on the small beach within whiffing distance of Jim and the Swiss family. The proximity of the girls made it impossible to ignore each other so communication was simply destiny. The blonde spoke first in native Portuguese to which Jim's confused face immediately sent her into English.

"Hello, how are you doing today? It is perfect day for a swim, yes?" The beautiful Portuguese girl said, already making Jim salivate with the application of sun tan oil. "Do you need some help with that?"

Jim asked rubbing his hands together in the water to show that they were clean and ready for service. She just giggled and the brunette chimed in with a far different accent to her English, yet with complete mastery of the language as though it was her first.

"Where are you all from?" She asked with what Jim thought was an Australian accent, but was actually South African.

Jim made three or four barrel roles to get closer to the girls and then extended his hand to the brunette, "My name is Jim. I'm an American who is seriously considering moving to Canada or maybe Portugal if you two will take me in. What about you two? It sounds like you are from different places?"

"My name is Stacy. I'm from South Africa. This is my cousin, Juliet, who lives here. I'm visiting her for the summer." The brunette was full of smiles and content to be in a conversation with the American. She was attracted to his dark tan and alternative look as well as his aggressively friendly personality. The blonde thought highly of Jim as well, but she could tell that her cousin was already entranced.

Jim then remembered his manners, "These are my new friends from Switzerland, Thomas and Monica, and all their kids that I don't really remember the names of, but I remember this cute little one is Vivian." He tickled Vivian. "They picked me up on the road out there. We all got lost trying to find this place and they saved my life with this beautiful picnic." The verbal communication helped break the ice and the group on the beach became one relaxed unit interacting like a peaceful family. The girls were extremely kind and outgoing. They immediately began to play with the children in the water and the brunette even jumped off the top of the waterfall with Jim earning the boys' ultimate respect. They thought it was normal for the brawny pirate to prove his bravery, but for the girl to be so sanguine was something they thought only their mother capable of. Jim wasn't admiring the bravery as much as the physique. He was pretty sure there would be an equipment malfunction when the itty-bitty bikini hit the water at full speed, but the South African beauty was savvy enough to hold tight to the top when she hit the water.

The day flowed by like a lovely shade of emerald green and the water refreshed everyone as if it were the fountain of goodwill and friendship. The girls agreed to meet Jim at Parrot Eyes for dinner and the Swiss family gave Jim a lift back to his luxurious seaside villa, as he called it. They left him with their Swiss address and demanded that he stop by and stay a couple days later on during his summer travels.

The girls needed a couple hours to make the transformation from swimming hole to night out with the dark, mysterious man. Stacy wanted to attack Jim in a sexual manner as soon as she could get him alone, but Juliet was the voice of reason and tried to restrain her cousin's nympho instincts. "You'll never see him again. I don't think it is good to make a habit of sleeping with men for the simple plea-sure of tasting another flavor, you'll end up like me, a single mother."

"He'd taste great though, don't you think? And there are ways to be careful you know – I can make him wear a condom. I mean what is life if you can't have a little variety?"

"Variety my ass, you keep your pussy in your pants. You can play with it when we get home, but I'm not letting you go home with him, he's a pirate for sure."

"A sweet pirate though, I bet."

Jim was spending his down time on his perch above the town toking on his favorite herb and dreaming of a perfect evening with the cousins. He was very attracted to both of the women and he figured that they must have at least found him interesting to agree to a night out. He wanted to shack up with both of them, but figured it a delusional fantasy because they seemed the sensible type, not the kinky type. He would try though – he would try to bring it out of them. Jim figured that there was a caged animal down inside of everyone and that he had figured out how to let it range free while others, like the girls, kept them in their cage. Jim dreamed at the far ends of a situation so that anything in-between was conceivable and his daydreams on the rooftop patio were quite fantastic. "The girls will make for perfect company, kinky or not. I'm lucky that such fine women will even be seen in public with me, much less take any of their clothes off. I've got to control my thoughts and figure out how to be civil. Maybe I need to put the tiger back in the cage—he's eating everything in sight." Jim thought as he made his way out the door all clean and respectable like.

The night began when the girls walked into Parrot Eyes in full make-up and in exquisite summer dresses. Their bare shoulders, exposed cleavage and radiating smiles turned the bar into a whole different place – a more exotic, avant-garde affair where the air buzzed with sexuality. The whole place gravitated toward them with their necks craning to absorb the youthful beauty. The shapely young women were more than the local patrons could handle and everyone seemed to be exposed with overreaching smiles. James made immediate work of getting the girls' drink orders and winked at Jim while doing so commending him for the high quality of accompaniment he had acquired.

"Ladies, it is my pleasure to have such stunning company. I will do my utmost to remain a gentleman, but if I should slide into a baser creature, please feel free to abuse me in any way you see fit. You both look absolutely fabulous by the way. I'm sure that I could scour the earth and not find a pair of cousins as mutually gorgeous as you two." Jim eloquently stated and the girls glowed with the compliments. The three then went on to get completely smashed, skipping dinner and maintaining a full-fledged liquid diet. They continued drinking deep into the night and were joined by James and Betty after they had closed the bar. From the fermented liquids came a courage and honesty that made the evening conversation unique and somewhat Freudian, being that Jim was taking a commanding role in most of what was said.

"So do women masturbate as often as men, and I mean like daily? James, do married people have to masturbate at all or do you just get sex whenever you want it? 'Cause I mean, if I were allowed to have sex whenever I wanted, then maybe I wouldn't have to jerk off so much and then my poor pecker wouldn't get all swollen. If I had a woman available all the time, though, like a wife, I think I would be fucking instead of jerking. I mean, when I get a girlfriend it seems like we're saturated in lust, humping all the time, you know." Jim exclaimed as the conversation was hovering around relationships and sex and had just been steered into masturbation by a guy with very little couth.

James answered with half sincerity and a huge grin, "She gives it to me enough."

Jim shook his head slowly from side to side claiming bull shit on James's statement and started staring directly at Stacy in hopes of getting the single girl to spill the beans about her masturbation habits. She turned bright red, but she was drunk enough to be forthcoming.

"I do it, not every day though. You do it every day?" Stacy diverted the conversation from her and threw the question back in Jim's face.

Jim ignored the question and went right back on the offensive, "So do you have toys or do you just rub yourself or what?"

Juliet jumped in, "I've got a vibrator. It always gets the job done and when it wears out you just change the batteries and he's good as new. I mean, obviously I have sex being that I have a daughter, but the vibrator is much less complicated."

Then Betty chimed in, "I've got one too."

"Oh shit." James said with a glowing red face, embarrassed by the development.

Betty slapped him on the arm and continued on anyway, "James knows I have it—he even uses it on me sometimes during foreplay. Our sex life is good, don't get me wrong, but a husband is not always around and I bet he would much rather me have a vibrator than a boyfriend."

"I don't have one, I guess I'm really missing out. You girls think I should get one, huh?" Stacy asked with drunken sincerity.

"So you use you fingers, right? Do you just rub your sweet spot or do you slide them in and out? Do you use one finger or do you bunch them up like this?" Jim put all his fingers tightly together like a torpedo and shoved them into his crotch. This action and statement finally put him across the line and sent the group into a spiraling laughter that ended with everyone in tears. After the laughter died down, Jim put on a very serious face and again directed the question towards Stacy, "No really, I want to know how girls do it. I just kind of rub the tip until it gets hard and then I stroke it full length, up and down, like I'm mad at it and eventually it will spit up all over me."

"Ooh, you're disgusting. So, it gets all over you?" Stacy asked with everyone giggling. Jim had lost all couth and was now floundering in an abyss of distaste, but the waters were comfortable and he didn't feel like he was drowning.

"Sure, if you're lying down it gets all over your stomach and chest if it's a really powerful shot. You can always catch it in a rag or sock or something if you're cleaned up and don't want to get it all over you, but I prefer letting it roam free, then you really get to finish it off. Sometimes I do it in the shower and just let it shoot down the drain – don't have to worry about clean up that way, but if the shit gets on you in the shower it sticks to you like glue. So you can be walking around later that day and find a big piece of cum all wrapped up in your leg hair. I'm just being honest, do you think it's too much? I really like some juicy details on a female masturbation session. I keep trying to get answers and now that I've bared all, I need you to depict one of your sessions in one of those exaggerated phone sex voices."

"I'm not doing that, you're crazy. I'll give you a little information, but just the basics, okay? I just rub the sweet spot, as you call it, in circles until I have an orgasm and I usually continue on to a second, but I don't stick any fingers in there, it's the sensitive area that counts. Men always try to stick fingers in there because they don't know what the fuck they're doing. Why do you think it works so well when you put your tongue down there, you're not sliding that in and out of anything, just titillating the sweet spot, right?" Stacy explained making Jim look ignorant.

"I haven't put my tongue anywhere yet, but if you insist I could probably comply." Jim said with a smug look at Stacy inferring that he would do it right there if she wanted.

The group went on to discuss more admirable subjects, but all of them created laughter. The five drunken members of the party were thoroughly amused by each other, but as the night wore on Jim began to put his priorities in line. Actually, there was only one priority on his mind and that was to pry Stacy from Juliet so that he could fondle her back at his luxury accommodations. It was Jim's last night in Portugal and he wanted to send himself off with a bang, literally, and Stacy had shown many signs of wanting to accommodate. Stacy and Jim had even went to the wash closet at the same time and about got the deed done in there, but were rudely interrupted by a thundering knock from Juliet. There was physical juices flowing, but there was a lid called Juliet on Stacy's cup. Jim was desperate when the party was finally broken up, but desperation doesn't look good on any man. "Please, I've been very lonely throughout my journey and I just need someone to hold me through the night. I know she wants to Juliet, she wants to hold me and be held, don't you Stacy?" Begging was unbecoming of Jim and as she began to slip away from him, firmly in the grasp of her cousin, he blew her kisses as gallantly as he could. They were both sloppily drunk and Juliet could see that the things they would do to each other in that state would easily be regrettable in the morning, so she drug her cousin to the car and made one last comment to Jim.

"She is coming home with me. You're not going to take advantage of her. She's drunk." Juliet said with a playful smile – she liked to watch Jim suffer. She could see his desperation fading to panic. He had tasted her and now she was being torn from his lips.

"So am I and that makes us equal. Anyway, I'm not going to take advantage of her. I'm going to let her take complete advantage of me. Right Stacy, tell her."

Stacy swayed in the Portuguese breeze outside Parrot Eyes. She embraced Jim, kissed him passionately, and slurred out, "I guess I have to go with July, sorry. I would prefer to see you naked, but it would be unacceptable on such short notice." The bomb had been dropped. Jim felt crushed like a tiny grease spot on the cobblestone streets. The rejection showed on his face so Juliet embraced him and kissed him gently on the cheek.

"A beautiful man like you will have many more opportunities to seduce women on your journey, just make sure they don't have a controlling cousin dragging them around. We had a fabulous time dear Jim." She said as the girls got in their small hatchback car and sped into the night.

Jim moped back to his spot looking like a dog that had just been scolded. He had lost and was going to go the night without the treat. He thought to himself, "It's always so difficult to pull one woman from another, especially family. If they weren't family, I could have kept them together and then the story would read so much kinkier. Oh well, at least it was a beautiful night with a beautiful crowd in a perfect magical moment somewhere in paradise – not everyone gets to experience that. I'll live another day to overcome the rejection." His drunken spirits somewhere between rejection and instant nostalgia for the place and people that he would be leaving in the morning, Jim hit his single mattress with a thud and lingered in dreams of his Portuguese visit. The world teaches men and women about love in increments, thoughts leading to actions, a romantic gesture that is embroiled in emotion, which always carries the logic out of the situation so that learning about love can only be felt and never explained clearly. Jim loved life and the characters in it, so he lay in bed, thought about Stacy and pulled one off in her loving memory. He would learn the delicate art of wooing one woman from another as he matured. He would also learn how to keep them together when the situation called for it. Jim would learn many lessons of lust, love and of the gray area in-between along the rest of his adventure.

Chapter 5
A TOUCH OF SPAIN

The sun was burning high in the sky when the train came to the end of the track in a sleepy piece of Portuguese countryside. A ferry would carry him across the river into Spain. He was refreshed by his time in Tavira, by the spirits he encountered and by the feeling of goodwill that seemed to travel with him from such an experience. The world was like a bright sunflower opening up to a smile, gravitating towards the sun, thriving in the light. Jim had his shades on, no shirt, his backpack strapped on, and his sandals protecting his feet from the radiating heat. His skin had tanned considerably leaving him dark enough to pass for a southern European. His dark hair pulled back in a ponytail, he looked like one of the Spaniards that waited for the ferry to carry them home.

There was another man about Jim's age standing on the platform in a similar get-up with backpack and shades. He approached Jim and began to speak in Spanish. Jim was quick to show his befuddlement, "Hold on my friend, no hablo Espanol. I sure as hell should, but I never paid attention in class. Habla Ingles?"

"Oh yeah, not problem. I wasn't sure, but you could pass for Spanish. Name's Carlos, you?"

"I go by Jim, Jaime in Spanish if you like. That's the name I used in Spanish class for the two years I attended physically, but was on some other planet in my mind. Now I'm in college and I avoid language like the plague because I have convinced myself that I'm no good at it when really I've never put forth any effort. Here I am traveling the world and I seem a little arrogant, and I'm sure a little ignorant, not speaking another language. I can confuse myself within my own dialogue, sorry. Anyway, it seems like most people speak English, so that's probably another obstacle to me learning another language, I can communicate with everyone already. Sorry to ramble on, just trying to justify my laziness and it's getting me nowhere. Beautiful day, huh"

Carlos obviously thought the wondering American was entertaining or interesting or odd or a combination of all of them. "Yes it is nice. Where you headed?"

"I figured I'd get myself to Seville for today. It looks nice. You been there?"

"It is called Sevilla in Espana and yes, I've been there and I'm heading there now. Stick with me. I can get us there by the cheapest method and show you around once we get there if you like. Tonight I am staying in Sevilla, tomorrow I go to Morrocco." About this time, the ferry pulled up to the dock and Carlos and Jim boarded with a new friendship intact. The two men hung on the rail of the small vessel and talked about their present travels. Originally Jim thought that Carlos could have been the kind of man that liked other men, but he directed the conversation towards sexuality and was quickly assured that the opposite was true. The misperception was only born through the extreme kindness that Carlos was showing Jim, which was received with open arms and returned with the same energy. For this reason, Jim thought that if Carlos was gay, that he was relaying all the go ahead signals to him and therefore had to steer the conversation towards his enthusiastic preference of women. Jim would have traveled with a gay man without a problem, but he did not want to lead him on. Carlos wasn't gay, though—he was just nice, and sometimes the word means the same thing.

Carlos, on the other hand, thought of Jim as quite unique—this lone American on the border of Portugal and Spain without a care in the world or a plan of where he would lay his head. Carlos enjoyed the free spirit and saw a reflection of himself in the bronzed American. He wanted a traveling partner for his trip to Morocco and was sure that he could convince Jim to come along by the next morning. Carlos was a tall lanky Spaniard with a clean-cut hairstyle of slightly wavy black hair. He had a five-o-clock shadow growing and was covered in a good amount of curled body hair. His complexion was somewhat fair for a Spaniard and he could have easily been mistaken for a member of Jim's family just as Carlos had mistaken Jim for one of his countrymen. The men were the same age and the more they talked the more they discovered that their interests were very much aligned. They enjoyed women, drugs, alcohol, music and especially the consumption of all of them within the same interaction—an internal combustion of emotion and adrenaline.

Once across the bay, Carlos led the two adventurers to a small restaurant, which just happened to double as the bus depot. Carlos bought two tickets and told Jim he could buy him a drink later on that night to make up for it. The bus was idling in front of the restaurant waiting for the ferry passengers before speeding off. "Good thing we made it; this is the last bus of the day." Carlos stated as they sat in the very back seat of the bus. The bus was more like a city bus than a long haul bus and did not have bathrooms so the back seat was spacious and comfortable without the stench of a bathroom. "The back of the bus is the smoking section if you know what I mean."

"You mean someone is going to light up a doobie on a public bus? No way."

"That's my prediction and if it happens we'll catch a buzz on the bus and get a little for tonight if they are willing to part with some." Carlos explained with confidence.

"Actually, I've got a little stashed in my bag, but it's too late now, we've already stowed our stuff. I was expecting it to be cool to light up on a bus. You really think someone will smoke one back here?"

"Oh yeah, most definitely. Espana is full of casual travelers like us. It is a festive place, Sevilla, and on the way there the passengers ought to be festive. We'll probably have the privilege of smoking a little Moroccan hash in this part of the country. It's even more abundant than grass itself. The back of the bus will come through for us my friend. Trust me, I've spent many an hour in the back of Spanish buses and most of the time, there was a nice buzz going around." Carlos had Jim to the point of salivation—he was so excited.

"What's this hash like? What does it look like? How do you smoke it, with weed or what?" Jim asked.

"You don't smoke hash in America?"

"I think it's there, but I haven't ran into it much."

"It comes in little compressed blocks about as big as a cigarette, but square and usually only about a quarter of the length, or at least that's how much I buy at a time. It goes a long ways. To smoke it, you just burn the end of the block, and it dries out and little pieces flake off that you can burn in cigarette tobacco. You could mix it with weed, but that would be really strong and unnecessary. I think hash is a more intense high than pot itself."

Jim told the story of his only experience with hash. "I smoked some hash in Portugal, at least I think it was hash, with this English guy from Germany. That sounds kinda fucked up, huh? Anyway, he said it was Nepalese hash and it was like a big glob of tar. He rolled it up like a snake and we smoked it in a joint that was twice as long as a regular joint—he called it a spliff. It blew my fucking mind and took me to another planet or solar system or beyond. We were in this zone with people in our train car from all over the world and everyone seemed to understand each other—we floated along in a kinda haze. I've never been that high in my life, but I was also juiced up on pills and drowned in beer. It was a train ride that skirted the boundaries of hell with evil cackles bouncing off the compartment walls with a feeling that sin was standard course. So you can see that my traveling experiences would definitely call for me to be seated in the back of the bus."

"No shit! It sounds like this will be pretty mild compared to that crazy trip. I've never got my hands on any of that Nepalese stuff, and I live a lot closer to the source than you. I've always heard that it's fantastic stuff. You're lucky you got some of that shit. It's hard to come by."

"Yeah, I stumble into some unique situations and I usually end up with a partying crowd. I just gravitate towards people of chaos." Jim's comment brought a slight smile to the lips of Carlos. He considered himself one of those people and didn't mind being put in that category.

Within twenty minutes of leaving the bus depot, there was the sweet smell of marijuana in the air. A couple that looked like they were straight out of the movie "Grease" lit up a hash-laced cigarette and began to puff away directly in front of Carlos and Jim. The prediction had come true and it couldn't have been a more convenient location for the couple to pass the joint back. The young man who lit it had dark-fifties style shades covering his eyes with his hair plastered back with a shiny substance, a tight pair of blue jeans and a tee shirt with a cigarette pocket loaded up with Marlboros on his chest. His girl wore a tough but playful scowl. She had a ribbon tying her ponytail in the air so that her hair fell down to her shoulders but didn't touch her neck on the way down. Her boyfriend turned around and raised his eyebrows with the joint slightly elevated as if to offer anyone a puff or to absorb any objections that someone might have. Of course, being in the back of the bus, he expected that the first option to be obliged, which Carlos gladly did with a subtle reach forward. The smoke wafted in the air like a burst of magic dust come to take those in the back of the bus to a fairytale world where everything was soft and fuzzy. Jim and Carlos were not the only takers on the smoke express, almost everyone in the last three rows lit up like a pervert at an elementary school when they were offered a drag. The group became so large that the Fonzy-looking dude lit up another magic stick so that there were two swimming through the back rows, being handed discreetly from one stoner to the next.

The two friends landed in Sevilla as the sun was beginning to descend. They were stoned on pot bringing them to a mellow place where the world spread out before them like a big cartoon. Their first touch of reality came when they had to strap on their huge bags, which were quite burdensome for two guys that wanted to float around. Carlos suggested finding a nice double room in a pension so that they could pay the least possible considering they were planning on spending a lot of the night drinking and chasing women. Jim was used to this arrangement since it mirrored what he and Joey had done. The reality was that it allowed the men to choose a nicer place than they could foot alone. They wove through the tight ancient streets of Sevilla with Jim amazed by the beautiful stone structures that were older than his entire country. Some of the buildings had pointed spires reaching into the sky depicting the influence on Muslim invaders hundreds of centuries before. The mixture of Western European with Arabic structures made for a unique skyline with domes and pointed spires mixing together and softening each other's lines. The city had a medieval feeling diversified with a very fashion savvy youth, which kept it in tune with the present, while its structures allowed it to tell the stories of the past. They found a spot in a nice Spanish home on one of the back alleys near the river and dumped their bags on the double beds, admiring the fact that they had been able to acquire extremely nice lodging for a very reasonable price.

The tranquil Gundalquivir River made for a fantastic background to an outdoor bar that was just around the corner from the pension. The river dissected the city and brought beauty to its every turn. The bar thrived with dance music and young people throwing back Sangrias, red wine fruit punch, like it was water. The festive drink was the preferred and the most economic drink on the boardwalk, so it was an easy choice for the weary travelers who needed liquid to put out toxic cases of dry mouth. They were probably developing a slight case of the munchies as well, but it was nothing that some alcohol and a little more pot couldn't quench. Carlos had acquired a small chunk of Moroccan hash from the couple on the bus and found a good spot on the riverbank to fix up a joint. The entire river near the bar was lined with steps that went all the way into the water and Carlos and Jim were perched one step above the quiet surface. Carlos demonstrated the charring technique—taking the chunk of hash and burning it until it would crumble off in pieces that could be spread throughout the joint. Carlos originally wanted to roll the hash with cigarette tobacco, but Jim was glad to prepare a little weed for the base, and so the concoction was thrown together. Both Jim and Carlos enjoyed going as far out as possible, and their high-level THC cigarette was just the rocket needed to launch to outer space. The result was two comatose dudes vegetating in a supposed social environment, but due to their state, they were entranced in a two-person ecosystem with other odd species wondering about.

"I like Espana, man, really mellow and the people are ultra friendly, like you for instance—you're a good man, amigo. No shit Carlos! I mean it—you're all right. Now work your magic with some of these senoritas cause I don't think I can talk and I'm not sure I can get up—I hope you can." Jim stated in an extremely slow, deliberate speech that made it seem like he was trying to talk to a young child.

"I think I can get us a couple more drinks, but I don't know about talking to anybody. Maybe we'll get lucky and they'll come talk to us." Carlos said in the same sluggish cadence.

"Here man, here's some pesos. Pick us up some more of those sangrias and a couple of hookers that own a liquor store." Jim added as Carlos struggled to dislodge himself from the steps. "Don't fall in, Holmes, you'll get the shit wet." Carlos wobbled to his feet looking as if he might tumble down the steps and into the drink, but miraculously he managed to balance himself and stride off, ever so carefully, towards the bar.

He returned twenty minutes later with two cups half-filled with the tasty wine beverage. "Man, what happened, you forget which one was yours?"

"What do you mean?"

"They're only half full. Did you spill it or did you drink it, not that it matters?"

"Oh shit. I guess I drank it. I was waiting for some change and scanning the crowd for those hookers and maybe I switched between drinks. Here, you have them both, I'll go get some more."

"No, no, no, take a seat brother. If you go back to the bar it'll be midnight before you get back. Let's light up another doobie and see if we can't attract a little company." Carlos sat down and both the men took a drink of their half-full sangrias. Then Carlos broke out his piece of hash while Jim tore up a little weed and together they made a marijuana salad that took the form of a stealth torpedo once wrapped in its smoking paper. "We didn't really need that room, we could have just slept right here. I'm numb, it wouldn't have fucking mattered, but I guess the bed will be cool, right? I mean, if we make it back." Jim stated as he sprawled out on the Spanish steps and lit up the torpedo. He took a hit and passed it to Carlos.

"We'll definitely make some friends with this, but I don't know if we'll be able to communicate with them." Carlos exclaimed as he stared down the burning torch before putting it to his lips. The young friends did attract a little crowd, and the night flowed to oblivion like the river in the dark.

By midnight the mixture of pot and sangria, along with a day full of travel, wore down the two hearty travelers and they had to retreat to their residence without any authentic senoritas. The mattresses were calling the Bohemians, and neither of them bothered taking off his shoes once he rested his head on the pillow.

The next day started with eggs mixed with salsa and chorizo sausage in fresh tortillas. The fiery combination brought Jim to his knees, but he ordered another one despite the fact that the flavor was worth a little burning sensation resonating on his tongue throughout the rest of the day. During the meal Carlos tried to coax his new friend into traveling to Morocco, which was only a short distance from Seville, but did mean exiting the European continent and that made Jim a little nervous. "I could get myself all fucked up and miss the beauty I'm supposed to meet in Zurich in a couple of days. I can't let her down and hanging out with you could be hazardous to my health." Jim stated as he walked Carlos to the bus that would whisk him off to the southern tip of the country. The two men parted ways at the entrance of the bus, embracing as if they were long lost friends. Carlos rode the bus south and then caught a boat across the Straight of Gibraltar while Jim wandered the streets of Seville all day.

Seville was the first Spanish city Jim had visited and the first major city he had had been in for a couple of weeks. The energy was back to being like a city, but nothing like Paris although Seville held onto the southern relaxed attitude. Seville had its token cathedral that was being restored, but it had a very different look with some eastern influences and a past that may have included a mosque at one point. The streets were tight and crowded and the ancient buildings were filled with modern garb. Jim didn't have any direction or conquests, so he spent the day wandering aimlessly. He didn't open his guidebook, but let the streets take hold and lead him to curious observations.

In different parts of the city there were castle-like structures built with stone blocks as big as a person and stacked upon each other as a child would stack the blocks of his imaginary fortress. There was a history in Seville, something deeper than Jim could grasp in one day of wandering, so he let it be. He decided he would take a night train to Barcelona trying to make some progress towards Zurich and to save a night's lodging by spending it on the train.

The night train took a little spirit out of the trip since a large piece of Spain would go unseen. Jim was in a slight rush through Spain, so every hour had to be used with his best judgment. He was willing to give up a little of the Spanish countryside for a taste of the twenty-four-hour beach city of Barcelona. Carlos had gotten Jim excited about the beauty of the women and the lifestyle that was standard in the city. The Portuguese beaches were beautiful, but the crowds were sparse compared to what he was about to experience.

Jim got off the train prepared for a day at the beach with many visions of beautifully bronze Spanish women dancing around topless as far as the eye could see. The spectacular thing was that his visions came true. It was like spending a day at the Playboy Mansion where clothes were a faux pas and breasts were able to breathe. Jim thought of American standards and laws and how silly they were. "How can the human body be outlawed?" He thought about some beaches where thong bikinis had been outlawed because they were too provocative. "This is more like it. Beauty gets to be seen for what it is. Who could reign in beauty like that? It must be some really jealous bitches that can't stand their men to turn their heads." Jim thought to himself as his head turned like a swivel at the constant specimen of pure exotic sunshine.

The day in Barcelona was pristine with the sun climbing through an utterly blue sky. The pebble beaches that outlined the city were jam packed with locals as well as tourists, and no one seemed to have any concerns beyond getting a tan and a buzz. Jim, of course, complied. Laying his towel within a couple feet of two Spanish sun goddesses, Jim watched their perfectly shaped breasts as they slowly absorbed the sun, turning a deeper shade of golden tan with each passing moment. The water slapped the shore lightly— the waves gently rolling in without threat. Jim hovered around the goddesses long enough to work his way into their company. After getting them stoned and much pleading and begging, he was allowed to apply suntan oil to their luscious bodies. The day continued on with Jim and the girls swimming, frolicking and sucking down margaritas at the beachside bar. Jim was being himself and the girls seemed to like it, so he began to insinuate that he needed a place to stay for the evening as the day wore on. The girls picked up on it quickly and offered him a place to stay without any qualms. They were actually very excited to show the foreigner the nightlife of their most beloved city. The girls lived together two blocks from the conglomeration of their towels. This moment was when Jim finally got a vision of what heaven was like in his mind—it was just off the beach in Barcelona, who would of thunk it. His meeting with Elizabeth was rapidly slipping from the top tier of his thoughts and it was replaced with blazing wanderlust. "Dear God, thank you for the Spanish sun and please help guide me to the Promised Land tonight." Jim's sincere prayer to his most high God was a request to swim in a lake of sin—to fornicate perpetually with two women at the same time. Somewhere on the sidelines of his mind, he also made a deal to sacrifice a great deal of pain and suffering later on in life—if he could just be allowed this complete gift of the flesh.

The girls took Jim back to their humble pad to show him the way before he jaunted off to the train station to retrieve his bag from a locker. By this point Jim had figured out the names of the girls. The auburn-haired woman was Melissa and the black-haired woman was Maria. He referred to the ladies as M & M, which they had heard before, but Jim liked to use it to get both of their attention at once. Melissa had endless legs while Maria was petite with an incredibly tight figure that bragged of muscle definition usually seen on professional athletes. Her breasts were in perfect proportion to the rest of her exquisite features, and her butt was tight and round like two perfect melons. Melissa, on the other hand, was long and luxurious with exceptionally large breasts and a supermodel sleekness that radiated a high-class beauty. Jim was fumbled into a dream encounter and he didn't want the bubble to pop. All the suns had aligned just right to put Jim in the perfect situation for a young male traveling about looking to experience a worldly city like Barcelona. For Jim, the finer things in life had everything to do with beautiful women and nightlife.

Jim arrived back at the girls' apartment with his bags and a bottle of tequila to continue the margarita tradition they had started at the beach. "Hola senoritas, daddy is home!" He bellowed out like Rickey Ricardo in "I Love Lucy".

"We're in here!" One of the girls shouted from the bedroom in the back of the apartment. Jim followed the voice, dumping his bag in the living room, but keeping the bottle to show the girls what he intended to make. To his surprise, both of the girls were wrapped in skimpy towels with nothing else on when he entered the room. "Put that down and get naked." Melissa said with a mischievous twinkling in her eye.

"You gotta be kidding me, no shit?" The girls shook their heads and let their towels slide to the floor as they lowered themselves to the bed with room in the middle for their American friend.

"We're going to make you our boy toy. Do you think you can handle it?" Melissa said with a smooth Spanish accent that was well practiced in English and sexy as hell. Jim jumped out of his clothes.

"Hallelujah, that's exactly what I always wanted to be." Jim said as he slid into the middle of the bed so excited that his body was physically shaking and his dick was already hard enough to hit a baseball. He slid his hand along the thigh of each woman as if admiring two fine automobiles.

"No touching, Jimmy boy. We're in charge." Maria said as she took Jim's hand from her thigh and pressed her naked body onto his with her knee coming up right below his balls. Melissa did the same thing on the other side of him and he was sandwiched between them with his penis being the dividing line. The girls kissed him on each cheek and then rose up above his head and passionately kissed each other. Jim wanted just a little juice from the kiss to drop down on his lips. He was in such ecstasy that he was worried about going off right there without performing any kind of sexual act.

"My lord, please allow me to perform, none of this premature shit." Jim prayed to himself knowing that the alcohol and weed should provide some numbness on his massively erect member, but this was the most erotic moment of his life, and his excitement was overflowing. The girls then kissed him on the cheek again, got up from the bed, replaced their towels and began bantering in rapid Spanish and laughing hysterically.

After having a good laugh Melissa finally spoke in English again, "Go take a cold shower, Jim. We just thought we would give you a little taste of what's in store for you later tonight."

"What about now?" Jim whimpered. "That's cruel. You can't get me all excited like that and then abandon me. I'll walk around with a hard-on all night if I don't fire him off one time right now. I believe I'm gonna have to masturbate if you girls won't help me."

Melissa walked into the bathroom to take a shower with Jim still holding his hard penis. Maria winked at Jim when Melissa went into the bathroom and reached into a drawer pulling out a condom. She threw it at Jim and his face lit up like he had just been pardoned from death row.

"Put this on, sexy boy, I'll let you play for a little while, but I don't think you can handle me for very long." Maria said rubbing herself. Then she picked up the bottle of suntan oil they had used earlier and poured it all over her chest letting it drip down between her legs.

"Don't I look like I can handle anything?" Jim exclaimed as he rolled on the condom in a split second. Maria stood over him rubbing the oil into her hard body. Jim reached for the bed, grabbed her hand and pulled her towards him. His face was still red from the embarrassment that he had endured just minutes before, but his mind had forgotten the situation and he was completely infatuated with the glistening body of Maria. She didn't hesitate to straddle him and allow him to penetrate her. As soon as he was in, she thrust her hips towards his and took all of him. The two fit together as if they were practiced lovers moving in a sensual erotic rhythm that matched one another's lustful passion. It was just sex, but it was the kind of sex that strangers can sometimes have but never duplicate once they get to know each other. Their hips swirled, grinding each other like it was the last thing they would do on this earth. Maria still had the bottle of oil in one of her hands. She poured it all over Jim's chest, rubbing it in fast and powerfully creating friction and heat. Jim pulled her towards him and their oily flesh met with her breasts caressing his chest. He kissed her and then guided his tongue around the silhouette of her lips. She pulled away and arched her back, placing her hands all the way back on Jim's shins, leaving his member pulling in an unnatural direction. But it hurt so good that Jim arched his back sending her back even further. Then, keeping him in her, she turned around so that she was on top and backwards and she rose and fell gripping tightly on Jim's thighs and began to make a sensuous moan. Jim reached up and got a handful of hair and massaged her shoulder with the other hand—providing pain and pleasure that mixed together like a gourmet dish. The oil mixed with the sweat and Jim began to breathe out loud as if whispering his lust.

Melissa stood in the doorway of the bathroom for at least five minutes after her shower admiring the two savage creatures. The two reached a momentous climax with Jim having both hands firmly dug into Maria's hips and ass and Maria digging trenches in Jim's thighs. Maria shook all over as Jim exploded into the condom. Her moans had ascended to a very high-pitched level while Jim had turned into a savage, grunting and roaring like a lion. "My God, you two looked like some wild beasts from a National Geographic show. That didn't even look human, but it did look like a lot of fun." Melissa said standing in the bathroom doorway with nothing on but a towel that was wrapped around her head. "You two are going to wear yourselves out and not even be into dancing later."

"I feel great. All refreshed and ready to get down." Jim said walking by Melissa with a hard dick and condom stilled glued on.

"Ooh, don't get that on me!" Melissa exclaimed as Jim walked by starting to unravel the loaded rubber.

He held it up between his thumb and forefinger and stated. "There are a lot of women that would die for the fine genetic material that I'm about to dispose of. You sure you girls don't want to freeze this stuff, so that you'll be guaranteed above average children. I don't mean to boast or anything, but this stuff would cost a fortune if you had to buy it on the black market."

Maria just smiled at the comments with a dreamy contented look that shouted satisfaction. She felt relieved of the world and all the problems that came with living fast. She felt like the three of them had been supplanted into a perfect vacuum of time, and while there, nothing could go wrong. She was completely comfortable with her naked body as she followed Jim into the bathroom and turned on the shower. She left the door of the shower open, waiting for Jim to join her. They showered together scrubbing each other's oil-covered skin and exploring every inch of one another.

While Jim and Maria were fondling each other in the shower, Melissa slipped out to the neighbor's apartment to pick up six high-powered tablets of ecstasy. When she returned, she whipped up an entire pitcher of margaritas on the rocks and even prepared some glasses with salted rims. She had enjoyed watching her friend make love to the mysterious American and figured that the introduction of more booze and some high-powered drugs would put the night on the extremely memorable scale, if things didn't get too cloudy to remember. Inhibitions had already been left at the beach somewhere around the third margarita, and the ecstasy would just turn everything a bright shade of red and make kinky, even kinkier. She cranked up the stereo with some electronic dance music with a Latin flair and began to apply her own stylish array of make-up.

When Jim and Maria emerged from the bathroom, Melissa was there to shove a pill in their mouths and put a drink in their hands. "Down the hatch." She said like a mother giving important medicine to a child. Neither Jim nor Maria hesitated in bringing the drink to their lips to wash down the sour tasting pills.

"That looked like a groovy little pill. You girls are my kind of foreign hosts. That's ecstasy, right? I did that for the first time just down the tracks, but I don't remember much of the night. It wasn't the ecstasy's fault though. I had put together this kamikaze mix of drugs and alcohol that could have killed a moose, but it put the old brain into overload. Anyway, I'm taking at least two or three drugs out of the equation tonight, so I think it will be a better experience—let's hope so. From the way this night has started, I want to remember every piece of it. You're not going to get me all fucked-up and then take advantage of me, are you?"

"Of coarse we are." Maria stated with satisfaction, winking at her roommate and slapping Jim's bare ass.

"Just smile and come along for the ride." Melissa added with a more viscous slap in the ass.

The girls got ready, changing into exotic summer dresses that were made with little material allowing their bodies to be the main attraction. They wore no bras and their panties were merely strings. The dresses had slinky little shoulder straps that barely held the cloth in place. They were low-cut on top and high-cut on bottom with the maximum amount of leg showing. With a little bit of sweat and movement on the dance floor, the light material would reveal the exact woman beneath. Both of the women pulled their hair straight back and clasped it in a ponytail to help them stay cool during the hot Spanish night.

Jim figured he had to look his best to accompany such a gorgeous couple, so he shaved off the shaggy goatee and pasted his hair back in a similar ponytail. He wore his one set of nice duds that he had taken the time to iron while the girls were getting ready. He turned on his best version of a Latin lover, put on his American smile, and took one girl in each arm.

"Off to Las Ramblas." Maria said as the three pretty people ascended into the night. Their eyes were beginning to feel a little crossed as they strolled through the sizzling night air. The world began to expand and contract. All the senses heightened, and everything they touched was unique and fine. They made it to the famous boulevard of Las Ramblas and looked both ways into the sea of sexy people offering their bodies to the night. Jim's pupils devoured his eyes as he stared at the luscious mixture of life intertwined on the walking boulevard. The party was on and everyone showed up. The ecstasy was beginning to add distance between the threesome and reality. They floated down the street, Jim's arms wrapped around both women as he walked in-between them. The night was like a giant lit sparkler, and all the people were flashing through the streets exploding light into the world.

Jim was the first to comment, "This shit is fantastic—it's like I'm in wonderland. I'm really parched, though. We should make our way to a beverage location."

"I need to dance." Maria exclaimed grabbing Jim by the hand and dragging the group into the nearest thumping disco-tech. The bar was full and the dance floor was beginning to show signs of life. The alcohol and drugs were beginning to put a spirit in the crowd that would last until the sun came up. The electric air and pounding music carried the youthful crowd to a fervor that kept gaining strength as more was consumed. Young people were expanding their already rampant emotions to levels beyond the human capacity with chemical alcohol mixtures that could send a rocket into orbit. Melissa and Maria headed straight for the dance floor while Jim careened into the crowd by the bar in hopes of securing three drinks. By the time he got to the bar he decided to order three margaritas and two shots of Petron. He left the drinks on a table next to the dance floor and carried the shots to the gyrating women who had already attracted two male partners. The men were kind enough to back away as Jim made his entrance with the shots. Tequila blasted down their throats and detonated in a bomb of ecstasy that sent their bodies into a frenzy. Jim moved to the rhythm as if the music was playing through him. The girls attached themselves to him, creating complete rhapsody between the three. It was downright funky in Spain that night. The music thumped and the threesome glided through the electric night.

At two in the morning, they took their second tablet of ecstasy and by three they were all naked in the ocean. They danced all the way to the beach and lost their clothes as if complete nudity was the only way to truly be free. The night was bright and Jim could see Maria's smooth black hair glisten in the moonlight. He was amazed at the perfect roundness of Melissa's breasts as they absorbed the moon's glow. Images of the naked women kept flashing through his head like a bunch of black and white negatives that he would develop in the lab—it was one perfect image after another. Maria was enamored by touch and her mind couldn't get over how good it felt when her lips met another set of warm lips or when her entire body caressed another warm, hard body—every touch sent her spine tingling. Melissa was feeling very turned-on. She had to pull herself into the web of Jim and Maria's physical pleasures. Maria was attached to Jim, kissing him passionately on the lips and then sliding her mouth down his neck where she could gently use her lips and tongue to show her affection. Melissa joined the group, swimming up from behind and grabbing Jim's ass while kissing the other side of his neck.

Eventually the group exited the water and made their way to an apartment complex near the waterfront that had a glowing swimming pool and hot tub. Jim hoisted the girls over the fence and joined them on the other side to enjoy the heated water of the Jacuzzi. Once they got in the tub, again without a stitch of clothing, the girls began to fondle each other. Melissa sat up on the top step spreading her legs and laying her body back on the wood floor of the deck. Maria kissed her thighs and then ran her tongue in slowly down her inner thigh until she was pleasing her roommate. This put Jim in true ecstasy while extremely intoxicated on ecstasy. What more could a self-proclaimed rock star ask for? Eventually Maria made her way over to Jim with the hot mouth that just left from between her friend's legs and began to please Jim with the same energy. Melissa made her way behind Maria and began to use massaging fingers to make Maria moan. They became one mass of eroticism moving from one to another involved in various sexual acts with their eyes closed and the hot water swirling around them. Jim entered both women at some point feeling their insides and wishing that the moon would stay cast forever. The drug and alcohol mixture was the perfect recipe for Jim to maintain exceptional performance without reaching the finale. His eyes rolled back in his head and his hands dug into the flesh in front of him—Jim maintained euphoria through-out the hot tub experience. Maria moaned and Melissa purred as the sensual touching, kissing, licking and fucking made the night stand still. The tub became more full of lust than water as the slithering threesome sent water out with violent movements of passion.

After an hour of unadulterated frolicking in the hot tub, Melissa and Maria lead Jim back to their apartment where they could escape any persecution. The three couldn't get enough water and ended up in the shower together as soon as they arrived back in the apartment. The girls would reach climaxes from time to time turning moans into screams and then gliding back into moans. Jim, on the other hand, was a never-ending sex machine whose drug-induced body gave him bionic capabilities. The shower proved to be another hour of fuck-ing where Jim did not climax, but continued to stay at full attention sliding in and out of one or another of his beautiful partners. He lay in the tub with Melissa riding him and Maria standing above with her crotch firmly planted on Melissa's face. Maria put her leg up on Melissa's shoulder and her back against the tile wall to steady her. She stayed like that for a while and then dropped down to Jim's face where she could make-out with Melissa while Jim pleased her with his mouth.

Jim was in a haze believing each successive moment was the best of his life. He was the star of his wildest dreams, and he devoured every second with his memory turned on extra-sensitive so that little would be lost. Many people have spiritual events in their lives that they can point out as their most satisfying moments—helping Habitat for Humanity build homes in less privileged parts of the world would be an admirable shining moment for someone—but for Jim this experience was the apex of his fast moving lifestyle. He perceived that having sex with two women at the same time was the ultimate achievement here on earth. Not to say that Jim wouldn't grow past this stage and come to value much more honorable things, but for this time in his life he was achieving the very mission that was always swimming through his mind. It wasn't that he even had to share the momentous event with any of his cronies back home. He just had to remember the glow he felt surrounding him as both of the sexy women wrapped parts of their naked bodies about him.

This was not a common event for the girls either. They sometimes fondled each other and would exchange deep, passionate kisses to shock onlookers when it tickled their fancy. They were playful, sexual creatures, but they had never crossed this line before; they had never fully pleased one another while sharing the same man. They had discussed the possibility of being completely open sexually when the right situation came about, and that both of them could be aroused by one another if there was a man involved as well. They had never imagined that once engaged in such an act, that it would come so natural or be so satisfying. It was safe with the mysterious American and could be locked in the moment and be left there without fear of exposure. The girls would feel a bit odd around each other for the next couple of days, but it was always awkwardness shared with a grin beaming from within. It felt so good to be so bad.

After the shower the logical progression would have been for the threesome to make it to the more traditional spot for sex acts, the bed, but instead they spread their naked bodies about the couch. Jim had still not achieved an orgasm from the sexual marathon and by this time in the morning, as the sun blared through the shades, he was desperate to produce just that. For Jim it was good that the girls were willing to help and even felt obliged to let Jim run the show in hopes that he could be satisfied. Jim rolled Melissa over to her hands and knees and slid it in and out from behind her. He slammed his hips into her ass over and over again while she screamed, "Keep going. Don't hold back. Harder, yeah, yeah, yeah!" After a while sweat poured down Jim's temples and his legs began to shake, yet he still could not reach the summit.

He pulled it out of her after he had pushed both of their bodies to the limit, "It feels so beautiful, like a never ending orgasm, but I can't quite get to the real thing."

Maria, who had been resting and watching the two for the last ten minutes, replied, "Well as long as you're willing to keep trying, we won't give up on you." She had a cute little smile on her face that begged him to keep trying.

"Onward to exhaustion." Jim thought as he hoisted Maria onto the kitchen counter. "I think if we increase the kinky factor that we can get this thing done." Jim said aloud trying to be funny. He got Maria spread out on the counter, pulled her to the edge and slipped it in her from his natural standing position. With every thrust, he felt like he could explode, but it was just building up waiting in the shadows. He felt pure ecstasy that was only a tiny increment away from the ultimate orgasm of his life. He continued to pound himself inside the little

Spaniard until her butt began to sweat and she slid easily back and forth on the slick countertop. Melissa got up off the couch and came to joint the sweaty couple. She was interested in being part of the finale, and she had a solid idea to bring it about. She didn't fondle Maria, she got on her knees and began to kiss and lick the cheeks of Jim's ass. Then it happened, she stuck her tongue right in Jim's asshole and the whole world turned pink. Jim jumped to his tiptoes, his eyes folded back deep in his skull, and his whole body began to shake violently.

Maria screamed, "Cum inside me, baby! Let it go, yeah, that's it, oh baby!" Jim let out a huge expulsion of air as his entire inner self poured out in machine gun fire. The shots fired for an eternity and Jim stayed up on his toes with his arms holding Maria in air as she had been pulled off the counter.

"My lord in heaven, thank you!" He sighed as he lowered Maria back down to the counter and lowered himself to the floor melting into Melissa's arms. "That sure was a surprise and it did the trick." Jim said with a giggle and a hug for his freaky friend. Melissa smiled and squeezed his bare ass.

The sexual extravaganza had finally come to an end, and then and only then, did the crazy threesome ever make it to a bed. They spread out across the bed, caressing each other softly, as they swept off to sleep some time around noon. Their bodies lay limp and spent like puppets that the master had dropped on the bed. The passion poured out of them, they sunk into the mattress for a hard day's rest.

Jim woke up in the dark of night and quickly came to the realization that time was running out to make his rendezvous with Elizabeth in Zurich, but he was not going to leave a perfect situation until there was just enough time to make a mad dash to Switzerland.

He would arrive on time, but he would still have the smell of the girls dancing with his skin. One more abstract sexual experience and he would be sexed up enough to hold out for a couple of days if Elizabeth made it difficult for him.

He got up to wash the previous sex away making his way to the shower not noticing if either of the girls was awake. Halfway through his shower Maria joined him. She turned off the lights and brought in two candles that bounced light off the walls, flickering like sporadic waves. The candlelight mellowed the mood and the veracious passion from the night before was replaced with a precise, deliberate and sensuous treatment of each other—gentle massaging hands and long slow kisses where lips stayed together as if they were stuck. Maria was developing chemistry with the American that was undeniable and Jim could feel it in her touch and in the way her eyes met his. The lust that had driven the first twenty-four hours of their relationship was melting into true affection and comfort. The water splashed on the naked flesh of yet another lovemaking experience and they both felt smiles brimming all the way through to their lips. Maria pressed up against the tile wall while Jim lifted her in the air slowly extended himself into her suspended body in a seductive shower dance that lasted until they both were completely satisfied.

They exited the bathroom to find the entire apartment lit up with a variety of candles creating a mellow, mystic setting. Melissa had a bottle of red wine corked, some Spanish music flowing through the air, and was making love to her wineglass as she danced about the room. She didn't stop when Jim and Maria entered the room—she just kept her body swaying and spinning with her eyes closed. She was wearing a long silk robe that revealed her slender body when the candlelight bounced off it just right. Maria poured Jim a glass of wine and joined Jim on the couch with one of her own. They watched the dancing beauty perform as the music enhanced her movements.

The night rolled by slowly with candlelight and music bouncing around their isolated cave. The three didn't leave the apartment that night. The music and the wine set a mellow tone. Melissa seemed washed away within herself—not expecting anyone to join her as she selected different music and danced to her own beat. The threesome was still entranced in their overall experience, but Melissa had stepped away for the moment. Her movements and sexy figure were mesmerizing for Jim and Maria to watch and kept them both gazing at what they both thought of as a wonderful creature. Eventually Melissa came back to the planet and settled herself on the rug in front of the couch. "So, can you handle both of us for another night or what?" She asked staring directly at Jim. A serious look of determination flashed across Jim's face, and then he crawled down on the floor and pulled the strap holding Melissa's silk robe and watched it slide from her milky smooth skin.

The next day, Jim woke up with two naked women again, but this time he had no choice but to make a mad dash for Switzerland. He had left himself just a sliver of time to travel a good distance—it was extremely difficult to put his leg over the side of the bed. Once he got the motivation to move, he gathered his things quickly, lightly kissed his Spanish princesses and exited the sacred walls feeling like the King of Spain.

Chapter 6
MEET ME IN ZURICH

Jim changed trains somewhere in the French Riviera. It was pitch black and he didn't really get a feel for the place. He jumped a train headed north to Lyon where he could finally get on a Swiss train that would drop him off in Zurich sometime in the middle of the pending day. By the time he got off the train in Lyon, the sun was beginning to brim over the Alps. His next train carried him around beautiful Lake Geneva and then began to ascend over the French side of the Swiss Alps. The scenery was absolutely breathtaking and Jim was glad that he had stumbled on the good luck to travel this leg of his journey in the wonderful morning light. Switzerland had the crispest blues and greens that Jim had ever seen and he wondered if his camera could even do justice to the pristine environment. Lake Geneva was wrapped in pine and the city of Geneva blended into the environment with the Swiss structures built form the very materials cleared away to make room for them. The pine and stone structures blended with their environment and didn't obstruct the beautiful scenery from which they had been built. As he ascended the Alps, the smile on Jim's face could not even be wiped away by the end of his mortal heart ticking—he was blissfully happy.

Jim made it into Zurich a day before Elizabeth was scheduled to arrive, which gave him one evening to get familiar with the city so that things would go smoothly once Elizabeth arrived. He wanted their journey to start off without a hitch and even have some shades of romanticism if he could produce it on a limited budget in a luxurious city.

He would not tell his friend of his Spanish conquests, but leave the descriptions of his trip so far in the most vanilla setting. His glow remained from Spain and may have produced an overconfidence that gave him the impression that he would have no problem luring his longtime friend into his open, loving arms. She would be open to exploring parts of her that she didn't know existed and leave the rest of the world, and all its rules, somewhere in England. He would make her feel an overwhelming exhilaration that would release some of the inner passion that she had been keeping bottled up for far too long— he imagined himself as the key to opening up her spirit. His goals were a little lofty considering the woman coming to meet him was in love with someone else, but these were just minor details to a man that was pretty sure he could satisfy two women at once.

What was Elizabeth thinking as she maneuvered the trains from London to Zurich? She certainly wasn't thinking of two naked bodies rolling around in the surf like Jim was, but she truly wasn't discounting anything either. The possibilities were endless and she wasn't willing to restrict the free spirited nature that the trip was based on. Was she as convinced of her feelings for Jim as his were for her? No, not really. She expected that he would push for a physical aspect to their relationship to develop, but she had no idea how she would respond.

Elizabeth was supposed to arrive the following day on a train from Paris, so Jim had a night to get aquatinted with the city and the Swiss people. He whipped out his trusty guidebook in search of a youth hostel. He wanted to save money on his first evening so that he could find a cozy little hotel room for Elizabeth and him the following night. He was going to waste no time on building the perfect situation for Liz and him to get intimate and, hopefully, stay that way throughout the trip. He didn't like resistance even though he knew that Liz was far too smart for just a sprinkling of simple charm—it would take a complex mixture of alcohol, charm, ambiance and some begging to win Elizabeth from the grips of her English mate.

Jim made his way to a youth hostel that was a little ways out of the city, but was located only a block away from the lake in what seemed to be an extremely nice neighborhood. Actually, everywhere in Zurich was an extremely nice neighborhood. After getting settled in the hostel, Jim went out into the clean, crisp Zurich night wanting to explore a little nightlife, as always, and get a feel for the Swiss people on his first night in town. The city was spotless with beautifully efficient street trolleys that made ordinary getting around much more entertaining than underground systems. Everyone was kind and helpful and for the most part spoke flawless English. Jim felt like he was in some kind of utopia until he received the check for his first meal. He enjoyed a fairly light meal at a restaurant that looked very accessible and not too extravagant, but he felt a little sting when the check came out to be more than he usually spent on food for the entire day in Spain or Portugal. Zurich was pristine, but at a cost.

Jim careened around the city that evening drinking frothy beverages and enjoying different views of the lake and river. He admired the quiet strength of the stone castles that bordered the peaceful Limmat River as it flowed into Lake Zurich. He stayed around downtown until nightfall and then made his way back towards the hostel, which sat on the far end of the lake from downtown. The busy area near the mouth of the river was full of pubs and bubbling over with people, which was hard for Jim to leave, but he knew it would be better to be close to his bed when he started drinking. The trolley car zipped him back to the other end of the lake in no time and dumped him off a couple blocks from his bed. He sauntered back into the lively hostel with a little beer buzz and his usual confidence. He bounced off the youthful guests and finally came to the consensus that most of the others were making their way across the street to a lakeside club that featured live music of the rock / punk style. Jim thought a live music show would be a perfect place to knock into some fellow stoners and pick up a bag of pristine Swiss marijuana.

The music wailed in the early evening, and the crowd over-flowed out of the barn-like structure into an extensive outdoor area that was littered with picnic tables. Inside, the band's music roared and reverberated off the wooden walls that were splashed with graffiti, and the people were bouncing off each other like ping-pong balls. Punk rockers in slashed clothing with heavy amounts of hair gel sending their unique flags of hair spraying every direction mixed with more moderately dressed, yet equally as soused, youthful individuals. Jim fit in his own category with the plaid leisure shorts, blue surfer's tee shirt, and his trusty sandals. He wasn't known to thrash around the stage, but he definitely could groove to some hard driving rock-n-roll music. The lyrics were in Swiss-German, yet Jim found himself singing along to the chorus. It seemed to jive perfectly well, especially after he made his way into the toking circle. The joint was passed to him as if he was an original part of the group, no questions asked and even served with a smile.

"Danke, my brothers." Jim exclaimed when there was a little lull in the music.

"Ah, an Englishman, yeah?" One of the rockers replied.

"American." Jim replied, unconvinced that he could ever pass for Canadian.

"You like the music? You understand? It's Swiss-German, much different, yeah? They sing songs in English too. Wait, you'll see." The Swiss gentleman replied not caring where Jim was from.

Later on, Jim sat outside with a group of locals that frequented the rocking barn and was able to get to know the individuals as well as learn a little about their country. The first band had played some fresh tunes. Jim was amazed at the quality of the band's English songs, which would have been hard to differentiate from an American band. Jim had embedded himself with a group of people that were traveling with the band and ended up helping to load instruments into a large Volkswagen van. After the work was done, everyone settled in at a group of tables near the water's edge. The breeze blowing in from the lake mixed with adrenaline from the live show, some booze, and pot creating an electric buzz that flowed through the air like blue molasses. There were five band members, five of their friends, and the newly acquired American sidekick. The conversation gravitated towards music with everyone spouting out his or her favorite bands and backing it up with reasons for their supremacy.

Jim put in his two cents, "The greatest band of all time is Led Zeppelin." Two females and a dude agreed. "Their music is timeless. If it comes on the radio today, you can't tell that is twenty or thirty years old—it is more complex and fresh than any of the new stuff. The Beatles sound dated, and some of that shit is just too cutesy —it sounds like a Brady Bunch theme song or something. I mean, the Beatles and the Stones are the only ones that you can put against them, maybe Aerosmith, they've been around forever, but all their shit sounds the same. Zeppelin has range, unbelievable staying power, and you've got to admit their shit is straight funky."

"What about Pink Floyd? Man, you've forgotten them. And what's the deal with all these English-speaking bands; we've got to put a couple of our own in there just to fuck you up. Swiss-German music is famous all over the world."

Jim asked a little girl with purple lipstick and pink hair what she thought. She blinked her eyes a couple of times, her head bobbed, and she tilted it to the side as if she was going to give a well thought out answer and said, "I think I need to be sick." Jim was quick to respond. He held out his hand and led her to the edge of the water in an area that was buried in the shadows of an overhanging tree.

"Let er rip, sunshine." Jim said, grabbing the girl's hair as she quickly got to her knees and began to spew straight liquid into the lake. Three deep breaths and three coughing, vomiting fits later, the girl was finished. She wiped her mouth with her sleeve and found some clean water to splash on her face. "You're all right, now you've got plenty of room for more. Probably need to get that taste out of your mouth, huh?" Another girl walked over with a glass of water, and the sick girl sloshed it around in her mouth and spat it out. Then she drank the rest of it like it was the last liquid on earth. After a couple glasses of water, she was ready to swallow beer again and with great courage, if you want to call it that, she got back in the game as if she hadn't missed a beat. She even began to articulate some of her thoughts on music.

"I think Echo is going to be the greatest band of all time." She said regarding the band that had just performed and was sitting amongst the group. "The music of right now is what I like best. I don't want to listen to the radio to tell me what my favorite music is—I want to experience it. I want to find it somewhere within my city so that I can feel it and live it every time I'm near. If you guys were to become world famous, then I would know where you came from, and I could support you on your top forty ventures, but I'm happy with you just the way you are. You're the best band in the world, my world."

"Wow, that was deep from the wasted one." One of the band members gleefully projected. "I really like what you said though, Sammy. Music is more than what is on the radio. It's part of your life, and the more you experience it, the more pleasant things are. Music is supposed to come from deep in the soul, and if we can play gigs where people feel us at all, then we should keep playing and keep making music. If I can hold on and make it part of the rest of my life, I'll be better for it."

"Your band is great, man. I mean—you could play anywhere. I think you've put together a chemistry that gels and a sound that is completely unique. Your English songs are as good as any band that I hear in America at places like this. You guys could go on tour in America. There is a million clubs like this and it's not too expensive to get a bus and a trailer. All you need is a promoter to find you gigs and you could spend a year touring America, letting your music pay the way. Maybe you get a record deal, and maybe you don't. Who cares—you'll get to travel and play your music. Just an idea, you know. I'm not trying to say that it is better to travel around America than Switzerland—just that it's so big, and there is a lot to see. I think it could be a really great experience, just like traveling through Europe is for me. Also, the English market is the biggest market for record sales, isn't it? You might as well give a shot at making a pile of money, right?"

"Usually, if bands want to make it really big, they have to cross over to the English, and that's why we are always developing our English stuff. We want to give some big summer festivals in Great Britain a chance—or actually we want them to give us a chance. If we can get on the bill at some of those monster shows, then we might have a chance to do what you're talking about. Some American or English promoter might see us and help us get on our way. Otherwise, we stay here in Switzerland and maybe travel to Germany and Austria a bit. We could get a pretty big following just in central Europe and sell some records, but it doesn't compare to going to America and getting the exposure to sell a million records. Touring over there would be a dream come true, but it's a long ways from where we are right now. There have been bands that have crossed over and had success with English music, mostly from Germany where you can make a pretty good living as a band. In Germany, some bands can achieve fame and wealth without crossing over, and that can happen here, but on a smaller scale. Usually, when that happens, the band gives a shot at crossing over anyway. There are famous Swiss musicians, but you'll notice when you turn on the radio that the Swiss and German music is always mixed with mainstream stuff from the States and England, so the music scene doesn't stand alone; it is propped up by top-forty music. English music sets the trends that our artists seem to follow. For some reason, American Pop-culture is everywhere even when you're halfway around the world, eh." The lead guitarist explained in a friendly tone.

The discussion continued well into the night with a couple of the crew always willing to speak to Jim in English while others chatted in their native dialect. The drunk girl with pink hair threw-up again, stopped drinking, and became the roller of marijuana cigarettes, which she gladly passed around once she delicately put them together. She took a liking to Jim and stayed by his side for the rest of the night. As she left she invited him to meet her at the park near the lake the next day. She was going to try to sleep off her hangover while sunbathing and smoking a doobie or two at the lakeside park near downtown. She figured the American would make good company. Jim told her that he had to pick somebody up at the train station, but until then, he would hang out with her at the park.

Jim woke up the next morning with a pounding headache and a body that reeked of alcohol mixed with sweat. He was in need of a shower and a joint—something to clear the headache and put a soft edge on reality. After washing his body thoroughly with soap and water, he jumped the trolley car to go search out a place for Elizabeth and him to stay that evening. The day was lovely, the sky stark blue, and the temperature just south of searing with a little breeze that tied everything together and made it just right. Mountains soared into the sky at most edges of the city, and the lake lapped against the shore like the whispering heartbeat of a magical kingdom. Jim floated through the streets wondering what the pink-headed Swiss girl would look like in a bathing suit, and if she could keep from vomiting if he took her for a drink. She was a cute little thing that seemed to be completely fearless. When she did speak, she had something fresh and unique to offer.

Jim found a hotel not far from the train station or the lakeside park, dumped his bag at the front desk, and was told that he could return to get access to his room at one-o-clock. He would be early to the park, so he went to find a swimming hole. The water was clean and cold. Jim swam heartily in hopes of pulling himself out of a hung-over funk, and the swim was just what he needed, reviving and refreshing his spirit. He wondered if he was going to mix the pink-haired girl with Elizabeth, or if it would be better to detach the Swiss rocker and do his best to attend to the needs of his old friend. He lay in the sun maneuvering the day in a variety of ways inside his warped mind and decided it would be best to blow off the Swiss girl once Elizabeth arrived. Pink hair would surely offend the sensibilities of his Oxford girl. He knew if he kept the Swiss girl around, he could be tempted to go home with her if Liz wasn't giving him the right signals. He wanted to concentrate on Elizabeth because it was a friendship he wanted to develop into something greater. If he kept the Swiss girl around, Elizabeth would encourage him to go have a good time causing the trip to start off with the wrong feel.

Jim knew, or at least had the opinion, that Elizabeth would not be easy—she would not roll over the first night they were together and say, "Fuck me." He remembered long conversations during their teenage years when she would describe the torture she put her boy friends through. The heavy petting she would allow to escalate until her partner's penis was ready to shoot missiles to Russia, and then the calculated cut-off point leaving his loins throbbing for her until the next time they met. She would laugh about this; she would boast about this, and he knew that she was stronger than him—she had a will that could make his quiver.

After his swim, he parked himself next to the statue that was to be the meeting place for him and the Swiss girl. Jim couldn't remember her name so he was planning on getting to that early on in their meeting. It was still an hour before they were supposed to meet, so Jim laid out his big beach towel on the cool green grass of the pristine park, slipped on his shades, and proceeded to take a hearty nap. About thirty minutes after he dosed off, the Swiss girl arrived and laid out her stuff next to his, which eventually rousted him. As he sat up, he noticed the park had come alive during his short nap—there were people playing games, walking dogs, and sun bathing. The park was like a vast green beach with pine trees instead of Palm.

"Hey, you been here long?" She asked as Jim began to rustle.

"Oh yeah, I've already had a swim and found a hotel for later tonight just down the way. I took a toke down by the lake this morning to try to combat the driving pain in my head—it seemed to work. The swim really helped too. How do you feel?"

"I had to bake too, but I haven't gotten the swim in yet. I could use one, you want to join me?" This was the first glance that Jim took of the young lady as she disrobed into her bathing suit, and now he could see why the girl had so much trouble holding down all that beer the night before—she was tiny. Her petite figure was not lacking shape, though, and Jim was mesmerized as the little, sexy thing extended her hand to help him up.

"I'm Jim by the way, I forgot your name, I'm sorry. I'll be glad to go anywhere with you in that little thing."

"Melinda is my name. So you like my suit, huh? It's a lot different than what I had on last night. I meant to apologize about last night. I'm surprised you even showed up after the ass I made of myself. I don't usually try to drink with everyone. I stay smoking, but I don't need to be drinking like that."

"I thought you were a real trooper. You didn't give up and, you could still roll a mean joint in-between heaving in the lake."

"Don't remind me. Let's get in this water. I need a big strong man with me in case the current tries to suck me under."

"Well, we better find one cause I have trouble keeping myself afloat." Jim smiled as he followed his little Swiss princess into the water—her pink hair melting to red as it got wet. Melinda swam a good distance out into the lake without fear and with a good stroke. Jim fell in behind her making sure that he was close enough behind to admire her exquisite shape. He forgot about Elizabeth for the moment, and hoped that by some miracle, he could get this beautiful little woman out of what little clothes she had on. Eventually she stopped swimming and turned around to catch Jim splashing right into her. She swung he legs around Jim's waist so that her breasts were staring him directly in the eye, and he had to tread water with powerful strokes to keep their heads above water. Melinda kissed Jim without hesitation and was pulled playfully under water as Jim kissed her passionately. They frolicked in the water discovering that they were both ridden with lust. Jim was surprised at the forwardness of the petite little Swiss prize and would have never imagined having to slip in a sexual rendezvous before going to pick up a woman that he supposedly cared for very much. This was proof that he sure wasn't ready for monogamy; even he could admit that, if confronted. His self-control was minimal at best, but he had no commitments in place with anyone, and, therefore, was willing to play the game the only way he knew how — wide open.

The couple made their way to the shore and to their cozy spot on their towels. Melinda needed sunburn protection that Jim was glad to apply on every inch of her tiny little body. They laid in the sun and enjoyed a freshly rolled joint enticing another couple near-by to join them for a communal smoke—it was international law that joints were rolled to be shared, and everyone in-the-know didn't hesitate to enforce the law. Stoners in the park once more – it was a common theme for all involved. The Swiss society treated the funny smelling smoke with a nonchalance that rivaled someone smoking a cigarette or cigar. Swiss people grew their own marijuana without fear of prosecution even though there were some laws on the books against it. The attitude of the people and the government was much to Jim's liking—there was a mellow attitude of acceptance that wasn't influenced by extreme factions on either side. The neutral aspect of Switzerland reigned in its people, as they didn't pass judgment or race to rash decisions.

As the afternoon crept forward, Jim hinted to Melinda that he needed to go check into his hotel so that he would be ready for his guest that was arriving later in the day. Melinda offered to come along, which Jim was hoping for, and they hurried off to the hotel. Melinda knew the guest was most likely a woman, but Jim had done a good job of skirting around the issue.

"So are you in love with this girl, your guest?" She asked unabashedly.

"How do you know it's a girl?"

"Come on." She said making a face that said she was no idiot.

"She's just a friend. We've never had any sort of romance or even been close to it for that matter. We grew up together and decided to do some traveling together. There's really nothing more to it than that."

"Sure." Melinda replied as Jim was given the key to the room. "A man like you doesn't just go traveling around with a woman without some sexual tension making its way into the equation. You're full of it; I can feel it in you, and it's not something you can just set aside. What does she look like?"

"If I told you she was chunky and homely, would you believe my innocence?"

"Is she?"

"I don't want to lie to you, she's almost as sexy as you are."

"So, you are going to take me up here and seduce me, and you are going to lure her into your bed later?"

"If I'm real lucky, yeah. But she's kind of a prude, so I may lure her into my bed but she'll keep all her clothes on. She certainly won't come on to me as convincingly as you have. Actually, she probably won't come on to me at all considering she's in love with some other man." Jim explained as Melinda listened with a mischievous grin on her face. She thought the whole situation was quite interesting. Jim could tell by the grin that it was Melinda who planned on seducing him, and he appreciated that very much.

As they opened the door, Melinda spoke for the last time to Jim, "I'm not usually like this, but there's something about you that makes me kind of crazy. It's the eyes, and the way that you can just pour yourself into me within twenty-four hours of meeting me. You're magic to me." She walked to the opposite side of the seventh story room as she spoke these words. Then she opened the drapes so that the bright midday sun burst into the room and drenched her luscious body as she poetically removed each article of her clothing.

An hour later, Melinda let herself out while Jim was using the restroom. She had enjoyed him. It was a spontaneous combustion of lust, but it felt like it was the only thing that could happen during that day. She had just enough of the man to leave a perfect image in her mind, of the body, of the spirit, of a slice of time, when two people collided, and all the parts fit just right. She didn't need any more or any less. Sometimes satisfaction is just a couple hours out of a beautiful summer day, but it lasts forever—that image of time standing still, and everything within releasing a deep sigh of complete and total satisfaction. Melinda grabbed onto that moment and locked it away as a sunshiny moment that would forever be useful when wondering if it was possible to be satisfied as a human being.

Jim felt a glow as well, but it was interrupted by the thought of his friend's pending arrival and the disheveled state of their hotel room. He had to make it looked napped in, not fucked in. He did his best to put the pieces back together again and jumped in the shower to wash off the sex. He had less than an hour to get to the train station and be the one-man welcoming party for Elizabeth, but he was still lost in the moment passed, the wistful couple of hours spent soaking up life with Melinda. He shook it off the best he could, however, it would just run down his skin and absorb back in—he couldn't get his mind off sunshine and nudity, the rays of light dancing around the curves of perfect flesh. His mind was a kaleidoscope of the few hours spent with Melinda, and it wasn't going anywhere else soon.

Some how his body carried him to the train station, and he ended up at the proper café with a beer in front of him slightly before Liz's train was to arrive. At least he would be in a fantastic mood to welcome his friend to Switzerland.

Elizabeth moved in quietly behind Jim, put her bags down, and slid her hands up under his arms grabbing his chest and kissing the back of his neck. "I'm here. All your dreams have been answered." She said in a sexy, smooth whisper in Jim's ear.

"Damn, you're a little cocky in your adulthood. My dreams, including you, don't have anything to do with train stations, and you're always completely naked."

"You would have to be a perv. You are not going to see me naked any time soon."

"Don't make promises you can't keep. I haven't even begun to start charming your pants off yet. Give me a little time, and nudity will feel like your natural state when you're in my company. We are going to some places where we can be naked all the time. You should revel in such freedom my dear. Would you like a beer or do you want to go drop off your stuff?"

"Let's go, let's go, let's go, I'm so excited. We're going to have so much fun." Liz said brimming with anticipation of the adventure they were about to begin.

Jim picked up Liz's pack, "You've got to be kiddin me; this thing is huge. You're going to lug this thing all over Europe? How can you possibly need all this stuff? Is there a fucking Lazy Boy in here or what?"

"You don't worry about my stuff, I can take care of it. Give me that, I'll carry it. You need to be more of a gentleman and not comment on a lady's personal things."

"I'm a gentleman, let me carry that thing, you'll have plenty of time for it. You better rest yourself because this thing is no joke." Jim said giggling at the enormity of Liz's backpack, which was at least fifty percent larger than his.

"I've got to maintain myself and have some options—we are going to Italy." Liz exclaimed as they exited the station and headed towards the hotel. "What if we go out? You want me to be presentable, don't you?"

"I'm sure you look gorgeous when you roll over in the morning, and there ain't nothing in this bag that can change that. You're just going to have to let me go through this thing and decide what's important. I'm sure I can get rid of at least half of this shit. We'll give it away to the poor."

"You will do no such thing, you awful man. I will carry my own bag, and you don't need to worry about what's in it. You can't threaten a woman's wardrobe—it just isn't right."

"Oh, sunshine, don't get angry with me. I'm just having a little fun. We're going to enjoy ourselves, and if you need all this shit to enjoy yourself, that's just the way it's going to be. You're probably going to have to worry about being seen in public with me. I've only got about three outfits so you might get a little tired of looking at me in them, but any time you want me to, I'll take them off." Jim said putting in another plug for communal nudity.

Both Jim and Elizabeth had notions of what the few weeks would hold, but their ideas of relationship bliss were not exactly cohesive. Jim believed that sex was on the horizon, possibly even that evening, while Elizabeth was looking to share an intimacy with her friend without the complications of sex. Elizabeth really didn't feel that she could fit into Jim's exotic life, but she wanted to be close enough to feel it—to have the rush of being bad without actually being bad. Jim wanted her to release herself to him and to experience his world without inhibitions.

They both wanted their dreams to be fulfilled, but their conversion to reality could not be done with a wiggle of a nose.

Their first night together would paint the picture of how the rest of the trip was going to proceed. Jim could have been completely insensitive and got a room with one bed, pressing the situation to his desired outcome, but even he thought that would be a little tacky. The two were familiar with each other's bodies since they had cuddled and rubbed each other through their adolescent lives, but they had never even as much as kissed. Their hormones raged for exactly what each other had—they could feel their bodies pull towards one another, but they always resisted. They enjoyed everything about each other, and both were willing to share a deeper form of intimacy, but Jim wanted to take it all the way while Liz just wanted to stick her toe in the water. Jim, or Jimmy in times of affection, was too dangerous. She knew what he was capable of—she had heard many stories during their high school years, not only from others, but also from his own lips. She wasn't willing to be another statistic even though being around him made her skin tingle with anticipation.

When they made it to their room, Jim jumped on his previously rustled bed to help hide the fact that a couple hours before, all the sheets and blankets had been ravaged to the point of complete debacle. Jim aired out the room by leaving the window open, and the fan running on high when he left, but he could still smell the sweet smell of the lotion he had rubbed on Melinda's body lingering in the bedding. If he were lucky enough to steer Elizabeth into bed later that evening, he would be sure to aim for hers.

"So, what have you been up to? Have you had a chance to scout this beautiful city? What do you think we should do?"

"I think we should go get drunk and then come back here and screw. I mean, we can still be bosom buddies, but we need to be friends that fuck. I think you're extremely sexy, and I want to be naked with you as often as possible. Doesn't it sound great: drinking, fucking, riding the rails, enjoying the flavor of Europe and each other. Now that you have had a successful sexual encounter, out of wedlock I might add, we need to expand on that experience. I want to help you, help me, and help yourself all at the same time."

"Let me drop my pants to the floor right now. You're so romantic that I just can't wait—take me now! Come on. Did you really consider that speech a form of seduction because it was way off the mark for me? I can't just have sex with you because it's fun and it feels good. There's a lot more to it than that. I need a lot more, and you know that, Jimmy, you know what I'm all about." Liz announced in a semi-convincing manner. She mused, "Maybe sex was suppose to be fun, feel good, and be convenient with life-long friends, or was that the stuff of television soap operas."

"You don't really believe that we can resist each other on this entire trip, do you? Don't you want to experience my world for a little while? I mean, maybe that's a little selfish expecting you to walk my way, but I'm wide open, and you've only got a small array of possibilities to choose from with your cautious approach. Maybe it's a way to keep from failing, but it's no way to experience the edges of the universe. Try to enjoy this little slice of time that we've been given and don't hold anything back. You don't have to prove anything to me or anyone else in the next two weeks. There is no one looking over your shoulder—no one to report back home to your beloved Danny—no one to hold you accountable for your impeccable Catholic values, which it seems you have already betrayed, not to rub it in or anything. Let yourself go. If you don't want to fuck me, that's fine. I'm not saying that fucking is the only way we're going to have fun on this trip; I just don't want you to set up any barriers that you might regret later. I want us to enjoy our time together and whatever happens, happens. I've had an amazing time so far, and you're about to walk on the edge with me. You know you want to try it, and I want you to be next to me with no expectations but to enjoy the world and the people in it." Jim's dissertation was heart felt and he hoped convincing as well.

"You're completely out of your mind—I guess that's why I love you so much. What are we really going to do anyway? I'm starving. Let's go grab a bite to eat, and then we can get hammered, but I'm not guaranteeing anything else."

"Ah, but the door is open. That's what I like to hear. You keep that attitude and things are going to turn out beautiful."

The couple eventually made their way to the stone streets of a very old section of Zurich, near the river, just down the street from their hotel. There were lots of restaurants and bars to choose from and they wandered in and out of them looking for the perfect atmosphere to spend their evening. The sky was a crisp blue above Zurich, and the air was a soothing kind of rich warm that seemed to be filtered by the fresh water near by. The serene environment influenced the couple to look for outdoor seating at the establishments they were scouting. It was too nice a night to be trapped indoors. Some of the quaint areas in this part of town had pedestrian only streets that the restaurants used liberally, scattering as much seating as they could on the cobblestone paths. The evening was

utterly perfect, and the couple felt like everything was going their
way. They had a utopian sense as they sat down at a large wooden
table outside a lively pub with a view of the river. They ordered
beers that reached their lips without having to pick them up off the
table and were swayed into local cuisine by a very amiable waiter.
The Swiss food was heavy on meat and cheese and didn't stray too
far from what Jim and Liz were used to, but it was definitely different and excellent with cold beer. Liz was thoroughly wrapped up in
Jim's tails of his trip to that point. She stressed her amazement of
what he was able to achieve in Oxford and was even more in awe
when he began to detail his Portuguese and Spanish exploits. He
told her about Joey and the crazy Scottish drug dealer and went on
about the beauty of the Algarve, but admitted that much of his first
week in Portugal was quite hazy.

"Why do you always end up doing drugs? Do you have some kind
of death wish or something? I remember when you used to climb up
on my back porch during the summers. Tina and I would be up there
in our sleeping bags, and we couldn't even get to sleep until you got
there. We knew that it would be late when you finally finished partying, and we knew that you would be way out there on something.
And you always showed up like you said you would with some outrageous story of what you had been through in the previous hours.
We would almost become intoxicated by your energy, and from the
smell permeating from you, but we could never imagine doing the
shit you were doing. It was always something we thought was for
degenerates - like LSD or cocaine. What about all the time you drank
whole bottles of cough syrup—what was that all about? We thought
of you like a character in a movie that we could touch, but we never

understood why you did what you did. All the drugs seemed over the top for someone that did so well in school, someone who was so successful in sports and all that. I mean, didn't you hear the warnings? I don't see how you couldn't be scared of overdosing or having some awful thing happen to your body from all those chemicals, or whatever it is, that you put in your body. Your body is supposed to be your temple—don't you know that?"

"I don't fear any of it. I live every day as if it will be my last; every moment I want an explosion of feeling. I don't shove needles in myself, and most of the drugs I do don't really have high rates of overdose. Heroin is the most dangerous, and I don't touch that shit. It's not that I don't want to—it's just that I've heard if you do it once, it's all over. I'm just a recreational drug user, and I switch it up a lot so that I don't go too over the top with any one drug. Oh shit, I sound extremely stupid trying to justify myself, don't I? I'm trying to rationalize my drug use when it really comes down to the fact that I have little to no self-control and would rather be a step or two outside reality. I like to live in a haze, a magic smoke that softens all the edges. The real world is this cold place that I can float above with the right level of intoxication. I stay a good distance from the harshness that way. I'm constantly in this liquid smile that wraps around me and keeps the boogey man out. I look at my parents I see what I don't want, anguished sobriety, so I go on these other exotic paths, and I never have any idea where I'm really going, but I'm sure as hell enjoying every minute on the road there. I gravitate towards people with the same interests on the same random path who don't care where they're headed—just how fucked up they can get along the way. I've found that there is a plethora of free spirits roaming the range, and we always get together and smoke a joint when we run into one another. I do drugs; it's just part of my functioning nature, and you might even witness some outrageous behavior while traveling with me. Don't do what I do, or what I say, because you might regret it and end up fucking my brains out while intoxicated. At least you've picked up drinking—I'm not sure that we could get along otherwise. A good drinking hole is always a central part to my traveling agenda. And the sex thing, I'm glad that you've jumped into that pond. I'm hoping that we will engage in such acts as soon as possible."

"I'm not responding to those final comments. Do you think you'll always be out of control, or do you think it's just your youth, and some day you will slow down?"

"Why? You wanta marry me some day? You wanta make sure I come home every night and do the responsible thing?" Jim asked with a hint of sarcasm scratching his voice.

"You've already told me that you have no intentions of ever getting married, so how could I even have such aspirations?"

"Women believe they can manipulate a man into doing what they want. They may think that at the right side of the rainbow, every-thing will work out, and all the things they love about you will take over with the undesirable characteristics melting away as if they were banished by the well- wishing woman. It's probably true—there prob-ably is some power radiating from between your legs that could put me in a trance and force me to mend my ways."

"It's my cunning intellectual aptitude that would overtake you. What's between my legs would just keep you happy. You can't handle me everyday anyway. I need constant attention, and you've never been the type to latch onto a needy woman. You would always be tell-ing me to stop whining, like you do now, and I would keep whining. Eventually, things would turn ugly, and you would go out on some run leaving me completely broken hearted."

"You don't have enough confidence in either of us my dear. I wouldn't break your heart, and eventually, your whining would turn into moans of ecstasy." Jim said as he leaned over and kissed Eliza-beth on the cheek.

For the next few hours the couple sat at the outdoor table ordering two-foot-high beers of which Liz was drinking one to every two of Jim's. They began to get inebriated becoming more lovey and touchy. Their hands began to explore each other, and it became clear where the night was heading. The alcohol definitely had a lot to do with Liz's flirtatiousness, which was beyond anything Jim had ever seen from his friend. They obviously had some of the same ideas in their heads about how this trip was going to proceed, or maybe it was just Jim's overpowering sexuality taking Liz's flirtatiousness and turning it into lust. Whatever it was, when the waiter came back with their change, he found them completely lip-locked and left the change on the table.

For a while on the walk back to the room, the couple let them-selves be a couple. Liz let Jim usher her as she fit just right into his outstretched arm with her head resting gently on his shoulder. Jim thought to himself as they strolled along, "I can't believe this is going to be so easy. She's going to fuck me on the first night, and we're go-ing to have a sexual revolution on this trip. I may be declaring victory far too soon, though. I can't take advantage of her if she's too drunk, can I? I mean, there's a million things that can happen between now and her having her pants off, so don't get too cocky Jimmy boy, and don't do anything that's going to fuck up the whole trip. If she's hot and heavy for the sex, then you've got to give it to her, but if she's not, you've go to keep your dick in your pants. Who knows what will happen. I've never been in this situation with her, and I've got to let her be the one making all the rules. If I start declaring what's going through my twisted mind, she might turn around and head right back to the train station." Jim kept bouncing different thoughts through his head, not knowing what to expect in a romantic situation with Liz, who had only been a friend to this point. He thought of her as a prude, yet he had all the respect in the world for the way she lived her life. He just wanted her to let it all out the window when she was with him.

Elizabeth was also somewhat confused and had a dialogue of her own running, "I can't do this—I can't just give him everything on the first night. I'm not going to have sex with him. I'm going to say something as soon as we get to the room. Maybe I should just sleep with him without the sex—give him a little of what he wants, but definitely not it all. He's so adorable. It feels right, but it's not what I expected. He's just too much for me. I can't do this—I can't do this—I can't do this!" She screamed to herself. "I love Daniel and I'm committed to him. Jimmy will just be in and out of my life in a flash. He has no intention of creating something lasting. At least, I don't think so. What am I thinking, he has told me hundreds of stories about being with women—just sleeping with them and going on his way. I've got to resist. I want him so bad, but life can't be this easy. I'll regret it in the morning, and the rest of the trip will be ruined. I've got to hold myself together." The sensible thoughts swimming through

Liz's mind differed greatly from the irrational mini-dreams plowing through Jim's.

The two points of view were bound to collide at some point. Jim's sex drive was his controlling force, while Elizabeth was fighting an emotional battle that left her gasping for the right answers. She had hormones too, but the alcohol wasn't enough to allow them full control. Jim could allow them full control dead sober, but he could also snort an eight ball of cocaine and go to church the next day, so you can't really compare the two.

They made their way back to the room, kissed in the doorway, and immediately fell on Liz's bed in an embrace. Liz's shirt came off with Jim's to follow, but as soon as Jim put his thumb and forefinger on the button of Liz's pants, the party was interrupted by Liz extending her arms up and pushing Jim away from her. Jim sighed before Liz even spoke, "Don't worry, I'll get over to my side. I had a feeling you might slow things down even though I think full exposure would be our best way to continue."

"You always try to over-simplify things when you know how I am. This is the first time you have even kissed me and you expect me to just melt in your hands and lose touch with all my sensibilities—I'm not that drunk. It takes a lot of work to get that button undone, and it's far too complicated to allow you full access when I have no idea how you're really going to act. I just can't do this right now, it's far more than I can handle. You're just going to have to stay Jimmy, my loving friend. We can't change things right now."

"We're going to keep it which ever way makes you happy because we're fixing to enjoy the next couple weeks together, and I won't put that in jeopardy. It has to be on your terms because mine are pornographic and would probably make you a little uncomfortable. You tell me how it's going to be and that's how it's going to be. If it was up to me we, wouldn't even be having this conversation right now because I would be busy kissing every inch of your naked body, making your hair stand up and your spine bend so that the only thing touching the bed is your shoulder blades and your heels. If I were still driving this action, we would be on our way to paradise. Now your paradise and my paradise might be two different things. Actually, I'm pretty sure they are because you stopped me cold on the way to mine, but I'm going to let you take over the driving, and I'm going to be happy with whatever road you take. I care for you, and I want you to have a great time and feel just right."

"I don't think I can handle us being involved. I don't think I can just give myself to you and feel like I have any control at all, because you've had a sex life that I can't imagine and don't think I'm ready for. It's not that I don't want you." Jim leaned over and kissed Liz before she could finish. He kissed her on the lips and gently on the neck.

"Don't worry about explaining. Let's just take it day by day." Jim said and kissed her one more time and whispered her a goodnight. He made his way to his ruffled bed that still had the slight scent of sun tan lotion and thought to himself, "I can't let her make any definitive rules, she's got to keep the possibility of us open. She's so beautiful and sweet. I've just got to make her unravel so that I can see what's in her core."

The long time friends slept across the room from each other dreaming of Italian adventures and wondering what the other was thinking. The next morning they would head south.

Chapter 7
VENICIA

The Grand Canal is the main thoroughfare through Venice, or as the Italians call it, Venicia, and is shown in a million postcards around the world as a serene river-like serpent with quiet gondolas, gently manned by their well-dressed captains, while a loving couple embraces on the way to their romantic destination. When Jim and Liz exited the train and descended the long stairway outside the station, there lay a very different site in front of them. The Grand Canal was massively busy with large motorboats acting as taxis to the swarming tourists. The cobblestone pathways that acted as walking boulevards were jam packed with foreigners strapped with cameras and camcorders or loaded down with their bags heading to or from the train station. The cinematic romance that had always been portrayed in American media was lost while Jim and Liz struggled to situate themselves in the summer mayhem that was Venice. Neither Jim nor Liz wanted to give up those romantic notions, so they pressed on hoping to put some distance between themselves and the mob.

"We're just too close to the train station, I'm sure we can find some place more tranquil than this insanity." Jim said looking back at Liz as he was wedged in between two people on a street that was just wide enough to walk three abreast. After the long train ride from Switzerland the couple wanted to unwind somewhere peaceful and were hoping to have a relaxing, possibly romantic, rest in the city of love. They had no idea it was going to be the city of chaos in the depths of July, but so it was and they would have to adjust. The frenzied swarm of tourists made it unlikely that a room would be easy to come by, but Jim had faith in his guiding abilities and led them on some quick zigzags down some less packed allies.

"Do you have any idea where you're going? It's going to be impossible to find a room—there's too many fucking people." Elizabeth whined in her trailing position, trying to keep up with Jim's brisk walk.

"Chill out precious and have faith in me. The Lord is with us and we shall not want."

"You can't possibly have a clue where you're going. You don't have a map and you keep making turns—how are we going to find our way back?"

"Stop whining and never question a man about direction. I know exactly where we are and looky there—that place looks perfect; don't you think?" Jim had wandered smack dab into a quaint little hotel that was a little off the main path so he figured it might have a room.

"We're too close to the station. There's no way they're going to have any rooms." Liz was in a whining mood after her romantic notions of Venice had been shattered.

"Have faith, my dear, you never know until you try. And lighten up for goodness sakes. We've only seen a fraction of this place, and I guarantee you, it will get better." Jim smiled reassuringly and bounced through the front door to check for a vacancy. He returned with his head down and a manufactured frown. "Those people in there said that there is no fucking way that we're going to get a room in this city tonight. They said you have to have reservations like a month out. We're fucked!"

"I told you! What are we going to do now?" Liz exclaimed on the verge of tears.

"I guess we can go up to our room and take a load off. It's just up that flight of stairs in there, only one bed, but I brought lots of rubbers so I think we can make it work."

"You ass—I was about to cry. Why did you do that to me? You know I'm fragile."

"Don't be such a sour puss. Tonight is the night we make sweet love in the city of love. I'm going to get you stumbling drunk and take advantage of you. The things I'm going to do to you, girl. By morning you'll be walking around buck naked smoking a joint and begging me to fuck you one more time."

"Get me to our room and I hope you know that you're going to have to sleep on the floor, no funny stuff in the bed." Liz was a little grouchy, but the stunt Jim had pulled and the good fortune of finding a room was enough to get her turned in the right direction. She and Jim would extract their own version of romance from the cobblestone mazes and aqua boulevards that formed the ancient city.

The duo made their way to their room that had two old large windows with detailed wood trim, small ledges sticking out from them and gargoyles guarding the edges of the building just outside the windows. Jim sprung into the room as if he had completely overcome the letdown that the thriving crowds had pressed upon him. "We will find a quaint side of Venice and we will make it ours. We will conquer this city and all the other great cities of Italy. The ordinary tourist will be lost in an abyss compared to our extraordinary experiences, my dear. Don't forget who's riding shotgun on your journey—it's not one of your wet-end boyfriends from high school and it certainly isn't one of those prim and proper Englishmen that you seem to fancy at the moment. It's me, Jimmy, the one and only master of chaos and multiple orgasms. I will lead you to the most entertaining ends of the earth free of charge. Do not fret, we will enjoy ourselves, or we will simply get on a train and leave. Do you feel me, sister? We are in control and we will not let the world drag us down."

"You're right. Thank you for trying to cheer me up. There are just so many fucking people; you can't even walk on the streets. Maybe later on tonight things will settle down and we'll be able to check things out better. I almost had a panic attack out there. I felt like I was going to get trampled. The damn water taxi was like a cattle barge and what was it to get in the gondolas—like fifty bucks? Screw that; we'll ride the cattle barge. We just need to find some place quiet for dinner. I'll get some wine in me and I'll be okay."

"That's the spirit—a couple bottles of wine, and it will be the paradise you envisioned." Liz dropped her bag on the floor and plopped herself on the bed. Jim cuddled up next to her and began to rub her shoulders. She closed her eyes and mumbled that that was exactly what she needed. After the massage, Jim got up and opened the two windows to the room. The musty air of Venice rushed in, but it was better than the dormant stale air that had settled in the old hotel room. The room wasn't bad, though, especially for coming upon it so easily during the busiest time of summer. It had brown carpet, gold wallpaper, and a cubbyhole-sized bathroom with a standup shower and a dinky sink.

Elizabeth begged for a shower and some time to get ready, both of which Jim had no interest in, but he figured he wouldn't fuss with her since he had just barely pulled her out of her pouting mood. He

planted himself on the second story ledge and watched the unsuspecting tourists and maybe a few locals. They careened off the stone
walls trying to find their way through the maze that was Venice. More
than once he heard the passersby exclaim, "I think we've been here
before! Doesn't it look familiar to you?" He could even swear that the
same statement was being said in several other languages because
the people shared the same expressions. An argument would ensue
as to whether the group or couple was on the right path or just going
in circles. Ten minutes later he might see the same people having the
same argument. Jim sat hovering above the pedestrians without anyone noticing him. Each person was possessed by their own tunnel vision, searching for their own perfect Venice—the art, the architecture,
the masterful engineering of a city sitting in the sea, the romance, the
music, the food—each person driven by the allure of what was around
the next corner. Venice slowed down a little underneath that window.
Jim was removed from the scene but so involved with it that he got the
feel of how to interact with Venice. The people that were the happiest
were not fighting to find their way, but letting the way find them, and
he could do that. He thought to himself, "We don't have to fight this
sea of people; we can modify our tendencies to enjoy ourselves without
struggling against the tide. I'll let her take all the time she wants to get
ready, and we'll eat later. Shit, we don't even know what's out there.
I'm sure there are some places to breathe." With those thoughts, he
laid down on the bed, and instead of being in a hurry to see as much
as he could, he took a nap knowing that being in a rush would only
invigorate the uneasiness the couple had felt earlier in the afternoon.

Before she jumped in the shower, Liz noticed what her traveling
mate was attempting a nap and decided to lay down with him. The

time during their trip was valuable, but the mood was even more precious, so a nap was a good call. She lay down on her side of the bed and did not attempt any physical contact. They both slept while the sun beat down on the stone, and the tourists jockeyed for position. The town went by under their two open windows with a slight hum not concerned whether the two were involved in their summer rituals of experience. Rest was a wonderful thing for the couple in their second story Venetian room with the gold wallpaper depicting a variety of seashells. The air dropped a couple of degrees and included the slightest amount of freshness as it stirred through the room caressing their waking skin. They stretched and yawned, and Liz made her way to the bathroom to begin her ritual of preparation. She showered and was standing in front of the mirror applying different formulations of Clinique when Jim walked into the bathroom butt-naked.

"Hey, I don't need to see that." Liz said extremely startled by the naked man almost brushing up against her in the tiny bathroom.

"I must bathe, and if I wait for you to finish, we'll never get to the restaurant before closing. Anyway, we need to start getting used to seeing each other naked because where we're going in Greece, all the beaches are completely nude. We can't be rude and not comply with local customs. We were born naked, you know—that is our natural state. You should feel more comfortable naked, and I suggest you start getting used to it as soon as possible. I think we should be naked whenever we are in the room from now on—that way we'll be completely comfortable with each other's nudity by the time we get to the nude beaches."

"I'm not taking off all my clothes on a beach. I might take off my top, but I'm definitely not going completely nude, no way."

"Oh don't be such a prude. It's just your body, and it's a fabulous one at that. You should be proud that you have such vivacious curves. You're absolutely scrumptious, and the rest of the world should get to share in your beauty."

"Yeah, and you with that camera all the time, I'm sure the rest of the world really would get to share."

Jim was angered by the notion that he would betray his friend like that, or at least that she recognized plans before they were able to hatch. "I wouldn't share those pictures with anybody. They would be for my personal enjoyment only." During this conversation, Elizabeth stood wrapped in a towel doing her make-up in the mirror of the bathroom. Right before Jim closed the swinging door to the shower he made sure to tug on Liz's towel causing it to float to the floor.

Elizabeth panicked. "You bastard!" She shouted as her reflexes caused her to drop her make-up and retrieve her towel from the floor. Jim was hoping for a sexy, straight-legged bend, but she disappointed him by using one arm to cover her breasts and by bending at the knees so that her nakedness would be least exposed in the crouching position.

"Hey! Don't be shy. Ditch the towel—I did."

"Yeah, well you're a slut and everyone knows it. I'm trying to hold onto a little dignity, and you seem to think that is unreasonable."

"Ah, don't resort to names. By the way, you look fantastic without that towel." Jim said with the water rushing over his head.

Elizabeth regained her composure with her towel back in place and continued her ritual face painting without acknowledging Jim's naked body just a few feet away.

"You're going to go naked on those beaches, aren't you? You're going to try to embarrass or shame me into it, and it's not going to work. I'll bet you there are still people with clothes on. They're going to wear clothes when they leave the beach. It's not like they walk around the entire island naked all the time."

"Well, you already said you weren't going buck anyway, so I guess we won't go to the completely nude spots. I'm sure it's a matter of choice. I might have to ditch you for a little while and go check some of them out. I'm not scared—just need a little sun block for my pecker."

"Ooh, don't call him that."

"What, you got a better name?"

"Just call him your thing or even penis is better than that."

"My thing, are you kidding me? How bout my cock, or dick, or slong? What do you think about Jimmy Jr? Would that make you more comfortable? Maybe you should get to know him a little better, and then you could come up with a better name for him. Maybe we shouldn't go out there with all those people anyway. Maybe we should just stay in here, butt-ass naked, and fuck like rabbits for the rest of the night. I really think that it would be the best way for you to loosen up and have some fun, and I didn't mean that literally."

"Is that all you think about? You never used to come onto me like this."

"Well you always said that you were going to wait until you got married. Now that you've broken the seal, nothing is sacred. I used to respect your decision to keep it in your pants, but now you're fucking, so I should be first in line."

"I told you that I would have sex with the man I married. I think I will marry Daniel. We've even discussed it already."

"Bullshit. You told me you wouldn't have sex until you were married. You're not married yet, therefore, that promise no longer guides my moral restraint. You can't possibly have sex with only one man your entire life—you'll never be satisfied not knowing what you're missing. Sex is a form of expression and it is a huge part of the contentment within a relationship. You haven't done it enough to know if this guy is even right for you. Now that you've allowed sex to be part of the equation, you have to evaluate the quality of it, and to do that; you're going to have to have something to measure against. That is where I come in. What I propose is that you let me seduce you in every possible manner that I can imagine in the next couple of weeks. I will do my utmost to make sure that your sexual experiences are fulfilling and exhilarating. I will show you why sex is on the mind of most people, most of the time. It is the essence of energy when captured just right. Trust me—I can make your body feel like it is completely outside itself, floating in a blissful euphoria."

"You're not going to talk me into it, Jimmy my dear. Remember, I held out for twenty years."

"If you make it too difficult, I'm not going to beg, but I'm also not going to spend my summer vacation without some intimate heavy petting, so I may wander off from time to time." With that Jim turned off the water and pulled a towel into the shower. He dried himself, stepped out of the shower with the towel over his shoulder, and kissed Elizabeth on the neck as she did her make-up. "I'm not going to say anything more about it; if you want some of this just come and get it. You can call little Jimmy whatever you want, and he'll be ready and willing."

Jim put on some boxer shorts and let the time pass peacefully, not demanding that Elizabeth get herself together in a reasonable amount of time. Eventually, Liz prepared herself, and the couple exited the room on their way to dinner. Jim dressed in his trusty plaid shorts with a dark tee shirt while Liz sported a light summer dress, which seemed to caress her skin as she walked giving a nice silhouette of her pristine shape. By the time they hit the mazed pathways of Venice, it was well past the traditional dinnertime as the sun was melting in the midsummer sky slowly bringing with it the dusk of night. They strolled slowly through the streets crossing lots of small bridges over backwater canals. Whenever they bumped into a crowd, they turned away from it. Their hunger and thirst kept them from exploring too much of the city as they quickly settled on a comfortable little restaurant. There was seating available along the walk outside the restaurant against the railing of a serene canal. Prior to finding the establishment, they had meandered by some more boisterous places and were glad to find a quiet restaurant with outdoor seating. They both preferred the fresh serenity of an outdoor dining experience, so there was no argument about where they would sit.

Elizabeth ordered a carafe of house wine, which she and Jim sipped in a somewhat vigorous manner—both of them needed to take the edge of travel off as well as deal with the emotional strain that one put on the other. Elizabeth felt a mixed bag of emotions as she tried to establish a firm position in her mind of how she was going to deal with the physical yearning that she felt for Jim. Across the table, Jim dreamed about her naked body and tried to nail down his best strategy for seeing more of it. He had to confront the situation and wasn't willing to play games, "Okay, this sexual tension thing is really on my mind. I know that I said I was going to leave it alone back in the room, but I think it would be better if we just talked about it. I mean, I thought we definitely shared a connection last night, even though it was interrupted by the emergence of rational thought. Now I think we need to treat this one of two ways, either we have a lustful affair, or we ride on out as brother and sister, much like we've done in the past. If we decide to go the brother and sister route, we can explain to those of the opposite sex why we are traveling with each other and maybe even assist each other in creating some romantic escapades. I prefer the affair, but somehow I don't think you're quite as sure of yourself. I can't get the issue out of my mind and would rather have a decision now than trying to figure it out as we go. I don't play games with my emotions as they're way too over the top." Jim exclaimed catching Liz by surprise with his directness.

She sighed and put some thought into her reply, "I, I think we... well I'm pretty sure we would be better if we didn't, you know. Don't you think it would be harder to deal with? We've known each other so long, and I don't want our relationship to change. I always want to have you to make me laugh and make me wonder in amazement at the other side of life. I could fall in love with you so easy, and then I would be lost, cause I don't think you know what love is. You'd admit that, wouldn't you?"

"What? I don't know what love is? Just because I've never told a woman that I love her doesn't mean that I don't know what love is. I haven't experienced romantic love yet, and I haven't been looking for it. I can't imagine allowing myself to get that deeply involved at twenty-one. I've seen my parents go through marriages like pieces of chocolate, chewing them up, swallowing them, and then going on to

another. I'm a little leery of love. I'm more into lust. It's straightfor-
ward and doesn't lie, and the energy from it blows me away. Don't
get me wrong, I don't want to lose what we already have either, but
I don't believe getting lost in a mutual physical adventure will hurt
anything. We've developed something that will last through good or
bad sex. It will be there when we wake up in the morning, and then
we can decide whether to do it again."

"If it was just that simple, Jimmy." She said with her eyes going
down to the table trying to decide how to proceed without completely
closing the door, but still relieving the pressure for the time being.
She was feeling a little turbulent within caused by the realization
that her long-time friend wanted her in the way that he did. He was
blatant and honest about it, and she could see in his eyes that he
truly desired her. In the past, she had felt that he was aloof of her
sexuality. Actually, he had always been aware of how he felt for her,
but repressed it to the point of coming off as she saw it. He liked her
pristine ambitions of purity and decided against using his cunning
ways to get in her pants. She was like a sister, because he decided to
treat her as such, but as she grew more attractive each year, he was
constantly reconsidering his position. Elizabeth was a woman that
he got along with and was stimulated by on every level, except the
physical, which he believed was also possible if the protective barrier
between them could be quickly demolished.

Jim had allowed himself to achieve a certain level of frustration
over the matter, and at that quiet little dinner table, he was having a
terrifically loud conversation with his inner self. "I can tell she wants
to let this thing die down for now, but we're in Venice for Christ's
sake. We should be naked in the room right now, entangled in each

other wherever we go, not worried about the rest of the world. My motivation is always directed from the wrong location. I am with a beautiful woman, so my body just aches to have her. She just wants to have all the warmness of a relationship without the sex. I guess that I need to grow up and have the kind of relationship that she desires. Maybe this will be good for me, holding back my desires for once. I really don't have a choice. Just let her off the hook; tell her what she wants to hear."

Jim's voice finally projected his quagmire of thoughts, "All right, you win. I'm going to stop pressuring you to do what I want and work on building our relationship as friends. I can handle that. You may not think that I possess any self-control, and you may be right, but I'm going to give it my best. Even though I do truly believe that Venice is the type of place that we should be making love a couple times a day. Whoops, I said I was going to stop that, didn't I? I'm sorry—I'm going to be good. I want you to be comfortable."

The food finally came and filled the table with a steamy aroma that made the couple salivate. They had avoided the traditional five-course Italian meal and had just ordered entrees, which was a nuisance to the waiter, but a necessity to the frugal travelers. Jim had a traditional tortellini in a white sauce; each homemade pasta exploding with cheese or meat, while Elizabeth had a ravioli stew, which made her taste buds dance. The food shut the two up, and they devoured it without making eye contact. They ate and stared into the water, both wishing that they could have the other on their own terms, but neither able to communicate well enough to secure their terms. The problem that had arisen between them had been unforeseen, and they began to guard their emotions, afraid to enter any level of intimacy. Jim had to constantly struggle to identify some shred of self-control that he had never really worked on developing before.

"That was good." Liz finally broke the silence at the end of the meal. "I think we need more wine, don't you?"

"Sure, get two of those damn things. There's only about three glasses in there, and I need at least that myself."

"You're a drunk. I'm only getting one at a time."

"Whatever, then we just got to wait in-between, cause you know you're going to drink at least two more. You're no angel. You'll drink your share." Jim said in a sarcastic tone that followed him wherever he went. They did order two more, one at a time, and then wandered back to their quaint room deep within the maze.

The sun came blistering into the room as they woke up on their own sides of the bed. They were not embraced, and both had clothing on, even though, in Jim's case, it was only a pair of boxer shorts that Liz demanded he put on after he tried to crawl in bed naked. She thought Jim way too casual with his nudity, while Jim was just used to sleeping like that, with or without a woman present. The windows were open, and the streets were already bustling with activity. The town was seriously drowned in tourists to the point where the islands felt like they could be overloaded and could sink into the sea.

The wine beat on Jim's head as he rolled out of bed. He looked over at Liz, and her face showed the expression of how he felt. Her petite features grimaced at the sun, and she showed no signs of appreciation for the nice day. Jim figured, by her looks, that he had two headaches on his hands, so he worked on altering his attitude to a more favorable position. His favorite technique for doing this was to smoke marijuana, and he knew there would be objections from his traveling companion if he were to fire up in the room, so he waited for her to go to the shower, then he smoked one anxiously hoping that she wouldn't interrupt. He thought of Liz as a square and tried to avoid confrontation, but at the same time enjoyed getting a rise out of her, just not too much of one. Jim shut the windows before lighting up so as not to catch a beef with any of the passers by, even though he liked to watch the puzzled look on people's faces when they got a strong whiff of Mary Jane in the air. The THC thwarted the wine hangover quite well, leaving just the slightest headache.

When Elizabeth exited the shower, Jim was smoking a cigarette to mask the odor of the marijuana. She coughed dramatically upon entering the room. "You need to air this place out. You were smoking pot, weren't you?"

"Maybe, you want some?"

"You know I don't do drugs. Put that cigarette out. I can't handle that this early, plus my head hurts and I'm going to gag on that."

"How about some pills?" Jim offered her some Advil, which she gladly accepted. "I'll go out and get us some snacks, orange juice, and espresso. I saw a little place on our way home last night. What do you think, you want something?"

"That sounds good, whatever." Elizabeth replied with little interest. Jim headed out to fulfill his suggestion and returned with a variety of pastries, a large glass of orange juice, and a beautifully made cappuccino with chocolate sprinkled in the froth. These gifts were genuine attempts to make his friend feel better. He wasn't sure what straight people did to get over hangovers. Marijuana was his perfect cure, but it was impossible to convince Liz that such casual use of an illegal drug could ever possibly be to her benefit. He was banking on caffeine, ibuprofen, and good old vitamin C combining to alleviate Liz's ailments. He knew from past experience that this cure was a much slower process and not always as sure fire as his way.

"You really should relax and smoke a little grass. It would knock that hangover out in a second." Jim said grinning in his early morning bake. "I know you feel like shit right now, and I have the magic cure, but it is not this scrumptious array of goodies from the corner bakery—it is simply a herb used by people of more reasonable times to promote peace and tranquility. Whoever vilified it was a fool. This here grass will get your head right in almost any taxing situation, be it a hangover or a stress-filled environment. What do you think? You want me to roll you one up so we can put a smile back on your face?"

"I don't need drugs to smile. Thank you for this stuff. It was sweet of you to try to take care of me. We drank too much last night, and my head is about to break in half." Elizabeth said ignoring the dissertation on the benefits of marijuana. Jim lay on the bed, keeping his distance from Liz as he ate and drank his breakfast.

Eventually Liz felt well enough to brave the new world. Jim and Liz entered the congested streets of Venice leaving their quaint, comfortable hotel room in the rear-view-mirror. Jim had acquired a one-page map of the city streets the night before and felt comfortable that he could maneuver them. Elizabeth wanted to see the cathedral at St. Marks Square while Jim preferred sniffing out a beer—the square would accommodate both requests. The day was alive with the streets bustling to a busy tune, but Jim was no longer uncomfortable as he had been the day before; his attitude had been adjusted. He nestled up and through columns of people bobbing his head and waving while smiling broadly to show his good will to the fellow tourists. Elizabeth followed, still in a slightly frustrated and hung over mood, but able to cope and was improving as the day progressed.

They entered St. Mark's Square with the noon sun beating down on the cobblestone surface. Camera shutters were a constant flutter as the crowds oohed and awed at the majestic Basilica of St. Mark, the huge bell tower, Campanile, and the lavish, white Dodge's Castle. The square was also lined with shops and inundated with pigeons that had the run of the place. There were vendors selling birdseed so that the brilliant tourists could have the lovely winged creatures eat out of their hands and shit on their head. Children were sure to enjoy it until they were overwhelmed with too big of a flock or bombed by the product of overfeeding. Jim chose to avoid the flocks and find a seat at an outdoor café, and there were many wrapped around the outskirts of the square. Elizabeth was repulsed by the thought of alcohol and chose to make her way directly into the church. The Basilica was open to visitors, and Liz took her time enjoying the luxurious art that enveloped her when she entered the building.

"Where are you from?" A gentleman asked that was seated next to Jim. Jim had been making friends with the gentleman's young child who kept running in and out of the square. The man was with his wife, and the three of them portrayed the perfect nucleus of a family traveling through Europe. Jim couldn't help but notice a very brash accent, New York, New Jersey or Boston—Jim wasn't well schooled in accents.

"Idaho originally, but I've been a student in Oregon for the last couple years. What about you, I definitely detect an accent of some kind, somewhere on the East Coast?"

"We're from Boston. Just trying to get in some traveling before junior here has to go to school. Wife and I always wanted to do Italy. What about you, where you headed, and what have you seen so far?"

"Been all over checking out Western Europe. Started in England, made my way through France, Spain and Portugal, then picked up a straggler in Zurich that I'd be traveling with through Italy and Greece. Then I'm back on my own to wander wherever I feel like going, maybe up north, Germany, the Netherlands. You got any suggestions for Italy, or are you just getting started?"

"We flew into Rome, thought it was kind of dirty, but there's a lot to see. Don't get me wrong—it's definitely worth visiting. But Florence is the place; it's exquisite, and you really should plan on spending some time there. We're also planning on heading out to the wine county when we leave hear, you know, Tuscany and what not. It's been a really nice trip, can't complain. Hey, do you mind getting a picture of us here?"

"No thanks. I don't like touching other people's cameras, never know if that snot nosed kid slobbered on it or something." Jim looked at the couple with a blank stair as if he was serious. "Just kidding, give me the camera."

"Ha, a wise guy, huh kid."

Jim thought that the only reason for the polite conversation was to secure a photographer for the family shot in Venice, but he could have been wrong. The family might have been comfortable with the familiar, another American, a comrade. Jim snapped a couple of pictures of the family with the Castle and the Basilica as a magnificent backdrop. Then, after handing the camera back to the family, he grabbed his own and shot photos of them discussing their next move.

They wandered off without noticing him, and he sat down and ordered another beer. The wide-open space in the square was refreshing considering the tight, crowded spaces of the rest of the city. Jim wasn't in any hurry to get out of his comfortable, people watching position. He drank and smoked, and from time to time, kept his eye on the doors to the Basilica to see if his friend would emerge.

"Do you feel closer to God? Did you experience something that I might need to get in on? I'm not opposed to this whole Catholic, thing if you think it will save my soul. Do you think I need to go in there, or do you think the place would burn down if I took a step in there?" Jim asked as his friend sauntered up in a much more congenial mood.

"You should go in there, Jimmy; it's beautiful. The artwork is magnificent. The insides of the domes are painted with beautiful mosaics, and the interior architecture is breathtaking. You really shouldn't miss it."

"I don't figure I need to go into that there church. I think she's mighty perty from here. Anyway, I'm holding out for the great big one in Rome, the one Michelangelo designed. I don't want to get burned out on churches, kind of somber for my liking. I'm much more intrigued by bars than churches. Sorry for my barbarian style, but you should have known what to expect. Sit down and have a drink. I believe this is the best spot in all of Venice. All the people of the world pass right by here; there is no need to wander the mind-bending paths when all will come to us. The guys with the wooden flutes are going to put out some tunes—kick back and enjoy the eclectic view." Jim stated with his feet up on the chair closest to him. Liz sat down on the chair opposite succumbing to his odd use of time and space.

They sat, ate, drank, and watched the world go by. The summer day brightened their spirits, and the alcohol lifted them past any frustrations. Jim commented on future plans, "I think we can pretty much get the flavor of this place with the rest of today and half of tomorrow. I think we should head to Firenze on an afternoon train. I just talked to some folks from Boston who just came from there. They said it was the highlight of their trip, plus you're excited to see some of the art there, aren't you? That statue of a naked man, isn't that what you wanted to see, David? You've already seen a perfect, live, naked male on this trip—the statue will probably be anticlimactic."

"You're no David. You need to shave your face and cut your hair and maybe get a little perm before you can be considered classic art. Right now, you're more like an abstract expressionist piece of work."

"I'm talking about the body, my perfectly sculpted physique that's just like a work of art."

"Yeah, right. Let's go tool around a bit, we've got to give this place a little more of a chance before we give it our final grade."

"I say we go back to the room, if we can find it, get naked, and give each other a chance."

Liz stuck out her tongue, flicked her shades down off her forehead and ignored the insinuation that her friend had made. "Come on, let's move about a bit. We can't sit around and drink our whole trip." She stood up with her hands on her hips expectantly, determined to get Jim to come along. He got the hint and followed her lead, taking care of the tab on the way towards the walk.

For the next couple of hours, they moved with the masses touring the city of Venice by foot, crossing bridge after bridge onto stone street after stone street. Jim had his camera out and was recording each move through the vast mazes. He took pictures of backhoes on barges dredging the canals with workers on them fixing the foundations at and above the water line. It was a constant engineering feat to keep the buildings maintained as the salt water splashed against them endlessly. Jim's camera focused on a large Italian worker pushing a wheel barrel by a Visace store, framing the man against the name as if he were a model, his white tee-shirt smudged with mud, a standard pair of blue jeans and a sun hat to keep his complexion sturdy but not washed out. The next shot was of a little kid trying on a carnival mask sticking his tongue out the hole of the mask. He made pictures of gondolas passing under pedestrian bridges with older, wealthier couples, gliding by as their dedicated gondoliers stood strongly behind them steering with long straight poles. The photos resembled his reality, completely scattered and without connection. They became his center on this day in Venice as they did on many days during his travels. He would step outside himself, detached in a way, not participating in what was going on, but trying to observe it and catch the essence of the place through his lens. Liz was rarely in the photos as Jim was trying to create art more than chronicle his vacation.

As the couple wandered through the streets, they became more and more comfortable with their unique vision on the city. It became easier to wash away all the people and stay in a bubble together expressing awe at the uniqueness of the islands of ancient buildings. Jim began to dance through the streets grabbing Elizabeth's hand and pulling her along into the fairy tale world. They ate outside at a public square where they watched local entertainment bounce around the space with wooden flutes and juggling balls or swords on unicycles. As they began to let their minds wander, it began to feel more like a festival than a city, and that is how they engaged it. At each stop, they filled themselves full of food and wine while watching the hoards of people discover Venice in their own way—a museum-into a shop-into a bakery-into a bar for a quick nip-back-to the streets, water taxis, and gondolas with the large Italian opera-singer serenading the rich, plump patrons from the back of one of the boats.

At the end of the endless day, Jim found a perfect little hole-in-the-wall restaurant that had the laid-back kind of staff that he was so drawn to at each of his stops.

"Come on in my friends and get drunk and eat until you can no longer move. We can guarantee you these things if you join us for the evening." Said the host as Jim asked to see a menu.

He put the menu down and announced to Liz, "We have found our home for the night—let's look no further." Elizabeth smiled and shook her head in agreement.

"I'm not going to hurt myself like I did last night. We've got to start our day out better tomorrow. You can't possibly put up with me in that kind of mood for another two weeks, can you?"

"Ah, my dear, with such beauty, I can always turn off the sound." Jim retorted. Liz stuck out her tongue and slapped him on the butt as they headed to their table. It turned out that the host was also the owner, and he showered the couple with kindness as he tried to extend their bill as far as possible. The problem was that both travelers were pretty savvy at keeping costs down and always preferred large vats of house wine to expensive bottles that were suggested at the outset.

The couple ate and drank for quite some time during their last evening in Venice. They were treated well by their hosts, who understood that they were just traveling students without huge budgets and began to make their suggestions accordingly. The day, which had started out on a rocky road, ended gay and full of authentic Italian flavor. "Tomorrow we'll travel, my dear. What do you think?"

"Yeah, I say on to Florence! Isn't that where you want to go too?"

"Sure. Onward to Firenze." Jim toasted his traveling mate as he made the statement, and it was decided that they should move on.

The next morning they woke, still not entangled with each other, and strolled the streets for an early morning espresso and pastry, as was the case many mornings, while they were traveling through Italy. After some nourishment, they loaded up their bags and headed for the train station—Jim letting Liz lug her gargantuan backpack. The train wheels squealed out of Venice on a one-way shot to Florence and made good time with a light load, plenty of seats. It was another sparkling summer day, and the Italian countryside whizzed by with beautiful clarity as the two were traveling during the day. The view out the window was worth burning a little daylight traveling. The night trains were convenient for connecting the dots between two places, but missing the entire space in-between was a big loss. Elizabeth and Jim sat across from each other in the train cabin, both in window seats, examining the view. Jim would hold his lens against the window and snap photos with a super fast shutter to catch the luxurious sunshine slapping against the landscapes of Italy. There were a lot of small towns as well, some warranting a stop, and others breezing by as if they remained asleep.

Jim started drinking early into the venture and was even lucky enough to get caught in a smoking circle with some rowdy teenagers in an open-air passageway between two cars. They asked him if he smoked, as he walked by double fisted with two beers, hoping that he would pass over a beer as appreciation for the toke. Jim gladly handed over both beers after the joint burned down to the fingertips and had to be discarded. He then headed back to the beer cart to replenish his supply. On his way back from getting the beers, he decided to pull into the coach holding the teenagers instead of his own. He made himself comfortable with the group that also contained two beautiful young Italian girls that Jim managed to lodge himself between forgetting about his traveling companion who was five or six rooms down.

Liz began to get bored with her surroundings after Jim had been gone for an hour. She wasn't worried about him and knew him well enough to assume that he had stumbled into a group much more engaging than her. She also knew that he was probably not going to come retrieve her. If she wanted to partake in the fun, she would have to hunt him down, which is what he expected her to do at some point. When she arrived at the coach with the laughing teenagers, she could distinctly hear Jim's voice. "No! No! No! Pot, grass, and marijuana—it's all the same in English. We call it weed, dope, smoke, or a hundred other names I think."

Liz made her way into the room with a smile. "What are you teaching these kids, bad habits?" As she entered, she saw Jim with one of the girls draped across his lap with only a bikini top on being massaged by his powerful hands.

"This is my sister, Elizabeth, everyone. We are traveling together."

Jim said looking at Liz in his cross-eyed way.

"Ah, good to have you with us, sister. Come take a seat. Jimmy has taken our girls; maybe you can keep us company." The young Italian boy with the best English clamored pushing one of the other boys off the seat to make room for Liz.

"How old are you boys? You've got to be kidding me, Jimmy. You're going to get locked up for drinking with these children. And let go of that girl, she is much too young to be groped by you. You're completely out of control." This statement caused an eruption of laughter from the coach as Jim held his hands up in the air to profess his innocence, but a guilt look was splashed across his face. His eyebrows raised, and a grin beaming from the corner of his lips, plead his case as only body language could.

"Hey, sis, you need to relax, take a seat and get to know the wonderful Italian youth. See the thing is, at this age there is absolutely no limits to the vision of these young people. Their values are instilled, but their ideas are not yet bounded by the miserable defeats they will incur later in life. They haven't been knocked down enough to even know it hurts. I love the freedom of sixteen; there's absolutely nothing that can stop you. These kids are going all the way to Rome for a couple of weeks, just free-wheeling it, riding the rails, not a worry among them. Remember when we could just jump in a car with a group of friends and had no idea what kind of trouble we would get in on the other end?"

"No, I don't remember. While you were out running wild, I was usually doing the responsible thing. Not to say that I didn't have a lot of fun and even show some spontaneity in my life, but my memories are probably not as raucous as yours. I was involved in religious activities, and we usually knew what was going to happen on the other end."

"Well now you're free from all those Miss Priss stereotypes, and you can let go and have a little fun with our very own youth group. I'm sure these are all good Catholic kids too, right?" Jim asked to the girl he had returned to massaging.

"Of coarse. We are home of the Catholic Church—we live it every day whether we want to or not. My mama attends mass every day; she is very full of faith. She thinks I am out of control, but I still believe as she does. I am Catholic and will always be, but not mass every day, only Sunday, and not while we're on holiday. We want to have fun with a little sin mixed in, and then later I will confess—later I will be forgiven. We've never been to Roma, who knows what will happen?" The girl expressed with her cheek squished against Jim's knee.

"I'm not a Miss Priss." Liz exclaimed, still dwelling on the statement Jim made previous to the young girls speaking her mind.

Jim replied, "Whoa! Where did that come from? Didn't you just hear this young lady spill her guts on how she feels about her faith, or have you just been sitting there boiling over that one little comment? Isn't this relevant enough for you? Calm down. I meant no harm. Now give this young lady your undivided attention." Jim said lifting the girl's head up and turning her face towards Liz. "And explain to her how important her Catholic upbringing will be in the future. You know, the abstinence thing, how to hold on until you're a senior in college and then give in to some pansy Limy, and when it comes to the man that you really need to roll around with, you're back to your old ways." Jim said all this with a definite cutting spite in his tone, but, of coarse, the Italian youngsters had no idea what he was talking about, or at least he thought they didn't.

Liz, frustrated and reddened by the comments, stood up and announced she was going back to their original cabin, and she would see her darling brother in Florence, if he cared to find her when they exited the train.

"Why did she go?" One of the Italian boys asked with a sad, rejected face, selling out his inner feelings.

The young lady in Jim's lap quickly clarified the situation without even checking with Jim. "She's not his sister." She read Jim's actions, understood the comments better than the others, and could tell the woman, whom he called his sister, was actually someone he cared for in a deeper way. She could tell the couple was sideways and denying anything intimate. The young girl could feel the tension in Jim's hands when Liz entered the room and knew that she could not possibly be his sister, especially after the passionate comments he made to her. "I'm right, yeah? She is too pretty to be your sister. She is your girlfriend, and you are arguing or something; is that it?" The girl asked getting up to look at Jim's face.

"You're right, she's not my sister, but she certainly is not my girlfriend either. We're kind of in limbo, trying to play it as friends, when really we both need a little bigger taste of each other. She won't let me in, so I make it hard on her. We're traveling together, and I'm going to let her do her own thing for a while. I'll let her follow her own direction and see if I can't find me a nice girl along the way. That will really piss her off." The group of youngsters laughed at this odd relationship and shook there heads somewhat lost at the meaning of it all. Jim didn't really make it clear if he had strong feelings for his friend or not, so they really weren't sure what he was after. The young girl looked into his face trying to distinguish his emotions, being that she thought he was quite intriguing, but she couldn't gather much more than the stoned, silly look his slant-eyed face flashed back at her. He wasn't trying to lead on a sixteen-year-old; he was just trying to enjoy the ride, which he always found a way to do. Now it was his turn for a back rub, and he made sure that the fiery little girls paid up.

Eventually, Jim left the young people's cabin wishing them good luck on their journey and getting the phone number to the flat they were staying at in Rome; it was one of the young men's brother's house. The youthful group encouraged Jim to stop by with Liz while in Roma. Jim hugged them all, wishing them well on their journey, but not promising anything. He made his way down to the cabin where Liz was and found her nestled up against the window quietly sleeping. The sun was starting to fade away, and the train would soon be arriving in Florence where he would have to do a little mending for chasing her off and not coming back sooner to patch things up. Jim knew the emotional variations that Elizabeth was capable of and assumed that she would be a little frisky once she woke up. He laid his head on her shoulder and found that his theory was right as she quickly shrugged him off.

Chapter 8
FIRENZE

The train arrived in Florence with just a slice of sun left in the sky. Jim and Liz scurried out of the train station hoping to catch a glimpse of the city, which other travelers spoke of so highly. They needed accommodations and were pointed to an inexpensive hotel by a friendly local at the wine shop where Jim was picking up an extra large bottle of the regions famous Chianti. He saw some others drinking wine in the streets and thought it not a bad idea, so he asked the clerk for an opener and shoved the cork in his pocket. Jim nudged Liz with the bottle; she hadn't said much since their arrival, and she took it and drank it as if drinking enough might wash him away. Loaded down with maximum baggage, they passed the bottle back and forth and marveled at the sights of the city as they lumbered towards the river following the directions of the Good Samaritan. They walked by the cathedral, which was even more intricate than St. Marks, and down the crowded sidewalks lined with old, important looking structures with terraces hanging over the streets with clay shingles as hats. The sunset added life to their wine and without knowing it their spirits began to rise as the sun fell.

They caught the final glimpses of the sunset from their eleventh story hotel room on a little patio that faced the river, but they were a few blocks away so it could only be seen in slices. They could see the top of the Point Vecchio, or Old Bridge, as it would be called in English, which spanned across the Arno River and was parallel to so many other bridges running down the length of the river. The clay shingles on the roofs of the shops of Point Vecchio were all that could be seen, but they would certainly walk across the bridge the next day and get the full effect of the little buildings on each side of the bridge. They drank their bottle of wine on the veranda, and both of them felt a wave of appreciation for where they were and how genuinely magical it was to be able to see the world in such a comfortable manner. For a moment the intensity of their relationship was not an issue, but they dwelled in the familiar warmth that they shared in each other's company. The home of the Renaissance embraced the couple and put their anxieties to the side or maybe it was the quart jug of wine they were swigging from the bottle.

"I'm sorry about giving you a hard time on the train. I didn't mean to piss you off or throw anything in your face. It's just that I really do want to be more physical with you and it's not easy trying to swallow the fact that we've already decided against that. My plans for this journey have been sabotaged. I really thought we would be together just to feel what it would be like, not leaving anything to chance. Then I keep stumbling on your perspective, which I completely forgot to include in my equation of us traveling together. Sounds kind of piggish, I know, but I need to work on empathy. I really figured I could steer you to my way of thinking—it seems to work most times when I get women drunk in beautiful places." Jim said looking directly at Elizabeth. It was his own twisted way of apologizing for the cutting sarcasm he broke out on the train.

"I'll try not to be so uptight, and you don't have to worry about offending me as I know you well enough to expect what comes out of your mouth. You're just driven too much by your hormones; settle down and enjoy the company. We can enjoy each other, you know, without sex even. We've been friends this long without it."

"Yeah, but that was before you really developed. Now you're all of a woman and I can hardly resist. Actually I can't resist. I feel like masturbating every night just to relieve the tension in my loins, but I don't want to upset you by rocking the bed. I'm just going to have to get laid at some point to keep my mind off of you."

"Well, let's go out then. Maybe you'll find someone to fulfill your lustful needs. I'll get ready; you know I can't go like this. I've got to get that train off me and start fresh." Liz said with a new sparkle in her eye.

Jim was glad she had come around and was ready to let off a little steam at a club, if they could find one. He didn't so much as look at himself in the mirror. Sure he was a little grungy from the daylong train ride, but if the world wasn't willing to accept him with a little train smut on him, they could fuck-off as far as he was concerned.

"Good attitude, Jimmy." He thought.

Jim's unwillingness to clean himself up cost the couple admission into many respectable nightclubs as Jim's rugged hippie funk attire was not good enough to pass any dress code. They had to lower their standards and look for a bar where shoes and shirt were all that were required. There were plenty lower class watering holes that put Jim at ease, but Liz was longing to see the Italians in their designer best sashaying through the clubs like a never ending entourage of soap stars. Jim's void of long pants kept them out of the clubs and out of the truly groovy scenes. They finally settled on an open-air bar that was two stories with the upper floor being on the roof of the building. The place was bustling with an eclectic crowd that was at least half local and the other half a miss mash

from around the world – all sizes, shapes, colors and languages.
The walls surrounding the hardwood floors were filled with Renaissance prints interspersed with popular culture photos and posters,
but the eye quickly moved down the walls to the grand staircase in
the rear of the place that wrapped around in a half circle and led to
the roof. The idea to put in the staircase and the rooftop bar must
have come quite recently because the stairs looked so crisp and
clean that they couldn't have been there that long. There was an effort to make them look as old as the building in style and elegance,
each step finished in hardwood and the banister ornamental and
antique, but there were no scuffmarks and absolutely no wear and
tear. The rooftop bar was more modern in design and had a live
band grooving some jazz on its stone tile floor with the moonlight
as its backdrop and the stars as its lighting. Jim and Liz could both
enjoy themselves in this environment and even though the staff
frowned a little at Jim's apparel, they did not refuse him service.
Once Jim flashed a kind smile at everyone, they realized that his
style was the chic dirty traveler and they were comfortable with that
because he was authentic. The reality was that he needed to wash
his duds and himself, especially his going out ensemble, but he just
didn't want to cut into his vacation time at a laundry mat, and he
surely wasn't flush enough to pay someone to get his stuff cleaned.
He needed money in reserve for doobage and alcohol, or at least his
twisted mind demanded such allocation of funds.

The couple got pulverized by the alcohol of the evening - don't
forget the bottle of wine they pounded before heading out - and
became friends with a couple that had just been married. The man
was from England, and his name was Eric while his wife was from

Switzerland, and her name was Mona. The couple was approaching their thirties, and they were collectively beautiful, not just each on their own, but as a couple, they radiated. They had asked Jim and Elizabeth to share their table as the bar was approaching maximum capacity. The musicians were on break when Eric and Mona arrived, so it gave the couples a chance to talk and get to know each other. Eric and Mona had been drinking before they arrived so they weren't far behind Jim and Liz, who felt like they could not get enough fermented liquid in them. The tipsy mentality of the four soldiers made it possible to build an easy relationship that had a miraculous ability to grow in leaps and bounds without the modern inconvenience of conscience.

Within an hour of the new couple's arrival, Jim had Mona on the dance floor while Liz and Eric were in a deep discussion about Oxford men and what they provided to the world. Eric himself was such an animal, and Liz was enamored by her beloved Danny whom she could gloat about to Eric, but couldn't even bring his name up around Jim. Mona and Jim were on the dance floor depending on one another to stay balanced, but still making movements that resembled dancing with Jim throwing Mona into a deep dip about every third turn, loving the dramatic flair and getting a giggle out of Mona each time. Mona could have been hung over the rooftop by her ankles and giggled at that point—she was lit like a Christmas tree and Jim was the electricity. Jim was extremely attracted to Mona, but he was just as fond of Eric, so he had nothing in mind except enjoying the evening with good company. After a while Eric took over with Mona and Liz joined Jim in his own jazzy groove that he had perfected on the little rooftop dance floor.

When everyone finally convened back at the table, Eric raised his glass, "Here's to love and a beautiful Italian night." He raised his glass as if he had said it all, not quite comprehending that Jim and Liz were avoiding love, or maybe he was saluting Liz's love for the Oxford man, or maybe he saw that somewhere in there was a spark of something that he already understood. There were no objections to the toast and both couples swung their glasses in the air spilling some of the sweet nectar on the table. After they had all taken a drink, Jim hoisted his glass in search of a toast more appropriate to his and Elizabeth's plight.

"To new friends and the value of each moment." He expressed with grace and a splash of charm not exposing the difficulty he was having trying to get on the same page with his traveling partner. Again, the group gladly drank to the appropriate toast in a direct attempt to become toasted. The wine flowed, and the couples got to know many interesting details of each other's relationships.

Eric was talking about meeting Mona's very rural Swiss parents, "To test my worthiness as a man, her father sent me to the goat pasture to milk one of the goats. He assumed if you couldn't figure out how to milk a goat you were going to have a hard time with the real complex issues in life or at least that's what he said. I was supposed to figure out which goat to milk and how to make it stand still while I grabbed its tits. I'm from London for bloody sake; how am I supposed to know how to corral a goat and extract its bloody milk? He was definitely fucking with me, right? But I can't really see in his face if he's jerking my chain or what, so I grab a bucket and head out to the pasture as if I know what I'm doing. I winked at Mona and said no problem to the old man. It can't be rocket science; I'll figure it out. Mona knows he's testing my character, not my farming skill, but she lets me wander out the door with no fucking clue as to what I'm going to do when I hit the pasture. I get out there—it ain't but a hundred yards behind the house. All the goats are grazing in a fairly good size chunk of land. I crawl over the fence with my trusty bucket, and I begin to search for the goats with the sagging tits. They won't let me get within ten bloody meters, so I figure I need some food or something to lure them to me; but there is still no way in hell they're going to let me grab their tits. It's not like they're fucking cows in a pen, right? I mean cows are all put in the barn to get the milk and I didn't see any pens in the barn designed for goat milking, so I saw no reason to corral one into the barn. I mean, I was really at a loss. Anyway, I figure it's all a big fucking joke on me, so I keep chasing the goats until someone comes to rescue me. I mean I got a hold of one once or twice, but there was no milk coming out—just a man against beast struggle that ended with the goat kicking me and breaking free. Mona didn't let me flail for too long, and as soon as she came to the rescue, the old man broke out in uncontrollable laughter. She had a goat tied to the fence milking it within five minutes. She cornered the whole lot of em, got a rope around ole Bessie's neck, and tied her to the fence where she was happy to have the pressure in her tits relieved. It was really amazing spending time on the ranch in the Alps. Her family makes cheese for a living, goat cheese, right. I learned the whole process with her brothers, and fell in love with the place and the lifestyle, at least for long visits. I don't know if I could really live it." Eric chirped away his comical, heart-warming story. Jim went on to tell stories about him and Liz growing up on the same street, but really existing in two different worlds. It was nothing like the difference between the Swiss countryside and the concrete jungle of London, but it was a profound difference in terms of their actions, their friends, the events they attended, and the morals and values that they acted upon in their lives. Eric and Mona didn't have these kinds of differences even though they were literally from different worlds. They desired the same things, were spiritually on the same kind of hippie page, and their intellects meshed into a stronger personality as they constantly pumped each other up. They expressed their love in almost every comment and were in complete adoration of each other via their body language. Mona's hand was always sliding to Eric's thigh, and his hand gently pushed the hair out of her face.

Eric had light chiseled features—his sandy blond hair, whipped in one-inch curls and would go bouncing around his head when he got animated. Mona had dark hair, also in curls, with smooth soft features that effortlessly blended with her flawless shape. The two looked like an ultra-pretty set of Raggedy Anne Dolls, almost alike and bursting with smiles. Jim and Liz found themselves lost in something they had never truly seen, a new, fresh overpowering love that devoured everything in its path. Liz's eyes glistened as she spoke privately to Mona, getting the details of the soul mates and their truest of love. Mona was so drunk she was quite exasperated in her detailed description of how the couple met while skiing in Austria, the instant love affair that followed, and then the uniting of the two very different families—one, goat farmers and cheese makers from the Alps, the other, blue blood bankers from a long line of city folk. Their love affair was something from fairy tails as was their evening atop the roof of the Italian bar being serenaded by a wonderful jazz band as the stars danced with them. The music had flavors of New Orleans, Paris, some African roots, and then just a splash of Italian flair. It was entertaining a worldly audience in a peaceful Europe, and the air was so full of life, laughter and music that time stood still on that rooftop.

The foursome got drunk, or pissed, as Eric called it, and stumbled their way back down the magnificent staircase to the street, where they parted on very loving terms, but not planning to spend anymore time together. They were too intoxicated to get each other's information and who knows if they would have such a wonderful aura together if they were to meet up again. As it was, they had a perfect taste of each other leaving a satisfied feeling that there are good people inhabiting the earth together. Jim held Elizabeth up, or vice versa, as they swerved back to their room. Jim couldn't help but picture Eric and Mona having some terrifically nasty drunk sex, and he explained his demented thoughts in great detail to Elizabeth who was shocked he could see their friends in such a light.

She decided to change the subject, "We should have made a better effort to stay in touch with those people. They were so nice. How can you defame them like that? I just want to be like them. They were so pleasant."

"I think I liked Mona a little too much to be buddy, buddy with that couple. I almost tried to make out with her a couple times on the dance floor—I couldn't help it. She's too damn scrumptious. I wouldn't be able to resist forever. I have no self-control; I'm pathetic, and I know it. It's like being friends with you. Sure it's great that we can enjoy each other's company, and sure it's great that Eric and Mona are wonderfully happy with each other, but where's my fuckin piece of the pie? You greedy bastards won't share any of it with me. You've got this pasty-faced English cocksucker that you're so infatuated with that you won't let me touch you. I earned you with all those years of letting you be you and waiting for you to catch up with me, to see the world just half the same as I do." Jim slurred, but with enough clarity and vigor that Elizabeth took the comments seriously. His language and his crass description of the man she was dedicated to offended her. She didn't let it cut too deep, though, because she could detect the slightest sweetness within her friend's sentiment even though he was overly dramatic in expressing it.

They were situated in the room before Liz responded. Jim stripped down to his boxer shorts and began taking pulls off the leftover Chianti earlier. Liz also had on boxers and a light tank top with no bra. "You know it's funny that you act so desperate to have me now that there might be some hope of sex. That was the deterrent before. It wasn't that you didn't want me before; you just knew it was forbidden. You say that you were waiting for me to see the world as you do, but you were just waiting for me to start screwing, right? You act as if I'm your property and you have first rights to me; and if you don't want me, then someone else can come along—well that's not the case. You're my friend and I love you and always will, but on this planet we're still in different worlds. You don't respect my values and I can't even make out yours. So stop bitching about not getting in my pants and stop looking at me like that!" Liz exclaimed with Jim staring at the light outline of her nipples as they barely pressed into her shirt. Jim had heard what she said, but he was too busy enjoying how she expressed herself to be concerned – the exaggerated movement of her arms, the way she twisted on the ball of her foot like a ballerina as she turned at each pace along the front of the beds, her long tan legs tightening with exquisite muscle definition leading to her little butt that made a flawless transition from legs to torso and filled out her shorts with the perfect shape. He realized that he was infatuated with every movement of his longtime friend.

"You need to come lay down with me on this nice soft bed, stop bitching, and have a drink. You look sexy when you're angry. Come here and let me give you a little rub and get some of that tension out. That might be the only way you'll let me touch you." Liz went over, took a drink of the wine, and put it down next to Jim fully expecting him to massage her as he had suggested. She knew that allowing him to caress her body was a cruel trick, but he wanted to and she wanted to be touched much more than she would let on. Elizabeth had some feelings aroused by the couple they had spent the evening with. She envied them and longed for such a connection, but she wasn't sure if the feelings swimming around were for her boyfriend or for her outrageous traveling partner who kept showering her with affection and then turned it into a club and beat her over the head with it. "Is he some kind of barbarian or does he really love me? I can't tell—he's too unpredictable."

Jim went and got some lotion out of Liz's bag, she had three different kinds, and squirted a large amount into his hand rubbing it together with the other one to warm it up. He pushed Liz's shirt up to her shoulders and began to work in the lotion on her pristine back. He covered every inch of her back, extending his fingers down her sides and gently caressing her breasts, then pulling her pants down slightly at the waste to get to the bundles of nerves at the top of her butt. Liz melted into the bed, letting every muscle of her body sink into the softness of the bed, allowing his pressure to be felt at her core. Jim had her on his mind and his hands, but he couldn't figure out how to make an honest effort into her heart. She sighed and let his hands wander wherever they felt the need to massage, which was almost every silky inch of her skin. He leaned over and kissed her neck. She didn't resist, but moved her head to allow more room for him to sink his mouth deeper into her tissue. His hands worked their way down her arms grasping at the top of her hands and kissing more passionately. He pulled her slightly to one side and she voluntarily rolled over to meet his lips with hers. Her shirt was slipped over her shoulder and his lips gently explored her breasts.

"Stop! We can't. You know we can't. We've already been over this. I shouldn't have let you get your hands on me." Liz said pushing him away and letting out a huge sigh as if she were releasing her emotions and letting her logic take back over.

What a shame, Jim thought, but he said nothing, rolled over and went to take a semi-cold shower.

His conversation with himself in the shower came to some bitter conclusions. "Fuck these games. Why travel with a beautiful woman when you can't taste her beauty? I know I'm selfish, self-centered, whatever. I know I have no class, but I can't help myself. This no touch bullshit is far too much for me to handle. I'm throwing in the towel and turning this game on its head. She's not going to get me even if she changes her mind. I'm just going to be myself without trying to win her over. She's playing some kind of game with me like she does all her other men, hard to get or whatever, but I'm not going for it anymore." Jim kept shaking his head in disbelief at his predicament and wondered what the point was for two people to repress their feelings when there was a cosmic pull making it impossible to stay apart. Jim wasn't someone to restrain anything; he lived life in a devouring mode and left little unsaid or undone.

In the morning the couple shook off their wine hangovers, Jim in his usual fashion and Liz with modern medicine, and headed out to the streets of Firenze to track down the Statue of David and many other sculptures by Michelangelo. Jim tagged along to the museum because he was earnestly interested in the work and even though he felt cold towards his friend for not letting him have what he wanted, he didn't want to show her that she was getting to him. He thought it would unveil a shallowness to his character that he knew truly existed, but didn't want to put on display. He felt that he could grow up enough to have a mature relationship with a beautiful woman without being able to trace her panty line with his tongue.

The sculptures were truly magical, human figures expressed in such smooth lines with exquisite detail and perfect symmetry. The artist's spirit glowed from each piece of work and marble was made into soft flesh. Jim and Liz wandered around the Museum in silence, in reverence to the master that left so much of himself here on earth.

After a couple hours in the museum, they made their way back into the busy streets of Florence to do some sight seeing and plan the rest of their trip. They didn't plan on spending much time in Florence, wanting to touch down in Pisa for a night and then make their way to Rome, which Jim was very excited to see even though he had heard conflicting opinions by various travelers about its overall cleanliness and allure. For Liz, Rome was the home of her faith and she longed to submerse herself in the rich traditions of the Papal City. Rome had all kinds of significance in both travelers' minds with all its history and Italian charisma, it was sure to be a fulfilling destination. The couple sat down for cappuccinos and banged out their plans. They would head to Pisa the next morning, spending a day and night, then head to Rome on a southbound train. They liked the route between Pisa and Rome because it went near the coastline and they figured the scenery from the train would be especially breathtaking. With their coffee drank and their plans settled, they decided to split up. Jim wasn't interested in shopping on the Old Bridge and he wanted a little time away from Elizabeth. Jim thought he might follow the river until he found a park, then kick back, smoke some dope and hopefully attract some righteously minded Italian female who would guide him on an authentic tour. He was always looking for experiences that included locals, where he could be exposed to actual life within a foreign culture, otherwise he felt like he was intruding on someone else's world. Following the hoards of tourists was quickly wearing on him, and he had to save some of his patience for Rome where there would be several tourist activities that he might have to buck up and partake in.

Elizabeth didn't mind splitting up. She felt a slight tinge of hurt regarding her traveling partner's request, not because she didn't want the reprieve, but because he was the one to suggest it. She didn't want him to have any kind of emotional advantage on her—she didn't want him to be driving her emotions. She made her way through the little shops on and around the bridge buying things that would really extend her bag to maximum capacity.

Jim was weaving back and forth across the river taking one parallel bridge across, then weaving back across on the next, going a few blocks away from the river then cutting over a block and coming back down towards the river. He was in a random cloudy haze that was his favorite form of travel and was looking for the right environment to get caught up with some natives who might take a liking to him. He settled himself in a little shady walking square where there were a lot of young people loitering in front of shops and cafes. There were some street performers, which always drew Jim in, and a wide variety of eclectic youth. The day rolled by and Jim had little luck acquiring any acquaintances, so he used his usual tactic when in need of companionship, he went to a bar. He had a little trouble finding the dark, dingy sort of bar that he preferred back in the states. He finally tracked down something with a hint of ding and smoky air, even though it was a little upscale for his taste. He was really looking for a friend who might be able to sell him a little more grass as well as smoke some with him. This was always a somewhat sensitive issue when approaching total strangers, but it had gone smoothly so far in southern Europe, which jacked Jim's courage to high levels. Jim also greased himself with a little liquid courage, the more of which he consumed, the quicker he got to the point. He began to search for a pothead who stuck out like himself, a flaming smoker who wore it on his or her sleeve. Jim wore the look, the straggly hair, the rocker goatee, and the semi-grunge slash retro clothing that didn't fit in any genre. He was the picture of the guy smoking pot on the war against drug posters back in the States. They cautioned, "Don't turn out like this!" Jim was shooting for that look, the anti-establishment free spirited dope smoker that would some day grow up to be an enlightened freethinker. He didn't really want to grow up, though, he wanted to laugh, get high and screw–like the Jimmy Buffet song but on a worldwide scale.

Jim met Vinny, a New York Italian visiting family in Florence. They hit it off instantly. Vinny in his jeans, tee shirt and shades – the same ensemble he wore every day, almost skin itself.

"Well fuck me silly, Jimmy. What brings you down the back streets of Firenze to my little haunt? Francisco here is a fantastic fucking bartender, doesn't speak English worth a fuck, though, he's liable to get you the wrong fucking drink. Let me get you a drink, anyway. What you having?"

"They still serve Absinthe around here, don't they? You ever drink that? It's supposed to make you crazy and since I'm already halfway there, I thought it might reverse the effects." Jim replied to Vinny who had immediately struck up a conversation with him as he sat down next to him at the bar.

"I've never heard of the shit, but let's see if old Franny here can hook you up." Vinny hollered out in Italian for Jim's drink finishing with the familiar word, Absinthe. Francisco smiled and produced a large bottle of green liquid from under the bar and splashed some slowly over some ice into a tumbler.

"Hey, hook me up with one of those too, I'm all for going crazy." Vinny exclaimed in English, but Francisco picked up on it without hesitation. Two antifreeze-looking drinks were dropped down in front of the new friends. While they sipped their smooth, florescent drinks, Vinny began explaining his existence in Italy. He was visiting his uncle for the summer, in-between jobs and struggling with the brash life in New York City.

"I even live in my Uncle's pad in New York. He raised me in America and came back here to retire. He left me in a sweet brownstone in the city and all I have to do is pay the fucking taxes, which ain't no shit, if ya know what I mean. I haven't been able to get my shit together, though, Jimmy. Sometimes I can't even get the taxes paid and my uncle bails me out and flies me over here to make sure that

I'm not a complete lost fucking soul. I really don't think I am, Jimmy. I think I can make it in this world; I just need a fucking break—ya know what I mean?" Vinny was spilling his guts and Jim loved it. Of coarse, Jim really didn't know what he meant and didn't know what it was to struggle to find self-identity or to actually have to pay taxes—to this point in his life, he had pretty much been completely void of responsibility.

Jim fed back a little of his current story. "I'm just randomly traveling through Europe. I've got a backpack and these here sandals and that's pretty much been enough to carry the old boy. The only complication is that I'm traveling with an old girlfriend from high school right now and things have bogged down a little. I'm trying to open myself up and get on with it without her being a factor. I can't allow the situation with her to keep me from being me; I'm not really interested in any stress on this trip. We split up for the day to get a little space, clear my mind, or at least distort it just the way I like. I don't think she could rationalize sitting in a bar in Florence getting high on Absinthe, but for me it's the highlight of the week. Our priorities are different, and I'm not good at making concessions and either is she."

"Sounds like you got pussy problems there, boy. I think I know just the thing to solve it. She's not giving it up, right? If you were getting some, you wouldn't give a shit about concessions or whatever the fuck you're worried about." Vinny spat out with his usual New York charm and bravado.

"You're right, I ain't getting any. She's in love with this boyfriend from England who she's known all of a pile of months while she's known and loved me all her life. She just hasn't been convinced of that yet – the loving me part. I've tried all forms of manipulation, honesty, and downright begging that I can muster, and I've made us both sick of the struggle in the mean time."

"I got just the solution. We'll have us a couple of drinks, these crazy fuckers or whatever, then we'll head over to a special little underground parlor I know about. You don't have to worry about a thing cause Uncle Giovanni will flip the bill. He gets all fired up when anyone will go to the whorehouse with him. He knows all the girls and they treat him like the fucking king of Italy in that place." Vinny explained with a glimmer in his eye as if Jim had woken his playful spirit and steered the day just the direction he wanted it to go.

They stumbled out of the bar in hazy evening light and made their way to Uncle Giovanni's pad. When they entered, Jim was in complete awe of the place. Uncle Giovanni had a decorator with class. Jim expected a dusty old place with bad lighting and Victorian antiques, but Uncle G, as he would endearingly become known as, had a snazzy modern spread. The house was three stories and everything had been opened up with the second and third floors being exposed to the first with wide-open balconies. All of the furniture was black and white leather while all the accessory furniture was in brushed stainless steel. There were abstract expressionist paintings jumping off the stark white walls with some modern pop art interspersed. The place was mellow with an inviting nature that drew any visitor in. The bar sparkled at the corner opposite the door with light spraying upward from inside the glass structure filtering through the liquor bottles and creating a kaleidoscope of color three stories above on the ceiling. On the second level was a huge screened television and on the third level was a full-blown art studio with works in progress wrapped around the balcony railing.

"Not bad for a piece of shit like me, huh?" Vinny expressed as Jim stood motionless taking in the unaccustomed luxury. "Uncle G, I brought home a straggler from the States. Poor bastard wandered into our little haunt. You here, Uncle G?"

"He looks like a fucking Hippie to me." A middle-aged man without a shirt and paint streaked black jeans expressed as he leaned over the top floor balcony assessing the new visitor. "Where do you pick up these vagrants? You can't just invite anybody to the spot. What if he's fucking psychotic or something; he looks like he could be off-balance." Uncle G continued his obviously good-hearted jibbing. "He's probably got a doobie on him. Why don't you two get one sparked up for old Uncle G. I could use a brain squeeze right about now."

Jim answered to Vinny, "I think he likes me already. Jim pulled his last little bit of pot out of his pocket and showed it to Vinny. " He had me figured out from thirty feet away."

"Put that shit away, youngster, we're going on a much finer ride than that. You might as well throw that mess in the trash bin and let me reload your stash. Uncle G is always packing the best shit in Italy. Fuck, he even left me with a sweet light set-up in the city. He knows how to do it, man, follow me." Vinny lead Jim to a small bedroom tucked in a distant corner down a long hallway on the second floor. When they went in the room, the door opened like a seal was in place around the door, which there was. Vinny told him that it had been built as a darkroom. All light had been shut out of the room and water had been piped in for the developing process. The room had a more urgent purpose, though. Uncle G grew his own high-grade marijuana, and as Jim saw, it had been developed quite well. There were three large bushy plants growing out of some rocky material with a constant flow of water running through the root systems and steady lighting directly above the plants. The smell was intense. Jim thought he had walked into a candy factory where the aroma sent him salivating. His eyes sparkled and he gave Vinny a big hug as if he had just lead him to enlightenment.

"What unbelievable fucking luck I have." Jim exclaimed after letting Vinny loose from his long embrace. "Who would of thought two big ole harry Italians would be packing such an exquisite stash. My friend, I bow at your feet for involving me in your supposedly fucked up life. I surely don't think you have it that bad, though. All that boo hooing at the bar and you bring me back to this fucking Shangri-La with all the booze you can drink and weed you can smoke, and you wonder why you can't hold down a job in the city. This is a fantastic situation—you just need to chill with Uncle G and stop bitching. We're going to get hookers later, right? I mean, what else do you need, sex, drugs, oh yeah, a little rock-n-roll; where are the tunes? Let's roll one up and crank the tunes."

Vinny smiled broadly at his new friend's excitement for the situation, but there was a sad look deep in his eyes. He felt as if he lived within his uncle's life and that every attempt he made to individualize himself failed miserably. He had spent his entire life riding the shirttails of his extremely talented and wealthy uncle, but had discovered no passion for himself. He had not discovered anything but the vast material and physical pleasures that he and his uncle constantly partook. His spirit was a little bleak, but the energy his new young companion was demonstrating was enough to breathe some life back in him. "The music around here will be straight blues, my friend; it's the heart of rock-n-roll anyway. This place is wired to the hilt, man. Uncle G will get it grooving once we spark one up."

There was a large round steel tray that had several large buds that had previously been clipped from the tenderly manicured plants. The luscious buds were dry and crispy and ready to smoke. Vinny grabbed one of the buds and led Jim back down the hallway where they plopped themselves in front of the big screen. They sat on a thick, soft Italian leather sofa that had a sturdy glass coffee table a couple of feet in front of it. Vinny picked up a teak box with the picture of a bonsai tree emblazoned on the top of it and put it in his lap. When he opened it, Jim peered inside and saw a vast treasure of pot paraphernalia and a mass of pot crumbs that had spilled into the bottom as joints were rolled on the open lid. Vinny's expert fingers rolled a long spliff that widened as it got towards the end and narrowed at the other end where he had installed a small piece of cardboard so that the weed would not be wasted as it burned towards their fingers.

"Wonderful work." Jim stated as he marveled at the professional craft that they were about to smoke. Uncle G came sliding down the spiral staircase from the studio with a white cloth digging at the paint on his hands.

"How you doing there. Call me Uncle G, just like Vinny here. That way I don't get too fucking confused. I'm getting kind of old or maybe I smoke too much fucking pot, I don't know. You tramping through Europe, huh?"

"Yeah, I am on a random path trying to find some enlightenment. Ran into Vinny here and so far he's proved to be the way to the truth." Jim said in a playful manner trying to demonstrate some wit, charm and a good sense of humor for a man that exuded those characteristics. Jim loved the way Uncle G bounced around with his "fuck-you-if-you-don't-like-it" attitude and wide-open face that always held a grin. "I started in England, made my way through France, Spain, Portugal, and Switzerland so far. Headed to Pisa, then Rome and then the Greek Islands, we're going to skip the mainland."

"Who are we? You traveling with someone else?" Uncle G asked as he studied the young man. He generally liked youth and its exuberance, and he genuinely got a good first impression of Jim who looked him in the eyeball when describing his travels. He could see the mischief in his eyes, and it matched his own kindred spirit. He immediately felt free to be himself, no worries or reservations.

"Yes, a woman who is giving me trouble, or at least I've made it a problem when it's really no big deal. She's sexy, though, and I can't handle keeping our relationship on the friendship level like we did when we were kids. I'm supposed to be able to handle myself like a gentleman, but that's just something I've never been. I can easily wander into thinking with the wrong head—actually I think that's my default setting. Vinny thinks if I get a little pussy, the temptation won't be so fucking fierce." Jim delivered the idea before Vinny to see how Uncle G would truly react.

"Well fucking eh right then, let's get us a little buzz, then go round us up a multicultural smorgasbord of beautiful women who bare nothing but our needs in mind. Ole Vinny here has been a stick-in-the-mud for the last month or so, and we haven't even made use of my membership to one of the finest establishments this side of the Alps. I learned the hard way never to keep a woman around. It's much cheaper just to pay for one when you need a little company. I get all the bitching and moaning I need from Vinny. If I had a woman around on top of that, I might have to hang myself and my work would definitely suffer." Uncle G stated with a pizzazz that made Jim believe that procurement of prostitutes might be the most efficient way to fulfill the male needs, but what about Linda, Maria and Melissa? They were all free, weren't they?

The joint was being passed around while Jim, Vinny and Uncle G were all sitting shoulder to shoulder on the comfortable sofa. They could have easily been family. Jim with his deep suntan, dark hair and broad shoulders fit in with the American Italians both physically and mentally. They were all children at heart who believed in intoxication as an art form to be maintained and expressed at all levels of consciousness. The joint burned down to the butt and all three men floated into mellow. Uncle G added to the tone with his selection of some Miles Davis blowing them higher into a groove of blissful sound. Vinny stirred up three gut wrenching drinks and the new companions toasted to the trumpet. After three more drinks all three men were dancing with their glasses— the brown liquid splashing around like a stormy sea—their eyes closed and the ear-piercing music digging into each piece of human tissue.

When the CD finished and the fourth drink became historical consumption, Uncle G started to rumble. "We must ready ourselves for the world. Vinny, you're going to have to provide our young vagrant with some threads. We will portray ourselves as gentlemen no matter what the case." Vinny shrugged his shoulders at his Uncle's comment and motioned for Jim to follow him. Uncle G took the staircase down and headed to the master bedroom where his wardrobe was unlimited. Vinny had quite a spread himself on the third floor down the hall from the studio. He opened the closet door, flipped on the switch and let Jim pick out anything he liked for a night of soliciting high-priced prostitutes in a completely polluted state.

"Why are you dressed so shitty when you have all these clothes to choose from? Why not ooze with style everywhere you groove." Jim said feeling quite good and a bit silly.

"Sometimes you gotta be just what you are, my boy. A tee shirt and jeans is Vinny and if you don't like Vinny in regular old duds, then you ain't going to like Vinny in fancy duds, are you? Anyway, I don't like dragging things to the cleaners when I can just throw my jeans in the machine every once in a while."

"Doesn't Uncle G have someone come pick up the dry cleaning? It seems like he's filthy fucking rich? This place, the art work, the clothes, supporting your vagrant ass, it's all too much for me." Jim expressed with a little curiosity that was able to peak through the buzz.

"He's got plenty of dough, no doubt, but there's never been no body serving us in any way. Uncle G is an amazing, man. He does all his own shit, cooks, cleans, shops, whatever; he doesn't want any help with anything. He decorated this fucking place himself, the furniture, artwork—every fucking detail is his own. Same with my brownstone back in the city, I've never changed anything that would detract from Uncle G's magic touch. The women fucking love it, right? He's got style and enough energy to run circles around me. A lot of times it seems more like we're brothers even though he's got twenty years on me. Anyway, you learn to take care of yourself around him. I just never received his Midas touch when it comes to cash generation, and he never gives me any stress about it. He always says that we ain't going to run out of cash in his lifetime. He's always giving me tons of cash and telling me it's better to give it away when he can see me enjoy it—I'm all for that fucking attitude. He loves me even though I'm a fuck-up, you know?" Vinny exclaimed as they both picked out their apparel for the evening. Vinny picked a crème colored suit made out of silky material. Jim thought the suit a little pimpish and let his friend know so, which made Vinny appreciate the suit even more. Jim decided to join in on the theme and picked a canary yellow suit that looked like it was straight out of an episode of Miami Vice.

"Pimps we will be, my man. I wonder if Uncle G will fit within the parameters of pimpness?" Jim asked.

"He always dresses like a nineteen-twenty's gangster. I'll bet you he's in pin stripes with a fucking cabby's hat on backwards; that's his look. Sometimes he even wears a bow tie just to set things off."

Sure enough when the group got together at the first floor bar for one last swig before they left, Uncle G was decked out in pin stripes. He also had on a stark white satin shirt with an oversize collar, no hat, no tie, and some shiny black Italian shoes with a large chrome buckle flashing on the side. His shirt was unbuttoned to expose his large hairy chest that still looked tight and fit with only a couple of gray hairs mixed in.

Elizabeth was sitting back in the room by the time Jim and his new buddies hailed a taxi in front of Uncle G's pad. Liz thought her friend would come walking through the door at any moment, and that they would get to enjoy the evening together. She truly enjoyed his company and was under the impression that he finally understood how to perceive their relationship. She wanted things to be on her terms, but what she didn't know was that Jim's attention span was so short that he couldn't possibly wade through a game of attrition. He wasn't willing to struggle for something that he perceived as his already. He knew that Liz was testing his sincerity and he wasn't willing to wade through any of that. She knew who he was, and he knew her inside and out. There was no need for any games in his mind. She waited until her eyelids grew too heavy and she faded into the abyss dreaming about the way things should have been going. She dreamed that Jim was well kept and consistently polite, attending to her every need like her well trained English lover.

By the time Elizabeth had faded, Jim was naked in a Jacuzzi with two black women that didn't know a single word of English. Vinny was in the same room, but around the corner on the king-size bed. Vinny stayed with Jim's theme of beautiful black skinned women, but he only had one while Jim was trying to handle two in the bubbling water. Uncle G had insisted that the boys be outnumbered, "You never know what's going to happen when you can't keep your eye on all of them—creates a real element of surprise."

Uncle G was part of an exclusive underground club where women from all over the world were pleasing men in all the ways men preferred to be pleased, and he was treating Jim to one of his first experiences with paid-for sexual pleasure. Jim had dove into the ancient realm of prostitution once before somewhere in the hills outside Reno, but he hadn't been able to afford the VIP treatment that he was now receiving. There were four bottles of open champagne dispersed throughout the room in ice buckets and to set the mood there were several candles burning along with incense that floated peaceful scents throughout the room. All that was needed was a disco ball and a revolving bed, and a pornographic movie could have easily been produced. Jim felt like he was transplanted to one of his most pleasurable erotic dreams where nothing could possibly go wrong, as long as he was functioning properly, and where smiles never left the

faces of the sensual women that were pleasing him in every physical way that one could imagine. There was some nice groovy Italian
music mixed with feminine giggles and masculine groans and every
once in a while Jim had to give a little play by play. "This one had a
tongue ring and she's been under the water for at least five minutes. I
think these women are superhuman. Vinny, are you alive over there?
I thought I heard you have a heart attack a little earlier. That roar of
yours seemed almost painful, you alright?"

"I'm in fucking heaven my boy. Enjoy yourself, but keep the trap shut.
I'm trying to concentrate over here, and you're breaking my stride."

"Sorry, just wanted to make sure you were still kicking. There isn't
enough thanks in the world that I could extend to you after this." Jim
expressed with a smile that reached all the way around his head. He
left Vinny to finish his business and started concentrating more intently on the full plate he had before him. One of the African beauties
began to spread hot oil all over Jim's shoulders as she sat on the edge
of the tub massaging him. The other came up from under the water,
turned away from him with her perfectly sculpted ass lowering on to
his lap so that he entered directly into her. His eyes rolled back in his
head and he leaned into the woman behind him as she continued to
deeply massage his shoulders and neck. The two women managed
to lift his body outside itself and turned it into the soft fluffy air it
breathed, light as a feather and completely fluid.

While Jim and Vinny were reaching ecstasy, Uncle G was practicing some good old fashion brow beating sex with the Italian Madame of the exclusive club. She took pleasure in giving one of their
most prolific customers the personal treatment. The Madame rarely
participated in the business herself, but when it came to the ultra-

charming Giovanni, she practically devoured him. He engaged her in a way that made him irresistible, adding to his status in the club and guaranteeing any of his guests' top-shelf service. Uncle G happened to be one of the finest and most respected modern artists in the city that exhaled art in each breath of its existence. He had retired as a professor of fine art at New York University, from which he had done guest work all throughout Italy. He combined photography and silkscreen imaging with his exquisite painting strokes to create some of the most breathtaking and complex work throughout the world. His paintings graced the lobby walls of fortune five hundred companies, ultra-rich patrons and museums in New York, Milan, Florence, Rome, and a host of other locations. His fortune had grown immensely since his retirement, being that he had more time for his work. He was not an old man, just past his mid-fifties and he was expressing himself with the freedom of a youthful artist who had been accepted with extreme passion by the art world and was being made rich by the appreciation. His commissions were in the millions and his work had brought him superstar-like fame. Jim had had the dumb luck of stumbling into his drunken nephew in the back alleys of Florence, and now he was living like one of the family.

The club was in a residential part of town. It had no exterior markings and looked like an apartment building from the street. The top three floors were personal apartments for the girls, while in the basement a luxurious gentleman's club thrived with life all night long. Members would call ahead and reserve rooms with girls they knew by name or simply by physical description, such as Vinny had done that evening. "You can't get so close to the African Continent without exploring some of its finest features." Vinny had exclaimed before they had arrived at the club. Vinny had seen the girls in the club and thought that it would make for an interesting night to keep them all together. Uncle G thought about joining the boys, but every time he got around the Madame, his blood began to boil and his dick got hard. Jim had been ecstatic about the opportunity to demonstrate his sexual prowess at an exclusive Italian brothel—it definitely wasn't an activity listed in the guidebook.

"What did you think there, my boy?" Uncle G asked as the three sluts got in their cab for the ride home.

"I think any man who treats a vagrant he just met to world class pussy is one of the finest men I'll ever meet. I can't believe I just experienced all that and someone else was kind enough to pay for it. I'm not going to ask how much it cost, but I surely want you to know that I appreciate it from the bottom of my loins." Jim stated, fired up on champagne and after-sex-glow. "I didn't even know places like that existed. Now I see how the other half lives and I'm going to have to find a little more drive so that I can make something of myself or I'll never get past those Mexican border hookers."

"Old Jimmy here had that water in that hot tub rolling like the fucking Red Sea. By the time he was done, that fucker was half empty. I walked around the corner to see how he was getting along, I had already had a glass of bubbly and smoked a dooby after I blew my nut, and there he is with his cock still at full mast. He had both of the women bent over the edge of the tub, butts up, him hitting one while spanking the other." Vinny's comment brought out a roar of laughter from Uncle G that shook the cab and was contagious to everyone in the cab including the driver who had to pull over to wipe the tears from his eyes.

"So you were making the best of the situation, huh, my boy?"

"Shit, I was on my third round by the time Vinny came to check out the show. I was burning up rubber like a drag racer. Vinny comes in there and hands me a glass of champagne while I'm fucking and asks me if I can switch booties without missing a stride, because he sure would like to see such a thing. As soon as I finish the drink, I do a complete spin, just for show, then slide right into the other one without missing a beat. The spin definitely gave me some extra style points." Jim stated trying to keep Uncle G's deep belly laugh continuous. Uncle G sat in the middle of the back seat with an arm around Vinny and Jim like a proud father who had just taken his two kids to Disneyland, his laughter filling the early morning air.

After the night had been recapped and all the chuckles that could be extracted were had, Jim finally came to the realization that he better get back to the hotel as to not alarm Liz. If he wasn't there when she woke up she might freak out and start calling authorities. She had never been integrally involved with the free-spirited young man's life, so she would have no understanding of his unique ability to get lost in an alley for days without explanation. Only Jim's parents truly knew what it was like to wonder what kind of chaos their son had wandered into, and whether he was coming out alive. Elizabeth was thrust into a life that she had only touched and viewed from the outside looking in. Now she was mixed up in the sorted affairs that her friend seemed to roust wherever he went. She had already got a closer look as his insanity in England and was a little leery of what the trip would bring, but it was a kind of leeriness that also teetered on the brink of excitement. She wanted to be able to lose herself in the moment, but there was always some hundred-pound test line reeling her back to her reality. Jim didn't want to cause any unneeded stress, so he had the cab drop him off at his hotel and bid his two new best friends farewell, promising to stop by the next day for lunch with Elizabeth.

"You can't say a fucking word about where we were. She couldn't possibly understand such a venture. I won't hold my breath, though, who knows what you two might drag me through. I'll be there, though, don't worry, I'll make it late afternoon. Grazie mille my friends."

Jim tried to sneak in the room as quietly as possible, but as soon as he closed the door he heard a sleepy perturbed voice, "Where were you? Thanks for leaving me alone in a strange city all night."

"I got a little carried away at a local tavern, met some of the natives, I'll explain tomorrow. Sorry." Jim said softly as he ducked into the bathroom for a long hot shower hoping that his friend would fall into a deeper sleep knowing that he was now back.

The sun began to peak up over the horizon soon after Jim laid his head on the pillow, but he remained glued to the bed. Elizabeth was up early and decided to go see a couple museums and take the tour of the cathedral. She knew Jim would not be getting up for several hours and he deserved a little disappearing act anyway. Jim understood that his friend would probably want to ditch him most of the day, but he wanted her to meet Vinny and Uncle G, so he had to engage her somehow.

He rolled over as he heard her stirring in the morning, "I've got a pretty interesting lunch scheduled for us. I think you'll really enjoy meeting my friends from last night. I know I don't deserve your company, but I promise I'll try to make up for it if you just come back around lunch time, please muy bella signora." She couldn't imagine where he had been all night, so the interest of putting the pieces to-gether would probably bring her back to the room. She remembered the stories he used to tell her on her patio late at night and her imagination began to piece together a night that wasn't too far from the reality. She really didn't feel that spiteful towards Jim, even though she was wearing it as if she did, and would reserve the final opinion for when she met the lunch dates.

Jim was just barely able to function by noon. He had made it as far as a shower and had put some shorts on, but still had to pack and get the rest of his clothes on. Everything hurt until he got right with a perfectly rolled joint that Vinny had fixed him up the night before. He had actually rolled him an entire cigarette package full of joints so that Jim wouldn't have to spend a waking moment sober if he didn't choose. Italy would be experienced in soft mode, and with the high quality of weed, little could go wrong as long as no one swiped his stash. He had the room full of smoke when Elizabeth burst into the room with a distressed look on her face.

"You can smell that in the hall, you know? You're going to get us in trouble."

"What are they going to do, throw us out, we're checking out today anyway? This is a smoking room. You see the little picture of the thing burning on the door, that's a joint. You're supposed to smoke reefer in this room, this is a reefer smoking room. You stick with me, and I'll teach you the ways of the road, baby. Take a little puff; it'll calm your nerves. It's the Uncle G kind, it'll blow you away."

"What about the police? Are you completely out of your mind?"

"Oh, calm down. We're in southern Europe and Mussolini isn't the fucking dictator anymore. I'm sure they would just take our shit and smoke it themselves. Anyway, I've got connections in this town; we'll be able to get out if they lock us up."

"I'm getting out of here, I'm not getting locked up." Liz said with a little panic and a lot of disgust in her eyes.

"Calm down, calm down. I'll put it out. I'm obliterated anyway. Look, I'm going to light a regular cigarette now so that it will cover the smoke of the other. Don't get your panties in a wad. I aim to please."

"You're completely ridiculous." Liz said as she grabbed her gigantic bag and headed for the door. "I'm waiting for you outside. You check out and don't take forever and don't forget that I'm out there." Jim looked at her with slanted eyes as she made her demands, his mouth half opened and turned up in a slight grin. He shook his head slightly with each demand, as to recognize and comply. He wasn't going to argue and was hoping to get her to lighten up with his silly half-cocked face. She didn't pay any attention, marched out of the room and slammed the door. Jim sat staring at the door for a couple of minutes, dragging the cigarette and wincing at her abrasive attitude. He had to get her in a jovial mood before they reached Uncle G's. He wanted to showcase her good looks, sweetness and charm, but first he had to locate those qualities and bring them to the surface.

He checked out of the hotel and made his way to the beautiful amber-haired American girl who was pouting on a bench outside the front entrance. She had her shades on and was looking away from Jim as he approached her. "Hey, Sunshine, put a smile on your face. We're in Italia and nobody knows or cares what we are doing. We must enjoy ourselves, my dear. We must enjoy each other—there is no time for strife. Let's go meet my friends and then we'll head out of this town. I think you'll enjoy them very much. We're going to see some beautiful art and see the artist who created it." This comment piqued Elizabeth's interest and she rose from the bench turning her head towards her friend. As soon as her head turned, Jim planted a big wet kiss right on her lips. She couldn't help but crack a grin. Jim had broken her down in an instant and she was whisked out of her foul mood that had been lingering from the night before. She remained silent as Jim led her through the streets to Uncle G's suave pad.

Giovanni opened the door as if he was expecting a long lost friend. He swung it open quickly with a broad grin and the hand holding his drink spread away from his body pointing inward. "This lovely young lady looks like a champagne type of woman." Uncle G said as Jim let Liz enter the house first.

"This is Elizabeth. This is Giovanni or Uncle G after a couple of drinks." Jim said introducing the two. Giovanni took Liz's hand and kissed it lightly like a breath of fresh air.

"This is s a beautiful place, did you decorate it yourself?" Liz asked.

"It is all inspired by God himself who has provided so well for me. Keeping the place current is definitely a hobby of mine. I can't get a damn thing out of Vinny, though. Vinny, come out here and meet the lovely young woman your vagrant friend brought for us to enjoy—she's stunning. I have no idea how she ended up with Jimmy here, but I think she'd rather stay with us than go any further with him. Fix us some mimosas too, would you? I think he brought back your pimp suit too. I think you should let him keep that thing, so I don't have to see you in it." Uncle G yelled at Vinny who was standing across the room in a pair of shorts with a button-up shirt, completely unbuttoned, and his hair slicked back into a black helmet. He popped the top on a chilled champagne bottle and followed his uncle's orders without as much as a peep.

As he walked up to the group, he made the one comment that Jim was hoping he would have the couth to avoid. "Did Jim tell you about our evening last night?" He asked as he handed Liz her mimosa complete with a half slice of fresh orange straddling the edge of the glass.

"No, he really didn't elaborate. He just said he had been out for a drink. There was much more to it than that, wasn't there?" Liz asked with Jim in suspense.

"So he didn't tell you about the Nigerian hookers, huh? I kinda figured he'd leave that out." Liz looked at Jim after Vinny made the comment. Jim was shaking his head from side to side as if Vinny was telling a complete lie. Jim even shrugged it off as if to say, ah, don't pay him any attention. "I'm just kidding, where you going to find Nigerian hookers in Florence anyway? I bet you that would be fucking impossible, especially if you desired two at one time. What do you think, Jimmy?"

"Whew, what an imagination." Jim said still shaking his head back and forth screaming no, no, no. "Uncle G just took us out for dinner and a drink on the town. I met Vinny in a little bar down the street. I was looking for some kind of trouble to get into and he was the perfect guide. This place is amazing isn't it? Mr. G is a world famous artist. You should check out some of his work up there in his studio. It's really amazing." Jim directed his comments towards Liz pulling her away from Vinny's viscous attempt to drag him through the mud. It worked too—Liz began talking to Uncle G and left Vinny out of the conversation sensing that he was trouble. Uncle G wasn't about to burn Jim, but he didn't bail him out either.

Jim and Liz had brought their bags to the house and were planning on heading straight to the train station from there. The house was comfortable, though, and the conversation went perfect with champagne and orange juice, which was in unlimited supply. Elizabeth was proud to be thrust into a group that lived so beautifully, tying her back to her home as well as accepting her into a different culture. Uncle G, and even Vinny were extremely enlightened individuals who knew the history of Italy as well as America and were able to tie them together in a way that made Liz even more comfortable being within the borders of a foreign country. There was so much to learn about food, wine and the arts that she was immersed in the dialogue and became more and more engaged as she drank. Uncle G and Vinny whisked her off her feet and made her feel so at home that the couple never left for their afternoon train. They stayed and talked about modern art, the auctions at Christie's and Sotheby's, where Uncle G bought more work for his collection and saw some of his own work pedaled. They talked about romance and the Italian way of life, whether in America or Italy.

Jim and Liz shared a king size bed in a beautiful guestroom that had all the amenities, including a Jacuzzi tub. "Come on and get in here with me." Jim pleaded with Liz as he soaked in the tub. He left the bathroom door open, as he was getting ready so that Liz could catch a glimpse of his naked ass getting in the tub.

"I'm not getting naked with you. You have no idea how to treat a woman." Elizabeth said with a little slur to her speech caused by her flat-out drunkenness. "You probably did sleep with hookers last night. I don't think Vinny was making that up. You were nervous when he said that."

"How could you possibly think that we had hookers last night— that's preposterous, Vinny was just trying to start some shit."

"So why did nobody bring it up the rest of the night?" Liz asked standing at the edge of the tub in her bra and panties. "I'm getting in, but don't get any ideas." She slid her long legs into the tub without taking off the rest of her clothes. She sat facing Jim with one foot resting against his naked butt.

"You really need to feel more comfortable naked. It would be a lot better for our relationship. I mean, I'm completely exposed here, and even though I can see your nipples through that bra, it's not the same as complete nudity." Jim said using his foot to explore Liz's body. She grabbed it and bit one of his toes. "What, you don't like being felt up with my sensuous feet? I thought you would love the sweet caress of my big toe." Jim was drunk and felt a desperate need to get his friend naked and have his way with her, but he knew that exposing such desperate feeling would be self-defeating, so he tried to maintain a playful attitude. Elizabeth was screaming drunk and would have allowed her friend more liberty than usual if he had made a move.

Jim had been shot down on many previous attempts and was skittish to make any bold attempts. "Why don't we dispose of the games and take advantage of each other?"

"You're supposed to be romantic, but I don't think you know what that means." Liz exclaimed ducking her head underwater and coming out with her auburn hair glistening, water dripping off her chin and her eyes blinking furiously in her drunken stupor. Jim recognized her belligerence and let her be for the evening even though he did spend some time exploring her body with curious hands in the pose of a massage. He had finally gotten her naked and had her melting in his hands as he rubbed various parts of her body, but by the time he got himself all worked up feeling every curve of her body, she had passed out in his arms. He pulled her out of the tub and put some shorts and a tee shirt on her before tossing her in the luxuriously soft bed that they would share. He thought about leaving her naked so that she would have to wrestle with what happened when she woke up, but his kinder instincts took over and he even spent some time drying her hair, as she lay out-cold. When he went to bed, he cuddled up with Elizabeth feeling it necessary to be close to her, and realizing he longed to overcome the obstacles of their relationship.

Jim woke up with the sun streaming through their only window, a massive arch shaped window that took up an entire wall, and Elizabeth was rubbing his back with her cheek resting on his shoulder. She realized that she passed out naked in the tub and that her friend had treated her with love and respect. She believed that there was some outside possibility that Jim could be the understanding, compassionate companion that she was looking for, and Jim was willing to oblige as long as he could take care of his physical needs somewhere else. He had an appetite for physical love, or actually the wild enchantment of physical lust, like he had experienced the night before at the exotic brothel, but it was always better if there was an emotional connection as well. He needed the intensity of passionate emotional exertion as well as the feel of a female body thriving and sweating against his. These are things that Elizabeth could barely grasp. She had not been one to feed into lust, but she did have desire, a deep seeded desire to drink from the cup that she had spent most of her life abstaining. Excesses in all things drove her friend while she kept grasping heavy objects to try to stay grounded and not be whirled into his unique unreality.

The champagne bubbles were still pounding in their heads when they woke the next day. Jim looked out the window and saw the sun high in the sky. "It must be noon already. We should make our way out of town pretty soon even though I believe I could stay at this house forever if they'd let me."

"Yeah, this place is beautiful, and those two are so nice that I bet they would let us stay around a while. It's amazing the way you befriend people. I can't imagine staying in someone's house the day after you meet them, yet you seem to pull it off all the time."

"It's called charm; you should ask your pasty faced boyfriend about it. I'm sure he'll unleash his charm on the masses when you go abroad with him, or maybe he'll be a rude, stuck up English snob and all the people will stay away from you like a bad smell. I don't mean to degrade your Danny boy, but I feel it is my duty to point out my strengths so that you'll be cognizant of what you'll be missing if you continue down this disastrous path with this Englishman." Jim explained as the couple piddled around in an effort to get ready to enter the main quarters of the house.

"You always have to ruin perfectly good moments with your self-absorbed, distorted comments. What gives you the right to judge Daniel when you wouldn't even take the time to get to know him."

"I'm sorry, my dear, forgive me for my vulgar display of egotism. I really didn't mean to be so nasty; it just comes out before thought intercedes. I don't deserve your company—please put a leash around my neck and keep a tight grip, so that I can't just wander around in public. Come on now, let's present ourselves to our hosts in good cheer." Jim said in a mocking English accent that immediately reddened Liz's cheeks, but she managed to transfer her anger to appreciation as soon as she set eyes on their host.

Uncle G greeted them as Jim had first met him, in jeans and no shirt with paint splattered on his naked chest. "You two have inspired me. I've been up since the crack of dawn working on something new, and you must come take a look." He guided Jim and Liz up the winding staircase to his studio. There was a large canvas that had been plastered with four extremely large black and white photographs. The pictures had been developed from the night before. They were of Elizabeth and Jim wrapped in each other's embrace expressing their loyal friendship in a completely drunken disarray of body parts. The photos were in a series, the first of Liz putting her arms around her friend, then two shots of her pulling him close into a hug and a final shot of her lips pressed against his cheek in a display of affection that summed up their relationship. Uncle G had snapped photographs of the couple throughout the night until they had become completely comfortable with him observing them. After a while they no longer noticed the flashes. Uncle G had begun to paint on the photographs, completely devouring the lines that existed between each piece of photo paper so that it created an intimate collage with the blackness between each image pulling you into the next.

Jim and Elizabeth stood looking at the piece in silence for several minutes. They liked the way they looked together, especially in such a playful state. Liz's legs were draped across Jim's lap, and her arms reached awkwardly around his neck to draw him close enough for the kiss. Jim's eyes were squinted, and his mouth was open in laughter as he submitted to her with obvious delight. "She's in love with me, isn't she Uncle G?" Jim expressed after staring at the images.

"If she isn't, then her eyes betray her my dear boy." Uncle G said with a sparkle in his eye that turned Liz a bright shade of crimson, and it wasn't anger that spurred on the change. There was a lot of truth to Uncle G's statement, but Elizabeth was only betrayed by her cheeks. Inside, she was still fighting a battle against her true feelings.

"Yes I do love Jim, but I believe you two don't understand the type of love I am displaying. It's a love full of trust and caring, not the sexual longing that seems to dominate your thoughts." She finished her comments with her eyes glued on Jim.

"No, no, no, I see lust in those eyes, you definitely want me, but are involved with some kind of cruel self-punishment that locks you into the first person you have succumbed to sexually. You have this life-long moral code that says you can only spread your legs for one man, that your love can only be singular, and once you've given yourself away, you can never take it back. It's not that simple though, my dear; you're going to have to give me chance or you'll spend the rest of you life wondering if we could have made a go of it. I mean, if you give it a shot and we fall flat on our face, then no big deal, you can go running back to Danny boy and all will be well—but if you continue to deny me, you are going to break my heart and leave yours scream-ing for a second chance." Jim said with his normal pizzazz about the tired subject. Jim was blunt about it because he was tired of fight-ing against it. The comments gave Liz a sour taste in her mouth and she turned her back on Jim. She changed the subject to her desire to have some of Giovanni's photos sent back to them in the states, even though Jim would probably be so mad at her that they wouldn't be talking once they got back. She could see that the more she resisted him, the more discouraged and indifferent he became. He was starting to look at her like a sister instead of someone he desired. She wanted to keep his longing alive, but she didn't want to have to deal with it physically just yet, which was completely counterproductive. Elizabeth had conflicting thoughts of where tomorrow should go, and the vivid pictures running through her head displayed a true emotional lust that steamed up the windows in her mind.

Jim got high with Vinny and became indifferent to the world. He backed away from closeness and put on his playful charm. After a couple of laughs and some final parting encouragement, Jim and Liz left their wonderful hosts and headed back out into the streets of Florence. "Sometimes you strike it rich with the finest people in the world, you know?" Jim said.

"Yeah, they were fantastic people with great big hearts. That was a great experience—thank you for dragging me in there against my will."

"I knew that you would be relaxed as soon as you walked through the door."

Chapter 9
SILLY PISA

They made their way to Pisa by afternoon train, barely speaking and enjoying the countryside. The trip wasn't long, and there was still plenty of sunshine remaining in the long summer day. Pisa was a small, quaint little town where they had decided to stay at a hostel that was recommended in their guidebook. They walked right by the leaning tower on their way to the hostel. "Well, there it is. It's kind of anticlimactic in person, huh?" Jim asked as they strolled by.

"Well, it certainly is leaning. I think it's kind of cute. Can we come back after we drop off our bags? I want to see if we can go up in there. You need pictures, anyway, don't you?" Jim nodded his head in disinterested agreement. He wasn't sure what he wanted and had somehow slid into a foul mood. Liz could barely detect this and was in such a jovial mood that she could not commiserate. "This is such a beautiful spot, I'm glad we came here. Look at all the sunflowers. They're your favorite, right. Come on, cheer up." The sunflower field extended from the hostel as far as the eye could see, and it was a happy sight like a million happy faces following the sun.

Jim had lost some of his energy and felt a desperate need for a little rest while Liz was revived and wanted to party the night away. The hostel provided the right environment to satisfy both attitudes. There was a large group of backpackers, many exhausted like Jim, and many with energy for a party, like Liz. The exhausted group stayed around the hostel drinking wine and conversing on the lawn, while the energetic group went into the small farming town hoping to find some mischief.

Liz found herself with a group of Australian men who were absolutely delighted to have her company and who were vying, almost viciously, for her attention. The winner was a tall outspoken chap with big round golden curls and an intellectual mind to go with his throbbing hormones. He spent the night intensely trying to seduce Elizabeth, and by the time they returned back to the hostel, extremely drunk on wine, he had succeeded in keeping her outside in the yard alone. "I fell for you the second I laid eyes on you, and I knew I had to keep those other savages away from you. They're my blokes and all, but they certainly don't know how to treat a lady. You're in good hands with me." The Aussie wooed as he bent down for his first kiss. She succumbed to his Australian charm; it was even bolder than the Englishman's she so adored. As the bright moonlight bathed the sunflowers, he succeeded in removing her shirt and bra as well as getting one button of her shorts dislodged. The Aussie thought he would easily conquer his prey, but Elizabeth would only allow the heavy petting to go so far. She melted in his hands just like a willing woman would, but she was very rehearsed at clicking off the yes and turning on the no.

The young man didn't know what hit him when she quickly launched him off of her and re-clothed herself. "I'm sorry, I can't do this here, not now, not like this. I've got to get to bed; we're headed to Rome tomorrow. I'll never see you again, anyway, I just can't."

"Never see me again, that's ridiculous. I'm Australian; I travel the globe as a hobby. I'll surely pop up at your back door in America.

You're a lovely woman; I'd travel half way around the globe to be in your company any day. You've got to admit this is a pretty romantic thing you're turning your back on - the moonlight, the flowers, and the cool Italian breeze with scintillating romance surging through it. We need to make the best of this time and this place or we'll never be able to duplicate it."

"You sound like someone else I know, but all the smooth talking in the world isn't going to get my pants off. Don't get me wrong, I think you're a wonderful man, but I'm not quite that free-spirited – I can't just have sex with a man I just met. I really enjoyed myself, and I'm sure I enjoyed the make-out session more than you did, but that's as far as I go, sorry." The young man wasn't that easily deterred and came in for another shot at a kiss, but only received a peck as Liz's iron will was stronger than his throbbing loins. He would feel the pounding ache surging through his body, as he lay in the bunk of the hostel wondering what had hit him so hard.

Liz had let herself get a little further out there than she expected or even really wished, but she felt no remorse for her actions and was glad to have had the session. It was easier dealing with a stranger than it was Jim, he wasn't willing to agree to just heavy petting and she had to look at him the whole next day. Liz could easily dismiss a make-out session in the grass as long as no bodily fluids, besides saliva, were exchanged. There was no offense and she could keep a clear conscience.

Jim woke up much earlier than his gallivanting friend and made his way through the quiet town in the early morning light to get some photographs of the Leaning Tower. The slanted light made for exquisite shadows and the early morning mist gave the images a fairy tale quality. From the tower, Jim took a stroll in one of the laughing sunflower fields. He shot photos of his favorite smiling flowers and enjoyed the quiet time alone to reflect. The quiet time lead Jim's mind to thoughts of Elizabeth going off with the Aussies the night before, and he tried to dispel any unhealthy jealousy. When the group had left, he could tell they were very pleased that he wasn't coming along although all got along well at the hostel. There were enough men, and they knew that if Jim joined them, they wouldn't have a chance at the girl. Jim knew Liz would lead them all on to gather as much attention as possible. "I don't blame her, I would do the same if I was imbedded with a lovely group of females. She wouldn't do anything with any of them, though, I'm sure of that. I mean, if she can resist me, there's no chance those guys could possibly possess more charm than I, and she certainly isn't giving anything up to me." Jim had some thoughts about what happened the night before, and the jealousy kept creeping in and torturing him with every thought. "She's not mine and I'm not hers; I've just got to drop it."

The morning was hot in Pisa, and Jim had sweat brimming from his forehead and running down his back as he approached the hostel. His morning walk had opened his mind and created an enchanting spirit that would thrive through the rest of the trip with Elizabeth. He came to the conclusion that his attitude was paramount on a trip such as he was on, and that it was the one thing he could control, so he would try to steer it towards the smiling sunflowers whenever it went astray. No matter what the situation was with Elizabeth, he would accept it on a day-to-day basis and work with whatever was given however little or great.

Liz wasn't ready by the time Jim arrived back at the hostel, so he made himself comfortable in the yard and watched the business of the travelers scurrying around as they prepared themselves to go to the train station. The young backpackers, who were seen all over Europe throughout the summer, were very similar in many ways, although they were from all different parts of the globe. There was always a sense of frugality as meals were thrown together from supermarket produce, yogurt and, slices of cheese, but it was communal with everyone sharing with complete strangers. A traveler was usually joined by a wide variety of others just like themselves with backpacks, cameras, and beaming faces, especially in Italy. The feeling of being part of an adventurous group was always sustained, and everyone was looking out for everyone else—telling each other the good places to stay, the most important cuisine or beverage to partake, and even warning about stricter locales that were better to travel through than stay. Jim had opened up such a sharing situation that morning as he had stopped by a local fruit stand on his walk and picked up a whole bag of fruit on the cheap. He made himself comfortable next to a small table in the yard and began to cut some of the fruit when a beautiful young woman came up to inquire where he had purchased his bounty. He said it was clear on the other end of town, but that he was more than willing to share what he had. She spoke in a thick German accent, but knew to use English because she had seen Jim around the hostel using it. "You are so kind. Let me get my friend, we will join you, we have some things to offer as well."

The young German woman came back with another that looked much like her, they were both good size, full-figured with large bosoms and long, straight hair, one brown and one dirty blonde. They wore loose fitting tops with no bras and did not shave their armpits. Jim had seen many women like this in the hills of Oregon—they were good old fashion hippies, and Jim loved the free spirit that came along with such a way of life. The girls added to the feast with crackers, cheese, and some exotic fruit juice they had picked up the day before.

Elizabeth found Jim squeezed between two full-breasted German girls having a backpacking feast when she finally stumbled into the bright light of the hostel yard. She felt a slight tinge of jealousy, but she was able to overlook it as she embedded herself with the large group of Australian men that she had gone out with the night before. Jim watched as the lanky Australian that had been taken to the brink of ecstasy the night before leaned over and gave Elizabeth a short brushing of the lips. Jim could see that the intimacy level was nothing to worry about, but it still turned his stomach the wrong way.

"Do you know her?" One of the girls asked noticing that Jim had been affected by the kiss and that Liz was heading their way.

"Yeah, she's with me. Not with me, you know, but traveling with me. We're old friends careening through the countryside together. It looks like she might have had a little luck with that fella, huh?" He asked in a lighthearted manner.

"I think you love her, but won't admit it," said the blonde playfully eating a piece of fruit as if she was kissing it. She had a feeling that this comment would get Jim excited.

"It is what it is. What it should be might be a different thing, but I ain't going to sweat it no matter what it is, or what it shall be," Jim retorted trying his best to baffle his friendly guests.

"What?" The brown-haired girl replied. Jim avoided the question as Liz was coming up to the table. He acted as if he hadn't even noticed that she had come out of the hostel. She walked up right next to him, but he didn't acknowledge her and continued to munch on his cheese and crackers. The two German girls took him out of his game by staring up at Elizabeth with expecting eyes.

Jim finally gave in and introduced Liz to the girls, "This is Elizabeth. We used to call her Liz, but now she's grown up and likes to be referred to by her full name; it's only proper. This is Hilga and Ethel; they are my new German friends, and they are ultimately more exciting than you. They are obviously traveling hippies, and I'm not really sure if they like boys or girls. You might want to be careful who you sit by, cause we're all desperate for a piece of ass." Jim felt the two girls would take his humor the right way, and he was right as all three women giggled quite excessively.

"I'm sure they get high. All hippies get high, right?"

"Sure, and we like boys and girls, so both of you better watch where you sit." Hilga, the blonde, replied.

"Hey we're taking these girls with us on the rest of our trip, don't you think we should?" Jim asked Liz with a straight face. The German girls laughed and shook their heads as if they were willing to fulfill their end of the bargain if only Liz would agree. Liz shook it off and sat down at the table next to Jim. The German girls were playing perfect roles for Jim's biting sarcasm, and he wasn't going to let her off the hook for sucking face with the Australian. He began to weave his web, "So, you had a good time last night, huh?"

Liz looked at him for a long second not knowing how to proceed and then simply said, "Yes."

Jim began a direct attack, "These girls have female instincts, and they said they could tell by the way you were slinging tongue with the shaggy Aussie, that you probably had shagged him—meaning, allowed him much more access than meets my approval. Now if these girls are right, and you let some stranger enjoy the fruits of my labor, then I might just have to lay down on the tracks at the next station and let the train run over me like good old Anna did. So let's have it, do men have to have a smooth foreign accent to get in your pants, or what?"

Elizabeth looked at Jim as if he had lost it and politely ignored him, if it possible to ignore politely, and directed a question to the girls. "So, where are you girls headed?"

Ethel answered, "We didn't say nothing about shagging. He's making all that up." All of a sudden the girls had jumped sides when he thought they would surely back him up.

"Oh ignore him, he doesn't have any manners. He knows better—I wouldn't possibly allow a stranger any more than I allow him."

"What are you talking about? I sleep in the same bed as you and don't get any of those sloppy kisses."

"You always want too much, more than a good girl like myself is willing to give." Liz replied making the topic much less fun than Jim wanted.

"Girls, why have you abandoned me? I really need some support here; this woman has ice running through her veins. She refuses my love and picks up with strangers."

"You can't condemn her without letting her explain herself. Relationships should be open for interpretation. Who cares what fun she had with the shaggy man; today she is with you. We're all young, and we need to be as free as possible. Don't try to chain her up and try to make her yours—that will only leave less of the world for both of you." Ethel's loud, persuasive opinion interjected. She believes couples should support each other's endeavors and savor every life experience possible within the realm of physical safety, sometimes risky, if the rush is extraordinary enough. Hilga and Ethel were completely out there, like savages feasting on honey from a hive with the stings just tickling. Their ideals were expressed in their open faces and forgiving eyes; they had no room for judgement, just acceptance mixed with bright optimism. Jim and Liz thought the girls refreshing, dropped their confrontational attitudes, and adopted the girls' fresh, optimistic outlook.

Hilga and Ethel joined them as they boarded their train to Rome, which was already beginning to show signs of festivity as it pulled away from Pisa with brimming cars. The train ride to Rome would be a long one filled with many stops and a constant surge of people. For the first half of the trip, the train was bursting at the seams, and Jim let the girls have seats while he sat in the entranceway with a rowdy bunch of Italian Nationals. Jim ended up in a game of charades with four Italian men of his age who had no ability to speak English and spent the train ride teaching Jim how to come on to women in Italian. Sometimes they taught him vulgar things to say, but Jim would try them on neighboring women, and when they almost hit him for his comments, he demanded his tutors not betray him. He wanted to be able to turn a girl's head in a good way and not have her rear up and swing at him. The laughter was intense as Jim chose different women standing throughout the cabin to practice his new lines. Two hours into the journey, all the women in the area had been used as bait for Jim's Italian lesson, and all of them became wise to his intentions. Sometimes he even spoke Italian to American girls fitting the Italian profile, and they would shoot back in his own dialect, "That's not going to work on me." knowing that he was an American imposter and having the savvy to understand the Italian language before coming to Italy. Jim did manage to entertain the cabin, and although the space was cramped, everyone managed to keep a smile on his or her face while Jim and his Italian friends practiced picking up on women.

The girls were one car away and had gotten a seat in a cabin, so were not aware of Jim's buffoonery. They were engaged with conversations with other backpackers and had come across some great information about traveling to Greece, which Jim and Liz planned to do, but had not yet come up with the itinerary. A couple, who had made the trip before, explained how it was extremely convenient to take a ship from the eastern coast of Italy to the western coast of Greece and then to take a bus across Greece if you wanted to go to the islands. These recommendations were written down by Liz and were later used as the blueprint for their travels. Even Ethel and Hilga were excited by the information, and thought about making the trip.

The train remained completely packed for the first three hours of their southern journey, but as they made more and more countryside stops, the thriving hoards began to relent, and the train slowly became a comfortable group of people. Jim had to say goodbye to his new Italian friends and did so with hugs as if they had known each other for years. After the boys had gotten off, Jim joined the girls in their comfortable cabin that had emptied out.

"I just learned how to tell a woman she has marvelous legs and a fantastic ass in Italian. I even tried it out on some of the locals and a couple American girls. It wasn't as successful as I'd hoped, but I think if I perfect the accent things might turn out better for me."

"What do you need those lines for when you already have three gorgeous women accompanying you?" Liz said with the other girls shaking their heads in agreement.

"I must spread my wings and fly. You women have teamed up against me and I'm going to have to find some slutty types to overcome your righteousness. Now, of course, I can imagine some beautiful interactions between the four of us, but my friend here only goes for smooth-talking foreigners. I've given up on her, but I'm more than happy to consider a sexual revolution with you two beautiful German queens, if you'll dislodge yourselves from the grips of Elizabeth and become engaged in a meaningless flurry of lust. I'm also willing to accept friendship; don't get me wrong—there is a lot more to life than frivolous sex, but if you're in, I can take kinky to a whole new level. I'm kind of shallow; I'm sorry."

"You don't have to apologize—you're just like every man, except you're a little more honest about your intentions. I wouldn't rule anything out except Ethel doesn't really like boys; she kind of prefers women if possible. Me, on the other hand, I encourage frivolous in the right circumstances."

After this comment, Ethel put her hand on Jim's knee and said, "Yeah, since you're having so much trouble with Elizabeth, why don't you let me have her, and I'll share Hilga with you."

"Hell yeah, you can have her."

"Wait, wait, wait, you forgot to ask me if I was willing. I don't think I'd really enjoy being with a woman. I mean I've tried the kissing thing and all, but I don't know if I could, you know, go down there."

"You never know till you try." Jim retorted with both Hilga and Ethel agreeing emphatically. "You need to loosen up and get high. We're going to smoke a doobie. We've got this car to ourselves—we might as well get loopy." Jim had finally succeeded in getting Elizabeth high at Uncle G's. It was the cool thing to do, and Liz took four or five drags in her champagne gorged state. The problem was Liz was completely sober at this time, so she was not as easy prey as she had been a couple of nights before.

"We can't do that on the train—everyone will smell it. Are you crazy?"

"We'll open the window and light a cigarette at the same time. If someone comes storming through the door, the joint goes flying out the window, or someone can swallow it, and the cigarette remains to suppress the scent. That's the plan. Girls, are you in?" Jim's face brimmed with excitement over his plan. In all reality, he had little to no concern about being caught. They were on a train within the borders of Italy, so there would be no officials checking passports for border crossings, and the ticket takers had already given up trying to contain the hoards of people hours before. He had traveled enough in Western Europe that he believed smoking a joint was the status quo. He lit up the joint before Liz could object, took a huge puff filling his lungs to overflowing extracting a massive, never-ending cough that sold them out much more than the smell. He passed the joint directly to Liz as if she was an old pro. She quickly passed it to Hilga, who looked eager to share, without taking a toke herself.

"Don't worry about it Elizabeth; no one will possibly give a damn what we do in our little cabin here." Ethel said taking the joint and inhaling as if she was sucking in her most precious breath of the day. She kissed the joint three or four times after her initial inhale, pulling just a little more smoke into her expanded lungs each time. She chugged, coughed, spat just a little and let a cloud of smoke out that surrounded them all. She smiled and tried to hand the joint to Elizabeth again. This time Liz took it and put it to her lips, her eyes darting around as her mind was on the verge of a panicked frenzy. She took a tiny bit of smoke into her mouth and swallowed it like a parcel of food. She coughed two gurgling coughs, and handed the joint back to Jim with her eyes down as if she was ashamed of herself.

"Peer pressure's a bitch isn't it?" Jim said through hits of his own. "Here, take another hit and don't be such a pussy with it. Suck on it like it's Danny boy's you know what; give her a good hard pull."

Liz turned bright red at the comment. "You're a fucking asshole of the highest degree. I should take this thing and burn a hole through your eye socket."

"Just smoke it, don't get hostile."

She grabbed the joint defiantly and gave it a petite hit, blowing out a tiny cloud of smoke just seconds after taking it in.

Ethel took the joint from her and began to explain, "That's beautiful, honey, really, I'm glad you're participating. It will definitely chill you out, but take the smoke like this." She took a drag of several seconds, very slow and deliberate. "And hold it down in your rib cage like this." She said with held breath. "Keep it down for a little bit." She continued with held breath. "A little bit longer, let it absorb into every living cell in your lungs." She slowly exhaled the massive cloud of green smelling smoke. She handed the joint back to Liz as if giving the pupil the piece of chalk to demonstrate on the board. "Try it like that."

Liz took it back, enjoying the attention, and took another petite inhale, but this time she swallowed it like a gulp of water and held her breath with extreme diligence. She couldn't hold it for long because a cough tickled her into a mighty exhale involving some stray bullets of spittle. She was truly getting stoned for the first time, her senses began to blur, and she felt like she was on a carnival ride as the train swayed about. Her previous encounter had just multiplied her drunkenness, but this time she was truly getting the feeling of the peace pipe. Jim told her that now she was prepared to get in touch with her true spiritual self, and she probably wouldn't need the Clinique to feel good about herself; her natural beauty would overwhelm the exterior coating. "Smoking marijuana will make you closer with God, He appreciates it when you make use of the herbs that He has provided for us. One time I got so high that I saw God and he told me, "Keep smoking my brother." He had dreadlocks, he was black, and he had a big smile on his face. You may get to see him someday, too. If you stick with me, things can only get better."

The cabin billowed with smoke, but no one bothered them, and the joint burned to the tips of Jim's fingers before he threw it down his gullet and swallowed it with a gulp of beer. "I don't want it to fly through someone else's window." He said after the girls looked at him for an explanation for his caveman behavior. That answer was good enough, and everyone became glued to his or her seat. They stared out the window at the lovely Italian countryside and had happy conversations with the rolling fields of smiling flowers.

Chapter 10
ROMA

The girls and Jim reached Rome after a daylong train ride. The four travelers' eyes looked like the setting sun, and they were desperate to get settled and eat Italian food until they exploded. Ethel and Hilga went their own direction, as they had plans to stay with a friend who only had a small flat, but they vowed that they would see Jim and Liz at the boat to Greece later in the week.

Jim and Liz didn't waste any time finding a place to stay, ending up within a couple blocks of the train station in an inexpensive hotel that suited their needs. They were in Rome, and they both felt as if they had conquered the world with a buzz—their Roman vacation was about to take off. So much history, yet the contemporary city so full of life that it pulled its visitors in with a unique texture that encompassed all of time and history meeting up with the present in a collision bursting with energy. The couple let the city envelop them—they wanted to be a part of the city and not strangers from a far off land. They dumped their stuff quickly and headed out on foot in search of some authentic cuisine, or really just the first place that smelled good—they were starving.

They ended up strolling right past the Trevi Fountain as they searched for a place to eat. Jim said, "What's all the fuss about? Look at all the people. This must be some kind of famous Roman landmark, and we must find out its significance, my dear, after we eat though." They walked a block from the fountain and found a restau-

rant that had nice seats on a walking boulevard. The cost was probably more than they could afford, but the decision making process was
hampered by the drugs they had ingested throughout the day. They
popped in like they were meant to enjoy fine dining abroad, and they
were sophisticated travelers with a broad palate. Jim was dressed in
plaid shorts and a tee shirt with Elizabeth not exceeding his classy
style by much, but the restaurant was not interested in turning down
such an exciting pair. They were obviously there to spend some
money, so they were seated with a few looks of puzzlement by some
of the other patrons.

"Yeah, we don't really blend in here, babe, but if we act civilized, I
don't think they'll want to burn us at the stake."

Elizabeth was barely paying attention. She was experiencing severe
dry mouth and a ferocious appetite. She ordered a bottle of wine and
had the first course of a five-course meal on its way in no time. It
would be their only such meal on the trip. They had shown reasonable frugality up to this point, saving the majority of their money for
what seemed most necessary - alcohol - but one extravagant Italian
meal was needed to round out their experiences in Italy. The anti-
pasta and the bread were devoured to the very last crumb. After that,
the food came in waves with two bottles of wine needed to wash
down the never-ending Italian saga/meal.

"I think the waiter is concerned we are not going to pay; he always
keeps an eerie eye on us. Do you feel it?" Elizabeth asked after their
entrees had been served.

"Shit, I haven't looked up from the food since we got here. Let him
sweat, we'll kick back and relax after we eat. We'll both go use the
bathroom at different times— that'll keep him on his toes. We'll drag

it out till we're the last ones here, then give the bastard ten percent for looking at us like criminals. Sorry, I don't have a fucking dinner jacket since I'm backpacking across the damn continent—it's a little difficult to keep everything pressed."

"No, I don't want to give him a hard time. I don't want people to think of us like that."

"Are you kidding me? We're halfway around the world at a restaurant in a fucking alleyway. How far can this asshole's opinion get, and how many times in our lives do you think we'll be coming back to this place?"

"Americans have a bad enough reputation without us adding to it. We want to leave a good impression everywhere we go. That should be the feeling you get within yourself, some respect, you know."

"The street runs both ways there, sister. We should be treated like welcome guests, not suspected of foul play just because I might appear a little rough around the edges. I mean, he surely can't expect you to be any part of a foul plot; you're so beautiful and innocent. I think I'll have a talk with him and clear things up." Elizabeth just shook her head not thinking that he was serious, but when Jim motioned for the waiter, she instantly began to stutter in panic, "No, nnno, no."

When the waiter approached, Jim addressed him while Liz kept her eyes glued to her plate. "Dear sir, my friend and I were just noticing how you seem to look at us with some concern, but I want to ensure you that even though we look a little disheveled by our travels, we are a very respectable young couple who will definitely tend to our responsibilities when it comes to this meal. You need not look at us in a condescending or suspicious manner, even though I am quite rough looking, my looks don't reflect my nature. I will not jump the barrier with my girl in tow and flee from the bill. I'm sure that may have happened from this particular spot in the past, but I can assure you that we are not such hooligans." Luckily the waiter did not take offense to Jim's speech, but was amused by it and actually filled the couples' wineglasses while Jim was expressing himself.

"Very good honesty, signore. I like honesty and truthful very much. I lose fares from outside tables, yes, as I have to work inside and out at same time. Youngsters make quite fun by jumping the fence, even in fancy clothes and good demeanor, I have no idea and then I am yelled at, no good. I keep my eye out, nothing bad meant by it, but I not worry about you two now. You speak truth and I accept."

Jim looked at Liz and said, "See, it's better to confront your uneasiness instead of letting it ruin your dining experience. Now we have an understanding. He looked at the nametag on the waiter's jacket, "With Angelo here. He knows we're not out to get him and it's put him at ease. It's the deviant youth before us that made him leery." Liz shook her head in complete disbelief of the entire conversation and kept her head down, unwilling to check up on the true emotions of the situation.

They enjoyed the rest of their meal, after Liz kicked Jim under the table several times, and even finished the evening on good terms with Angelo. The gracious waiter directed them to some interesting nightlife that wasn't out of their league and gave them some good advice on how to experience Rome without being in a constant summer line. He got a twenty percent tip for his bravery and good service.

The meal was enough for the couple, and they spent a short time sitting at the Trevi Fountain, learning a little of its history and watching the people flow in and out of the site. They were tired from their long day of travel, and their stomachs were completely bursting with five full courses of Italian food and two sturdy bottles of wine. Elizabeth had come crashing down from her stoned buzz and was ready to go back to the room and get a good rest before taking on the city. They took a little extra walk on the way to the hotel, cutting down to the Tiber river to see a little more of the city, and then cutting back towards the train station to their humble, yet comfortable, hotel.

The next morning, the streets were buzzing with a mass of foreign tourists covering the sidewalks in all directions, while the locals darted around on their scooters avoiding misguided tourists like cones set up on an obstacle course. There weren't a lot of horns blasting, since most of the traffic was scooters, but there were large swathes of traffic circulating throughout the city. It wasn't just a tourist Mecca, but a working, thriving city of over two million people, which was doubled by the number of camera toting vacationers. The European family vacationers, the masses of youthful backpackers, and the buses of senior citizen tour groups turned the streets into a festive, chaotic place, where entertainment could be provided by simply engaging one's self with the mass of humanity.

Liz and Jim had no agenda for the day except to wonder the hollowed ground of St. Peter's Basilica. They would spend their day on foot staring at the Coliseum and working their way through the ancient Roman ruins until they reached St. Peter's Square. The day was bright blue and steaming hot, like many of their summer holidays had been, and they let the hot blue turn up their spirits as well. They followed the paths through the gleaming ruins of the Forum and other long forgotten Roman government structures. Jim was intrigued by the ancient buildings, both standing and dilapidated, and saw them as larger than life considering years of history courses with pictures of these exact areas as examples of a lost empire. Walking among the ruins was like visiting a place that had been visited many times in his imagination, and he was trying to connect the two in a way that made sense. Where were the togas? These people were dressed in designer clothes. The Roman Empire of old may have been dead, but as soon as they stepped into St. Peter's Square, it was revived and to a new, magnificent standard. St. Peters was more than any picture could completely detail; its presence alone made the Coliseum seem like a playground toy. Jim's camera snapped the sights, as well as the most interesting of characters, as they converged on the world's largest church.

As they mounted the steps to the gigantic church, they made note of many famous scenes they recognized from television including the quarters of the Pope, where he would wave to the masses in St. Peter's Square. They were quickly directed to a tour group led by an elderly English nun who was a very hospitable tour guide and brought the Basilica alive with the detailed history of every major piece of the Church. Jim wandered from the group with his camera amazed by the available light that could be used to make beautiful photographs without flash, which was strictly prohibited. Michelangelo had designed the church with large clear windows around the dome making an immaculate display of sunrays that poured in while the sun was high in the sky. Jim leaned against a column to steady his hand while he let his camera shutter stay open a little longer than normal so that the dark areas around the rays would have a chance to show some detail. These shots would be some of his most beautiful work from the entire trip, the sunrays slashing into the church highlighting the gift given by the divine.

The church itself did not represent Jim's spiritual side, but he felt very comfortable within it. Liz, on the other hand, was drinking the history and description of every part of the church by the lovely tour guide; she clung to her side and asked many questions. The tour continued for about an hour with Jim staying on the periphery, and Liz being the main patron. The camera shutter continued to snap at the amazing light that flooded the church and allowed Jim's camera to absorb as much intricate beauty as was allowed. The tour worked its way around the entire church finishing at another magical Michelangelo creation, The Pieta, the statue of Mary holding the dead body of Jesus across her lap. The statue was guarded behind a bulletproof barrier because someone had attacked the beautiful creation with a hammer and had caused some damage. The tour came to a close with both Jim and Elizabeth truly enjoying their time in St. Peters. Liz was amazed at how much Jim enjoyed himself even though they had to take part in a tour group, which Jim usually shunned—actually, he had gotten quite friendly with the savvy nun by the end of the tour.

"That place is amazing, that unbelievable light. All the other old churches we have been in have nothing but stained glass—it makes them so dark and dreary. That place is so huge that it needs light, and for Michelangelo to understand the concept of that space before it was built is amazing. It brought the place so much more life. The beauty is there too; don't get me wrong. That's what makes the light so useful displaying all the exquisite detail that comprises every inch of that structure. The light seemed like it was designed to reflect off certain points, like the gold behind the altar with the eagle; it was glimmering and almost looked alive. That place was really amazing. I guess we'll have to see the Sistine Chapel as well. I'm amazed at this Michelangelo guy—he's everywhere in Italy, and everything he did is completely remarkable. He must have been God's artist. There had to be some kind of divine connection. Did you love the tour or what—it's a really magnificent place, right?"

"Yeah, I'm happy! It's your turn—lead us wherever you wish. I'll definitely be content the rest of the day." Elizabeth replied as they marched down the steps into St. Peter's Square.

"Let's just check out the city. We don't need any appointments or schedules. Let it take us where it may, forward, never straight, but forward."

"I knew it would be something like that; you're probably going to lead us to a bar." Liz said playfully.

"My dear, we must study the people as well as the places where the artistes are most likely drowning their aching thirsts. We must find the artists, the poets, the painters, and the starving photographers wrestling with their demons. There is much more than just a bar in front of us. We must be willing to discover the essence of the people, the hearts of the artists, and the souls of the common folk. All these things may be found in a bar, yes—you have to see it as more than just plaster and stale beer." Jim explained as he twirled around the square telling his story while dancing to his own beat. Liz grabbed his hand, and they made a waltz out of a summer day in Rome. Jim finished the maneuvers with a delicate spin and a soft dip, putting his lips close enough to feel the breath of Elizabeth.

They walked the boulevards of Rome in a random, unhurried pace, finally settling on a restaurant with a perfect view of the city street

as the world passed by. Jim was thirsty, so the lunch extended into
a relaxing drinking session for him, while Elizabeth checked out the
shops in the nearby area. They were having a pleasant day in Rome,
not getting bogged down in the drama that sometimes managed to put
a wedge between them. They allowed each other space without com-
menting or demanding the other's attention. It was a pleasant existence without any stress or expectations. Jim was in a carefree mood,
which rubbed off on Liz, and let the two adjust to the world separately.
Jim made some concessions giving Liz half of each day, the morning
jaunt through St. Peters being her half for this particular day, and the
second half of the day, she would have to provide willing accompaniment to whatever Jim chose to do. The next day, they would try to see
the Sistine Chapel in the afternoon after he was granted the morning
to schedule whatever he wished. The only thing was that Jim preferred
to never make a schedule, but to enjoy each location as it presented
itself, going wherever savvy suggestions took him. That day, his wandering techniques brought them to the Gallery of Modern Art and the
Zoology gardens, which were all part of the beautiful Villa Borghese, a
large park on a hill overlooking the whole city.

The climb up the hill was just a natural progression of Jim trying to
find the best spot to make good pictures of the city. Once in the park,
they realized that they had stumbled on serenity within the madness.
The park was calm, and people were lounging and strolling like they
do in parks, while the buzzing of the city gave way to the sound of the
breeze and a dog or two barking. They continued around the outer
edge of the park, as Jim was making pictures of different angles of
Rome, and eventually they ran into the Gallery of Modern Art and
the Zoological Gardens. The random wandering had been a success-

ful technique in creating a perfectly interesting day. They marveled at some of the world's finest art without having to wait in line or fight big crowds. From the museum, they entered the Zoological Gardens and began to wander around the paths with some of the most exotic creatures in the world. Jim took the opportunity to light up a marijuana cigarette while Liz was meandering down a different path. He didn't want to involve her because he knew she would make quite a fuss about him lighting up in public, especially a zoo full of children and concerned adults. But Jim was sly and no one was around, so he lit the joint, took a couple massive hits, quickly extinguished it, and replaced it with a French cigarette. "Nothing better than a buzz when in communion with a Hippo." Jim thought while watching the massive animal smelling another giant hippo's butt.

Jim's trip had made quite a bit of headway, and adding Elizabeth to the equation was working out, although, he hadn't quite won her over like he had hoped. He still had time, especially with the Greek islands yet to come, but he wasn't as concerned about it after being shot down so frequently. He really didn't understand her and had given up trying to get in her head. She had given him just a hint of a taste, and then given some random stranger the same taste, so he knew that he hadn't earned anything too sacred. He wasn't going to make any bets on getting her to suddenly roll over, drop her pants, and profess her love for him. Elizabeth had baffled him with her individual perspective on the way things should be, but her beauty and spirit still intrigued him and drove him crazy with longing.

They came back together in the wonderful maze of pristine gardens with Peacocks scurrying on one side, and Zebras lounging in the shade on the other. Even with the cigarette, Liz could smell the slight scent of marijuana that graced Jim's skin and clothing like permeating cologne.

"You're nuts lighting up that stuff just anywhere. You think you're some kind of modern day hippie, don't you? You sure look like one." Liz stated with a puzzled, questioning look smeared to her face. Why had Jim grown his hair so long and ignored his appearance when in the past he was always clean-cut and impeccably dressed. His appearance had changed the way she perceived him, but he hadn't changed underneath the odd skin—he was still the same carefree, kindhearted man, who gently massaged her back, while telling of his wild life back in their younger days. She wasn't sure if his new grunge style bothered her or not. She wasn't sure if she wanted a bad boy, especially one that wore it like a proud coat. Her English lover was superbly manicured with the most refined manners and vices that stayed within the acceptable realms of society. He got pissed quite often, but he didn't smoke pot at zoos or snort cocaine in Portuguese bars. The two men were so far removed from each other that Elizabeth had no way to measure them against one another and was much more comfortable in the safe world that her English aristocrat provided for her. She liked the bourgeois life, not the bohemian, but she loved Jim in a way that she couldn't quite grasp.

"You can call me what you like. I am what I am, and I find no insult in your words, but my appearance and my extracurricular activities cannot stereotype me. I'm not a hippie, a deviant or even a rock star, although I would like to be; I'm just Jimmy, the man with the true heart who loves every breath he takes and almost everyone he meets. I am evolving to what the universe desires of me, a product the kind planet earth, who tends to live every second with nothing but love for it all. Now, if a little marijuana helps me achieve such goals, hallelujah!" Jim replied beginning to skip through the park like a small child. Liz loved him in such a mood and was easily shifted from concern to joy; his recklessness faded and was forgotten.

It was a fine day in Rome with everything proceeding smoothly. The couple walked around the entire Villa Borghese and ended up lead back into the city by descending down the famous Spanish Steps. Jim didn't know the story of the steps, but Liz explained a famous scene from a movie where Fred Astair was dancing, and Jim could picture the scene and began to do his own jig. The tourists chuckled at the outrageous American spinning and dancing among all the people sitting on the steps, but the locals moved to the sides in fear that the large lumbering man might misstep. Liz shielded her eyes and sat down on the steps ignoring her traveling mate in hopes that others would not associate them, but when he reached the bottom and started calling for her, she had to claim him even though she felt like running back in the park and hiding.

"You can't embarrass me in front of half of Rome, you're completely insane!" She said as she quickly skirted by him at the bottom of the stairs.

"Dance with me, my dear. We are in Rome and are meant to dance, drink wine, and make love." Jim was being dramatic and silly—it was natural and fun.

"You wish." Liz said to the reference of sharing each other's bodily fluids.

"Hey! Look! There's a McDonalds, the Spanish steps and McDonalds, what a strange mix. I think we should try a Roman McDonalds.

What do you think?" Jim asked already heading for the door of the burger joint.

"Sure, get us off this street, since everyone is staring at us." They walked in the door of the very sheik McDonalds. The interior was marvelously modern and quite upscale for a burger joint. The floors and walls were made of dark marble, or something made to look like it, giving it a palatial feeling. The place may have looked quite classy with its exquisite interior architecture, but at the head of the restaurant on the marble countertops were the same McDonalds cash registers, with the same mix of young and old attendants with funny hats, and the same soggy wax covered paper cups carrying the beverages to the tables. The fries were still cooked in animal fat, whether they admitted it or not, and the burgers were still tiny little discs of beef hidden in fluffy buns and condiments. They ordered their food and brought their bagged grub back to the Spanish steps to eat it along with many of the Italian youth.

The day was winding down, and they were ending it with a much less complex meal than the previous night. Burgers and fries on the Spanish Steps—who would have thought it. They roamed the streets well into the evening hours stopping to have a drink and watch a wedding procession performing a unique ritual at the Trevi Fountain. The crowd cheered the bride and groom as they made some kind of wedding day wishes. The whole wedding party was gathered around the fountain all decked out in their tuxedos and once-in-a-lifetime dresses. The many colors of lights in the water, and the way they worked off the spraying streams made for a poetic backdrop to the ruckus wedding party. People were gathered all around the amphitheater seating trying to catch a glimpse of what was happening. Jim and Liz corked a bottle of wine at a nearby store and made a toast to the marrying couple with their paper glasses, which the shop owner had so politely donated to them. The wine sat on the burgers quite well, and the day ended with general satisfaction from the European traveling duo.

The next morning, they woke early after a full night's rest. As soon as they walked outside the hotel, they were immediately drawn to a scooter-renting operation with a very charismatic salesman pushing his services in the streets. Within minutes, Jim and Liz were strapped on a brand new shiny red scooter with plenty of scoot. Now, whether this was at all safe or not was not of much consequence and was not reviewed by either of the travelers very consciously. They just strapped on their little helmets and got on their death trap of a vehicle and sped away. The population of Rome was expert at operating high-powered scooters, and Jim believed that his many years on snowmobiles was plenty of preparatory experience to operate such a device on the trails otherwise known as the Roman avenues. He had no fear, and Elizabeth was almost giddy as she put her arms around her trusted chauffeur. The scooter company had given them an excellent map of Rome and the surrounding areas, which Jim shoved in his pocket, and then they made way for the hills.

They were immediately drawn to the congested streets of the city center, making there way to the promenade in front of St. Peter's Square. From there, Jim guided the scooter to a more remote road, which extended around the Vatican heading up a steep grade. Jim had raced through the city streets weaving through traffic and using his high-powered scooter to beat the others off the line at the traffic lights. He drove like a seasoned Roman, not letting the sea of

scooters in front of the cars at each light intimidate him. The remote terrain was much more exhilarating because the scooter wasn't
hemmed in and could breathe and move much quicker. As they
skirted up the hills, Liz began to laugh uncontrollably at the danger
they had lived through and barely noticed. "The city was completely
insane—they drive like maniacs shot out of cannons. We better not
tell our mothers we did this." She giggled into Jim's ear.

"We're perfectly safe, my dear; you have absolutely nothing to
worry about with me at the controls. Our mothers would be proud
that we can adjust to anything. Well, maybe not, but what they don't
know won't hurt them. I say, we haul all the way to the ocean and
check out the beach. What do you think?" Jim asked with his head
swiveled back, but his eyes still half on the road.

"You're driving." Liz replied with a carefree spirit. So the scooter
pushed up the hill extending to the west, or at least what felt like
west, as far as Jim was concerned. He got his original bearings from
taking a quick peak at the map at the scooter rental place using St.
Peters as his landmark. He stopped at the top of the hill overlooking the majestic city, new and old splintered together in a functional
unit, and pulled out the map from his pocket to see if it was feasible
to take the scooter to the sea. He and Elizabeth decided they would
go for it since they were enjoying the ride, and they wanted to see
more than just the city center.

The scooter shot up to fifty, sixty, even seventy kilometers-per-
hour without a hiccup, and they had a smooth ride to the seashore.
The sun was raining down on them, and the traffic was split with
quick bursts of scooter speed. They parked the scooter at a seaside
parking lot and locked it to a pole with the chain and lock, provided

by the rental agency. Liz carried Jim's daypack, which carried her bathing suit, Jim's camera, and some of Elizabeth's essential make-up and grooming tools. Jim had mentioned the possibility of heading to the beach that morning, which caused the packing of the daypack accordingly. Liz headed off to the beachside bathroom to change, while Jim waited on a bench. The beach was packed with tourists and Italians alike. The Mediterranean Sea produced short waves that lightly slapped the shore and made for exciting water play for the little ones. The beach was somewhat coarse, much like Barcelona, but once in the water the ocean floor was smoother. Jim couldn't help but to compare each beach with the Portuguese Algarve and its deep, soft sand that made for the best sort of barefooted beach strolling.

The playful spirit of the beach grabbed hold of Liz and Jim as they began to stroll down the waterfront ankle deep in the surf. They walked for miles, getting further and further from the masses even though the beaches would stay populated throughout. They caught themselves holding hands from time to time, the comfort of each other leading them to need one another's touch. From a distance they looked like lovers lost in their environment, lost in each other, not needing a constant dialogue yet always communicating. They dropped their stuff from time to time and took swims in the cool water to cool off from the powerful midsummer Italian sun. When they got in the water, Jim wanted to embrace his traveling partner with her legs wrapped around him as he stood up to his shoulders in water. But he couldn't force her actions, and he couldn't even imagine what she was thinking. He wanted to kiss her with the taste of saltwater on her lips and explore the curves of her body under the secret blanket of the sea. She, on the other hand, wasn't thinking of physical attraction, she was thinking of her emotional connection with a man that was so mysterious she couldn't possibly succumb to him. She avoided looking directly into his longing—keeping her eyes from entangling with his desire. He wanted her so bad, but remained the friend, only engaging in physical contact upon her lead.

As they continued walking down the beach, they ran into a charming stone building surrounded by a meter high stone fence and looked like it had grown up out of the sand. Upon closer inspection, Liz noticed three women dressed in long skirts.

"I believe this is a convent." She said as the ladies approached a gate in the fence that lead to the beach, and as they came closer, it became very clear that the women were indeed nuns dressed in long white habits.

"I wonder if they have their swimsuits on under those." Jim said loud enough for the women to hear.

"We swim in the nude." One of the nuns replied, giving Jim a startle that she spoke at all and in such clear English too.

"I don't think nuns should talk to such a horrible sinner as me. I'm not worthy of your good humor." Jim said sharing the same good nature with the quick-witted nun.

"Are you children lost? You're quite a ways from home, aren't you?"

"Actually, my friend here was thinking about becoming a nun, and someone told us about this here beach convent, said it was the best convent in the world and all, nestled right up on the beach. So my friend and I took off from America in search of the convent on the beach, and here we are. I guess I'll just leave her with you ladies and be on my way. I think I would take her straight to confession if possible. She probably needs to clear up a couple things with the big guy." Jim succeeded in turning Elizabeth red, but the nuns didn't take his sarcasm in a negative way and kept up the charade.

"So she wants to be a nun, does she? Well then, toss her over the wall, and we'll take care of her." The nun, who was obviously from the east coast of the United States by her accent, exclaimed, as she held out her arms as if to catch Liz.

"He's insane, I really shouldn't bring him out in public. That's why I try to keep the places that I'm seen with him to distant countries. We drove a scooter here from Rome, and we're just enjoying our day on the beach. This is a really beautiful building, so we just came up to get a closer look. I must say, this is a pretty fantastic place to be a nun—I mean if I really had any intentions of becoming a nun, I would definitely like to be at this spot." Liz exclaimed with the red draining from her face and the comfort of meeting new friends beginning to sink in. The American nun was in a group of three, her being the only one truly proficient in English; she was also taller and younger than her two companions. She came up and leaned on the stone fence exposing her kind, chiseled features and her sturdy figure, including a large bosom that pushed her robe out from an otherwise thin figure. Her hair was barely visible, but her light eyebrows exposed the fact that she was naturally blonde. She was quite stunning and drew Jim's complete attention as she began a conversation with Elizabeth. Jim had no couth when it came to his thoughts; he was able to begin undressing the nun in his mind without any moral objections. As they got closer to the woman, Jim thought that they were truly meeting an angel. The inviting, open nature of the nun made her float in her flowing robe. Her older attendants kept their distance as the beautiful nun engaged the couple as if they were long lost friends.

"I haven't seen any Americans in a while, as not many wander down this far on the beach. Usually when people see nuns, they back away and leave us be—it's as if they fear us. I like to talk to others, though. Sometimes I even walk the beach to find some interesting conversation. Our order is not as strict as some, and I'm even allowed to go into Rome quite often. So where are you two from? Are you enjoying Italy?"

Liz replied as Jim gawked, "We're from the northwest, Washington State, not Seattle, the other side of the state. I did go to school in Seattle, though, and Jim goes to school in Oregon. I've been at Oxford for half the year, and he just decided to come bum around Europe. I've joined him to add some culture to his diet. We grew up together, and we're trying to remain friends while traveling together. I'm Elizabeth by the way." She stuck out her hand to the sister.

"I'm Olivia from New York. I love the northwest, though. I traveled through there when I was in college. I spent an entire summer in Seattle volunteering at a convent, a beautiful place in the heart of the city. I taught a summer camp for children with the nuns and became intrigued by their lifestyle. So my choice to become a nun really came from my experiences in Seattle, what a coincidence, huh?" Olivia's distinct accent was expressed in a much softer tone than most New Yorkers. The other two nuns had scuttled away from the interaction, too shy to converse with the half-naked tourists. Olivia, on the other hand, was open to the whole world, unwilling to be included in any stereotype, yet still very comfortable in her role.

"You are an absolutely stunning woman. I'm sorry my mind is always processing the visual evidence first and, your beauty is captivating. I just had to comment, I'm not trying to get fresh or anything, but when I first saw you, I was sure you were an angel. Sorry, I'll get on with it. So, what is it like being a nun anyway? Are you committed to this thing for life,or can you put in a couple years and move on? I can always help you get re-assimilated if you choose to move on. I'll come back and pick you up on one of these rocket scooters like the one we've got today, and we'll shoot off into the sunset."

"So you two aren't sweet on each other?" Olivia asked ignoring Jim's strange comments.

"She's in love with someone else, and my natural born charm isn't winning her over."

"Well, I believe I will be a nun my entire life, and I don't think your charm will have much luck in changing that either. God's charm is much more unique; you are quite predictable."

"He is. He thinks of one thing, well maybe two, and both of them are sinful behaviors. I'm trying to lead him in the right direction, sister, but he is incorrigible. His mind stays in the gutter, and he is quick to load toxins into his body. He really does need to find the light; he's a lost soul. Do you think you might be able to help him?" Liz expressed, with a smirk on her face, enjoying making Jim the butt of the conversation.

"Wait a second here, I'm not a lost soul, and I'm very secure in my spiritual self. I do sin on occasion, but have no problem asking for and receiving forgiveness. I'm not really sure that we as humans can define sin anyway—at least I believe it is used for too broad of terms and always with someone pointing it out with their sinful fingers.

If human beings are defined as sinful creatures, which one among us gets to clarify who's in the right, and who's in the wrong? I feel confident that God is the pure life force within me, and I understand that force requests a certain direction out of me, which sometimes I ignore in order to appease my physical self. In the process, I neglect my temple, but again there is forgiveness available for such lost souls. I love the world and the people in it without stereotypes or divisions. I feel quite sure there is meaning to every second I exist and have little fear I will rot in the ground with my spirit dead for eternity. I am forever an optimist with some morbid thoughts and actions, but otherwise, out for the good of the whole, if my flesh isn't crawling with too much desire. Maybe that's rarely, but I do digress." Jim talked himself in a circle, but the grin on his face expressed he was happy with his tirade.

"I'm not much of a proselytizer, and I'm no saint either. I've become a nun because it felt right to give my life to something I believe in and never turn back. I am what I am, and you are what you are. What I'm trying to say is that I can't change you with a second's encounter or even with a weeks long moral teaching. I don't have the answers to do that. I can tell you to ignore your flesh and live for God, but how many steps would you take like that, and would I really want that for you, a life like mine? I assume you are happy in your own skin; at least you come off that way— and that can lead to a greater understanding of people and all the love they possess. Your charm is an asset. Your comments on my appearance are well taken, and I can only assume that your intentions are to make others feel good about themselves—this characteristic is a virtue. The purity in your heart is felt permeating from your wide-open smile, and I'm sure that your morbid side isn't that far from natural." Olivia stated in a flowing, almost musical voice, never removing her slate blue eyes from Jim, as he turned red trying to return her kind gaze.

"You're giving him way too much credit Olivia. He's a wolf in sheep's clothing. Actually, he looks like a wolf in wolf's clothing, so I don't know why you're giving him so much leeway." Elizabeth stated trying to bring some reality into the conversation.

"How about joining us Olivia? We're going to keep on strolling down the beach. We'll just go a little ways and then flip back here." Jim asked.

"No, I'm sorry, I can't. We have a full day ahead inside; we just had a short break to get some air. We're in the middle of studying the saints, and it's quite intense, so you can't let your mind get too far off track. It was very nice meeting you. It's good to see my fellow countrymen learning about the world. I'm not so sure that you two don't belong together, though. You would make a beautiful couple." Olivia said as she squeezed both Liz and Jim's hands.

"That's what I say, but she's set on some English guy. I think she believes he will behave better in public; he's already potty-trained and what not."

"Don't listen to him Olivia. It was wonderful to meet you, and you might want to pray for us a little—we're probably going to need it." Elizabeth said with a satisfied look on her face. Olivia made her way back to the convent. Her two friends were already indoors. She waved at the door with one last gesture of her gentle spirit.

"Who would of thought it, a nun from New York on a Roman beach, prophesizing that I will probably be the savior of man, or the second savior of man as it may be."

"What? She didn't say anything that could have possibly led you to that conclusion."

"What are you talking about? Were you a part of the same discussion I just took part in, or were you off somewhere else?" She said I was virtuous, pure of heart, and I would probably extend an immaculate love all through humanity. This love, my dear, will be the savior of man. See—God is love, and it is my job to spread that love, like Olivia said, with my pure heart and kind intentions. She saw the real me; maybe you should pay closer attention." Jim grabbed Liz's butt at the end of his statement. "See, love pats, I'm spreading the love already."

"Boy, you sure can twist words and drop them on their heads in some new configuration. I'm pretty sure that her kind words didn't offer any implication that your are going to be the next savior."

"But wouldn't it be a lot more fun if they did. Won't you ride along on my rocket ship? We'll go to heaven and back, and I'll open your eyes to a whole new world. Don't be scared; I've got plenty of fuel." Jim exclaimed as he pulled out another of his potent marijuana sticks supplied by his friends from Florence. Elizabeth passed, preferring the crystal clear day, which she was truly enjoying. She made no judgements or complaints and allowed Jim his freedom as long as he didn't demand her to join him. She had become used to him breaking the law in public, and her nerves had become a little more acceptant although they still twinged a bit. They existed in each other's space for a while in southern Italy, neither crowding nor forcing the other out of their comfort zone—there was balance for an instant.

The scooter fired back up as the day hit its hottest point since the couple had had their fill of salt water and steaming hot pebbles. They sped back to Rome with the hot breeze stinging their parched skin.

Their plan was to make a tourist stop by the Sistine Chapel before intoxicating themselves with Italian food and wine. They arrived at the Chapel in the late afternoon, locked up the scooter, and added themselves to a lengthy line. Further up the line they could see a couple furiously waving at them, so they walked up outside the rope to see who it was. The newlywed couple, Eric and Mona, from Florence, was already entrenched in the line.

Eric excitedly commented, "You two are completely insane to be riding around on that scooter. Those things are death traps. Please, go return it immediately and use the public transportation, like reasonable people. Are you both drunk, or what?"

"Scooter travel is the only way to go, man. You can't be shy or polite; you gotta get on the gas and leave the suckers in the dust. We drove that bad boy all the way to the beach; she's the Harley of Roma, and she'll beat a car off the blocks every time. We didn't get on any freeways, just the scenic country route, it was phenomenal."

"This is amazing, seeing you two here. We should get together tonight—it's meant to be." Liz added.

"I don't think you two will make it from back there. They're fixing to close down. We might get in. The line is moving really slowly; they only let a few people in at a time. As some come out, they let some in, but it's been a very slow go so far." Eric explained.

"Do you want to meet at the Trevi in a couple of hours and have dinner, actually about an hour and a half—what do you think?" Liz asked. Eric and Mona agreed, and Jim and Liz headed to their scooter, not really disappointed that they had bumped into their friends.

"It's my turn to drive." Elizabeth exclaimed as they were unhooking the scooter.

"You want me to hold on to your little ass on our way right into the heart of the city? What if I get a boner? Is that going to throw you off? I'm with you, baby. You drive. It's just the gas and the brake—don't mix em up." Jim said letting Liz take the drivers position.

"You're going to let me, no shit. Okay, I can do this. If you can do it, I can do it. You're half fried; at least I'm sober."

"Here," Jim turned on the engine, "Try it without me on back first and get a feel for her before I jump on there." Liz jumped on, hit the gas like a pro, and jetted off up the hill returning in an instant ready for her passenger. They sped down the hill into the busy streets near rush hour with Liz at the helm. Jim put his arms around his pilot and licked her neck just for effect. She kept her eyes forward and let the wind dry the saliva. She had entered a war zone of scooter traffic, and she was the one they were all gunning for, the American girl with the stoner on the back. Weaving in and out of traffic, almost careening off a couple cars as other scooters pushed her around, Elizabeth fearlessly maneuvered the speedy red scooter. Jim sat on the back making gestures to other drivers, warning them to keep their distance, like a moving traffic cop looking out for the better interests of his driver. Liz sped out of traffic and into the Bourghese to have another look at the beautiful park and spend some time at the top of the hill, which provided a wonderful vista of the city they had conquered. They had braved the hoards of scooters and had maneuvered like experts, but they still were not going to share the experience with their mothers. Within the park, they were able to catch a clean breath of air, away from the emissions of the jam-packed city. They harassed a fellow backpacker to take their picture while cozily wrapped around

each other on the scooter with Liz at the controls. Jim held on as if
fearing for his life, which wasn't the reality as Liz had done a fine job.

The scooter was returned before the couple made their way to the
Trevi to meet with their old friends, well not exactly old, but not brand
new either. It was an extreme coincidence running into them, but
did make some sense because most outsiders would converge on the
Sistine Chapel at some point while in Rome. The night the two couples
had shared in Florence was very much a pleasure, and there was no
reason not to repeat such an occasion. The night didn't go off quite
as smoothly, though. When Eric and his new bride showed up at the
fountain, they were hardly speaking and both wore serious frowns.
Eric had had his wallet stolen while exiting the Sistine Chapel, of all
places, and he had just turned a large amount of travelers' checks into
currency leaving them out of cash and completely bummed.

"Can you believe that, leaving the Vatican? A big crowd bumping and jostling and someone lifted my wallet—I'm sure it was there
because we haven't run into anyone since then. The son of a bitch
picked my pocket in the holiest place I've ever set foot in. I sure
wasn't expecting that, perfect spot for the bloody bastards, though.
We'll have to pass on going out tonight; I've got to take care of can-
celing a credit card I had in there. Good thing I left the rest of them
and the rest of my travelers' checks in the hotel safe just in case
something like this happened. You here lots of stories, so you prepare, but you never really think that you will be the target."

"Yeah, you two look clean-cut and loaded. You should let yourself
go like me, and then they think you're a fucking bum and leave you
alone. I don't think you guys should give up on the night, though.
Just go back to the hotel, take care of the credit card, grab another

and enjoy the evening out with us. No reason to let the crooks ruin your holiday. I've actually got a cure for what ails you. If you'd like to numb the pain of your loss, I've got several finally rolled marijuana cigarettes straight from the heart of Italy."

"Yes that's exactly what we need," Mona exclaimed, "and don't be a square, Eric. You know you like to get high every once in a while. Come with us back to our hotel, and we can smoke in our room. It won't take but five minutes to call the credit card company. I've lost one of Eric's cards before, and it's no big deal. He's right, sweetie. We can't let the criminals ruin our holiday." Eric just shook his head as if he was confused by the whole matter and not really sure if drugs would improve their situation, but he gave into the plans without a fight. The friends hustled back to the hotel to take care of business and medicate. They had already told their story to authorities at the Vatican, who promised to contact them at their hotel if anything turned up. Eric had been smart by leaving all his personal items in the safe so the only loss was a couple hundred pounds worth of currency and the one credit card; his passport had been in his front pocket.

The phone call was made regarding the theft, and Mona called down and ordered some champagne to get the night started and drown the sorrows of the day. The two bottles of chilled bubbly soon arrived, and the first top was popped quickly. The liquid gold was poured generously into each elegant glass. After the attendant left, Jim went to the door of the room and stuffed the crack under the door with a towel preventing the pungent order of what he was about to light waft under the door. Eric and Mona were on their honeymoon, so the accommodations were exclusive, and their honeymoon suite had a view of the river and the great dome of St. Peters.

Jim lit the joint and passed it to Mona immediately as she was the most excited about the prospect of getting high. "My family grew their own plants in Switzerland. On the farm, we always had five or six gigantic plants with their luscious odor rushing through the autumn air. My brothers would cut them down in the fall and hang them in the loft of the barn, and they would last us until the next fall. Even as a child, I liked the smell, and when I first smoked with my big brother when I was thirteen, a woman he said, I so enjoyed the taste of that aroma. It has become something almost spiritual for my family, getting in a circle to smoke—everyone does it, even mom. The first time Eric joined us, he thought we were completely out there, some hippie family from the Swiss countryside, but he has grown to feel the connection as well. My father always told us that marijuana was a peaceful plant from the earth and not to categorize it as a drug. He said that human hands must process it to be a drug, and we should avoid such substances. He also liked wine because the grapes came from the earth even though the alcohol was a little poisonous if drunk in excess. Stay away from the chemicals of the cities, he would say; they have no good direction, no peace." The joint fueled Mona during her entire speech, taking three huge hits in-between the recollection of her fond memories.

"How about passing that to your husband, my dear? You speak of the family circle, but I believe they have strict rules about taking a hit and passing." Eric commented, coming up behind his wife and placing a soft kiss on her cheek while reaching around and taking the joint from her hand.

"I've got plenty." Jim said. "Smoke as much as you like. Smoke until you're cross-eyed and fish-lipped, and then we'll go bump some uglies with some Romans. I think we need to go out and dance to-night, get high, and go out and boogie till we drop."

Elizabeth folded under the pressure as Eric passed her the joint; she hit it, gagged, coughed, and passed it to Jim who wore a huge grin of appreciation for his friend's efforts. "She's coming around. My little dove never smoked a thing until this trip. I think your spiritual speech tilted the balance in her mind towards the smoking side; it was so genuinely pro-marijuana. She hasn't shown a lot of enthusi-asm for my lifestyle and wants to maintain her own character, which I believe is a little too rigid. Getting high, my dear, is a way of life. You don't have to buy-in completely, but I want you to get a glimpse of the generosity and peace involved in all my clouds of smoke. It is not simply a distraction from the cruel intentions of others—it is a standard for communicating in a completely free environment where your personal hang-ups are blown out with the first exhale. Now, don't get me wrong. Some people's hang-ups get magnified when they get high, and they get paranoid and delusional. Such people should probably back out of the circle."

The joint had made the full circle and was back to Elizabeth. She took much greater care this time, touching the paper to her lips and inhaling slowly and steadily, not pulling too hard as to extract a cough, but keeping a good steady glow going, until her virgin lungs burst under the pressure, and she choked and coughed and spat and doubled over laughing at her own outburst.

"That's my girl; you're already a pro. Take a drink of that there champagne, a little chaser for your troubles." Jim exclaimed beam-ing with adoration. The joint was puffed to oblivion, and another was gingerly ingested; everyone started to float. The room became a smoky dungeon with Eric and Mona sprawled out on their bed, Jim doing snow angels on the carpet, and Elizabeth staring at herself in the mirror concerned that she was melting.

"I think I did too much." Liz said. "Can you overdose on weed, because I'm pretty sure that this is as messed up as I've ever been from any substance."?

"You'll be okay. Come lie down with us, you need to relax a little. The world is soft right now; don't try to analyze it—just let it be." Mona gently explained waving Liz towards the bed. Liz dragged her feet over to the bed and dived onto the mattress causing everyone to giggle. "Now you got the hang of it—just let yourself go."

"We must not vegetate too long." Jim said. "There are places to go and worlds to be conquered. Rome is ours for the night, and we must not let this small sliver of time pass us by. Everyone, down the champagne, and we will march on. A good buzz should be shared with the world. We must exchange greetings with the natives. We must leave Rome a small piece of our legacy—just one outrageous exchange with its ancient walls."

"Coo, Coo." Sprung from Liz's head buried in a pillow. She then rose up, "You're insane if you think I can go into public without looking completely retarded."

"He's right. We can't allow ourselves to vegetate; we must take on the city with our heightened senses. We are not retarded—we are special. We have partook of the magic fruit, and now we must share our vision with the world." Eric exclaimed popping up off the bed with his finger in the air as if making a profound point. "Elizabeth, we shall go on an adventure. Do not fear your state—embrace it. We will be there for you; don't worry."

"I'm high as a kite and ready to fly." Jim stated with exuberant joy. Eric was already washing his face in cold water as if preparing to make his way to the outside world. Mona was sitting on the side of the bed rubbing Elizabeth's back encouraging her to face the night. Jim was doing push-ups on the floor to get the blood flowing and to keep himself from falling off the ledge to lazy.

"I can't go out like this. I've still got beach sand in-between my butt cheeks." Liz stated without embarrassment.

Mona quickly came to the rescue, "You can take a quick shower here, and I've got plenty of clothes that will fit you. I've got enough stuff for any taste, plus you'll feel a lot better after a shower; it will refresh you."

"Hey, do you mind if I jump in with you? I'm pretty sure I've got sand in-between my butt cheeks too, and I can help you reach the spots that you might have a little trouble getting to."

"Jimmy, you will not fondle my naked body. You will not succeed in getting me drugged up and taking advantage of me. He's been trying to do that this whole trip—he has no shame."

Mona was already placing different outfits on the bed next to Liz, pushing her ever so slightly to get on the same page with the group and embrace the idea of engaging the city. "Come on, sweetheart, let's get you cleaned up and ready. Don't worry, I'll protect you from the silly man." Mona dragged Liz off the bed and pulled her into the suite-sized bathroom with the oval tub and the stand-up shower.

Jim and Eric poured more champagne and toasted to their women. Jim joked about his frustrating relationship with the beautiful Liz, and explained he could no longer allow his emotions to be so affected by how their relationship was moving along. "It is what it is, you know. She ties me up in little knots. Whenever I think I've got her figured out, I get myself a little untangled, and bam; she grabs both ends and jerks me tighter. What I want from her, and what she wants from me are two different things. They keep colliding and knocking each other off coarse, so neither gets what they want. Eventually, we'll strangle each other or maybe we'll just leave one another alone. What do you think Eric? She's definitely worth pursuing, don't you think?"

"Don't bang your bloody head against the wall, mate. If she's going to make it hard for you, keep your eyes open and lasso you some European beauties."

"I've had my share of them before I met back up with her. Shit, I even ended up shacked up with one at her place back in Oxford. She came home with her man, and there were four of us in one bed—it was fucking brilliant, really. I'm sure that image is still clear in her mind too, and that's why she is being so bloody difficult. Maybe I don't deserve her because of my complete lack of morals, but for some reason I always thought we'd end up together—that it would just come natural, and I wouldn't have to fight for it. I'm not really ready for any kind of commitment or anything. I want at least another five years to run wide open. Maybe she'll burn through this English guy in due time, but it looks like she's planning on getting married, and I can't see that being productive for our relationship. My vision of being able to snap my fingers five years from now, after my body and mind are tired of raging, and have her show up at my doorstep ready and willing doesn't fit well with her agenda. Either I'll have to take her away or let her go, and I figure by the end of this trip, I'll know which way to go."

"You think you can take her by force if needed, eh mate. I commend you for your confidence. She is a little feisty and I'm pretty sure you've got your hands full." Eric verbally expressed, but deep down he believed they would end up together. Their chemistry was a natural yin and yang. Eric couldn't see how two people who didn't want to be together would travel through Italy and the Greek Islands together. They were in serious denial—at least Elizabeth was.

The hot summer night embraced the four as they left the swanky hotel and ascended into the Roman night. The boys had a good alcohol buzz to compliment the marijuana haze as they had polished off the final bottle of bubbly without help. The girls had emerged from the bathroom looking sexier than the boys could live up to, but Eric lent Jim some clothes, so that the foursome could get into even the most stylish Italian club. Everyone felt like rubbing elbows with style.

"We need some culture." Jim professed as the group headed into the night. "We need half-naked, sexy people drinking too much with loud music and synchronized robotic lighting. If we dance, if we really dance, then and only then, we will exist." Mona let out an excited shriek of approval and Eric twirled her around a couple of times to help add to the festive mood. The setbacks of the day had been forgotten, and the pollution of their minds was on a perfectly numbing scale, making the world a soft flurry of lights and life.

They entered the club four abreast, Eric again flush with cash after visiting an ATM, and headed to the bar to dampen their throats. The club was already starting to roll into the late night fervor that comes with extreme alcohol consumption and a thick undercurrent of lust. Jim tossed down two drinks and immediately ascended onto the dance floor, not bothering to notice if anyone came with him.

He just found a spot, closed his eyes, and began to let the music flow through him. Before he knew it, his friends had joined him, and the whole dance floor was thriving with energy—everyone with their hands in the air letting their bodies slide off and on to others with complete acceptance. The night was alive, and the group of traveling friends got lost in it. Jim and Liz found themselves soaked in sweat with their bodies almost molded into one enjoying each other's fluid movements. Sometimes their lips would touch lightly as a reflex to their bodies being so engaged. There was electricity between them that could not be denied, although the current was cut off from time to time.

Eric and Mona devoured each other on the dance floor. They were the real deal; the mature love already fully pronounced and committed. Their lips were constantly entangled and their hands constantly exploring each other. From time to time the couples would switch partners with both of the women maintaining a closeness designed for a comfortable partner. Mona enjoyed Jim's antics, his hippie swagger, and the same smooth English element that attracted Liz to her man. When the group would drop off the floor for a while, their table overflowed with interesting characters, which were drawn to the energy of the group. Sometimes there would be a four-way split as the group was pulled to the dance floor by different entities from all over the world. Jim liked the sassy Italian women, while the American men fought over Mona and Liz, and some rather tall Swedish girls sandwiched Eric making him stay on the floor for several songs. The eclectic table constantly surged on and off the dance floor, and the accents of the half-shout-ed English varied, but were defined enough for everyone to communicate. The night was a magic mixture of people where toasts rained like a Texas downpour, and laughs were always tickling at everyone's throats. Cigarettes burned and conversation breathed in and out—everyone was excited to get a sliver of someone else's life, and they were grateful for each encounter.

The club never died down as the night reached the wee hours of the morning. The group that had assembled at the table didn't want it to end, so everyone ended up stacked in Eric and Cindy's hotel room, where several bottles of wine had been gathered on the way home from the club. There was a vibrant crew consisting of Swedish girls, an American man traveling with his Mexican wife, and an Italian couple who had spent time studying in America. The Italian couple maintained that they were just friends, much like Jim and Elizabeth. They had the same problem with misunderstanding each other, or fear of losing control.The two couples got along great and ended up in a long drunken conversation regarding the awkwardness of their relationships.

The American man and Eric were constantly trying to incorporate the two Swedish girls into an orgy with their perspective wives, but the Swedish girls were so innocent that they didn't even masturbate, much less participate in lewd sex with married couples. Mona and the Mexican woman became fast friends and ignored their husbands' constant references to everyone relaxing a little and taking their close off. Eric even went as far as to fill the whirlpool tub with a monstrous bubble bath at which point Mona slipped up behind him and dumped him in fully clothed. In any case, the Swedish girls ended up squeezed into Mona's swimming suits, their oversized figures filling out the suits and then some. Everyone took turns in the tub, and at one time, there were six people lounging in and around the tub, with the water overflowing into the bathroom floor drain. Bottles of wine were passed around without any glasses, each person taking a swig and passing on the bottle. Liz, Mona, and Carmin, the Mexican woman, were all in their underwear, not bothering to be modest at four in the morning. They were completely hammered on wine and marijuana. Jim would light up a joint from time to time, and everyone, even the proper Swedish girls, pulled expert tokes off the flaming pot stick. With everyone half-naked and dripping wet, the atmosphere was like a drunken fraternity party gone just right.

Jim exclaimed, "Eric, my boy, we need documentation of this. I hope you have a video camera tucked away somewhere. I've got my camera, but streaming video would be fantastic. The scenery is better in here than it was on the beach today. I think we could make some money on a thirty-minute video, if everyone will just do what I say."

"I do have a camera, but I don't think this is what my parents would expect from a honeymoon video. My mom might have a bloody heart attack if she saw this footage." Eric replied stripped down to his boxers with a bottle of Merlot in one hand and a Swedish princess nestled in under the other arm.

The Italian couple had finally succumbed to each other and had made a bedroom out of the walk-in closet. The conversation regarding their true feelings for each other made them realize that they really wanted to fuck, so they did, and no one had a problem with it. Jim and Eric even took a peak to fulfill their own morbid curiosity.

"Now why can't Liz give in like that—I'm surely as charming as that old boy there. What's his name, I forget?" Jim looked at Eric for an answer.

"No fucking idea. All I know is the Swedes are Heather and Becky, and I was thinking of naming all four of their enormous breasts, but I think Cindy might get jealous because I don't have any names for hers." Jim and Eric stood dripping on the hotel carpet surveying the suite, trading a bottle for a joint, and enjoying the fact that everyone was half-naked and so wasted they didn't have a care in the world. Heather and Becky bounced around with never ending energy and a gigantic thirst that was never quenched. Jay, the American guy, had befriended them and was playing quarters for shots of wine on the coffee table with them. All three wrapped in towels with the girls feeling a little chill that was noticeable to all. Liz, Cindy, and the Mexican girl, Anna, remained in the tub with the jets roaring and a bottle of wine still being passed between them. They were talking about love as all of them had supposedly found it. Their words were slurred, and they were getting emotional about the subject as Jim and Eric rejoined them, back from their peaking mission.

Liz was slobbering something out, "I know Danny loves me and trusts me, cause he let me come on this trip with that mongrel." She pointed at Jim with the tip of a bottle of wine she had tightly grasped in one hand. Jim winced in pain and asked her what she knew about love. "A hell of a lot more than you, who thinks with his dick only. That word doesn't even know your lips, not for me or any other woman. You've never said it and meant it. Shit, you've never even said it; you told me. Tell me you love me. Tell me in front of all these people and then maybe we'll talk. You can't—you can't do it. You'd love to fuck me—you can say that, can't you?"

"I didn't ask you to fuckin attack me Calm down sister. I asked you what you know about love, and for your information, I do love you.

Now does that mean that I love you love you or does that mean that I just love you? Of coarse you know that I'd love to fuck you, but that has nothing to do with me loving you. So tell me, do you love me?" Jim said sliding down next to her and pulling her into his lap.

"You're too reckless, Jimmy. I'm too scared to love you. I'm too scared that my heart might get trampled on during that journey. I don't understand you. Even if I did love you, I wouldn't know how. Your world is this dangerous, chaotic place where love can get lost or misinterpreted or mistaken by lust. I love you just like you love me, you figure that out." Liz exclaimed not looking at Jim but scanning her group of female counterparts for some moral support.

Anna, in her slightly Latin accent, took the queue and made a comment. "You two are so in love that you're both blind to it." This was not the kind of comment Liz was looking for.

Eric jumped in to take the edge out of the air. "Love is something that happens on a grand scale, and you can't avoid it. It's like trying to cross and eight-lane freeway in L.A. without getting hit by a car—it's an overwhelming rush that can't be avoided. It's a force that draws you together and won't stand to be ignored. Like when I met Heather and Becky earlier this evening, I knew they were the girls for me." Mona grabbed for something of Eric's under the water. "Did I say Heather and Becky? I meant Mona, my wife, of coarse. Anyway, when I met Mona, we had no choice but to be together. It was like two pieces of a puzzle sliding together and then becoming one. It shouldn't be a struggle—the pieces should just fit. Maybe it's not that simple, but for us it was, I think. Am I right, baby?" Mona moved up on his lap and gave him a kiss as her reply.

"It was really easy and natural. I don't know about you two, though. I mean, you just told me how much you love this Danny guy, and then Jim shows up, and he's so different from how you described the other that it's difficult to compare the two. And if you're in love already, maybe you should just stay friends with this one, because he does seem quite dangerous."

"If she's in love with this Danny fucker, why was she rolling around with some Aussie in Pisa? I mean—she's obviously testing the waters here. She doesn't know what love is, and I don't expect her to. I don't have a fucking clue either; I know that, but don't bullshit me with the love thing. Give it a couple years, and that's all I'm saying." But Jim wasn't taken seriously because his eyes were fixed on Anna, as she crawled out of the tub to go join her husband, who was sandwiched between Heather and Becky and losing decisively in the drinking game.

"I've got to go rescue my husband before he falls in love with Heather and Becky too." She decried as she pulled a towel down to dry her petite, well-toned, olive skinned, body. Eric was smart enough to keep his eyes to himself, but Jim lost a lot of ground by drying Anna off with his eyes.

"See, I can't take you anywhere." Liz said.

"What, I'm just keeping an eye on her in case she slips." Anna noticed Jim's eyes and quickly covered herself with a towel. Jim showed no remorse and waved as she headed to the living area. "Any woman in wet underwear deserves to be admired, and I feel no shame in admiring a woman's beauty. Eric, are you going to be upset when I check out Mona, or will you be honored at the fact that your wife is so beautiful she deserves admiration, or am I just a drunken fool who should keep my eyes to myself?"

"Looks are free, mate, but I'll have to charge you for a feel."
Again, Mona grabbed for something, but Eric countered with a
pinch in the butt that sent her off his lap and splashing in the center of the tub. A water-splashing wrestling match ensued with Eric
being pushed under water where he stayed providing nibbles on
various places of Mona's lower body. The water was wildly splashed
around, while Mona squirmed in every direction to fend off her at-
tacker. During the action, Jim gave Elizabeth a surprising pinch in
the ass to instigate what he hoped to be a very physical confrontation. Jim figured a drunken wrestling match with a beautiful, half-
naked woman was going to be as close as he was going to get to sex
for the evening.

By the time the four-way battle was finished the tub was only
half way full, and both woman had their tops removed by their
semi-victorious rivals who would have yanked their bottoms off
if the girls hadn't united and worked together to slither away.
The girls were so elated with having evaded their captures they
jumped around the bathroom slapping high fives and hugging.
The hugs were the highlight of the night for Jim and Eric. Their
women's' naked bodies pressing against one another was better
than a "Girls Gone Wild" video.

The night had escalated into drunken antics, but the wine was running low, and everyone had to fall at some point. Once everyone did
fall, the room looked like a battlefield strewn with corpses. Bodies fell
on the floor and couch, and all four of the bathroom wrestlers ended
up snuggled in the king size bed. The do not disturb sign and the
tightly pulled drapes kept the room cut off from the world, and the
drunken slumber rolled on until noon.

As Jim and Liz left the hotel, their vicious hangovers collided with the hot Roman sun, and there was no place in the world that was truly appealing to the haggled couple that day. They crawled back to their hotel room, vomited a couple of times, and slithered under the sheets communicating only in moans. Water and pain pills became their romantic Roman supper, and they watched 80's movies on the English language station. The pain started to subside a little later in the evening, so Jim smoked a joint and hit the streets just long enough to secure some provisions for him and his hurting traveling partner. They had had a wonderful evening, but they were paying dearly for their excesses. Coke, sweets and greasy food were what their hung over bodies craved, and Jim was acquiring such things at a very slow pace—every few steps forgetting what he left the room for. His neurotransmitters were not firing right, but he managed to arrive back at the room with pizza, soda, and some groovy Italian pastries.

His ailing friend was delighted by his progress, although she could only show her appreciation through a half-tilted smile. "You're good to me even though I make it hard on you." She said when he set her up in bed with food and an iced drink.

"When in Rome, eat like an American." Jim said as he shoved a piece of thin-crusted pizza into his mouth.

Jim and Liz were planning to leave Rome the next morning and head to Brindisi, where they would meet up with Ethel and Hilga and catch a boat to Greece. They had to get themselves together, figure out a train schedule, get packed, wash the puke off themselves, and focus on the next adventure.

Chapter 11
THE BOAT

Walking down the main boulevard of Brindisi, Jim and Liz ran into a classmate from their high school that had just got off the boat that they were about to board. "No way, that's Cheryl, what are the odds." Liz exclaimed as Cheryl came strolling right towards them on the Italian sidewalk. "Hey girl, fancy seeing you here. You just came from Greece? How was your trip?"

"I can't believe this, seeing you two. This is just too weird. We're halfway around the world, and we just run into each other. What a small world—so very cool. How are you two? It's good to see you. You're getting on the boat, huh? You're going to love it. I was traveling with Matt Simons. You know Matt, right, from high school. He had to go back, and I'm just checking out Italy. Where are you guys planning on going?" Cheryl shot out excitedly. She toted a big bag, wore Birkenstocks, and had increased freckles and golden skin from all the sun she had absorbed. She looked like a happy Raggedy Anne doll with a tan.

Elizabeth, who was friends with Cheryl in high school, did most of the talking and soon all three were seated at an outdoor café getting the lowdown on each other's journeys. "We're just going straight to the islands, taking a bus to Athens, catching a cab to port Piraeus, and then catching a ferry to one of the islands. What do you suggest; where did you go?"

"We pretty much did the same thing. Athens is kinda grimy,

so we didn't stay long. The islands are beautiful and an absolute blast. There are so many of them, and they all sound like fun. We went to Paros, Syros and Santorini. Paros is the first place most of the ferries go, and then you can catch a boat to any of the islands from there, or at least, that's how we did it. Paros is more of a commercialized island because of its big port, but it's a great place, and you can totally get away from the town and explore the island. Santorini was completely insane. The parties went all night long, and the beaches always had people on them—it is definitely the shit if you like to party. Syros, we caught on the way back to the mainland, and we were worn out, so we just chilled and didn't do much, but it was a nice place. The beaches are all beautiful, and some of them are only accessible by boat. People wear less and less clothes, the more secluded the beach. You've got to carry a lot of sunscreen for those areas that don't usually get a lot of sun—you've got to try it ala natural." Cheryl explained with Elizabeth jumping in at the insinuation.

"I'm not getting nude; I just can't do it. Do you have to, I mean, does everybody?" Liz squealed in a high voice.

"Don't be shy. What have you got to be ashamed of? It's nothing I haven't already sneaked several peaks at anyway, and I'm all for seeing more of it after my initial research. You did it, didn't you Cheryl?"

"Sure, I've got no problem being naked, and when am I going to see any of those people ever again? Look." She pulled down her top along with her bikini top that was on under her shirt. " No tan lines. Now that I know I might run into people from back home, though, I might be a little more modest, but it can't possibly happen again, right? Don't worry about it Lizzy—you'll get to see Jimmy's little weenie getting burned up anyway. Matt's sure did. It was funny as hell. The second day we went to the nude beach, Matt is walking around with all this sun block on his little red pee pee."

"I'm sure as hell not modest. If people are getting naked, and there's ample source of liquid courage, then I don't think there will be any problem with me swinging bare dick on the Greek sand. And if the gays show too much interest, I'll just have to show them what kind of man I am and let Lizzy here be my demonstration piece. You're going to have to show them that I'm only interested in the female touch. I'll let you apply a little lotion to the forbidden area, and they'll see the truth. What do you think, there, sunshine? Oh, and I'll be glad to apply your lotion as well, I'm here for you, baby." Both girls were worked up into quite a giggle.

"See, that's why I'm not getting naked; he's a pervert. I'm not worried about the tourists or the locals; it's just the obscene man that I'm traveling with that concerns me."

"He's just a man. Don't let him intimidate you, and it doesn't really matter if you get naked or not; there's always a mixture. Some people keep their clothes on and, others, you just wish would. The least modest are the least exciting to observe. Liz, the nudity is not a big issue; just go enjoy yourself. The islands are wonderful, so full of life. The food is great, the night life is fantastic, and no body's in a hurry—you'll love it." Cheryl stated as she finished her drink and readied herself to take leave. She had a train to catch, and Jim and Liz had a boat to board. Jim and Liz gave Cheryl a couple quick pointers on Italian travel as well as their impressions of the cities and towns they had visited. They encouraged Cheryl to check out some of the countryside; something they had not done, but had meant to. It was hard to fit all of Italy into the short time they had allotted, but they had done well and had thrown several coins into the Trevi fountain to assure their return. They both hugged Cheryl as she bid them farewell and then hurried themselves down to the docks to start their new Greek adventure. Cheryl swaggered off to fall in love with Italy, to be her own sunflower shining through the Italian summer.

The boat was more like a small ship and was comprised of three interior levels of cabins, some small duty-free shops, and dining areas. The cheapest fair did not include a cabin, but left a slew of backpackers to fend for themselves on the exposed upper decks. There was a rush to find the best spots to lay down sleeping bags and claim as camp for the next twenty-three hours. The top deck had a corrugated plastic roof that would shield its passengers from the rain if it were to come, while a lower deck at the rear of the boat was exposed to the sky creating a never-ending vista of sky and water. Jim and Liz decided to make camp on the back deck and trade beauty for the security of staying dry in a storm—there were no clouds as far as the eye could see. The back deck was also nicely accommodated with a shack that served beer and wine, and maybe food, but no body noticed that.

The outside decks were crawling with backpackers, and Liz and Jim had acquired prime real estate, in the rear corner of the ship, where they had the walls of the two railings abutting their little square patch of deck. They would sleep under the stars, nestled up to a wide array of young travelers, or maybe they wouldn't sleep, because the wide array of young spirits preferred to spend the twenty-three hours getting to know each other. Jim was in his element, while Liz was concerned about what affects the salt water might have on her hair. She had also turned her bottom lip up a bit, showing her concern that Jim was abandoning her for the excitement and adventure of the crowd. She shoved her nose in a book keeping her peripheral vision extended in Jim's direction, as he befriended all their surrounding shipmates. He wore a direct path to the bar and bled his enthusiasm for alcohol on the surrounding crowd.

Ethel and Hilga were set up next to Liz, but they were seated next to Jim, holding cold beers, greeting the new passengers as they settled themselves on the fast filling deck. Liz's attitude purposely left her isolated from the crowd, as the afternoon wore on, and the boat began to chug along. Her nose was in a book, as everyone else smelled a beer. Next to Jim's spot, a large contingency of Italian women set up camp, nine in all, with beaming smiles and electric enthusiasm. Both upper decks were full of youthful travelers, setting up their little groups together, and leaving small aisle-ways between camps, so others could pass by. People began to stray from their camps early on, and the decks turned into a traveling festival, where people from countries from all over the world were in attendance. Everyone mixed like the colors of a kaleidoscope. Most people were in a festive, social mood making it an environment conducive to meeting up to a hundred people in the space of a couple hours. The conversations varied and were rarely limited by language, since most of the educated Europeans were schooled in several languages; they were able to adapt.

Jim bounced around the decks, getting sidetracked on the way back from the bar, or getting stuck at the bar, making new friends at almost every turn. Of coarse, he was most interested in the Italian contingency that also took a liking to him, making him their new, scruffy, American mascot. The girls were lead by a charismatic med-school student named Stefania. Her personality dominated the crowd, and her enthusiasm reached levels beyond her bouncing American counterpart. She was a character with beauty and an explosive sense of humor. The amazing thing about the group of Italian women was that they all rivaled Stefania's looks—not one lacked an appealing figure or pleasing face. Stefania was naturally blonde, and many of the girls shared her natural big curls. Her golden locks reached her hips, and her smile extended to her ears. Her first question was straight to the point she most needed to clear up.

"Who are all these women with you? Does one of them possess you?" She asked having pulled Jim into their circle.

"Possess, are you kidding me? No woman possesses me. She can take me on loan for a while, but I'm not signing myself over to her."

"You know what I mean; are you free for the taking?" She asked again playfully, taking Jim's arm as if claiming him already.

"The German girls, I'm pretty sure they prefer girls. As far as the other one, she's definitely indifferent; she's committed to some English wanker. We're old friends doing some traveling together is all. I'm sure she'll loan me out, if your motives are acceptable to her value system, which is in question at the present moment." Liz heard these comments because they were especially audible for her, and she shook her head with a renewed pouty indifference. Stefania paid no attention to her now that she knew she wasn't a threat and laid claim to Jim in front of all her friends by her gracious attention and constant touch of some part of Jim's body. She would lean into him when she laughed, put her arm around him when she asked him a question, and put a hand on his leg when thanking him for a beer. Jim had no choice but to accommodate. Originally, he wanted to meet all nine Italian beauties, and make his determination, through careful observation; but the best chose him, and he relaxed into the role without a struggle.

"You are golden brown like beautiful Italian man. We thought you were Italian when we first saw you. I told the girls, you were off limits. It is even better that you are American, as I don't have to put up with Italian macho. You are kind with that smile, yes?"

"Kind, generous, respectful, caring, understanding and extremely romantic when I need to be. I'm pretty sure I'm the perfect man if you ask me. What about you, besides being beautiful and wonderfully vibrant, what are your most redeeming qualities?"

Stefania kissed Jim's cheek, "Yes, I am all things woman, and I absolutely adore life. You will get to know me, Jim—you will see who I am." This girl, who had taken possession of him in the first hour of their meeting, amazed Jim. She was not overbearing, and as the evening wore on, and the sun began to set over the Mediterranean, it was not their relationship that grew, but their teamwork that pulled together a massive crowd. Everyone who looked fun and engaging was pulled into their web and made to join their circle of fun.

As the evening wore on, the sea completely silent as if sliding along on a piece of glass, Elizabeth put down her book was drawn into the boisterous crowd. Jim made his way to her, as he saw her show some interest in the world. He was already good and drunk and asked her what she would like to drink. She wanted some wine, so Jim suggested that they go to the duty free shop, as many other passengers had, and pick up a bottle or two much cheaper than buying it by the glass. Jim made leave of the group and escorted his friend to the shop, making sure to pick up a bottle of Jack Daniels for himself to share with the giddy Italian girls. He wanted something truly American since the girls had taken a liking, for a change, to his Americanism. Elizabeth secured two bottles of red wine and was seen slurping the red nectar from the bottle with a host of companions all evening. Her beauty drew drunken male suitors from time to time, but Ethel and Hilga would eventually shoo them off when they tried to get a little fresh. Elizabeth had little fight in her at the time, and she was allowing herself to get bombed.

Jim befriended a Chilean aristocrat disguised as a backpacker. His name was Pepe; his parents owned half of Chile, and were in total control of the masses. Pepe's father had just been elected president in a semi-democratic election. His family had been instrumental in getting the former military dictator ousted and was now enjoying a peaceful reign at top. He humbly brought these details into the conversation via Jim's constant pounding questions that got deeper with each revealed secret. "So your father is the president of Chile and you're out sowing your royal oats. You're filthy fucking rich. Well, that's none of my fucking business; I'm sorry. Do president's kids get high? Don't you have some kind of body guard, secret service or something?"

"Our house had many rooms, and I've smoked in them all; it's common to smoke in my country and the stuff grows very well almost anywhere. You have a lot of smoke on you? Because if you do, I suggest we smoke it all before the boat docks. The penalties are insane in Greece for possession of marijuana, it's not like Western Europe, I mean, they'll lock you up for a while if you get caught."

"I've only got a couple of joints left, but they're real dynamite; we're going to need some help. I know Ethel and Hilga will get high with us. I don't know about the Italians. I would assume so though, at least a couple of them. We can get back in my corner and blow it over the back of the boat, and no body will know the difference. We'll buzz our brains out, drink this bottle of Jack, and then I'm sure we'll be ready to fly, or at least water ski behind the boat. We'll make the front page of the Santiago times, jumping naked off the back of an Italian cruise liner—just what ma and pa expected of their wayward son." The plan was put into action with eight of the nine Italian girls joining Ethel, Hilga, Jim, and Pepe in a huddled mass near the end of the boat toking one joint after another. The toke circle grew after the first number, and pretty soon the whole bottom back deck sat in a huge circle glassy-eyed passing around different bottles of liquor and puffing cigarettes and pot. Pepe expressed his knowledge of the Greek drug laws, which he had learned from a close Italian friend. After learning about the Greek laws, many of the other smokers broke out their stash and began to consume.

Pepe and Stefania were the bookends at each side of Jim, while Elizabeth was receiving undivided attention from two Czech travelers that looked a little older than the average member of the group. The circle extended around the entire bottom part of the outer deck, which was about a quarter of the length of the entire ship—this is where the outspoken alcoholics opened up the all-night Mediterranean tavern. The shy and timid fled to the upper deck with their sleeping bags and backpacks, while the rowdy tumbled down the stairs to the rear deck and joined the raucous festivities. Jim, Pepe, Stefania, and one of her friends, Barbara, got cozy in the rear corner of the ship, and the conversation rattled away with furious pace and no boundaries.

Stefania, with her squinted eyes and constantly animated expressions, was the master of ceremonies. "For all of us to be together on this ship is magical. The whole world mixed on a boat, and everyone loves one another. There is no strife, no problems. Ah, the spirit of the traveler, the adventurous spirit and the kind heart—everyone matches this, yeah? We are the future; the whole world as one—you'll see. The world is so accessible now. I'm going to see it all and take time to understand each culture, to let myself be absorbed into new people everywhere. That's why I'm going to be a doctor, because I will be able to help human beings, and I can do that anywhere."

Jim was easily pulled into the conversation. "Such optimism—It makes you even more beautiful. You amaze me, my dear. I couldn't possibly go to school that long, and I smoke way too much pot to have a very good memory, so I'm pretty sure that no one would want me standing over them with a scalpel. I do like your worldview, though, and I hope to join you in seeing and experiencing everything I can. I'm studying to be a journalist so that I can communicate with the world. I'm full of words, and I love my camera, so I can't go wrong. I may not save the planet, but I will do my best to find the truth, if there is truth. I just want to be floating around free, forever. I could continue this trip forever if my bank account looked like Pepe's here. Is that right, Pepe? Are you just going to continue circling the globe until you find the meaning in life?"

"I think I'm going to go to school forever, or until someone tells me that's enough, or maybe until I morph into a professor. My heart lies in learning and traveling. I've studied at Harvard and Oxford, and I've only absorbed a tiny bit of what is offered. My father will eventually want me to get into politics, and I have no choice, but I don't think it is for me. Maybe I could be an ambassador; that would be cool, but to make a bunch of important decisions, that millions rely on, is too much for me. I might grow up though, but I really don't want to. My father expects a lot from me, and sometimes I just stay away to not face it. I wander aimlessly, and I really don't know if I'm looking for the meaning of life. This is my fifth time to Greece, and it's just like this monstrous party—the islands are anyway, and so maybe I'm just hiding from the meaning of life. I'm kind of a lost soul is what I'm trying to say. I don't have the beautiful vision of Stefania. I don't really know what I want to do with myself."

"Not everyone knows what to do with themselves. Just take it day by day and do what your heart tells you to. There's nothing wrong with partying in Greece until you're forty, if that's what feels right. Someday, when you're passed out on the beach, you'll wake up to some vision of what you are destined to do. Maybe Zeus will come out of the sky and direct your future personally. Don't get down on yourself, Pepe, you can do anything you want in the world, literally, right?" The spunky little Barbara sitting by Pepe's side added. She found Pepe's dark Chilean complexion and tight curly hair attractive and different. His light splash of freckles was intriguing for a Latin man, and although he sometimes talked in a desperate manner, there was always an undercurrent of strength emanating from him. Pepe was humble, and he may have been unsure about his future, but he really knew how to live in the now, and a large smile was never very far from his lips.

The night wore on, and eventually the deck bar closed, but the duty free liquor and wine had taken over anyway. Pepe had secured two bottles of Crown Royal, and someone had been brave enough to buy some 151 and was daring the fittest to take a shot. Jim had settled into his back corner with the whole group of Italian girls giggling close by. Ethel and Hilga, who hadn't approved of her foul-mouthed Czech male suitors, and ran them off with threats in German, were guarding Elizabeth closely. Liz was swaying in the wind after gracefully finishing one bottle of wine, and not so gracefully, downing her second. Someone had a boom box playing a female German rap group, who somehow turned the art of German rap into catchy dance songs, succeeding in making a rough language sound smooth and fluid. Since the Germans were the only ones with music, everyone showed extreme enthusiasm for the limited resources, and the music brought many drunken travelers to their feet to dance inside the massive oval created on the back deck. The top deck had settled to a slumber hours before, while the lower deck had no intentions of sleeping until they were knocked unconscious by the booze, which started to wield blows around two a.m. One of the first casualties was Liz, who ended up giving Ethel and Hilga rather intimate kisses goodnight, before passing out in a human snuggle with Ethel and Hilga directly behind Jim's position in the human oval. Jim made sure that his friend got wrapped in her sleeping bag, and her head rested on her pillow, instead of Hilga's chest. She would certainly have no recollection of kissing the girls, but Jim would have a crystal clear picture of it, since he spied the occasion from the dance floor, where he was showing off his nifty feet to his Italian admirers.

Stefania made a comment about Liz's actions later in the evening, "So your friend likes girls, that's why you two aren't together, huh? She's beautiful, and it just seems if you are traveling together, you should be together, but if she's like that, I understand; it's nearly impossible to change them if they're like that. Olivia, see Olivia." She pointed to one of her friends with short hair and passionate eyes, "She prefers girls, but we always try to send the most attractive men to her to see if maybe we can change her intuitions, but she is very firm and, sometimes, even pulls one of the girls her way. You know, when we're really drunk, she'll take advantage of our curiosity; next thing you know, she's getting exactly what she wants."

"It sounds like you've been caught in her web." Jim pried, wanting to get some details.

"Yes, yes I have, but I don't blame it on alcohol. I was just confused and wanted to explore my sexuality. I enjoyed the times with her, but it just really confirmed I am full-blown heterosexual. I like men best; they awaken my spirit, while time with a woman is just physical entertainment. My emotions don't release with a woman—I need the strength of a man and a dick for sure."

"Stefania, you can't talk like that. You forget you're a lady." Barbara added being silly, but shaking her head in agreement the whole time Stefania was talking. "Don't talk to men about dicks. It will go straight to his head, and he will have the edge knowing that you can't wait to get a hold of that thing. Oh, look, he's blushing. I think we've embarrassed him, or made him not, one of the two."

"Your interest in my male anatomy is great, and I'm surely willing to let you at it whenever you want. If you think it would help Olivia to get a little some, I'd be sure to oblige, if she just wanted a test run."

"No, she's a pussy type of girl. She's all tongues and fingers, and she likes ice cubes and hot oils. Anyway, I think Stefania has already claimed you, and I'm not sure she's willing to share—she shares everything but her men."

"That's fine, I can be with Stefania's, but you can all share me if you like. I've kind of been nursing a fantasy about being with you all. What man wouldn't want to be with nine beautiful Italian women at once, especially if he had the dumb luck to stumble into such a group traveling together. You've got to understand that I'm sitting very close to my fantastical heaven, the mystical place that I dream about is forming in my reality and I'm downright giddy. If we could just pull this together on some remote Greek beach where we could be free and naked, I'm sure that we could restart the sexual revolution."

"You couldn't handle all nine of us. You're not even going to be able to handle me, if it gets that far. Don't think it's going to be that easy, though, you can't just come in here and charm all of us thinking you have a free ticket into our pants. I require romance for such exploits, a genuine effort to sweep me off my feet." Stefania claimed taking a swig of Crown Royal passed to her from Pepe.

All the members of the circle, the ones remaining upright, were completely sloshed. Pepe sat cross-legged with a huge smile on his face, but he was unable to communicate verbally. Barbara and Stefania sat on each side of him passing the Crown Royal through him. He wouldn't take a drink; he would just pass it back and forth between the girls and sit there glowing at his company. Jim got into babble mode, completely excited by the talk of group sex, but easily distracted into other topics, mainly involving his trip to that point. Stefania stayed by his side and expressed great interest, as Jim became a storyteller describing Joey, Neil, the drug-soaked days in Albufuera, the old fishing captain in Tavira, and the oasis waterfall just outside of town. He liked to talk about himself, and in the wee hours of the night, his stories were the most coherent things going.

The music had been turned off, and many of the bottles had been drained when the last of the rebels on the back deck finally fell to their sleeping bags for a short rest. The sunrise wasn't far away, but the party didn't quite make it to the magical moment of the sun peaking over the horizon. There was another magical moment, though, which was the bar opening, mainly for snacks, but the Amstel Lights were still cold and available. Jim was one of the first early morning patrons to wash down his hangover with a cold Amstel and some Crest toothpaste.

When Elizabeth finally rolled over into the bright morning light, she found her friends, Pepe, Ethel, and Hilga already sipping cold beers in their swimsuits as though they were sitting out on the beach. To Liz's astonishment, the two German girls were a little more natural than she expected—their long armpit hair was a little shock as one of her first morning visions. She knew it would not be polite for her to show any disgust, but a slight bit of it was smoldering in her throat.

Jim choked down the first two beers with gut-wrenching effort. By the third, he was beginning to feel a rhythm, and his insides weren't in total mutiny. The sun-drenched sea surrounded the boat in every direction with a beauty that demanded to be celebrated. The crystal clear blue water was so flat that the deck could have been used for a gymnastics exhibition. It was steady and still, and there was no reason to experience any kind of motion sickness, yet many of the young, weary travelers looked green as they rose from their short slumbers. As they woke, they were immediately greeted by Jim who professed the hard-to-swallow cure of getting a couple of quick drinks down the gullet.

The Italian contingency was tough and did not complain; rising and drinking was okay with them. Stefania's mass of frizzy curls bounced around the deck with the same vigor and energy she had shown the night before, and the face she made after her first swig of beer looked like a scene from "I Love Lucy"—one of those overly dramatic facial gestures that Lucille Ball used to bring the crowd to their knees. Some of the other girls were even more fearless and ended up taking shots of Pepe's last bottle of Crown Royal. They claimed it a quicker way to the same goal of calming the nerves and restarting the drunk. Jim envied the girls, had a shot himself, threw up five minutes later, and washed the taste out of his mouth with another beer and a ham sandwich.

The boat stopped at Corfu, an island off the Western coast of Greece, to let some of the passengers off, and to pick up some others heading to the mainland. Many of the passengers discussed the famous hostel on Corfu called the Pink Palace. There were stories of a twenty-four hour beach party with barely dressed people everywhere, which was almost enough to lure Jim off the boat for a night's stay, but he certainly didn't want to loose the Italians. The boat left Corfu after an hour in port and headed to the mainland city of Patras, which was the final destination of the magical "Love Boat". The rear deck became quite a spectacle, as it had the night before. The bikini tops and shining suntan oil created a club-med atmosphere, fueling the anticipation of arriving at the world's playground—the Greek Islands.

When the boat docked in Patras, there was so much chaos that most of the travelers from the back deck were split up. Jim concentrated on keeping Elizabeth intact and did not pay attention to the surging crowds, as they were herded onto busses heading to the East Coast. He assumed that the other travelers from the back deck would be on the same bus, since everyone had the same plans as Jim and Liz. In the back of his mind, Jim was very concerned about losing the Italian females. He didn't pay attention for a couple seconds, and found himself on a bus where there wasn't a whiff of the Italian beauties; he thought he had lost them for good.

He looked at Liz as the bus began to move, "What have I done. Somehow I've kept track of you and lost nine Italians—somehow I think my priorities are really fucked up." He sighed and shook his head back and forth, distraught and utterly alone.

"You're an asshole."

"Yeah, well you're a prude, and I'm pretty sure I could have got laid if I would have kept track of the posse. Just looking at you makes my nuts throb—do you know that? Do you have any idea what throbbing nuts can do to a man? They can send him over the edge. Is that where you want to see me, in some asylum drooling on myself all day trying to rub the throbbing sensation out of my nuts?"

"Oh, that's charming! Why don't you just put your jacket on your lap, and I'll crawl under there and suck you off, you twisted pervert."

"Really, I knew you'd come around. Make sure you swallow, I don't want all that sticky stuff caught in my hair down there, you know."

This comment was the last that Elizabeth could take, and she got up to try to find another seat. There were none, but she ran into Pepe on the top deck of the bus and begged him to go sit with Jim. Pepe was easily persuaded. After all, he and Jim were good buddies from the boat. He could see that Liz was angry or frustrated about something, but he thought it better to ask Jim than her. He made his way down to Jim's seat and asked what happened.

"I think she's had enough of me. We could use a little time apart. I'd much rather have my Chilean friend sitting with me anyway. I thought you would have been smart enough to keep up with the girls, what happened?"

"It was just one big line, and they were only a couple of people behind me, then they cut the line off right after me and started loading the next bus. They're not far behind. I don't think we'll lose them forever. Have faith my friend; I wouldn't let those wonderful creatures get too far removed. We'll end up in Piraeus on the same boat to the islands later tonight. It will be just like the boat over here, except a little smaller. We will dance with our harem of Italian women tonight my friend. I hate to say it, but it is probably good that you have alienated your friend, so that she will not want to tag along."

"She'll be glad to have me out of her hair for a while. I'm just going to leave her alone on these islands, and she'll find some man to treat her like a queen. We'll go our separate ways, at least while the Italians are around. We need to do a better job of taking care of those ladies, Pepe. I'm serious; we need to make their happiness our number one priority. You feel me brother. We have already infiltrated the finest looking group of human beings available on the entire chain of Greek Islands. We have access to the Goddesses, and we must serve them faithfully."

"I'm in my friend—don't worry—I'm on the same page." The two friends went on to discuss how amazing it was that nine such women would all be traveling together, not one being unattractive, and all having incredibly likeable personalities. They had somehow received favor from the Gods and made a vow that they would not lose track of the girls from the minute they exited the bus.

Elizabeth sat on the top deck peering out the window feeling a little bit put out, but not getting too down, considering the part of the world she was about to experience. She thought to herself, "He can't possibly treat me like that for long, I'm too cute and desirable. He just has no shame or couth. He cares for me, but if everything doesn't go perfectly his way, he just turns his back. I won't give him what he wants, and I won't give in. I'll show him—I can be a bitch if that's what he wants. He's impossible; I didn't want things to turn out this way; we shouldn't be fighting. I don't know what to do. I can't let this ruin our trip. Just have fun Elizabeth, and keep a smile on your face whether you feel like it or not. Don't let his crass bullshit throw me off. That's what he wants to do—get me rattled so he has control."

She kept the thoughts rolling back and forth as the hilly Greek countryside flashed by without much notice. The bus was cool and fairly smooth, although the bus driver drove it like a compact car. The bus did not have a bathroom, so halfway through the trip, Elizabeth got to watch an older gentleman take a piss right beneath her window, after convincing the bus driver to stop. The bus driver had little patience, though, and when the old man took his time, the driver began to pull away slowly. This caused the old man to shake quickly violently, creating quite a comedic stir on the top level of the bus. The comedy helped Elizabeth out of her fixated trance, which was starting to drag her down. She laughed at the old man's dilemma and was able to shift her mind away from conflict towards building a resolution. "Maybe I haven't treated him how I should have from the beginning. If I would have just let myself go, we could have had a very romantic time. That first night together should have been without rules, and then the whole trip would have taken on a completely different dimension. I came down here so fixated on Danny, and so determined to stay true, that I blocked myself from exploring my feelings for Jim. Now I sit here pissed off because I've completely turned the situation on its head. I still believe in Danny, but Jim is trying to show me how to live with a completely free spirit, and I just keep rejecting his perspective. If I let myself go, though, I will definitely end up giving myself to him, and then what sense does maintaining my strong will for so long make. Maybe I'll just let him seduce me, if he tries again; I don't know." This conversation with herself was the beginning of a dialogue that began to discuss the possibility of letting Jim in—all her previous conversations with herself to that point had been focused on diligently keeping him out—keeping up the defenses, so he didn't sneak in. But at the lowest part of their relationship during this journey, she was starting to open the door, although he was distracted and wouldn't notice for a while.

Jim was on the bottom level with Pepe, and the last thing on his mind was reconciling with Liz. She could pout for a couple of days for all he cared. His mind was fixed on Stefania and her traveling group of wonderful women. He had to concentrate on them and wash his mind clear of Liz, so his emotions would be at a heightened sense of clarity, when he was reunited with the girls. He needed to be sincere and couldn't have thoughts of Elizabeth trashing his concentration. Stefania was pure estrogen and could detect a man's wavering sentimentalities a mile a way.

"Pepe, you're going to have to pull out your best Latin lover impersonation, unless maybe that is your true character, and take

the conquest of these women very seriously. These women breathe
romance. Their level of compassion and skill at manipulating
the male heart are beyond our comprehension, so we are going
to have to be extremely charming to remain on their level." Both
men had already forgotten about Liz and were concentrating on
the task at hand.

When the bus finally reached Athens, there was another round
of mass chaos, as those heading for the islands rushed to grab
cabs to Piraeus to catch the last ferry of the night. Jim, Pepe, and
Liz shared a cab, while the Italians haled down a minivan taxi and
somehow shoved all nine precious bodies and their backpacks into
the steaming cab.

The sun had already set by the time everyone was loaded on the
ferry, which was headed to the central island of Paros. Jim was kind
of sad that he had to leave his marijuana habit in Italy, so he made
his way to the beverage stand to start the intoxication process and
numb the loss of his close friend. Pepe joined him, still smiling and
very willing to celebrate another voyage. Liz decided to take it easy
for the night aware she was being totally ignored. Hilga and Ethel
were already drinking and smoking on the top deck when Jim and
his fellow travelers arrived. The Italian girls arrived with quite a
bustle, nine voices chatting away, mixed with a newly purchased
music device, the idea borrowed from the Germans on the last voyage. Somehow, Italian rock music had also been purchased with the
device, and it blared at a generous level, while Stefania was boister-
ously spreading her charm. "Jim, I've missed you my love, it's been
so long since we were last together, and now we are together again,
and again on the Love Boat, yeh! You do love me, right? And you're

not scared of me, right? I mean I only bite if you touch me in just the right spots; other than that, I'm harmless. You're not scared of a little nibble anyway, are you?"

"Of coarse not, my dear—nibble away. I think you'll like my flavor." Jim answered with a beaming smile glad to be reunited with the woman he had feared losing. "Look Pepe; the girls are back, and you said we had lost them forever. Yea have little faith. Watch out! It looks like Olivia has a grip on Barbara; save her before she goes to the other side."

"I'm completely liberal with sexuality, I don't take sides, and I lavish myself with the best from both worlds." Barbara announced while grabbing Pepe's arm, but not letting go of Olivia who was snuggly wound in the other arm. "Don't make me choose, my Chilean prince, as that would be such a drag."

"Don't worry, princess, I will be there to fulfill your every desire as well as obey your every wish. If you and Olivia wish to use me as a boy toy, then I will be the best in that capacity. Like I said, whatever you wish, I shall comply."

The boat churned into the Adriatic Sea, another smooth palette torn in half by the bow of the ship. The group settled on the top of the boat with only sky above, and they left plenty of room for anyone wanting to join them. The group expanded to include a couple of Dutchmen who turned the journey into a wash of classic guitar songs, most of the relaxing James Taylor, Neil Young, or Eric Clapton type, which turned the group into a sing-song from time to time. Energy and spirit from the first voyage remained and even grew a bit in anticipation of finally setting foot on a much renowned Greek Island.

Jim really didn't know what to expect of the islands, but with the company he had been lucky enough to accumulate, there was no doubt he was going to enjoy himself. He had managed to wipe Liz completely out of his mind. Whether that was wise, considering they were traveling together was yet to be seen. Even if he could have been sensitive to Elizabeth's feelings, it would have been almost impossible for him to ignore such a large group of lively, beautiful women. He was completely absorbed into the Italian entourage and became engrossed in their stories as the night wore on. The conversation, instigated by the Dutchmen, after the guitar playing had ended, was pulling out all kinds of information about the diverse group of Italian women. The Dutchmen were very open and invited personal conversation in hopes of getting to know each of the women. They really only had four to choose since Barbara was happy with her combination of Pepe and Olivia, and Stefania was definitely set on Jim. They couldn't tell what was going on in any of their heads, so they solicited them all. How could anyone resist such a lovely group of vibrant, educated, and downright sensuous young women?

Stefania told stories of tearing apart cadavers as part of her anatomy class, causing the other girls to shutter, but gave her a tough-girl bravado. One of the young ladies studied music and proved her skill by taking one of the guitars and playing an old gypsy folk song, which she accompanied with mesmerizing lyrics. Another young lady was a writer for Italian television; she had a knack for comedy and admitted that much of her material was generated within this very group of traveling Italian beauties. Olivia was an artist, an accomplished one at that. She had embraced technology and was sought after for her skill as a graphic artist, photographer, and painter. Barbara was on her way to becoming a broadcast journalist. She had the face and energy for the job. It would just be a matter of time for her to work her way from the back rooms to in front of the camera. Two law students and a flight attendant from Air Italia rounded out the group. Stefania and the two law school students were the most relieved to be on vacation, and they showed a great deal of vigor for their holiday, which rubbed off on all their friends who were more used to leisure time than they were.

The group was drawn closer for the couple of hours they shared together on the boat. The comfort level had built up over the two voyages, and the women were constantly joking with Jim and Pepe who had infiltrated the group with genuine interest and would remain a part of it. They drank, smoked cigarettes as if they were air, and told stories to each other about the fantastic parts of their lives. Jim told stories of traveling across the United States with friends from college and high school. Pepe told stories of his never-ending college career, and of his intention to continue such a lifestyle into his thirties, if he could possibly pull it off. The journey was full of camaraderie, and everyone opened up and was completely honest about their past and their thoughts on life. Most of the conversation was lively and upbeat. Nobody really wanted to address any stressful topics. Nothing was wrong in the world for the travelers. They could find no faults in their lives or in their courses to reach their dreams—everything was attainable, and it would be achieved without too many setbacks.

"I don't believe that the world is a bad place. Granted, we all come from western countries that are advanced and wealthy, and that probably has a lot to do with my outlook. But I truly believe that I can accomplish anything, and anyone here can be exactly what he or she set out to be. The hardest part is focusing on what makes you tick—what it is that your heart actually desires because in the end, if you have a passion for what you are doing, the energy within you will continue to multiply. I could get caught up and lost in a million directions, sure, but I have faith that destiny will clear things up for me. The circle of life will work its way around to unity. There will be an instant in my life when everything is perfectly clear, and I can see the path I'm supposed to follow. I'll just have to stay sober long enough to catch a glimpse of it." Jim expressed within the flow of the conversation.

Pepe was the next to speak. "It would be easy to get lost in a never ending encounter like this. I just want to wander and meet people that love life as much as this group. It's the people that make anything real and worthwhile, so you're always searching for the situation, where the people you are surrounded by, are the ones you want to continue to be around. That's where I'm at now, in this bliss of life where I don't really want to go anywhere else." The group continued to fully enjoy each other's company until the boat finally lurched into port. Their sea legs wobbling onto shore, everyone was ecstatic to set foot on their first Greek Island, Paros.

Chapter 12
PAROS

The night had grown late, and the day-and-a-half of straight traveling had taken a toll on the travelers. They would not head out to the popping nightlife of Paros that night, but would look for a place to lie their heads down. The girls, via their guidebook, had chosen a campground along the beach for their residence, and the men at the docks quickly pointed them in the right direction. The campground was close by, and Stefania pointed it out to everyone. She made it clear they would be easily found the next day by scouring the beach in front of the camp. The complexion of the island was hard to see at night, but it was easy to make out an endless beach extended from one side of the port and the town to the other. The Greek Islands are not tropical locations, but desert affairs with white adobe buildings lightly splashed into the landscape. Jim, Liz, and Pepe were not equipped for camping and set out to find their own lodging. Liz wanted a real bed, so an inexpensive hotel was chosen for she and Jim, while Pepe had a much fatter budget and preferred the finest lodging on the island.

Elizabeth and Jim found themselves in a little tiled room with two single beds pushed against separate walls with a small space between them and a tiny bathroom with a stand-up shower. It would do, even though it was tight quarters for a couple that were barely speaking to each other. Liz had already been sleeping a little on the boat and made a direct dive into bed. Jim was drunk and had slept very little the night before, so he crashed just as hard.

The hotel room only had one small window, which was covered well with a drape, so they both slept well into the next morning without disturbance. Liz rose first, feeling refreshed and not hung over like her traveling mate surely would. She headed out to get some exercise and see some of the island. Jim happened to get up while she was gone and figured that she had probably had enough of him and had ditched him for the day. Whether that was the case or not, he didn't really care; he just wanted to get back into the company of the Italians and get a drink to combat his hangover. He showered and realized that the long sleep had revived him quite a bit. He dressed in swim trunks, a tank top, and his sandals hoping to head out on the beach and quickly sift out Stefania. The whole group in bikinis on the beach would have to be the most beautiful site on the island. He allowed plenty of time for Liz to make her way back, if she was just out getting food, but she was obviously out doing her own thing, so Jim felt free to do the same.

Liz jogged up a winding road heading towards a small cathedral, which could be seen from town. Actually, it was more like a tiny chapel that overlooking the town as if it was keeping watch on the moral integrity of the people down below. Elizabeth found herself in a very tranquil spot, and her mind began to engage her faith and what it meant to be in love. The little picturesque white chapel, with a small cross attached to the roof, invoked emotions in Liz that were much larger than the place of worship. Elizabeth pulled on the door handle and was glad to find that it was open. She entered an empty sanctuary with six rows of pews and a small alter facing them. Each side of the chapel had a large window, done in dark shades of stained glass, so the space was quite dim. Elizabeth took advantage of the

solitude in the unique place. She knelt and prayed for all those she
cared about and asked God to give her some clarity in her thoughts,
some ability to decipher the whirlwind of emotions that were constantly surging through her. It was a nice moment, and she felt much
more at ease when she exited into the bright light of the Greek summer. She observed the little town below and the expanse of crystal
clear blue sea. She saw locals fishing in one direction and crowds
starting to gather on the beaches in the other. She thought of Danny
in Oxford, and for a moment, she longed to be with him instead of in
an impossible situation with Jim. But they didn't have sunshine or
beaches anywhere in Oxford, so she allowed herself to become immersed in the beautiful world around her, let down her guard, and
became free from everything that kept the chains rattling around her
ankles. She knew Jim would head straight for the Italian girls, and
she didn't blame him a bit, so she avoided going back to the room
and took a long run up the mountainside road. She was at peace with
the situation and the moment.

Jim scribbled out a note before he left. "Went to find Pepe and
the Italians. We'll be on the beach; you can't miss us. Drinks are on
Pepe—come one; come all." He then headed over to the finest accommodations on the island searching for his Chilean buddy. He was not
in his room, and there was no sight or sound of him, but there was a
well-stocked coffee bar with croissants and Danishes left unguarded
that Jim pilfered ferociously. He walked out of the hotel with a croissant, Danish, cup of coffee and some breath mints to boot. The day
was a dandy one for searing the skin at the beach, and he headed
directly down the avenue that lined the beach in the shape of the
curving island coast. The campground was only about a quarter-mile

down the road, and it was easy to spot the Italian contingency and the tight black curls of his Chilean friend's hair. Pepe had arrived earlier on a rocket scooter and had already secured two more, so groups of three to six could go for rides whenever they desired. Pepe was very kind with his unlimited cash flow, and the drinks flowed from a beach side bar on his tab. There was no arguing with him or paying him a dime. He observed his role as the financial backer of the Bohemian movement, and he even reveled in it.

Stefania saw Jim strolling up and ran to meet him causing him to stop in his tracks. She was in a red bikini made mostly of string and covered so little of her that the imagination had a very short distance to travel. Her breasts were larger than the shirts she wore on the voyage showed, and her hips were shaped in such a curvaceous manner that Jim's jaw dropped to the pebbly beach. She was stunning and already perfectly golden tan. Her womanly shape made some of the other girls look like girls.

"My God, you're gorgeous!" He immediately articulated.

"Grazie, my love." She replied, planting a kiss directly on his lips. The tender gesture was genuine, and Stefania's blue eyes sparkled with the excitement of her feelings for Jim. She grabbed his hand and pulled him to the crowd, which was a reincarnation of the boat trips, especially the second one. The Dutch guys were part of the mix, and Ethel and Hilga were finally winning over Olivia to some extent. Pepe was concentrating on Barbara, rubbing her shoulders, getting her drinks, while Stefania already had Jim and her day planned. They were going to have a couple of drinks, a swim, and then jump on one of the scooters and disappear. The day was like candy, and everyone was nibbling on it, keeping a sweet taste in his or her mouth at all times.

Pepe made sure that Jim understood the concept of the scooters. "Take the woman on a ride; you can't beat the feeling of having her glued to your back with her arms wrapped tightly around you. Take one of the scooters; take it for as long as you like." The invitation was open, and Jim would surely whisk Stefania into the horizon as soon as he refreshed himself a little.

"I went by your hotel. That place is nice. I had breakfast and nobody even fucked with me. I asked for you when I got there, and they rang your room. I guess that's why they let me scavenge the place; they knew I was associated with their V.I.P."

"What do you want to drink, I'll get it?" Stefania asked. Jim decided he would have two shots of whiskey and a beer, and he would be ready for a swim after that. Stefania served Jim on her big beach towel. She drank a large iced Pina Colada while he drank his hard-boiled drinks. They smoked a cigarette, which was the natural accessory to alcohol, and talked to the group in a smooth relaxed tone reflecting how they felt. Stefania put some oil on Jim, and he gladly took the bottle from her and began to apply it slowly and meticulously to every inch of her body. She giggled at his thoroughness, but she certainly appreciated the soft touch of his massaging fingers. They got comfortable languishing in the sand, sipping cold drinks, and sticking together wherever their bodies touched. There was laughter, and a playful spirit emerged from the large sunbathing group. The air was filled with the luxurious scent of their summer: suntan oil, a waft of smoke, and with each breath, a touch of alcohol.

The temperature of the Aegean Sea was just right, perfectly refreshing and easy to stay in and frolic as long as one would like. The sea floor was smoother than the pebble beaches, as if the pounding serf had finally broken the pebbles into sand. Jim sprinted into the water, diving in headfirst, and turned to watch Stefania make her ascent. She wasn't as aggressive, but she was much more graceful. She wasn't even concerned about her mass of golden curls as she dove in headfirst as well. She met Jim in the water and firmly embraced him planting her hands firmly on his butt. Jim picked her up and spun her around as if they were dancing a waltz in the crystal blue sea.

"You fit just perfect." Jim said with Stefania in his arms. "That wonderful smile never fades, does it?"

"Not when I'm with you." The day was theirs' and they were completely lost in each other. The large group had dissolved into a dot on the sand as they swam out further, so they could show affection for each other without being ribbed by the crowd. For a while they kissed standing on the bottom with Jim's chest being stroked by the waves, while Stefania was barely able to keep her head above the bouncing serf. To solve the problem, Stefania lifted her legs and wrapped them around Jim's waist connecting her to him while their lips and tongues explored one another's.

After a good amount of serious groping, Jim thought it might be a good idea to break away from the others. "It's time for a little ride, don't you think?" Stefania agreed with a nod and jumped on Jim's back so that he could swim her back to shore. They looked like a couple and felt so comfortable with each other that their bodies were always touching. If they were walking, they held hands; if they were standing still, Stefania leaned into Jim's chest; and if they were sitting on the towel, Stefania would be propped up between Jim's legs using his chest as the back of her chair. The ease in which they fell into each other was comforting to all their friends, except for Elizabeth, but she hadn't arrived to witness the evolution of the relation-ship. Other couples took the cue and began to intertwine with each other as well.

After one more shared Pina Colada, Jim and Stefania mounted one of the scooters and slowly scooted away from the scene. They headed down the paved road that lined the beach with no idea where they might end up. They were just enjoying each other's company, and with the lack of an agenda, ended up carrying on for some time. The ride felt exhilarating once they got out of town and opened up the throttle tracing the rode with a tail of golden lochs flapping in the breeze. They pressed forward for at least a half-an-hour taking in the breathtaking scenery of the coastline and enjoying the spattering of orchards and farmhouses. Jim steered off the road onto a dirt road that led to a very isolated beach. Once they pulled up to where they could see if there were any others, they were surprised to see a line of cars and scooters parked over a dune. Off in the distance, there were the owners of the vehicles enjoying a beautiful beach void of clothing. "Are you the modest type?" Jim asked.

"Not really, but don't you think you'll get excited if we're naked. You sure were standing at full attention when we were out in the water. I don't see anyone walking around like that."

"I can always roll over and lay on my belly and hide the beast. Any-way, don't you want a little privacy down the beach a ways? We'll just walk down there until we're alone."

"You can't possibly get me naked on our first date."

"Sure I can; it's Greece, and you're supposed to be naked. It's like part of the culture or something. You can't insult these people and leave your clothes on." Jim grabbed his partner's hand and escorted her down the beach making sure to not stare at the different sizes and shapes and all their exposed genitalia. Stefania brought her small pack full of necessities, which included sunscreen that would be pertinent to the virgin skin they were about to unleash to the sun's rays.

"I can control myself as long as you don't touch me in any sensual manner, maybe." Jim commented as he dropped his shorts to the beach.

"Well, I'm going to have to put lotion on your little butt cheeks; they're bright white. And little Jimmy, he needs lotion too."

"If you touch little Jimmy, he'll be big Jimmy really fast." Stefania giggled and turned around motioning for Jim to undo her bikini top, which he gladly did. "Ooh, you're going to need lotion on those for sure. Go ahead, take them off." Stefania had hesitated at the bottoms and sat with her thumbs looped inside the elastic, but hadn't made the leap of pulling them down yet. Jim's courage was helpful, but his ridiculous white midsection looked like a swimsuit, making her hesitate, fearing she would look just as silly. But she took a deep breath, giggled a little, and dropped her bottoms to the ground. They were both completely naked in broad daylight for the first time in their lives, at least in public. Stefania was used to taking her top off at the beach, but to be completely naked was a little unsettling. They weren't drunk enough to make it feel completely natural. Jim was enjoying himself so much that his huge smile was infectious, and Stefania was easily loosened up as Jim rubbed lotion onto her most private of parts. His hands were gentle and sincere without being too promiscuous. They lay on Stefania's big beach towel and took turns massaging each other, offering little butterfly kisses from time to time and enjoying a relaxed conversation about summers past. They became comfortable in their nakedness and didn't budge when others came close to their camp. They would march in and out of the water for the whole world to see without even noticing anyone but each other. There was no sex, but the intimacy grew to a fervor pitch with constant shows of affection.

A couple of hours on the nude beach was an enjoyable experience, but there was no bar or friends to share the day with, so the couple redressed, hopped on the scooter and headed back to the main beach. This time, Stefania was at the controls. Jim suggested that she take over, remembering how much Liz enjoyed the driving experience in Rome. Stefania hadn't thought about it, but once the idea was pitched, she believed it was brilliant and immediately took the helm, her dramatic Italian features lighting up like the sun.

Liz spent her morning in a quiet manner, avoiding the others, and trying to bury the awkwardness that was creeping into her thoughts and feelings. She made her way back to the room and read Jim's note, which was exactly what she had expected, but not what she wanted. She wound herself into a lonely depression for the next couple of hours, trying to avoid the group altogether. She went to the beach with a book and her thoughts, but her thoughts won out, and she couldn't just rest and read with all the fun people within reach. She longed to be part of the fun, and eventually meandered in the direction where she knew she would find everyone. By this time, she was feeling sorry for herself for no apparent reason. She made her way, semi-pouting, to the bar where she had spotted Pepe cuddled around Barbara on a single bar stool.

"Ah, Elizabeth, what a wonderful sight." Pepe decried with just a touch of slur to his words. "You must have a drink. Everyone is here; we've missed you. Jim has disappeared on a scooter; I've got three of them if you want to go for a ride. I think everyone is too drunk to scoot now, so you may be the only one who is safe to drive. Why so glum? Have a drink—cheer up."

"Do I look glum? How unattractive. Maybe I should drink; I need to snap out of it."

Barbara grabbed Liz's hand and kissed it, "Don't be sad. It's time to play. The water is fine and there are golden men everywhere. A beautiful girl like you can have your choice."

"I'm taken. Maybe that's my problem. I've come on this gorgeous trip just after I've committed myself to a man. How stupid, huh?"

"Oh, sweet dear. You have found your love, and that is a precious thing. Don't worry about the men; they are mostly trouble anyway, especially if you have a keeper. No worries, stay with us, we'll cheer you up."

Liz sat down next to Barbara smiling gratefully and ordered a breezy beach drink, something with fruit juice and vodka. "So Jim just drove off by himself on one of those scooters?"

"With Stefania." Pepe replied. "They've grown quite fond of each other. They were way out in the water entangled with one another for a while, and then they came back in for one drink and were off on the scooter."

Liz frowned a little on the inside, but gave a look on the outside as if it was inconsequential. Liz got more comfortable as the vodka made it's way through her veins, and she began to loosen up a bit. She swam in the ocean and engaged herself with the group. The jovial attitude spread easily, and after four stiff drinks, she forgot that she came to the island with Jim. The Dutch men became more and more attractive, and pretty soon, she was doing an array of drunken gymnastics on the beach. The swirling around gave her a rush and was precise enough to elicit admiration from the group. As she finished her twirling exhibition, which included a couple of cartwheels followed by some perfect back handsprings, she was happy to hear a light splatter of clapping. The dizziness she had created within her own head made her lackadaisical when it came to a set of feet approaching at an unnaturally rapid pace. It was Jim, and it was too late for her to react, as he easily grabbed and lifted her off her feet.

"Let me go you man whore." She shot out as she was being whisked to the sea. Jim got out to his waist and quickly hurled her over his head into the coming waves. She gurgled and came out gasping for air.

"What did you call me? Where did you get such a vehement slang of my character? Are you upset that I've found a beautiful woman that enjoys my sexy body? Are you jealous that I've just come from rubbing lotion all over her curvaceous naked body? Oh, you poor thing, I didn't mean to hurt you. Let me help you." Jim picked her up again, but this time cradling her in his arms like a little baby. She squirmed violently and spit saltwater in his face. "Ooh, I like it when you're feisty."

"Let me go, I have new friends now." Liz decried as she finally escaped her captor. "You ditched me all day. What kind of friend are you?" She put on her best pout, her bottom lip sticking out with her hands firmly on her side.

"You're a grown woman, so don't give me that baby shit. You know that I have certain needs, and you're unwilling to fulfill them, so let me enjoy myself, and don't give me any attitude." Jim said, pinching Liz in the butt as he walked by. She jumped a few inches off the ground and couldn't help but grin.

"Ouch, why do you abuse me?" Liz was loosened up a little, though. Jim's playful spirit was contagious and he was right. Why not let him have his fun, and then there wouldn't be so much pressure on her. Elizabeth stayed with the group for the rest of the day as they tried with all their might to drink the small beach bar dry. Jim and Stefania remained close, sharing the same towel and taking long swims together away from the group.

"So, what do you think about a romantic night out, just me?" Jim asked Stefania as they were wading in from a swim. We can have dinner and wine in a quiet spot and fall in love as the sun sets."

"Yes, Jim, that's exactly right, that's exactly what tonight shall be. What time should I be ready?"

"How long do you need? It doesn't take me long?"

"Eight is good, and we won't miss the sunset you're talking about. I'm going to look my best, so you be ready."

"You always look your best; all you have to do is smile. I'll be proud to be seen with you anywhere, and I'll do my very best to show up looking like a gentleman, however much of a stretch that might be."

"You are a sweet man. You are taking me on a date; that is very sweet. You are very much a gentleman." Stefania said giving Jim a kiss on the lips and turning towards the campground to go get prepared for the impending date.

Now Jim had to maneuver without getting his somewhat agitated friend too upset. She had no good reason to be upset, but he could tell that if he neglected her too long she would get combative and make the rest of their traveling experience much less enjoyable. Somehow, he wanted to please both women. Stefania was something special, but he knew within a couple of days, they would be parting. She had plans to go to a remote island and camp with her girlfriends, while Jim and Liz had already picked some of the more mainstream islands. Jim had many different scenarios flash through his head as to how he could extend his time with Stefania, but all of them would be offensive to his traveling partner. He cared for her too much to suggest anything that would almost certainly infuriate her, such as him going to one island for a couple of days while she went to another.

"Her mother would kill me if she found out that I ditched her daughter in the middle of the Aegean Sea." He thought to himself as his mind tried to drum up an acceptable plan. The conclusion was that he would have to make the best of his time with Stefania, giving his best effort at creating a magical night that would last until they met again, a never-ending sweet memory. The setting was exquisite; it only needed the true light of romance.

After a hard day in the sun, the group began to disperse around dinnertime with everyone making plans to go to the Hard Rock Café for evening cocktails. The standard night on the islands called for heavy partying, so places such as the Hard Rock, thrived with little regard for closing time. The young world travelers that gravitated to the Greek Islands were looking for long nights and hot days. God provided the latter, while man made the former with cocktails and rock-n-roll. The Italian tribe had grown to almost double by displaying their bikini bodies on the beach all day, and many of the girls had told more than one man to meet them at the club later that evening. Liz had wedged herself in with the Ethel and Hilga group, and all of them were joyously planning their night out. The distraction was good for Jim; he could fly under the radar getting ready at the room with his traveling mate, and then breaking his plans quickly and strategically as they got ready to leave. This would leave Liz little time to dwell on the fact that she would be going to the club alone. "So you're ditching me again. I've got to go out alone and look like some desperate female searching for someone to be my friend."

"You've got to be shitting me, there's going to be twenty people that you spent the whole day with there. How can you possibly put a guilt trip on me?"

"Walk me over there at least; you're supposed to take care of me. And what if I get drunk and make a fool of myself; you won't even be there to protect me. I'm not even going to go. You don't love me."

"You won't let me love you. Now get your shit together, stop pouting, and I'll walk you over there. Pepe will take care of you, he's a good dude, and he won't let anything happen to you. As far as making an ass of yourself—that's a given, but you'll forget about it by morning." Liz scrunched up her nose and stuck her tongue out at Jim, but she was already dressed and had done her make-up so she wasn't going to give up on the night, and Jim knew it. "Come on, you can do some heavy petting with one of the Dutch guys. It'll make you feel better. You know you want to."

"I do not; I'm not going to do that anymore." Liz grabbed some money, shoved it in her pocket and stepped outside, waiting for Jim on the other side of the door. Jim still had plenty of time to walk Liz to the club and still meet Stefania. The others had decided to eat at the Hard Rock Café, or to simply have an appetizer with their liquid diets. Jim actually got Liz all the way to the bar and was able to toss back a drink before heading off to his dinner date.

As Jim was walking down the beach boulevard, Stefania came walking his way. Jim had to gasp for breath, losing it at the sight of her. She was wearing a black dress that was one piece of cloth wrapped around her body snuggly, cascading around her neck leaving her shoulders bare, and then tied at the waste. There were Asian landscapes printed on the dress in white, gardens with petite pagodas floating on the black material turning the corners of Stefania's sensuous curves. She had her hair tied up so that her curls flowed over like a fountain. There was a very light splash of make-up, just enough to bring out her natural, elegant beauty causing Jim to be breathless. He kissed her cheek, took her hand, and spun her around as if they had begun a dance to the music of life.

Jim had bought a new shirt, deep black and smooth enough to be dressy, which he wore with his only pair of slacks and a pair of cheap dress shoes he had picked up along the way. He was prepared to try to accommodate her stunning beauty, but his efforts fell far shy as she turned every head on the island, while most looked right through him. He knew that she would come looking far better than he could possibly fix himself up to be, but at least, he did his best to get the wrinkles out of his attire. Stefania was further gone than he and could have cared less what Jim was wearing. He could have shown up in shorts, and she would have felt just as comfortable. She never lost touch, completely accepting the world as it happened, and she was glowing as the excitement within her bubbled over to her exterior.

"You look marvelous. I'm surely the luckiest man in all of Europe to share your company on this perfect evening."

"You're so sweet. You look fabulous as well, and we look great together in our matching black. You didn't realize that I could clean up so well at a campground, did you? They've got really nice facilities and the girls and I know how to live on the road. We can live wonderfully on very little money. We've been making our way for years, and I don't think we really want anything to change."

"I surely don't want anything to change tonight. I'm exactly where I want and with whom I want to be." The couple walked hand in hand to a little restaurant that Jim had stopped by on the way back from the beach. He had spent a little time perusing the menu, engaging the staff, and was quickly assured it was an extraordinary group of people with a wonderful fare to offer.

"This little place is charming, I stopped in earlier, and the people really brought the place to life. They assured me there was no better place for a romantic interlude."

They sat at a little table along the window, a candle lit between them, and a cold carafe of fabulously smooth and sweet Greek wine instantly delighting their palates.

"Sir, the house wine is as good as any on the island, and you can drink a lot of it and still have money to go out. I took the liberty; do you like it?" The dark haired, blue eyed, Greek waiter said. It was the same man Jim had spoken to earlier, and he continued to let off a perfect energy that made the night even more exquisite.

"It's perfect." Stefania said. "And please pick the most authentic, tasty Greek meal for me. I'll eat anything; you could not possibly fail in your choice."

"Yes, I'll let you guide me with your choice as well. I have complete faith in you." The waiter was so kind and had such a purely beautiful look about him, that both Jim and Stefania felt he would treat them like family. The night was moving along with a mystical flow creating a romantic cloud that shut the world out except for positive sensations that would seep in for pure joy. The sunset on the water, the light music in the background, the flickering of the candlelight on olive colored skin, the smell of wine and fine food, and the wonderful hospitality made it feel like home.

"What do you think he'll bring you? What do you really want? Jim asked.

"I want you more than dinner."

"Fantastic. Waiter, can we get the check? Just kidding, just kidding—she's just getting a little hot, and I'm not sure we can make it through dinner. Can we make it?" Jim asked Stefania with the waiter grinning widely in total understanding of the youthful passion.

"We are looking forward to the meal. We are in no hurry; the atmosphere is perfect." Stefania said to the waiter who then went off pleased with the young couple, their enchantment wearing off on him.

"You are a good man, Jim, and this is such a nice evening. I want it to last. I'm definitely not in a hurry. We will be together tonight, right?"

"Where are we going to stay?"

"I've got that taken care of. The girls have made sure that we have our own private suite. They will be out most of the night anyway. We will have a beautiful night under the stars in my tent—we don't need luxurious accommodations, not us. I am ready for us; don't worry. You have done well with the meal, and the rest of the night is mine."

"You have such an ease about you, as if the world is a garden, and you're the gardener who knows exactly how to tend everything to make it live a perfect life. Those girls follow you and rely on your sense of things to make the best decisions for all. They are all different kinds of flowers with different needs, and you've got it all figured out. I'm amazed at how much they respect and love you. What do you think it is that makes you so comfortable in this world?"

"I have balance in my life. Nothing consumes me except for love. With the girls, they follow me because they are relaxed and do not want to make decisions. They tell me before we depart on holiday that the decisions are mine. Actually, most things were decided before we left, and so I take charge of only the little day-to-day things. It's easier for all of us if one person takes the lead so that we can stay a little organized. Most of us grew up together, and I was the outspoken one, the one who stood up for any one of us. I am very emotional, unable to hide how I feel, so my friends always know where I stand on everything—there's no hiding it. I try to be there for all of them, and they have faith in me."

"You said, 'nothing consumes me except for love'. That is one of the most wonderful statements I have ever heard. I can't say that I'm as good as a person as you. I'm selfish, but I'm just like you in the sense of being an emotional person. I'm transparent in that way. I can't hide anything either. I can't lie or steal, and I get very angry when I am attacked or criticized. I need to grow up. I try to take a little piece of the best attributes from the people I meet; sometimes they don't leave me anything but the bad, though. I only hope that you'll grant me a little piece of your kindness."

"You are the kindest man I have met in a long time, and being emotional is a good thing. Your enthusiasm for life pours out of you, and everyone around you is infected."

"No, that is you. You were the one that infected the whole ship. You were the center of the energy on both of our voyages. Everyone was drawn to you, especially me. Maybe we are a lot alike, though. Maybe that is why it is so easy and natural to be around one another. Hey look, I think that's our food." The plates arrived and each customer was elated with the waiter's choices. For Jim, there was rice pasta with lamb and a wonderfully light, buttery, tomato sauce. Stefania was served a fillet of fish with a local array of vegetables and elegantly prepared rice. The second carafe of house wine was served with the meal. It was perfect, and there was no reason to change. The couple fell silent for a while as they enjoyed their meals thoroughly.

"Take a bite." Stefania extended her fork with a piece of fish smothered in a creamy white sauce. Jim took a bite and returned the gesture.

The night was dark, and the restaurant was starting to empty by the time Stefania and Jim finished their third carafe of wine. Their tongues had really opened up with the help of the alcohol; not that either one of them really needed help to talk. Every once in a while the conversation would stop, and they would lean across the table and gently kiss the other, not in an obnoxious display of public affection, but in a classy gesture remaining couth in the public space. The waiter had become their friend and had spent more than his fair share of time chatting with the couple. He didn't hurry them out and encouraged them to stay and enjoy their wine as the staff cleaned up. The waiter was the son of the owner and brought a fourth carafe of wine to the table, on the house, and sat down to drink it with his favorite patrons of the night. The bill ended up only including two of the four carafes.

"Italy and America together, very beautiful. That is what makes our island so great; the world melts here. You two have just met here, yes?"

"Well, on the way here. We were on the same boat from Italy. Stefania was the spirit of the voyage. She pulled everyone together and claimed me for hers, and I didn't resist."

"And now you fall in love at my restaurant, yeah?"

"Love, yes, I could love this man. He could earn my love, yet we are in paradise, and nothing can possibly go wrong. Things might be different if the circumstances were more strenuous, but for now, he is the perfect man to spend the holiday with. As for the future, I will give him a chance and hope he comes through. I could look at him forever; he is beautiful, and his eyes are like magic candles always burning."

"If I was smart, I would just follow her home to Italy and never leave. What do you think Stefania? Would your parents approve of a longhaired American photographer with very little potential? Actually that's not true. I will make my way in this world. I will be successful. Would they like me?"

"Sure, my parents love everyone. They are both bubbly people, always happy; they would not judge you by your appearance or your profession, just by your character."

"So I can move in. I'll learn Italian and get a job at a newspaper in Italy, or maybe I can correspond to an American rag and do some writing as well. Yeah, let's go call your parents right now and tell them the good news. You've picked up an American straggler, and you're pretty sure with a little love and care he'll turn out okay."

"Yeah, they'll love that. You probably won't even remember me by the end of your trip much less make a commitment to live in Italy. Don't tease me like that; I would love to have you move in. You'll go back to America, back to university and to all your girlfriends."

"You two look beautiful together. Don't worry about any other night, just concentrate on tonight. Go take a walk in this perfect night, and everything will take care of itself."

"What, you trying to get rid of us?" Jim exclaimed.

"No, no, no. I have nowhere else to be. I just suggest that when you leave here, you take the women on a moonlit stroll. The sky will be magnificent, and the sea will make the air taste sweet."

"He's right, let's take a walk on the beach." Stefania said taking her last sip of wine. The bill had already been paid, and they all rose from the table at the same time. The couple's new friend escorted them to the door, gave them both kisses on both cheeks, and bid them farewell at the restaurant steps.

Jim and Stefania headed down the beach hand in hand with their shoes held in their opposite hands. They found a bench facing the sea, and Stefania sat on Jim's lap and kissed him passionately. "You will stay with me tonight." Stefania demanded more than asked as she came up from the kiss.

"Where else in the world would I want to be?" Jim said returning the kiss with a more gentle, subtle flavor. They sat looking into the starry sky and gazing into each other's eyes. They felt an inner warmth that allowed them complete relaxation and comfort. The time on the beach was short because they were itching to explore each other more fully, and there was too much traffic for that. They made their way to the campground and to the compound of tents that the Italian girls had set up in a circle. The girls lived as one unit, and they had made preparations for the night to come, leaving Stefania her own tent, which she had made into a romantic setting. She had candles set up around the tent and had removed the rain flap revealing the sky through the open mesh top.

The campground was nearly silent when they got there. All the girls were still out, and there weren't a lot of campers other than the Italian contingency. Stefania lit the candles and produced a bottle of cheap champagne with plastic champagne glasses. Then she pushed play on the small compact disc player, and a petite Italian voice softly floated over the festivities. Stefania was a classic romantic, and she had created an irresistible atmosphere. Her radiance was the highlight of the ambiance. She leaned up against Jim and they sipped champagne. He untied her dress around her neck and began to massage her shoulders with his free hand. They could only get through the one glass of bubbly before the lust took over. The candles were blown out, and the moonlight became their guide. Jim's hands unwrapped the fabric from her body. A strapless bra quickly unhooked, panties slid to the ankles, and then gently tossed to the side. Stefania worked as effectively having Jim's shirt and pants thrown to the side in an instant with an extreme urgency of getting to the skin. Getting their bodies naked against one another was a huge relief; their clothes were a heavy impediment to their true desires. Jim took his time exploring the perfect craftsmanship of God, using his lips to record every inch into his memory forever. The music reached a fever pitch as they made love with the Greek sand as their mattress and never-ending stars as their blanket. Stefania spoke in Italian whispers and Jim understood it all—their worlds had been brought together, and no translator was necessary.

Sometimes sex is something brewed by lust, and sometimes it is something spiritual, mind altering, and numbing. For Jim and Stefania the sex was definitely a gravity defying experience —they floated out of the tent to a place where they were the only two life forms. Nirvana, utopia, whatever you want to call it; they were suspended in pure ecstasy. Their bodies pulsed with life, and the steamy night air brought with it a liquid layer that lubricated their bodies, so there wasn't any friction, but a pure, uninhibited motion moving in perfect rhythm with each other.

There were climaxes reached, and rests taken with another glass of champagne to wet their throats. Then, they were back into a second coarse that never wanted to end. They didn't grow tired, but were more and more enamored by each other's touch. They sat facing each other, Stefania on top, dropping her hips down slowly to meet Jim's, a light kiss, then deeper with a fluid twist of the hips. They would evolve from one position to another exploring points of pleasure that neither had reached before. Inexhaustible sex continued until their bodies finally heaved into one last orgasm, which shook their consciousness to a point of disbelief. Their bodies finally drained of every last ounce of energy, and their insides still shaking, they fell asleep still entangled.

The morning came with the sound of young Italian women chatting incessantly around a small crackling fire where coffee was being brewed. Being professional outdoors women, the girls had life on the

land figured out and were completely prepared to survive as meager-
ly as possible. Their frugal behavior extended the length of their holiday, which had to be their ultimate goal, because they were generally
pretty cash strapped. Jim rolled over to rub Stefania's bare back, not
making a sound to let on that they were stirring. Stefania rolled over,
exposing her perfect naked body in the early morning sunlight, her
curls popping out in every direction and their golden color glimmering in the sunlight. Jim could tell she wanted him again, right there,
with the girls stirring about. He didn't say anything; he just began to
rub between her legs, slowly and precisely, until her back began to
arch slightly at every move of his fingers. He opened up the fifth little
silver package of the night, sliding on a condom before entering her.
They were nearly silent, Jim moving his hips very slowly, his shoulders raised up in the air, his hands pinning Stefania's wrists to the
ground. She wanted to come up and kiss him, but his strong upper
body kept her head and shoulders on the ground. She relented and
smiled at his controlling efforts. She closed her eyes and let him have
his way. He stayed fully inside her as though their bodies were glued
together at the waist. He moved his hips slowly in circles keeping
the intense pressure between their bodies. He finally dropped down
to have his chest meet hers, sliding his hands from her wrists to her
hands entangling his fingers with hers. He hands free, she wanted to
pull him even closer; her hands dug into his backside, and she pulled
him with all her force further trying to pull his whole body within
hers. She moaned, maybe loud enough to hear, but it didn't matter.
Jim pressed his lips to hers swallowing the passionate sounds. She
pulled her left hip off the ground bringing them both to their sides
then expertly completed the maneuver putting Jim on his back, the
sunlight charging her golden curls. Jim relented completely, and

soon she had her hands on his chest, sitting straight up with all of him inside her. Her golden curls cascading over her shoulders and gently caressing his chest. Jim's hands roaming up her stomach to her breasts then back down her sides tracing the curves of her hips where they stopped and tried to pull her even closer. She began to breathe heavier as Jim squeezed tighter and tighter with his hands. Jim could feel her starting to tighten around him, and his body reacted immediately causing his back to do some arching of its own and his arms to pull her lips to his. She gave one last powerful thrust with her hips and her whole body began to shiver. She held her breath, and bit Jim's lower lip to keep from letting out an undeniable sound of enjoyment. They stayed wrapped in each other's arms for several minutes—eyes closed sharing light airy kisses from time to time. "You are an amazing woman. I don't need to leave this tent for the whole day if you don't want me to. You're the sexiest woman I've ever encountered, and that smile is the purest thing on earth, I'm completely lost in it."

"Aw, my beautiful Jim, you say such sweet things. Our bodies are made for one another. I've never felt so good with a man; I've never been so fully pleased. The whole night was magic. I'm also lost in you; we can never forget each other. I don't want to lose contact with you; I want to see you again, some beautiful day in Italia. I know we are going different directions, but we can not deny the chemistry, and we can not resist reuniting some day."

"Don't worry, my dear; I would be glad to relocate some day. I'll always be in touch." Jim didn't know he was a liar, he really believed this girl was worth keeping in touch with, and he wanted to will himself to be better than he was.

They both knew the night was very special, but that their perspective groups were heading different directions later that day. The entire crew would be scattered about the Aegean, everyone having a different agenda and visiting different islands. Jim could not change the plans Elizabeth and he had already made, and Stefania definitely couldn't alter her plans with eight others tied directly to them. "Let's go take a shower together." Jim suggested.

"We can't do that; there's girls and boys bathrooms."

"Yeah, I was in there last night. I think we can get away with it in the boys showers. They're private, and their ain't no kids around here. No one is going to care. We'll slip in and out of there, and no one will notice. A little adventure will be good for you." Jim had a mischievous smile on his face and a determined twinkle in his eye.

They got dressed, Jim in his pants from the night before, Stefania in more appropriate attire of shorts and a tank top; she didn't bother with a bra. They emerged from the tent with large smiles and were met by a group of gleaming women, who were satisfied that their friends were satisfied. They had a small aluminum pot boiling their morning tea in the fire and were all sitting around in about the same outfit as Stefania. Their hair tied up in mass tangles and creases still streaming down their faces depicting where they had laid their heads the night before. Jim and Stefania were the stars of the morning, and the Italian statements flowed like wine at Stefania, demanding details about the evening. Jim was in his slacks from the night before, but nothing else, and he was barefoot and shirtless with his hair and face looking just like the girls'. He sat down on a large stone and was offered a styrofoam cup of steaming tea and was given a couple cubes of sugar upon his request. The girls surrounded Stefania kissing her on the cheek and getting details about the night.

Then, they pounced on Jim, "So, you had very much fun with our girl, yeah? She says you were very romantic. Will you come back to Italia? You have brothers, yes? You bring them with you. Maybe you come to Italia, and Stefania take care of you; she is our golden mother and she thinks you are fantastic. So do we. You should come travel with us; you will have more fun. You and Stefania can have your own tent, no problem." One of the girls, Jim wasn't sure of her name, said with enthusiasm.

"I'd love to come with you all, but I can't leave my friend, and we already have plans. You girls are going some place where there is only camping, and I don't think Elizabeth could handle that as she's not quite as one with nature. We have been friends a long time, and I have to treat her well."

"Ah, yes, Liz. She was with us last night; she is a good girl—you be good to her. She can not rough it, yeah?" The same bubbly girl asked.

"No, we didn't plan any of that. I'll make it to Italia to see you beautiful ladies again. How can I resist." Stefania was now behind Jim rubbing his shoulders. She had two towels over her shoulder and some soap and shampoo in her hands. "Ah, my dear, time to bathe. Excuse us, we must bathe." Jim slurped down what was left of his tea and took the shampoo and soap out of his mate's hand in order to be helpful. The girls looked a little puzzled as the couple walked off, but they said nothing and only smiled at the prospect.

Jim went in the bathroom first. There was one man taking a shower in the first stall, but it would still be no problem, at least in Jim's demented mind, for the couple to sneak past him and go to the last shower along the wall. Jim went and grabbed Stefania's hand and dragged her into the bathroom; she didn't have time to object. They were quickly past the man and behind their own curtain where they were out of view. The only way they would be found out would be if someone peaked under the curtain and saw two sets of feet instead of one.

"You're insane, there's somebody in here." Stefania snapped in a whisper.

"He'll be out in no time. We'll have the place to ourselves. If we get caught, I believe we will be admired, not frowned upon, we are conserving water, right?" Jim kissed Stefania's lips as the water cascaded over both of their faces. They went about washing each other until they heard the man leave and then they enjoyed one last sexual encounter. Jim lifting Stefania up and pinning her shoulders against the wall just under the shower nozzle so the water sprinkled down between them. After the sex, they washed each other once again and emerged from the bathroom an hour after they had entered. They walked out as two men with towels over their shoulders sauntered in. They looked at each other oddly, smiled and shook their heads. All is good on the Greek Islands.

Elizabeth woke up with a sizzling headache, crawled to the bathroom and swallowed four pain pills and crawled back to bed with a glass of water. She moaned and felt lonely and sorry for herself for a moment. She wanted Jim there to take care of her, to rub her back, and to help her through the hangover cure, which he was a pro at administering. She wished she hadn't drank so much, so she could have gone on the same nice run she had gone on the morning before. She wished the world suited her in a more congenial manner, and others would translate her thoughts into actions. She wanted the world to conform to her vision of it. She thought it not too much to ask that she should be princess of the world, master of the minds' of men. Liz's fairy tale world floated through her thoughts and passed into her dreams, as she fell back to sleep with just a little less pain than before.

Jim walked in with espresso and pastries in hand and a smile beaming on his pleased face. "I'm here to save the day sweet princess."

"Ah, that's more like it." Elizabeth thought, struggling out of a dream that Jim just entered.

"You can't sleep all day, we are set to make another voyage. We must set sail to Naxos; we must fulfill our destiny."

Liz finally realized it was reality and not her dream. "Leave me alone."

"Leave you alone. How can I possibly leave such a sexy young vixen alone? How bout you sit up, drink a little of this java, which has been specially made to your liking, have a couple bites of Danish to settle your stomach, then I'll give you a relaxing rub to get your day started right. I will not accept a poor attitude on this day."

"I can't move."

"Oh, you can move; I see you squirming around under there." Jim moved on to Liz's bed and began to lightly tickle her sides.

"Don't touch me!" Liz snapped, but Jim persisted, his mood much too high to get knocked off track. "You're impossible—stop touching me."

"So you don't want a rub?"

"You're not rubbing; you're tickling, and you're pissing me off."

"Ooh, pissing you off, you're so foul, and this isn't going to work.

You must lighten up, get up, and get yourself together." Jim stopped tickling and went to a more conventional tactic of gently rubbing her shoulders and back. She could not reject this and he knew it. "There you go, relax, let Jimmy's magic fingers soothe your soul. I'm going to take care of you. You don't need to put up a struggle. I'll get your shit ready. All you have to do is get out of this funk, and get yourself ready for the next voyage." Jim continued to rub. Liz mumbled satisfyingly, but said nothing distinguishable. After a long, pleasant rub, she finally sat up to drink her coffee and make an effort of shaking off the remains of the margaritas she had made love to the night before.

"So did you get lucky with the Italian? I suppose so, since you were gone all night." She asked as Jim was packing their bags.

"What do you want me to leave out for you? What do you want to wear today?"

"I don't care; you pick it. So?"

"An honorable man does not kiss and tell, my dear."

"Okay. That's fine—you don't have to be honorable. As a matter of fact, you told me about the Spanish girls, and I saw you naked in my flat with three other people. I'm not sure that any of that's honorable. And what about the story from Uncle G; it's probably true. You're a slut, and you can surely fill me in on the details. Honorable men don't sleep with women every time they step off the train, or boat, or whatever. Actually, I'm sure you'd sleep with them on the train, or the boat, if they'd let you."

"Do I sense a bit of envy?"

"More like disgust. So what happened? I know you want to tell me."

"I don't want to disgust you with the details of lustful sex, it wouldn't be right to subject such a pure women to such immoral behavior."

"Oh bullshit. If I can't do it, I at least want to hear about it. I can live vicariously."

"You know it doesn't have to be that way. We should be having our own sorted, hot, love affair. I would be glad to show you, up close and personal, how I can make your whole body tremble. There were a couple times last night when she was coming so ferociously, and her insides squeezed together so violently that I thought she was going to cut off all circulation. Look!" Jim pulled down his pants to display the deep slash marks that had been left in each of his buttocks. "Whenever you have wounds that could develop into permanent scars, then you've got to say the night went pretty well, don't you think?"

"Are you sure you weren't hurting her, and she was just trying to pull you off?"

"Come on now, Elizabeth, when a woman digs her nails into your flesh and pulls you closer with all her strength, the last thing she is feeling is any pain. Anyway, we had a very pleasant evening that ended in a lustful furry of mutual affection. I have to go tell her goodbye in an hour or so. They are going to some rinky dink little island with an extremely rustic quality as I understand it."

"So that's it. You're going to see her off, like out of your life forever, or is there something there or what?"

"Who knows what happens tomorrow. She's definitely a special girl, and I would be crazy to forget about her. I'll try to write, but I know I'm not very good at keeping up with that, and maybe I'll see her again some day. It was definitely more emotional than that kinky stuff in Oxford with Linda. The Spanish girls were just gifts from God. He understands that I am a connoisseur of women, and He was kind enough to allow me a fantasy experience. Yeah, I like this girl, and she might turn into something—you never know."

"You're so detached. You can just share the most intimate experience there is with a woman, see her off, and then you would probably sleep with me tomorrow night if I let you."

"I'd sleep with you right now if you'd let me, then go give her a kiss goodbye right after we got finished. I don't see any problem with that, I mean we're young, and we've got to feel while we can. Eventually we're going to grow old and numb, and when that time comes, I'm not going to have any regrets."

"You will, if you catch something, and your dick falls off."

"Nice. I wore a rubber, not necessarily because I wanted to, but all the same I was safe."

"You brought rubbers with you on your date? You're kind of cocky, aren't you?"

"No, I didn't bring any. I forgot. She had a whole box. Those girls are prepared to enjoy their vacation; and they're extremely sensible, smart, and sexy. So, do you want it really quick before I go say goodbye. That way you can kind of feel like you got one up on those girls."

"Nice try, like that bullshit is going to get me to drop my panties. You're so romantic I can't wait to jump your bones, come on." Liz was starting to lighten up and enjoy the rhetoric. "I'm sure you'll find another woman on the next island who will accommodate your endless lustful desires, but I'm not going to give in that easy."

Jim got their bags packed and headed back out the door to go see the Italian contingency off at the docks. When he got there, he noticed Pepe had loaded up with some nice camping gear and was going to make the journey with the girls, as any sensible single man would have done. Jim envied Pepe's freedom of movement and would have loved another night in the company of the Italian troupe. "Pepe, you're going to rough it? What about your five star hotels?"

"Who needs five star hotels when you have five star women."

"Exactly, you're so much smarter than you look." Jim left Pepe to ponder while he headed for his favorite Italian. She came running towards him lit up like a fire truck and jumped on him with her legs wrapping around his waste. They kissed, a long deep kiss, but did not say a word. A little glimmer flooded into Stefania's eye, but it was happy and soon retreated as she walked away. She was the last to place her foot on the boat before the crewmember connected a chain across the entry. Ropes were tossed onto the decks and the huge engines began to churn. Jim waved, feeling a little choked up, but not allowing the tears to well. He felt good, like everything inside him had been taken out and cleaned—he was completely refreshed. "That was a good woman." He thought, watching her fade away in the noonday sun. "Now what do I do with the mysterious one that refuses to join me in my fairy-tail land."

He walked back to the room crisscrossing the women in his head, Stefania's ease of being with Elizabeth's hard headedness. Stefania began to win the imaginary battle, but in the end, he was just as attracted to Liz; maybe because she had remained forbidden. He wanted to share extreme intimacy with her, but they viewed it on two alternate plains, and it was going to be hard for them to ever get into the same world with their bodies intact. Her set of morals and her long-standing tradition of abstaining from sin were not aligned with Jim's free-love spirit. She couldn't digress down the evolutionary ladder, and he couldn't promise her something he didn't even understand. He believed that if two people were attracted to each other, they should explore those feelings completely, sexually and emotionally—fate would join them for eternity if all the chemistry were perfect. Of course, this was naïve as Jim had never had to work through the slightest complications of true love because he had never allowed his heart over to another; he had never given control to anyone else. Jim had trouble seeing things past the present. He couldn't fathom the concept of time any more than he understood why people got married.

Liz got herself together in the room while Jim was gone. She showered and dusted on a little make-up, not her usual application, but enough to get her by, and was waiting for Jim with both bags outside the hotel when he got back.

"My oh my, you certainly did get motivated. There must have been something magic in that coffee."

"I'm not going to be such a bitch anymore."

"Whoa, who said you were a bitch? I haven't made any complaints. We're getting along okay"

"I've been pouting the last couple of days. I wanted you to notice me or pay more attention to me, or whatever, but that was selfish because I'm not providing you with what you are looking for. I shouldn't get in your way, and I shouldn't get upset when you find what you want."

"I want you as bad as anything or anyone. You could just succumb to my charm, and we wouldn't have this problem."

"In a way I want to. I wish I could. I wish I could just let go and have fun with you and not be so stuck in my ways. I can't think like you, though. I can't breathe life so freely, I have to analyze it and be true to what I've created inside. That doesn't mean that I have to be difficult, though. I really want to be more laid back; I really want to see the world through less analytical eyes, but I'm stuck in what I know, and what I know is to be cautious and sensible, not care-free and horny like you. Even though I've got to admit that there are times when I want to eat you."

"You want me as bad as I want you. You're just practicing some form of self-denial that is consistent with what you've been taught all your life. I don't blame you for who you are, and I don't even think it's a bad thing. You're just programmed different than I am, and if we're made for each other, the programming will go out the window. Just relax—we're going to be fine. I'm not going to be so selfish. We both need to make efforts to keep each other satisfied. We're on this trip to learn about people and the worlds that shape them, and we'll learn a lot about each other too. Maybe that will really be worth something, but we can't force anything to happen—we've just got to let things unwind." He kissed Liz on the cheek. "The not being a bitch thing was very nice, I appreciate it." He hoisted his bag to his shoulders, lifting hers up as well. They felt good in each other's company for the first time in a couple of days and were in good spirits when they stepped on their ferry. They were heading to the island of Naxos, not for any particular reason other than it was a short boat ride and a big island with lots to explore.

Chapter 13
TRUE LOVE?

Their choice of islands was a good one. Naxos was the perfect place for them to get a good taste of culture without being blinded by an overbearing party. There was a good mix of culture and holiday activities, and they would get a taste of both while on the island. They had also found an interesting, inexpensive hostel located on the beach just at the edge of town. The sleeping quarters were large airy rooms with mats strewn around for sleeping bags. The windows were always wide open letting the sea breeze flush through the room. There were several people lounging about, but not so many that they were piled on top of each other. Each person had comfortable space, although, it really didn't matter because when you walked out the door, you were on the beach. The hostel was set up to enjoy the beach with volleyball courts and a large recreation center with all kinds of beach equipment available for rent cheap.

Jim and Elizabeth set up camp in a corner underneath a large window and headed for the bathrooms to get in their beach gear as quickly as possible. They were both in the mood for rest and relaxation on the beach, and this was the place to do it. There was an open-air bar next to the hostel making alcohol accessible, one of Jim's criterion for quality living. The couple decided they would spend what was left of the day reading and kicking back on the beach. The afternoon was kind of gray, but the air was hot, and the breeze was just enough to keep the sweat from accumulating. Liz got settled in a lounge in front of the bar, and Jim put his stuff down and headed directly for the barkeep, which turned out to be a lovely Australian female. Actually, the only two employees at the bar were two extremely friendly Australian females.

"So, do you speak Greek?" Jim asked after he had been greeted in the Australian's native English tongue. He was the only customer snuggled up to the bar for the moment. There were a couple of other groups outside the bar ordering drinks from their tables with umbrellas. It was a mellow atmosphere that Jim liked a lot.

"Don't know much Greek. Been here all summer, and learned a little from our boss and the cook, but they both speak good English so they don't usually bother. Very rarely do we have a Greek customer; they have their own beaches. This is a tourist beach so they hire us for the summer plus a month or two before and after and then shutter the place for the rest of the year. The hostel keeps a steady stream for at least five or six months. It's been full the whole time we've been here, and everyone spends the money they save at the hostel drinking." The barkeep replied. The other girl, who was the waitress at the outside tables, came and sat next to Jim at the bar.

"So what gave you two the idea to come to Greece to find work? How did you come across a gig like this?"

"We're Aussies, and that's what we do. Most Aussies go on a roundabout before they start university. Sometimes it lasts two years or more. We travel around the whole world stopping from time to time to work, usually in the tourism industry. There's a network set up over the years. You always know someone's big brother or sister who has already been on their trip, and they give you all kinds of tips: where you can work, where you can live cheap, and have the most fun, all kinds of stuff. It's part of our culture." The waitress answered this time.

"I love that tradition—that's a beautiful way to start your adult life. I think I would end up wandering like that forever. I've been on a trip all summer, and I don't want it to end. Eventually I'm going to run out of money, though, and I've got to get back to school. You've got both of those issues covered; I'm envious."

"What's your name sunshine? I'm Amber and this is Cookie."

"Cookie, you do look good enough to eat." Jim said, trying to be funny, not crude.

"I've heard that one before," Cookie answered.

"Yeah, I know, I'm very creative and original; all my friends tell me so." All three shrugged it off and settled in for a comfortable conversation. The girls even sneaked themselves a drink while the threesome talked about journeys around the world. For girls in their waning teenage years, they had done everything Jim could throw at them plus a plethora of other ill-advised shenanigans impressing Jim. Jim got so engrossed in the conversation, he accidentally forgot about his partner on the beach. He was supposed to bring her a drink, so eventually she came wandering in.

"Oh, how easily I'm forgotten." Liz said, coming up behind Jim unnoticed.

"Ah, ladies, this is my friend Elizabeth. She is traveling with me, but she refuses to give me any sex, so I usually claim her as my sister. I'm sorry I forgot about you, my dear; I was just learning about these two lady's roundabout. They're from Australia and they're quite friendly. This is Cookie and the beautiful barkeep is Amber."

"He's a never-ending flirt. I should have known there were females in here. I can lose him really quickly if there are pretty girls around.

All of a sudden he gets amnesia and forgets all about me." Jim ordered Elizabeth a sex-on-the-beach, for a joke, and because he knew she would like it.

"So you two are traveling together, but you're not together. Isn't that kind of difficult? When you get a little loaded, things change a little bit, right?" Amber asked.

"I've tried to get her toasted. She might let her guard down for a second, but it never lasts."

"I'm in love with another man, and I think I'll probably marry him. I'm trying to be good. I want him to trust me." Liz said.

"Oh bullshit, what about the Aussie?" Jim retorted.

"Well, there was a lot of wine, and as noted, your judgment gets a little impaired."

Cookie jumped in. "Wait a second, who was the Aussie?"

Jim replied, "Some guy she was rolling around in the grass with in Pisa. She won't take a tumble with me, but some shaggy haired, smooth talking Aussie got her panties in a wad really quick."

"I didn't sleep with him; it was just a little heavy petting. It was a mistake, and I haven't done it again."

"Australian men can be complete snakes. You should watch out for them, sweet; they're only looking for one thing." Cookie added as she got up to go check on her customers.

"This one's the same; it doesn't matter where they're from—the male is genuinely driven by hormones alone." Liz pointed at Jim with her glaring eyes to make her example well known.

"Hey, do not degrade me in front of Amber and Cookie. They were my friends first, and you all can't turn against me with this male pig thing. I am a man who respects women very much and spends most of my waking hours trying to give them what they want. I am not simply pleasure seeking for myself."

"We're not going to turn on you, dear. Relax. We're very fond of men; they have their place." Amber said, grinning ear-to-ear enjoying watching Jim squirm. Jim thought he might be on the verge of becoming the butt of a female blasting session, and he needed to change the subject quickly because Liz had years of dirt on him.

"Anyway, Liz and I are friends from way back, and we had decided to come on this trip before she fell for Romeo at Oxford, but we were never romantically involved, so it wasn't like she was betraying me or anything. We used to live on the same street when we were younger, and we enjoy each other's company. I thought we would finally get a chance to expand that enjoyment on this trip, but I was overly optimistic. The sexual tension is a byproduct of us not being kids anymore. Actually, I thought she was really sexy when we were younger, but she was committed to her abstinence program, while I was in the free love camp, so we just compared notes and rubbed each other's bodies a lot."

"We're not romantically involved because he's a man whore and will be one always, and I would just end up getting hurt." Liz said trying to dig her way out of being a prude.

"Ooh, low blow. I would never hurt you. You just need to have a little different perspective."

"So, if we were to have sex, you wouldn't just consider it another casual encounter. If I sleep with someone, I'm definitely going to expect to be involved in a relationship. You have no intention of making any commitment to anyone. I know you, Jimmy, and some-how you want to convince me that casual sex among friends would be good for me—that we can make each other feel good whenever our paths cross, and as far as the emotional attachment, it would just make it that much better when our paths do cross. Am I right?"

"See, you're already coming around. You try to blame me for that line of thinking, but you've already got it all figured out, and I didn't put any of those ideas in your head."

"What are you talking about? You've been putting those ideas in my head for years. You've told me story after story about your affairs with different women, and how it's okay to have sex with different women on different nights of the week without any attachment to anything but the physical pleasure."

"Elizabeth, number one, I was never speaking of you within any of those stories. I don't see you as just any other girl. I already have full comprehension of what kind of person you are, and I have no intentions of taking advantage of your sentimentalities. Number two; I never said anything about just enjoying the physical contact. There was a lot more to it than that. In most cases, there was con-versation, friendship, the sharing of the beautiful intimacy of life. And sometimes there was a genuine emotional attachment, it just never lasted that long because you figure out it's just lust after the shine wears off."

"See, I'm supposed to take part in some lustful affair with you?"

"Sure, why not?" Jim winked at Amber behind the bar. "Do you have lustful affairs, Amber, or are you like Liz here and maintain a set of morals and values that are unrealistic?"

"I'm a realist, baby, and I ain't afraid to get a little hot and bothered every once in a while, but I don't just pass it out to anyone either. All in all, though, I do like the emotional adrenaline that lust provides. Sometimes it feels great to just let go with some beautiful man and see where it leads, and with men that almost always leads to shagging. I'm not looking for relationships, though. Hell, I'm traveling around the world; I don't need to give some bloke the wrong idea and have him try to tag along. I can understand though, honey, if you choose to value your body and not just give it up to any loser."

"Hey, hey, hey, this is winner material here. I'm offering her a perfect little slice of bliss, and she can choreograph it anyway she wants. Lust is the best drug on earth, my dear, and with the chemistry between you and me, we can take it to levels that your earthly desire has never experienced."

"Boy, he's cocky." Amber shrugged towards Jim and winked at Liz. Jim shook his head and gave up his fight for the time being; he could beg later. Jim had acquired an air of indifference when it came to him and Liz getting together. He was still riding the high of the time with Stefania and was, therefore, content to peck away at Elizabeth little by little in hopes of eventually making a breakthrough.

The day at the beach was very pleasant. The sky was gray, but the air was perfect bath water warm, and Jim and Elizabeth caught a little buzz, took several swims, and played Frisbee on the beach. They didn't have a concern in the world, and the lack of being part of a large group, brought them closer together. Amber and Cookie were sweethearts and provided tourist guidance, suggesting a good restaurant and a nightspot for drinking and dancing. The money they were saving by staying at the hostel could be spent on a good meal and a night out.

They eventually walked back to the hostel, showered and dressed in shorts and tee shirts, and headed into town for a meal and a night out together. The clouds had finally cleared by the time they reached town, and the sunset went on forever. The silhouette of a fisherman stood out on the shore against the bright sunlight. Jim had his camera and caught the image for good. The glistening evening light lit the island up, turning the quiet rocky landscape into a dancing reflection of light catching the sagebrush on fire with reds and oranges. It was a great night to dine outside, as was the habit of the traveling couple whenever it was possible. Naxos had a large boulevard bordering the sea that was perfectly set up for the restaurants to offer almost all their seats outside. The Greek meal was perfectly tasty, and the unique wine was refreshing and intoxicating. They enjoyed another night in splendid drunk, not too much, but enough to free the feet and hips on the dance floor in the little open-air bar that sported a DJ. There was a comfortable size group of young people at the bar including Cookie and Amber, who had closed the shutters at the beachside bar hours before.

The group spent a mellow night at the bar dancing and enjoying one another's company. Yet another Australian native ran the bar treating everyone like locals, and he had selective amnesia regarding how many drinks had been served to each person. It was part of the international network, and Jim really wanted a ticket to join the flow. He got drunk and worked on his Australian accent, but there was nothing authentic to it, and eventually he was told to give it up. Liz was more accepted by the girls than she was by the Italian entourage, but her attitude was on a much sunnier side, so it was easy to love her.

The night wound down without too many major events breaking loose; Jim wasn't making out with some other girl, and Liz hadn't seduced the barkeep. Amber and Cookie made the suggestion that the couple rent a scooter the next day. They had a guy they would send them to, who would give them a local kind of deal, if they just dropped the Amber and Cookie's names. The scooter could take them to some remote areas on the island, where they might find themselves alone on a vast beach with sparkling blue water reaching out to eternity.

The next morning, Jim and Liz were at the scooter dealer before noon, which was plenty early by their standards. They were not suffering from their usual thumping hangovers since they had spent a lot of time dancing the night before. After a light breakfast of yogurt and fruit, they were ready to explore the island. Amber and Cookie had stopped by the scooter rental before heading to work and had lined up a steal on a juiced-up scooter. Jim and Liz were pros on the two-wheeled machines and were quickly a good distance from the town on the winding blacktop road, which dipped down to the shore and rose up the mountainside as it worked its way around the island. The day was crystal clear, and the hum of the little motor and breeze rushing past their ears was the only sound as they cruised at the maximum speed the scooter would allow. The road was deserted as they headed down a valley next to an orchard full of plum trees. There was a little sandy road splitting off from the main road that cut through the orchard and reached down to the seaside; it was just the kind of spot that Amber and Cookie had told about. Jim steered the scooter down to the beachfront and was amazed to see the largest beach he had seen in all of Greece, and there was only one solitary couple clear at the other end of it.

"This is our spot." Jim declared as they parked the scooter when the sand began to get deep.

"Do you think this is someone's private property?"

"Na, those people's car is parked over there; it must be alright. No one owns the ocean. If we get evicted, we'll jump on the scooter and scram. We can't pass up this paradise." They spread out their towels right in the middle of the vast surface of sand. Liz put lotion on her front side, rolled over, and asked Jim to apply some to her back—maybe he would give her a little rub while he was at it. This is the first time that they had been isolated as a couple for quite a while, and there was a slight awkwardness that came with it. They didn't know what to do with each other, and they still hadn't resolved it in their minds. Jim applied the lotion undoing the back strap of Liz's top. "You should take this thing off, anyway—you don't need those nasty tan lines." Surprisingly, Liz reached behind her neck and untied the other string that held her top on. It fell to the ground, but she was firmly pressed to the towel.

"Wow, I can't wait till it's time to roll over."

"This whole thing is crazy you know—us—just kind of floating in space scared to bump into each other."

"Whoa, who's scared? I'm all for bumping. Actually I've been begging for it since Zurich."

"Well, I guess it's me then. I don't know what to do with you, and I feel if I let you in and you win, I'll lose all control."

"We're not playing a game against each other. It's just life, and in the end, we'll learn a lot about one another—that means we both win. Don't be afraid of me or us; those are the last things you have to worry about. I'm not going to hurt you. I'm not going to take you anywhere you don't want to go. I might take you some places you've never, been but they're places you have to see before you commit your whole life to someone else. I give you a hard time, but that is just a defense mechanism. Deep down, I have this burning desire to be with you, but you have to feel the same way for it to come alive."

"I do." Liz rolled her head towards Jim and looked into his eyes. He met her lips, as she came up off the towel, and they kissed a long, soft, free kiss—the kind that tastes so sweet, it never wants to end. She rolled over, and Jim pressed his body against hers looking into her eyes for a glimmer of what the future might hold. He didn't push anything; he just kissed her softly again and again, keeping his body entangled with hers until the hot sun and their feelings for each other boiled over, and they had to take a swim to cool down. He picked her up off the towel and carried her to the ocean, slowly walking into the water and continuing to kiss her as he went. Her guard had come down, but neither of them knew if it would stay that way.

An hour later, they had turned down their affair and were relaxing on their personal paradise beach, when an older gentleman came sauntering out of the orchard. He was wearing shorts and sandals with a towel tossed over his shoulder. He looked completely delighted with himself, smiling from ear to ear while munching on plums from the orchard. His hair was a curly plume of gray, and his belly was very well fed. He came out of the orchard about fifteen or twenty feet from where Jim and Liz were planted. Liz flinched for a second and covered her breasts with her arm, but then realized that she was being silly, as the man took no notice of her. Actually he was all for nudity, dropping his drawers and towel about halfway across the beach on his way to a refreshing swim. Jim and Liz watched as his wrinkled butt, without any tan lines, jiggled down to the shore. The old man was strong and happy to be in the water and attacked it as though he were stronger than the current itself. The man was completely at ease in the sea. He swam for a while and then turned on his back and floated taking in the rays of sun like he was bathing on the beach. Jim and Liz watched him for a while and then went back to reading their books, leaving him in his own world.

After a while, the man came walking back onto the beach in all his glory, walking straight into the orchard without stopping to dress or dry off. Jim and Liz forgot about him, suddenly he appeared right next to Jim. "Whoa, naked old dude, how do you do?" Jim stuck out his hand to shake the man's hand even though he was a little stunned at his appearance. His grin was still huge, so Jim figured he meant no harm. The man couldn't shake Jim's hand because his hands were full of plums. Jim asked the man if he spoke English, but he just shook his head and offered Jim a plum, which Jim graciously devoured. Liz and Jim ate a couple of plums apiece while the old man remained seated next to them. He spoke a couple of sentences in Greek, waving his arms to towards the ocean. He told them if you always swim in the ocean, you will stay young, and if you eat the plums from his orchard, you will always be happy. Although the old man spoke to them in Greek, Jim and Liz got it. They could see the meaning in his eyes, his smile, and his graciousness. Jim and Liz had feared that the owner of the land might come to the beach and make them leave, but the reality was the owner of the land only wanted to share whatever he had with the rest of the world. When he got up to go, he reached out to shake Jim's hand, his ancient pecker staring

Jim right in the face. Jim squeezed the man's hand and returned the huge smile, almost converting it to full out laughter. The old man went back to his towel to lay down, his naked butt a little bit warm from the scalding sand next to Jim.

"Well if Gramps can do it, so can I." Jim dropped his swim trunks to his ankles. He stood facing Elizabeth, arms akimbo, as if to ask, "what do you think?" He nodded his heads towards the water.

Liz slid her sunglasses down her nose taking a long look at her partner. "You're already burnt down there, you must have been skinny dipping with Stefania. You didn't tell me about that." Liz continued to examine her friend's overall physique. "You know you're pretty sexy, but you could use a little more butt. I like the dimples in the cheeks, though."

"Well, lets see the dimples in your cheeks and go for a swim."

"I will not." Liz exclaimed, but Jim had sprung down on her and had his fingers under the elastic on her waistband before she could react. Her bottoms began to slide down her thighs. She squeezed her knees together in protest, but Jim landed a kiss inside her thigh making her shudder and stop resisting. The old man leaned his head up at the ruckus, smiled, and then clapped at the progress. Liz's face was as red as Jim's sunburned ass, but she got up and scurried into the sea to hide her body below the surface of the water. Jim saluted the old man and headed for the water.

They came out of the water some time later, much less innocent than they had entered. The old man had sauntered back through his orchard. This time Liz walked slowly out of the water allowing Jim to enjoy the way the sun didn't leave anything to the imagination. The curves of her body glistened like the perfect pieces of fruit hanging in the orchard. She was ripe and succulent, and for the moment, perfectly at peace with the world. She didn't feel any sense of betrayal or unjust, she just felt an inner glow that blotted out the rest of the universe. Jim walked slowly behind her taking in the beauty of the moment, and of the little sliver in time, when all things were in balance. The couple spent another hour together lying on the beach wrapped in each other not saying a word.

Their stomachs began to rumble after a while, and they needed more than plums for sustenance. They packed up what little supplies they had and headed back up the dirt road on their scooter. Liz hung on tight, her cheek firmly pressed against Jim's back, not wanting to let go and not wanting to think about anything else. Life would be so easy if they could just continue their journey for eternity. She didn't want to think of anything beyond that island, so she let her mind go back to the water, back to his soft touch, the knowing movements of his body. Jim could feel her reliving the experience as her fingers gently massaged his chest.

The daydreams were put to rest as Jim pulled into a county restaurant that was a simple country house nestled up to the blacktop at a curve in the road. There were a couple of wooden signs and a Pepsi sign in the window, which gave it away. They walked up a set of stairs to an old style wooden porch running across the entire front of the home. The screen door guarded the front entrance, but the main door was wide-open letting in the sea breeze. Once inside, the house was gutted out in front to make one big room with the kitchen at one end, but in open view—it was like walking into your grandma's house for dinner. Jim and Liz sat down, and a plump little woman made her way to the table with two menus, and they were in Greek, with no pictures. Jim asked if she understood English, but she only smiled and took the menus back understanding the situation. She grabbed Jim's hand and pulled him to the kitchen, and Elizabeth was beckoned to follow. Once in the kitchen, the woman pulled out a large pan with a wonderful looking lasagna type dish that had been recently baked. The patrons shook their head in approval and were soon served salads with the dish chopped in huge squares and warmed up in the oven. They drank Pepsis out of a glass-door cooler along the wall and smiled at their host, as their food was delicious.

During their meal, a large group came into the restaurant in a festive mood. It was a large family, children and all, and they had to put together four tables to fit them together. The activity was quite exciting to Jim and Liz, and their curiosity was shared with the little children from the big table. The children wandered around the restaurant staring at Jim and Liz, wondering where the strangers came from. With the group, finally there was an English speaking person, a young man who had been educated in the United States and still did business there often. Somehow, Jim and Liz were engulfed by the family and made a part of the festivities. They ended up staying at the cozy little restaurant for hours, sipping wine and celebrating a vibrant grandmother's birthday. By the end of the evening, Liz had children sitting in her lap practicing English words and eating sorbet.

It was dark by the time the scooter headed back down the road, Jim and Liz kissing both cheeks of the entire Greek family before leaving the parking lot. Even the owners saw them off with exuberant waves. They were not drunk, but stuffed to the gills with ten different kinds of foods and desserts. The festive meeting with the locals was the perfect ending to a perfect day. Neither Jim nor Liz needed to analyze the day too thoroughly. They had come together, as was inevitable, and did not need to look any further than the day. The night air was still hot, and the scooter pulled the breeze by at just the right rate keeping the couple refreshed.

They made it back to the hostel, having to keep the scooter for another day, but were not ready to retire. They locked up the scooter and headed straight for the beach for a moonlit stroll. They found an isolated cove and laid down their towels together. Jim kissed Liz as they settled down in the sand, and she lightly pulled back from the kiss and looked in his eyes, her hazel eyes looking golden in the moonlight.

"Do you really think we should do this? Is it safe?"

"Safe, huh? I don't know anything about safe, but it sure does feel right."

"It feels right with someone in every port for you. I mean, am I just another one of many?" Liz splashed a sad defenseless look on her face to drive home the point.

"Come on, we've known each other too long to have any fear of what this is. It's always been there, we just hadn't acted on it. Enjoy it, it's not in a cage anymore; you don't have to hold back. I'm not going to hurt you. I'm not going to break your hear because my feelings for you are genuine, and I'm not too good at hiding how I feel. You'll always see the truth in me. I'm not treating this like a game of conquered souls, and I truly don't mean to do you any harm by expressing my inner feelings towards you. I can't stand just being your friend; you're too damn gorgeous. Every time I look at you I want to kiss you. Here we are traveling around the world together, we get into a hotel room, we share the same bed, and all you'll let me touch is your back. I can't handle that, so of coarse, I'm going to be with other women, if that's how it's going to be, but if you give me access, you're all I really want.

"I'm in love with someone else."

"Whoa, whoa, whoa! You can think about someone else later. Why don't you try this for now; it can't hurt. I'm afraid you're going to settle for something without any idea of what's possible. Just give the next week and don't hold back—no promises, no plans, just the now. You may find something that you're missing, or you may just have a really good time that you'll never forget. Neither option is bad."

"What about this option: me falling desperately in love with you?"

"Love is a good thing, right? That's another good option if you ask me." Jim smiled and caressed Elizabeth's hair.

"What about this option: you fall madly in love with me, and I decide to go back to Danny?"

"Don't think negative thoughts—it's not good for your emotional health. Anyway, I can handle a fair fight. I'll risk losing as long as I get to play. I've got an option for you: we have a great time together, you go back to Oxford with an open mind and not in a rush to marry old Danny boy, I go back to Oregon to get this school thing finished, and at that time, we re-evaluate the world we're living in with each other in mind. No promises of life long commitments; you need to live a little to know what you really want in this world. There's hundreds of options, really, and we could sit here all night dreaming up outcomes for our future, but we would miss tonight—tonight is the best of all." Liz laid her head on Jim's chest taking the advice of being comfortable in the now.

The night wore on, and they had no reason to return to their mats in the hostel. The beach provided the perfect hammock for a peaceful night's rest. They stayed in each other's arms sharing a spectacular view of a sky full of stars. They didn't talk anymore, and the future wasn't flashing through their minds. They were just relaxing in the warmth they provided each other. The waves of the ocean lightly breaking on the shore slowly serenaded them to sleep.

Jim woke up as the sun started streaming over the horizon turning the vast ocean into a melting pot of orange, red and blue. The air was warm, there wasn't a bit of chill, so he took off his shirt and rested Elizabeth's head on it, and got up to take an early morning swim. Liz stirred, but did not wake. Jim made his way to the water and dove head first into the morning surf. He swam hard into the waves chasing the sun. The water helped clean some of the confusion from his mind.

He was sure he was feeling something much stronger than he was used to feeling. Women were his favorite drinks, but until that instant, he had liked all the flavors and had gone onto the next with great appreciation for the last, with no need to try it again. He knew that his friend was more than he could handle. She was too serious for him, but she needed to be lightened up, and he needed a reality check, so the moment was just right. "I can ride this out and make it right for both of us—I have to." He thought, but he couldn't think for both of them. He couldn't control anything; he just had to let it happen.

Elizabeth eventually rolled over with her eyes slit ever so slightly adjusting to the blinding light. She finally focused on her long-time friend in the water. She could tell that he was asking the sun impor-

After lunch, Jim and Elizabeth swam along the edge of the shore until they came to an isolated beach that could not be seen from the road. They had not shown a lot of affection for each other throughout the day, but both of them were aching to be close. Jim swam up on the beach, laying his back halfway in the water and Liz swam up right between his legs and put her body on his. She had taken the lead with this move, and Jim was very pleased they were feeling the same. He succumbed completely to her control. They made love in the cool seawater for the second day in a row, except this time there were no inhibitions, no uncertainties or holding back. Jim couldn't tell she had had little experience in sexual activities, as her hips moved with a firm desire knowing exactly what it wanted. Their eyes stayed open as they both enjoyed the beauty of one another, the miracle of two bodies being one with the vastness of the sky and the ocean surrounding them. It was something that they both wanted to imprint in their minds forever—making love in the bright sun on their own secluded piece of earth with only the sound of the lapping water and their own air erratically being thrust in and out of their lungs.

When they finished, they laid naked in the water, swimsuits and snorkeling gear thrown up on the beach, and watched the ocean turn to vapor in the air. They relished the time bathing in complete serenity. The gulls would make some far off screeches from time to time, and the ocean was constantly whispering to them.

"Do you feel as good as I do?" Jim finally broke the silence.

"Yeah." Liz rolled over from her spot in the sand and threw a leg over Jim's resting her head on his chest. They were quiet for a long time after that, just soaking in the freshness and freedom of the moment. They made love one more time before getting dressed and back into their sexy fins and goggles.

Back to the scooter, they zipped into town and got themselves ready to make way to another island. They would take the evening ferry to Mykonos, a much smaller island known for its nightlife. They felt like kicking up their heels a little bit after having relaxed for a couple of days. Upon arriving in town, they returned the scooter and walked back to the hostel where their bags were already packed for departure. On their way to the docks, they stopped by the beach bar and said goodbye to Amber and Cookie. They wished each other well and exchanged addresses, the girls saying they would be through the states the following year and hoped to make it as far as the west coast. Jim was a little too excited about entertaining the girls state-side and received a firm shot in the ribs from Elizabeth after showing such enthusiasm. "Now you want to fight over me, when a week ago I was barely allowed to touch you."

"You were too busy with the Italians, remember?"

"A week ago we were in Rome, and there was definitely no hanky panky, remember?'

Cookie added. "You two sound like an old married couple; stop it. I think you're going to fall in love and end up with your hands all over each other." There was a glimmer in Jim's eye that told the rest of the story, and his grin completely exposed himself. "You two have already been wrestling, ain't yuh, no shit. Look at this Amber; I think they've finally crossed the line—we knew it didn't we? I told her the other night at the bar you two would end up knocking boots, and I was right. Look at her—she's blushing." Cookie pointed at Liz, and Amber looked on with her mouth wide open in a sort of amused amazement.

"You two didn't?" Amber gasped. "After all that whining and moaning about staying friends and being in love with the English bloke, you went and did the nasty anyhow. How fucking beautiful is that, eh Cookie!" Amber was delighted with the outcome. "You two are meant to be together; you ought naught fight it. If the force that brought you together is worth anything, you need to pay attention to it.

"So was he any good sweetheart?" Cookie asked.

Elizabeth was so read that her face looked severely sunburned. She didn't want to expose her secrets, but she already had. "I can't believe that you can just tell. It's your fault." She jabbed Jim in the ribs again.

"Answer the question, sunshine—was I any good or not?" Jim exclaimed without remorse. He knew that it would elevate her embarrassment, but he was enjoying watching her squirm.

"I'm not talking about this. You people have no couth." The original color came back to Liz's face, and she rested a hand on Jim's leg affectionately.

"That's amazing; he got in your pants. Cookie said it was going to happen, but I didn't agree. I said he was too reckless for you. But I'm glad it did. Like I said, I think it will work out beautifully."

"We're going to take it one day at a time. She could back out on me at any moment, especially with the way I'm harassing her, so I've got to be gentle and understanding right now. I don't want to scare her off before we get to spend a night in an actual bed. We've been staying at that hostel, which is pretty much communal living. Last night, we actually slept on the beach just down the way. We're going to catch a boat to Mykonos and get a room and really get this thing heated up. I've been trying to get her in bed since we were teenagers, but she always wanted to talk about her boyfriends or her sacred virginity or some other ridiculous moral standard that I could never live up to. Now she's drifting into my world and her next trip to the confession booth is going to be a real doozy." Jim didn't score any romance points with his dissertation, but he had little practice at holding his tongue for the benefit of others. It would take many years for him to gain such savvy.

After some more laughs, some drinks, and couple of hugs, Jim and Liz hoisted their bags to head off to the boat, which had already blown its whistle to get everyone aboard.

Chapter 14
TOO MUCH IS
NEVER ENOUGH

They docked in Mykonos some time in early evening, as the sun was leaning down into the horizon. The docks were right in the heart of the precise little town of Mykonos. The buildings were all white adobe like on the other islands, but in Mykonos, everything was tighter and more integrated. The buildings looked neat and everything looked freshly painted. The streets were like narrow winding car-less serpents bustling with people in more refined clothing than had been seen on the other two islands. The shops were designer stores and trendy bars with a flurry of lights and attractions. Affluent couples walked the streets with large straw summer hats and flowing silk garments. The young people were already dressed in long pants and scanty summer dresses, boys with their hair sculpted with gel and girls with impeccable hair and make-up. The people looked pretty, like they had walked out of the pages of a fashion magazine. Jim felt threatened by the formality of it all, but Elizabeth was at ease and knew that she could make them both blend in. Jim did like the looks of the nightlife, though. There was already quite a mixture of music in the air, and there were a variety of bars and clubs lining the streets. He concluded that the nightlife had to be pretty extensive to keep the large number of places thriving.

"I bet this place goes off in a couple of hours. We're going to get down and dirty tonight, baby."

"I'm your baby now, huh?"

"Sure, why, don't you like it?"

"I like it; I think it's sweet, sweetie."

"Ooh, that's not very masculine. I don't know if I can handle that."

"I like it so you'll deal with it. You know we're going to have to clean you up to go out in this place."

"Wait a second—you're already trying to re-engineer me. You're just going to have to learn to love me how I am, because I'm not likely to change because of these fancy pants people. I can handle them on vacation, but I'm not going there. I've settled on this grunge, hippie thing for now, and I really don't want to rise out of that distinction. People just let you float around and be if you're a hippie, and they don't try to tell you what to do because they know you're a nonconformist. It's the best point of perception, removed from the whole. I don't want people to expect too much from me. If I try to blend in with the pretty people, I'll just be an imposter."

"No, no, no, you can't limit yourself to one stereotypical category. You need to be versatile so that you can blend in with all sorts of people and get a real sense for humanity. Don't limit yourself, my dear."

"Ooh, I like dear better than sweetie, much more manly; can you go with that? You know that I can blend in with anybody, and I do find value in that—it's just that I believe I can be an effective person as my old musty self. I'm still capable of having something to say to any social stratum, even the pretty people."

"Yes, but first impressions can make or break you. How can you be heard when you've already been outcast as a vagrant? You're very capable of being pretty yourself. I remember when you used to be quite a little prep. I'm not asking for much. If you shave that thing off your face, you're right back in the game. Put your hair in a ponytail, get an iron to your nice clothes, and I think you'll be presentable, even sexy."

"So what you're saying is that you want me to shave?"

"Right."

"If we can shower together, then I'll certainly shave before such an event takes place. A little give and take."

"You want to shower with me?"

"Exactly, and no more goatee."

"Okay, I'll make sure you're spotless for tonight."

"I want to make you climb the walls of the shower in complete ecstasy. We've stayed with the water theme if you haven't noticed, eventually we'll get to a bed, but who needs one when you're on the Greek islands."

"Yeah, we've been fine without." They asked a shop owner where a good place to get a room at a fair price would be, and he directed them across a small bay. They marched around the bay, which was lined with a small beach, but it was nothing that could handle the throng of people beginning to fill up the town's streets. They got a room at a small hotel, which opened up right on to the little beach and overlooked the town. The little walk around the bay made it an overlooked gem. The room was perfect, and for the first time, the couple felt comfortable with a single queen-size bed. They wouldn't have to avoid each other in the small place, but could enjoy the closeness.

Jim went straight to shaving once in the room hoping for the shower to quickly follow. Liz tried to press a skimpy black dress she had brought along as eveningwear. The backpacks were not gentle on folded clothes, and she had not had the dress out since Rome. After shaving, Jim pulled out his one pair of dress pants from the bottom of the bag creased in a hundred different directions.

"I hope it's dark wherever we go because I don't think these things can be salvaged." His shirt was in better shape, and Liz was able to revive them both quite well considering the circumstances. "I'm sorry I can't iron; I've just never had the patience." He admired her handy work and had to add, "I knew I brought you along for a reason."

"Don't push it, or you'll be washing your own back."

"Just a joke, sunshine, I'm thankful for your abundant skill." He rubbed her shoulders as she struggled with the never-ending creases in his trousers. Once she was finished, she flung herself on the bed for a rest. Jim joined her. "You want to try out the bed, we can still shower together afterward." He kissed her lips and neck and slowly began to undress her. She did not resist him.

The couple walked out of their little room a couple of hours later completely refreshed and in the mood to show the world how they felt. Dancing and drinking were at the top of their agendas; they would save eating for breakfast. They couldn't resist the first bar they reached, even though it wasn't the thriving club they were ultimately looking for—they were too thirsty. First they would fuel themselves up on liquid courage so that they wouldn't waste any time once they arrived at the club. They were in the mood to dance and needed the fluid to lubricate their moves.

Hours later, in the dead of night, a large club still thrived with patrons including Elizabeth and Jim. They were glued to each other on the dance floor, both of their bodies covered in sweat with completely soaked hair and moist clothes. The yearning had been let out in a passionate dance. Their bodies mirrored one another twisting and turning to the same internal beat, skin firmly pressed against skin with the clothing only for show. They didn't make any friends or have any conversations; they were completely lost in one another. They were drunk on each other and only drank for thirst. Eventually the club began to slow down, and the music followed the mood, a slow, romantic flavor to end the night. The couple danced cheek to cheek until the last song; their hearts were beating much faster than the music. They walked home hand-in-hand underneath the bright moonlight trying not to smile too broadly, as they didn't want the other to know how completely satisfied they were to be living at that moment.

They made use of the bed in a wild, chaotic manner that left the sheets and comforter spread out in different corners of the room. The passion was high octane, and the bed didn't have enough room. Jim hiked up her dress and ripped the panties down her never-ending legs. She spread her legs wide across the bed and let him enter her without taking off the dress, the sweat starting to stream again. Each kiss was like an explosion, ripping into each other's lips, tongues desperately searching for a taste. Eventually, he pulled the dress over her head and tossed it in the corner with the comforter. The bra went to the other corner with the sheet. He picked her up, set her on the table, and let his tongue dance between her legs until her breathing turned into short powerful explosions of breath. He shoved himself back in her at the exact moment the contractions inside her began to pulsate, and the moisture between her legs multiplied ten-fold. She was coming for the first time in her life with a man inside her, and the power of it all was enough to make her scream, which she did in obvious ecstasy.

Jim still wasn't finished—he was planning to deliver more than one powerful orgasm to his lovemaking partner. He stood her up and bent her over a chair, her legs wobbling a little, but letting him have complete control. He slid himself in her and grabbed her hip with one hand and slid the other around to rub her pleasure center. He got into a rhythm, continuing for several minutes, stroking and rubbing and pulling her tighter towards him. Sweat began to roll down both sides of his head, and Elizabeth's legs became completely unstable. She reached for the bed and collapsed face first, as Jim never lost stride from behind. Her body began to warn of its second orgasm, with Jim's hand still pinned underneath her massaging her tenderness. He penetrated deep inside her and circled his hips as her body began to quiver; he felt the convulsions starting inside her, and this time she shrieked into the pillow to muffle the full power of her lungs. They drank in each other's emotion as if it was a shot, firing it down and ordering another. After a while, they were able to slow down and enjoy each moment as though they were having smooth, sweet liquor, sipping it and enjoying the entire flavor. They explored every piece of flesh with fascination and delight. He kissed her neck and rolled her over wanting to see the pleasure in her face and take in the beauty of her entire body. It was her turn to make her partner shiver, and she took the lead by sitting up and positioning herself on his lap, facing him, looking deep into his eyes. She grabbed him and inserted him back inside her while in their sitting position. She kissed him slowly and passionately, thrusting her hips forward to meet his. Then she arched her back putting her hands behind her for support, and she began to work her hips back and forth along the full length she was allowed. He was able to kiss her breasts and help with the power of her hips by placing both of his hands firmly on her ass and pulling her towards him when she made her thrusts. She came back for one more taste of his lips then pushed his shoulders down to the bed taking the top position. She placed her hands on his chest and began a sensuous attack that was designed to bring her partner to the same ecstasy she had already experienced twice, and in doing so she set off her third orgasm. This time the contractions within her brought her partner through the roof. His shoulders heaved and his hips surged to maximum contact as everything within him tingled in a luxurious sensation. They came together with barely enough air in the room for them both to suck in, the walls shook and everything bubbled out of focus. Jim and Elizabeth had found each other's purest pleasure points.

When they finished, their bodies had been expended of all energy; they lay in a heap with a sheet wrapped around their drained bodies. They were entangled as one, their lips lightly touching, Jim still inside her not willing to break the connection. "That was everything— that was it—years of wanting you colliding into one massive moment. Did you feel that? I couldn't even control my body; it just wanted more of you." Jim whispered as their bodies began to cool from the overwhelming heat.

"I lost all control. It didn't seem like we were really here. It was like we were in some other world, some magical place, where all the barriers we've ever set up against each other were indistinguishable. I just want to float around in it a little longer. As far as understanding it, I can feel what it was, what it is, but I can't verbalize it. The newness and freshness of the emotions are screaming at me, and it's a good message, but I'm not sure what it's saying yet. It's not audible to anything but my shaking insides. You've drawn everything out of me and replaced it with your own mystical spell that makes me feel like I'm floating. Even at the club when we were dancing, I felt it, and now I'm completely saturated in it."

"Oh it's mutual, except the spell isn't solely mine; it's created by our chemistry, and it feels so good, I want to live in it. I knew once you got the hang of it, you'd be a little feisty, but I never expected such pure passion. I'm glad we made it this far, because it would have been a shame to have never gone through with this, to have never known what it would feel like to be together. You were amazing; there's no way I could ever get enough of that—it's got to be better than heroin and a hell of a lot healthier."

"Don't do heroin, okay? I worry about you and your drug escapades. You might have to clean your act up a little if you're going to continue to get this drug."

"Whatever it takes to get my next fix, I'm cool." Jim squeezed his mate in one last hug before their bodies gave out to exhaustion. They slept hard well into the next day.

A light knock woke them up sometime around noon the next day. Jim grabbed a sheet off the floor, wrapped himself in it and answered the door. The cleaning lady was sent away after a quick exchange of towels. Liz rolled over and began to stir as the bright sunlight flooded in through the door. They both felt good and refreshed but were extremely thirsty—not so much from the alcohol the night before, but from the pounds of sweat they shed dancing in and out of their clothes.

"What do you want to do today, sunshine?" Jim dropped his sheet and stood naked in front of Liz with his hands on his hips. Liz slid over to the side of the bed and put her arms around Jim's waste and kissed him right above his belly button and then pulled him down on top of her.

"We can stay in here all day if you want." They picked up where they left off the night before, except this time it was at a slower more methodical pace, as the sunshine fought through the blinds revealing even more exquisite detail of each other's bodies. They took their time harnessing the passion into a more succinct, deliberate love making causing Elizabeth to dig her nails into Jim's flesh and Jim to bite Liz's bottom lip with a tender longing that multiplied infinitely with each passing moment.

After the slow, intimate love making session, the couple showered together and leisurely put on their beach wear. "The beaches are called Paradise on this island. Remember from last night, that guy said we had to take a boat to get to them, but that it was more than worth it—they're spectacular. There's Paradise One, Two and Three. He said they get more provocative as you move down the line. Three was the most risqué, the best party spot, less clothes, and a rocking beach bar; I think we ought to go there."

"That doesn't surprise me, since you're going to be hiding behind those sunglasses staring at every naked piece of ass on the beach." Liz looked at Jim accusingly.

"Even dudes let it all hang out at this beach. There will be plenty for both of us to appreciate. A little admiration of the human body never hurt anyone. Anyway, you're as sexy as anything this world can provide. If I can get you stripped down, I won't have to look very far. The fat old people are the ones that feel comfortable being naked, and the beautiful people are too self-conscious—some wicked psychosis that human beings are hampered with—the better you look, the more ashamed you are of yourself. I just want to go have a good time with the beautiful woman who has honored me with her companionship."

"Yeah, I'm all for a good time, but we must feed and hydrate ourselves, or there may be a disaster ahead." Liz stated as they walked out of their hotel arm in arm. They were happy, not just with each other, but with everything. The world had come to a perfect apex for both of them at precisely the same moment, and no one was going to be able to take away their glow.

They ate heartily and drank as much water as they could. They picked up two large bottles of water before jumping on the small commuter boat that taxied people to and from the isolated Paradise beaches, which were not accessible by road. The boat made its way out to sea, keeping close to the shore and skirting the large rocky crags jutting out of the water and lining the shore. It was hard to imagine how luscious beaches could exist on such a rocky island. The first beach took about twenty minutes to reach and was, as promised, a little piece of paradise cut out of the side of the towering landscape. The remoteness of the beach was unique, as it was a large u-shaped beach completely surrounding with rocky cliffs and only accessible by boat. There was no bar or outside services at this beach, and it was mainly local families that got off the boat. Paradise Two was much the same in the way that it opened up around a cliff-shrouded corner, but it was much more crowded and had a bar with electricity being dropped down over the cliffs. About half of the crowded boat unloaded at Paradise Two, mostly older generation folks who had heard the lore of Paradise Three and its rather risqué affairs. Twenty minutes later, the boat finally wrapped around its last corner revealing the legendary beach at the end of the line. The beach was smaller than Paradise Two, but it was obvious from the moment they pulled around the corner that its inhabitants were of the more boisterous kind. The speakers at the bamboo bar were stacked on top of one another and met the arriving boat with U2's Joshua-Tree album clearly stating that it was time to leave your inhibitions on the boat and let it all hang out. There was lots of nudity, and the bartenders and waitresses could barely keep up with the flow of customers. There were people perched all over the rocky ledges around the bar with little to no clothing, depending on how much they had had to drink. The sand was so hot that sandals were required, but for many that was their complete attire.

"It's time to get naked and dance in the sun, baby." Jim exclaimed as they jumped off the boat. Liz stared at the scene in awe—it was like a college fraternity party with a nudist theme.

"This is completely uncivilized. I think those people are doing it up there. Do you see that?" She pointed to a couple just above the bar on a rock. The woman was sitting on his lap while the man sat leaning back on his hands with his eyes closed and his head tilted back as if he was really enjoying what was happening on his lap. The woman had a thong bikini on, which could have been pulled over just a tad to allow her partner access.

"Sex should be free to do in public; it's perfectly natural." Jim displayed a grin that was wrapped around his head.

Jim and Elizabeth found some beach chairs that were together; the whole beach was strewn with lounge chairs that were for the public to use. The chairs were necessary to stay out of the scorching sand. "You're going to have to let those babies breathe; it's almost mandatory around here." Jim said as he reached out to untie the back of Liz's bikini.

She stopped his hand, laid down face first, and untied it herself.

"That's completely against the point. Roll over so I can put some lotion on those things, you don't want them to get burned."

"Why don't you drop your drawers, and I'll put some lotion on little Jimmy and the boys."

"Okay." Jim began to untie his shorts.

"No, no, no, no. I don't want you walking around here with that thing free—you might just stick it in anything close."

"Well then, just make sure you're always closest." Jim slapped Liz on the butt and followed it up with a big wet kiss on the same spot he had slapped.

"Look at that man. He doesn't have any hair around his; he shaved it all off." Liz exclaimed without pointing but leading Jim to the man with her stare.

"I think he thinks it makes it look bigger. Do you think I should shave mine?"

"No. You could trim it a little, but I don't think it's necessary to get rid of all of it—I think it looks kind of funny naked like that."

"Yeah, he looks kind of lonely without his little fuzzy friends." Jim left his shorts on, as many of the men did. Liz left her top off, and after a few drinks, didn't even seem conscious of it anymore. She let Jim apply the lotion.

By dusk, they were both well oiled with liquor, and they had consolidated to one beach chair with Jim sitting in the back and Liz laying on him. They began to get a little sentimental as they watched the sea catch fire with the sunset.

"We're in paradise, and we're happy together, right?" Liz asked.

"Happy, very happy. I've always wanted you. I was heartbroken when I got to Oxford, and you were so infatuated with Danny boy. I wanted to strangle him and get him out of the way. The first night in Zurich, you kissed me and I thought he was forgotten. You made it more difficult than it had to be. There didn't need to be the Australian dude or Stefania for that matter—it could've been us the whole time."

"Yeah, that would have been nice, but I really believed in Danny, and I and thought that it would be the perfect test to try to resist you. Then I saw you with that girl, and I began to boil inside. I knew I had to do something, or I'd go the rest of my life wondering why you made me feel so much. I was safe with Danny, though, and you're so dangerous. Now, I don't know what to do—I mean about tomorrow; are we just doing this, or is it something more?"

"Only your heart knows the answer to that one, and mine throbs for you every second. To be honest, I don't want to let you out of my sight. I don't want to live life without this magical feeling. Danny has got to go. It needs to end quickly and efficiently. Let him know you had a good time at the ball, but you found out you were Cinderella and your prince has always been just down the street. I'm not willing to give you back to him."

"I'm not your property to give or to take. You'll get me if I decide to let you have me, or you'll have to go to Italy and hope the blonde med-student will take you. Right now, the only thing I want is you, but I'm drunk and half-naked in paradise—what will I think tomorrow?"

"I don't mean to claim you like property. I just wanted you to know that I'm being real about this. Actually, I've been thinking really hard about what happens next, and I've got a really good idea that is definitely dangerous, but could be the best thing we ever did. It sounds cheesy, really, but I actually believe it will work."

"What." Liz sat up a little and tried to raise her level of consciousness for Jim's reply.

"I want to run away together. We've played by all the rules so far. We've done exactly how society and our parents have dictated, and I think right now, we have an opportunity to put a twist on things that we'll never forget."

"I can't just run away with you. I've still got to finish school. My parents would strangle me, no, they would strangle you."

"We're adults, right? We've got the rest of our lives to finish school and start careers, but right now we have this little window in youth where the world will accept us as Bohemians, as curious travelers out to understand the meaning of life. I want to get on a boat to Turkey, maybe spend some time in Africa, see Israel, Russia, China, Indonesia, Singapore, Australia, New Zealand, Japan, the Philippines, all of it. I want to see it; I want to experience it. I want to talk to Buddha, Muhammad, and Jesus. I want to see where man began, Lake Victoria, the Nile. I want to climb the foothills of the Himalayas and stroll along the Great Wall. If we don't do it now, we'll be sixty-five when we do, our joints will ache, and we'll be in some awful tour group. This is our chance to take the path less traveled. The Aussies do it— they go on a walk-about. They see the world, and they make enough money along the way to make it to their next destination. Our parents might freak out at first, but we'll have material for the rest of our lives, and who knows, we might stumble across some calling for which we were genuinely meant. It sounds scary, I know, but think about it a little, maybe even when we're sober."

Liz was staring out at the water listening very intently to Jim's words, she wasn't scared, and she was burning up with the sensations of mystery. She liked adventure as she had shown by striking out to go to Oxford, and by traveling through Europe with her long-haired friend who had always given her the tingling sensation of love.

"You're insane." She said.

The next morning they rose at a decent hour, having spent the sunset hours at the beach, but not the twilight hours at the club. They meandered through the little town in search of a little breakfast. It was another perfect summer day—they hadn't experienced too much else on the Greek Islands. They found a little café bustling with morning patrons and were seated on a veranda mounted above rocks being splashed by the sea. It was an exquisite spot for conversation and replenishment. Jim had thoughts whizzing through his head about how to pitch his ideas sober, how to let Liz know he was serious about traveling the world, and how to sell it to her, so she would have no choice but to accept the challenge.

"I can see your mind churning. What is it? Do you really believe we can make it? Do you really think you can handle me for years instead of weeks? Do you really think we can leave everything we've begun? It's kind of insane; don't you think, irresponsible?" You're not still thinking about whisking me off, are you?"

"That's exactly what I'm thinking. We can further our education infinitely by actually experiencing the world, by maneuvering through it. We can have someone send us some more Clinique if you run out. We're not completely isolated from the world. It's the information age; there's Internet cafés almost everywhere, and with that comes the ability to use our writing skills to help support us. We'll try to sell our writing and work in the tourist trade like the Aussies. Heck, I'll even do manual labor for a month if it will get us to the next spot. We've got to be creative and fearless. I'm not afraid that this thing will work, but it only sounds sexy if you're with me. They'll be plenty of surprises although we've known each other forever. We'll surely fall more in love each step of the way as we support each other in the depths of humanity. If we go back to what we had, we're going to be worlds apart with not time to develop something, which I believe is worth a trip around the world."

"I never took you for a romantic. I'm not sure it's that easy, just sailing off and leaving all our troubles behind. I've got all kinds of stuff at Oxford, and I was going to move in with Danny next year. Breaking those plans and taking care of all my crap isn't that easy."

"I'll go back to Oxford with you—we'll sell all your stuff, grab your laptop, say goodbye to Danny, and get back on the road. While we're in Oxford, we can do a little research on perspective employers in different parts of the world, maybe sketch out a possible route. It's not as complicated as it seems; we're not really tied down to any-thing. I've completely destroyed your purity, so why not let it all out and live on pure passion for a while. I'll keep you safe, and if there is any kind of emotional crisis, we'll work it out as a team, one beautiful unit with excellent communication skills."

"I do want to experience the world with you. I have fallen for you over Danny, and I can face that, and I can face him. I really need to think about what you are proposing, though. There's something to it, something so unique and real that I am truly drawn towards it. I always thought I would see the world after I made it, you know, after I was already successful in a career and had financial independence to do it. But I understand your point of view—we can take this with us, all the knowledge about the world before we ever get started."

"Right, we can get involved in so many things along the way. We can get to know the academic worlds, learn some languages, learn about other political systems, and become worldly in the literal sense. There are really no limits. We can volunteer and maybe get some shelter for it—who knows. There are whole continents to explore, and I really believe that the adventure will last more than a lifetime, we'll leave material behind for our children and grandchildren."

"What about us though? We're just babies in this thing, and you're already talking about children and grandchildren. We've been to-gether for days, not weeks or months. I know we've known each other for a lifetime, but who knows if we're compatible beyond this week. We're in paradise, right; how hard can it be to get along? It might be different if we're stuck in some rain-drenched village in Africa. There will be days when it might not be so easy to love you."

"Don't fear our relationship, it's organic, and it'll grow pure and clean. I'll make you one guarantee, and I'm not one for promises— I won't give up on us; I'll never stay mad. If you can just make it through my emotional outbursts, I'll always come out the other side with an open mind. I know you, all the little pieces that make you up, all the little egocentric behaviors that comprise your daily necessi-ties. I have no fear that I can keep you happy, even in a driving mon-soon in Africa. They'll be times when we both feel like crying, that's just life, but there is nothing wrong with letting out some tears and having the courage to help each other bring smiles back to our faces. I want to keep you warm when it's cold and share everything it is to be alive with you. It's easy for me to love you cause I always have."

"You can talk like that. You can tell me everything I want to hear; it's too easy for you."

"What do you mean? You don't think I'm sincere? I am—this is coming straight from the depths of everything I believe. I believe in you and me, and I don't have to think twice about it."

"I love you too." Liz said searching deep in Jim's eyes for truth.

"I'll love you forever."

There was a long silent pause as they gazed at each other realizing where they had come and where they were about to go. "Yes, I'll do it. I'll go to the end of the world with you, but if we fall off the edge, you're going to have to call my mother."

www.ingramcontent.com/pod-product-compliance
Lightning Source LLC
Chambersburg PA
CBHW051435260626
47162CB00001B/107